KASSANDRA FLAMOURI

The Chalice and the Crown

Acknowledgement

First, content warnings: Although full of magic and love and beautiful things, this work also contains depictions of violence, assault, slavery, family and animal death, and references to sexual and physical abuse.

Second, many thanks! My heartfelt gratitude goes out to all those who helped turn this book into a reality: My husband, who has supported me through all the crazy ups and downs; my mother, whose eagle eyes have caught so many typos that mine did not; my beta readers and critique partners, whose insight never ceases to humble and amaze me; and, last but far from least, my Kickstarter supporters without whom this book would never have been published. I'm so thankful for each and every one of you, and I can't wait for you to see what your generosity has made possible!

I

Act One: Lacrimoso

"And those who were seen dancing were thought to be insane by those who could not hear the music."

-Friedrich Nietzsche

Prima

For years, I've wondered why people say *dream* when they really mean *wish*. A dream come true. A dream of a better life. It's so much clearer in Russian: *sohn* for a picture you see in your sleep, *mechta* for a wish or a hope. It's an important distinction to make, because my dreams have long since turned into nightmares... and the very last thing I want is for them to come true.

For years, I've watched the night fall like a condemned prisoner counting down to the hour of execution. I've raced through sleep searching for dawn and safety only to collapse with exhaustion upon waking.

Today is no different. I wake in darkness, disoriented, with my heartbeat pounding in my throat. Where am I? A drop of sweat trickles down the side of my face and onto my neck, making me shiver. A ragged breath shudders through my chest. A second one, and a third, until the air flows smoothly. I rest for a moment, the memory of my dream gnawing at me like a dog with a bone. It overtakes me and pulls me under again, as if once just wasn't enough.

* * *

My name is Sasha.

I struggle to hold onto even this small bit of knowledge as I try to remember how to open my eyes.

A dull but intense pain hammers against my temples and makes my stomach churn. But finally, I succeed in pulling my gummy eyelids apart and then squint, trying to make sense of the strange pattern of blue and gray and black that shifts and sways above me.

I'm not alone.

There are other bodies stirring nearby. Though I still can't see through the mist, I hear them with perfect clarity. Some are coughing and gagging, some gasping and scrabbling in the leaves. The sound of other people getting sick triggers my own gag reflex and I turn my head to vomit, unable to move my whole body.

I squirm away from the cooling bile trickling down my neck, but I don't get far. Dead leaves and twigs dig into my bare flesh, scoring tiny, burning lines across my skin. My muscles twitch and jerk, refusing to obey as I scream inside my head. Finally, I give up. I lie still, gasping and trembling, and try to collect my scattered thoughts and senses into some semblance of order. But my eyes, though open, are useless. Or maybe not. I can see—there's color, texture, depth, movement—I just don't know what it means. All I know is that I'm cold and scared and naked except for a small, cold weight on my neck. A necklace, I realize, and it seems important, but I can't seem to grasp exactly why. I put that aside for a moment and return to what I know for sure:

My name is Sasha.

I breathe slowly, carefully, as if I can coax the memories out of hiding. My head is spinning and throbbing, like I've had too much to drink. Is that it? Am I drunk? Or hungover, maybe? But no, that's not right. I've never been drunk in my life. I'm responsible, I'm careful—I'm a dancer. I seize on this, relieved beyond measure to have something more than a name to cling to. I'm a dancer.

It's enough for now. It has to be, because I think I'm going to be sick again.

I force myself to roll over, only to find myself staring into the empty eyes of a little boy. I reach out and brush trembling fingers across his cheek, only to snatch them back as I realize the truth: The boy is dead.

My stomach heaves, but nothing comes up except a thin dribble of bile. This time, I succeed in dragging myself a few feet away. I squint, forcing my eyes to focus until I find a clean patch of leaves. I press my face into them and suck in a shuddering breath. The leaves are cold and clammy, and they smell like rotting things—like death.

* * *

My eyes open slowly, reluctantly. What will I see? Will I see at all, or will I be lost again in a wash of color and fear? But it's alright. Though the lighting is dim, it's enough to illuminate the jungle of props and old furniture. My face is stuck to the arm of an old leather couch that smells like years of dust and deodorant and sweaty dancers, not dead earth. I'm wrapped in an oversized sweater, tights, leotard. I'm not naked. Not cold.

But I'm still shaking.

My hand twitches against my sweaty cheek. I tuck both hands under my arms and take another breath. I've just fallen asleep backstage, that's all, and I've had another dream. A nightmare, nothing more. It doesn't mean anything. It can't.

There's no time for nightmares now, no time for fear. A flock of beribboned, giggling dancers dressed as swans flutters by. The glances they cast at me range from speculative to envious to outright hostile. Would the Swan Queen's handmaidens have looked at her like that, if the story had been true? Would they have hated her for being the one chosen to break their curse?

Perhaps it's fitting then that the other dancers should ostracize me as they do. They all wanted this role, and I was the one who took it from them. That's how they see it. When my grandmother announced that Nikolaev Academy would be putting on *Swan Lake* for the spring production, no doubt each one of them imagined herself dancing the role of Odette.

I've heard the whispers. They all think the role was handed to me because I'm Nadia Nikolayeva's granddaughter—the heir to the Academy, the crown princess of the East Coast ballet world. They have no idea, any of them, how hard I've worked, the hours I've spent practicing the same minuscule gestures over and over again until each motion is perfect. They don't know how much this role means to me, what's expected of me.

Ballet is my life. My past, present, and future. But it's the present that matters now. It's time for my duet with Prince Siegfried.

I push myself to my feet with a groan that isn't entirely for my sore muscles and aching feet. Prince Siegfried—also known as Loathsome Dave—is possibly my least favorite person in the world. He's not a bad dancer, of course. He would never have been cast otherwise. But he would never have been cast if Simon Cantor hadn't thrown out his back a week before the audition, either. Dave knows it, too, which makes his swagger and insufferable smugness even more unforgivable, the ungrateful little toad.

Dave greets me with a cocky grin as I join him onstage. I give him a tight smile in return and take my position. James, our director, rattles off our instructions and gestures to the rehearsal pianist.

The music begins, a deceptively delicate theme that carries an undercurrent of tension. Well, I have plenty of that. It's the delicacy that's been eluding me, no doubt because I want to slap that smug little smile right off Dave's—

"Hold it," James calls to the pianist. "Sasha, stop scowling and *relax*. Remember, the audience shouldn't be able to see how hard you're working. Your job is to make this look effortless. Ethereal. Right now you look like you're going to murder someone. Not good. You are a beautiful swan princess, not Lord Voldemort in a tutu."

A smattering of giggles from the surrounding swans only makes me scowl harder. At James' raised eyebrows, I take a deep breath and force my face into a smooth, blank mask.

"Good enough for now," James says. "Again."

The pianist begins again, and I rise *en pointe*. My arms float above my head and back down, graceful as a swan in flight. If James wants effortless, I'll give him effortless.

I move like sunlight on water, my feet barely touching the ground. My every motion is controlled, secure…until Dave puts his hands on me. My whole body tenses as he lifts me into the air, my leg pointing straight up and my back arcing toward the floor.

"Loosen up," James calls, but he doesn't stop the pianist. "Melt into it—Sasha, *relax*—"

I realize Dave's going to drop me a split second before I come tumbling down, and I twist in a vain attempt to catch myself. The hard planks of the stage seem to rise to meet me and slam into my side. I hiss against the pain, but I don't cry out. The pianist cuts off in a tangle of notes, and a chorus of gasps sounds from somewhere offstage.

"Oh, God." Dave reaches for me, his face beet red. "Sasha, I'm sorry—"

I smack Dave's hand away then push myself to my feet, ignoring the shocked whispers of the other dancers.

"I'm fine," I mutter.

James rushes over and takes my elbow to examine the scrape and incipient bruise. I breathe deeply through my nose as his thumb presses into a particularly sore spot and wait for him to finish. He pokes and prods around the joint a few more times until he's satisfied and then crosses his arms and scowls at me.

"Jesus, Sasha, it's no wonder he dropped you. You're so stiff, and you're shifting your weight too soon. Don't be in such a hurry to get down." He throws his hands up. "You're supposed to be in love, for God's sake."

Dave shoots me a wink that's probably supposed to be charming but just comes off as creepy. But underneath, I can see he's frustrated.

Well, so am I. Why did Simon have to go and take himself out of commission? We've danced together for years. We would have been unstoppable.

"Again," James barks.

"Come, my love." Dave sweeps a ridiculous bow and extends his hand to me.

I grit my teeth and take it.

* * *

After rehearsal, I make a beeline for the dressing room and throw on a pair of sweats over my tights. A moment of rummaging in my duffel bag yields a protein bar, which I shove into my mouth without tasting it, and a necklace.

My breath eases the moment my fingers close around the silver and moonstone pendant, a tiny replica of the crown waiting for me at home—the very same crown Baba Nadia wore for her debut performance of Swan Lake. I straighten up and fasten the chain around my neck, sighing as the pendant falls into place just below my collarbone.

The necklace is my most treasured possession. It's the most beautiful, too: two delicate, silver swans inlaid with pearl and moonstone face each other with their necks arched to form a heart. Baba Nadia gave it to me after I was cast as Odette. It had been a gift to her as well, she explained, to commemorate the very same role.

She never said who gave it to her, though, no matter how many times I asked. Just that he would want me to have it.

At first it was annoying, but her evasiveness did lend the necklace a certain mystique. I've worn it every day since, and now it's more than an accessory. It's my personal talisman, a charm to protect me from all manner of evil that lurks in the shadows of my world: cattiness, jealousy, laziness, complacency, despair…and, of course, failure.

James catches me at the door with a laundry list of notes he's thought of in the time it's taken me to change. Most of them are things he's said already, but I nod and try to look like I'm paying attention. He walks me to the car, drilling my ear all the while with an endless stream of critique. Finally, he runs out of notes—out of breath, more likely—and I make my escape. I drive home and stomp into the house, too irritated and too tired to close the heavy oak door with any amount of care. It slams behind me, making the whole frame shudder.

"Watch it," Emily shouts from somewhere out of sight. "You'll bring the house down around our ears."

Emily has been managing the Academy for nearly ten years, and she's been with my family even longer—ever since she was twelve or thirteen or something. She was one of Baba Nadia's students, and she sort of adopted me, watching me and playing with me while Baba Nadia taught lessons. Eventually Baba Nadia hired her officially as my babysitter, and she taught me my first ballet steps herself until I was ready for Baba Nadia to take over my instruction. Emily's been a best friend, sister, and mother all rolled into one for as long as I can remember.

I find her sitting on the floor of the living room, surrounded by charts and schedules. I drop onto the floor next to her and rub my eyes.

She peers at me with pursed lips but doesn't comment. "I was thinking you could give this a shot," she says instead, indicating the schedules with a wave of her hand. "Get some practice."

"Isn't that what we pay you for?" I ask wearily, then grimace. "I'm sorry, that came out wrong. But seriously, you do a great job. Why sully your work with my ineptitude?"

She raises an eyebrow. "May I remind you that I was also paid to change your diapers once upon a time. That didn't stop you from learning to wipe your own ass."

I can't help but laugh. Emily always knows how to pull me out of a bad mood. She grins and pats my knee with a sheaf of papers.

"Come on. The studio will be yours one day, and you need to know how to run it."

"Quite right," Baba Nadia remarks from in the doorway. She crosses to the high-backed armchair, her cane tapping lightly against the hardwood floor.

I sigh, wondering if I'll ever achieve the grace that comes so naturally to my grandmother. Baba Nadia always seems to glide, somehow, even with a cane, and she looks like a queen as she settles into the chair. I turn my attention back to the schedules, but I can feel her eyes on me.

"Now, then." She pokes me with her cane, and the illusion of royalty fades a bit. "Tell me about rehearsal. Emily says you had a difficult day."

"How—" I cast Emily an annoyed glance. "James told you."

She grins at me, her blonde curls bouncing as she cocks her head. "Dating the director has its privileges."

"It was awful." I let the schedule slip to the floor and groan. "I can't dance with Dave. I can't stand him. My body just rebels."

"That's no excuse," Baba Nadia says sternly. "He's your partner. You don't have to like him, but you do have to trust him."

"How can I?" I protest. "He's an arrogant ass. And he sickles his feet."

"You'll meet a lot of arrogant asses, I'm sorry to say." Baba Nadia shakes her head and taps the forgotten schedule with her cane. When I pick it up again, she continues, "You don't have the luxury of choosing your own partner now, and you won't for many years to come—if you ever do. Trust doesn't just happen, *kotik*. It isn't even earned, not really. In the end, it's a choice. You must choose to believe that your partner will catch you, or you will never fly."

"If nothing else, you can trust that he has more to lose than you do if he lets you fall," Emily adds helpfully.

That makes me laugh. And she's right, too. If this performance is my big shot, it's even more of an opportunity for Dave. He doesn't have the contacts I do or the many, many performances under his belt, or the scores of audition invitations already lined up. This is Dave's first time cast as a principal. If I can't trust *him*, exactly, I can trust his desire to not fuck up.

I study the schedule I've created. Are four classes too much for me to teach? Emily and Baba Naida have both been asking probing questions about my grades as we get closer to the performance. I can't deny that their suspicions are justified—in fact, I have an English assignment due tomorrow that I haven't started yet. I haven't even opened the book. *Henry IV*. Or is it *Henry VI*? I don't even know. I don't care, either. After I graduate, I'm not going to go to college.

I'm going to dance.

"It's a start," Baba Nadia allows. "But you must try to do better. Is there nothing you like about the poor boy? It's a love story, after all."

"People keep saying that," I complain. "But it's not!"

Emily looks up with raised brows. "*Swan Lake* isn't a love story? How in the world do you figure that?"

"It isn't," I insist, wrapping my arms around my knees. "It's about freedom, not love. Odette is cursed by Rothbart to turn into a swan until the moonlight hits her, but she can break the curse by getting a man's pledge to be true to her, right? So she does. She plays along and gets the prince to fall in love with her. Maybe she falls in love too, maybe not. But love isn't the point for her. When Prince Siegfried betrays her, she could forgive him. Yeah, she'd be a swan forever, but she'd still be with him. But she doesn't. She'd rather throw herself into a lake and drown. Because it wasn't about him. It never was. What she wanted more than anything else was freedom, not love."

Emily blinks. "Well that's…painfully unromantic."

"Oh, I don't think so," Baba Nadia says, unperturbed. "Let the passion be for freedom, if that's the way you see it. As long as the passion is there."

I consider this. Maybe I can deal with Dave if I don't have to pretend to be in love with him. "I think I can work with that."

"But I still want you to get to know Dave," Baba Nadia says, and I groan.

"Fine… I'll call him tomorrow." I wrinkle my nose. "Happy?"

"Satisfied," Baba Nadia corrects me.

I snort, and she flashes me a smile and a wink before she leans over to straighten the old photographs on the little table beside her armchair. First, the picture of my mother, Lara. Her gray eyes mirror my own, though her hair is honey to my dark chestnut. Then my grandpa Robert, straight and proud and proper. Then the grim-faced man who scared me once upon a time but whose name I share. Aleksandr—Sasha, my grandmother's first husband.

They're all dead, and to me they're just faces. But to my grandmother they were—are—real. Painfully so. I can see her love for them in the gentle way she tidies the frames and the tiny catch in her breath as her gaze moves from one to the next.

My own gaze is tense as it passes over my mother's features, so like my own. I barely remember her, and the memories I do have are overshadowed by a vague uneasiness mingled with sharp stabs of longing. It's always made me uncomfortable to think about her...so I don't, usually.

"I'm going to bed," I say abruptly and hand my attempt at the next week's schedule to Emily. "Here, I don't think there are any holes, but I'll try again tomorrow if there are. Goodnight."

"'Night, kid," Emily says, and reaches over to squeeze my foot. "Sleep tight, and don't worry. Tomorrow's a new day."

I smile wearily, trying not to wince as I get to my feet. "Thanks. I'll try."

"Have a shower. You'll feel better, you'll see." Baba Nadia leans down to caress my cheak. "I'll be up in a few minutes."

"Are you ever going to stop tucking me in at night?" I ask, rolling my eyes.

"Someday I won't be able to," she says. "So I will take care of you while I can."

* * *

Baba Nadia is right, as she so often is. The hot water washes away my frustration and leaves me so tired that I think I might actually fall asleep tonight.

I spend a few minutes stretching, scribble out a few perfunctory sentences that might pass as homework, and then crawl into bed with a sigh, too exhausted to move. But though my eyes drift closed, I don't sleep. The light is still on, for one thing, and I don't have the energy to do anything about it. And Baba Nadia hasn't come to say goodnight yet.

She doesn't keep me waiting long. The door creaks open, and a puff of light perfume tickles my nose. I open my eyes as Baba Nadia sits beside me at the edge of my bed. She brushes back my hair, her hand cool on my cheek.

"How are you feeling, Sashka?"

The familiar pet name comforts me, as does her presence. Though I might pretend to be embarrassed, I secretly cherish our bedtime routine. I wouldn't trade it for anything.

"Better," I mumble.

"I'm glad, *kotik*. I have something for you."

Her smile deepens the lines around her eyes, but nothing can hide the sparkle there. My eyes fall on the box in her hands. I shoot upright, my exhaustion forgotten.

"What is it?"

"I suppose you could call it a token of faith," she says, and opens the box.

Inside, a finely wrought silver crown studded with pearls and moonstones glitters against a bed of blue velvet. My breath catches, and I reach automatically for my necklace. My fingers close on empty air—the necklace is hanging on a peg next to the bedpost—but my hand stays at my throat. It's Odette's crown, the one Baba Nadia wore sixty years ago. The one my mother would have—should have—worn but never got the chance. Will I wear it? I tear my eyes from the crown and look at Baba Nadia for permission. When she nods, I carefully lift the crown from the box.

"It's so beautiful," I murmur. "And so delicate."

Baba Nadia's smile is wry. "It's heavier than it looks. But you're strong enough to carry it, Sasha. Never doubt it."

A lump rises in my throat. I blink against the pressure building behind my eyes and focus on a glistening pearl until the pressure eases.

"*Spasibo*," I whisper. "Thank you, Babulya."

She pulls the crown from my unresisting fingers and settles is back in its box. With a brisk pat and a smile, she shuts the box and sets it aside.

"Time for sleep now, *kotik.*"

I lie down and snuggle into the covers with a contented sigh. She starts to hum, then to sing, and I hum along with her.

> *"Bayu bayushki bayu*
> *Nye lozhisya na krayu*
> *Pridyot serenkiy volchok,*
> *On ukhvatit za bochok*
> *I utashchit vo lesok*
> *Pod rakitovy Kustok."*

Like all lullabies, it's pretty morbid if you stop to think about it: *Baby, baby rock-a-bye, on the edge you mustn't lie, or the little gray wolf will come and bite you on the side. He'll tug you off into the wood, underneath the willow root.*

It never scared me, though, because I knew even as a child that Baba Nadia would never let a wolf or anything else take me from my bed. The wolf took her baby, she told me once, but she'll never let it get me. Never.

Baba Nadia's kiss, when it comes, feels distant and faint. Like she's far away—or I am. Panic flutters in my chest. I reach for her, struggling against the fatigue dragging me under.

Baba Nadia was wrong. I'm not strong enough. I fall back into a well of mist and shadows.

And I sleep.

a la Seconde

That weekend, I meet Dave at a little diner a few blocks away and find him lounging in a secluded booth with his arms draped over the back. He whistles appreciatively as I drop into the seat opposite him.

"You look great," he says, nodding to my low-riding jeans. "I'm not sure I've ever seen you in anything but dance gear."

I frown. We're here to have a serious talk about our partnership, not to flirt. Does he think this is a date?

Dave runs a hand through his carroty hair, smiling languidly. *Bozhe.* He *does* think this is a date. My nostrils flare. The urge to reach across the table and smack that self-satisfied smirk off his face is nearly irresistible. I take a deep breath and force my fingers to unclench themselves. But I let go of my water glass and sit on my hands, just in case.

Dave clears his throat. "I was surprised to get your call."

"Baba Nadia thinks we need to get to know each other," I mutter.

Dave grins, his gaze drifting down to my chest. "I like the sound of that."

My jaw clenches so hard I think it might crack under the strain. I level an icy stare at Dave. His shoulders hunch a little, and he sinks lower in his seat. The cracked vinyl of the diner booth creaks in protest.

"What?" he says defensively. "Why did you ask me here if my company is that offensive to you?"

"So glad you asked." I give him one more wintry stink eye, then force my tone into something more conciliatory. "Look, we suck together. Everyone knows it. But no one else can dance Siegfried, and I'm not going to let this performance suffer because we can't get our act together. We need to trust each other. My grandmother thinks getting to know each other will help, so I promised I'd try. But if you're going to be a creep about it—"

"No." Dave's expression turns serious. "No, you're right. I'm sorry. I get stupid when I'm nervous."

Now I smirk. "And I make you nervous?"

"You're *Sasha Nikolayeva*," he says. "Of course you make me nervous. But the idea of fucking this up makes me want to puke. So if you promise not to eviscerate me with your eyes, I promise not to be a creep."

"Thank you." The tension in my shoulders eases just the slightest bit. "So...you go to St. Bart's, right?"

Dave makes a face. "St. Fart's, more like."

I wrinkle my nose. "Charming."

"But fitting."

"It's really that bad?"

"Worse." Dave looks away with a scowl. "It's nothing but a cattle yard for jocks and meat heads. If they ever found out about—all this—life wouldn't be worth living."

I blink. "No one there knows you're dancing Siegfried?"

"They don't know I dance at all. As far as any of my so-called friends know, I drive up here three times a week to meet with an SAT tutor," Dave says with a humorless laugh.

I sit back, silent. How can he—how can anyone—live like that, hiding his talent as if it's something to be ashamed of? Because he *is* talented, even if he's not Simon. And even if he does sickle his feet sometimes.

"I learned my lesson," he adds. "I'm not making that mistake again."

I frown. "What do you mean?"

"I started at St. Bart's as a sophomore." He bites his lip, then says, "Do you remember Chelsea Dunn?"

"I think so." I tap my finger against my glass, trying to place a name with the face. "She graduated a few years ago, right? She went to Julliard."

And killed her career, I always thought. She could be a principal by now if she'd signed with a company when she had the chance.

"That's her. I went to Mooreston High with her." He scowls. "And her little brother. She gave me a ride home one day and asked me how my solo for the winter showcase was coming along. We started talking about the Academy and her college auditions and everything… Her brother had this shit-eating grin on his face the whole time but didn't say a word. The next day he and a bunch of juniors found me in the bathroom. They pinned me down and wrote all over my face in permanent marker—you know, 'fag,' 'fairy,' shit like that—and then kicked the crap out of me. Bruised three of my ribs."

"That's why you were out that year." I shake my head, remembering how I sneered at what I thought was his lack of commitment. "I'm so sorry."

"Don't be." He shrugs and fiddles with the zipper of his hoodie, then looks me in the eye. "I just—I want you to know that I take this seriously. I don't want to screw things up for either of us."

"I appreciate that. Really, I do." I offer a tentative smile. "Maybe my grandmother was onto something."

"She's a smart lady," Dave agrees, and we lapse into silence.

It's a relief when the waitress arrives with a burger and fries for Dave and a cup of chicken noodle soup for me. I dip my spoon and pull it out, trying not to wrinkle my nose at the thin skin of congealed soup that dangles off the end. Dave nudges me under the table with his foot.

"So what about you?"

"Hm?" I pull my eyes off the soup-snot and raise my eyebrows. "What about me?"

"I told you my deep, dark secret," he says lightly. "What's yours?"

I look away, fiddling with my necklace and wondering what to say. It's not that I don't have anything to share—it's that I have too much. But it can't have been easy for him to tell me what he did, and I feel obscurely indebted to him. I slip the swan pendant onto my pinky and hold it up, considering. My heart squeezes as I remember—as if I could ever forget—that my mother was supposed to wear my necklace. And my crown.

"Well," I say slowly. "You know my real name is Aleksandra."

He blinks. "I didn't, actually. Is Sasha your middle name, then?"

"No, it's just Russian. A nickname for Aleksandra." My necklace seems to grow cold between my fingers. "I was named for my grandmother's first husband, Aleksandr Nikolaev."

"As in Nikolaev Academy?"

"Exactly," I say. "My grandmother never changed her name. She always says it's because she'd already made a name for herself as Nadia Nikolayeva, but I don't know…both her babies are named after him—me and the Academy."

"That's your big secret?" Dave asks, amused. "What, did your grandfather throw a fit over it?"

I smile faintly. "No, Grandpa Robert had already died by the time I was born. I never met him. But I always wondered why my mother would name me after someone *she'd* never met instead of Roberta or Bobbie or something, for her own father. And why she'd give me my grandmother's last name instead of her own—she was Lara Chantry, not Nikolayeva. Sometimes I thought she was ashamed of me, and sometimes I thought—I hoped—she wanted the Nikolaev name to bring me luck. Or opportunity. Something. It wasn't until later that I realized she didn't name me at all. My grandmother did."

"Is that a Russian tradition or something?" Dave asks, looking confused.

"No." I take a deep breath and steel myself against the words pushing against my teeth. "I was born in a psychiatric hospital. My mother didn't want anything to do with me. Everyone kept telling her I was her baby, but she didn't understand… She died when I was four."

Dave stares at me, seemingly at a loss for words. Well, he wanted deep and dark. I stare back, unblinking.

"Baba Nadia always said she was sick—that it was a medical problem, not psychiatric," I continue. "But I don't know. A year before I was born, she was one of the top students at the American Ballet Academy. I've seen videos of her dancing. She was…amazing. It was Swan Lake, you know. She was going to be Odette. But then she tore her Achilles tendon."

I nod at Dave's wince of sympathy. "Her career was over. It wouldn't be that surprising if she just went mad," I finish. "I wouldn't blame her if she did."

That last bit is the only lie I've told him. The awful truth is that I *do* blame her, and I always have.

"What do you mean by sick?" Dave shifts, making the booth creak again. "What—you know what, never mind. It's none of my business."

"No, it's okay." It actually feels kind of good to talk about it. I wasn't expecting that. "I don't know much. She stopped sleeping and eating, and she started believing things that weren't true. And then my grandfather had a heart attack and died. It must have sent Lara—my mother—over the edge. She disappeared for weeks and came back completely cracked…and pregnant."

"She stopped sleeping," Dave repeats slowly.

His eyes rove over my face, and I go cold. I don't need a mirror to know what he sees: pale, papery skin and dark shadows under my eyes.

"Yes," I whisper. "Nightmares, I think."

I haven't told anyone about the nightmares, not even Emily. Not even Baba Nadia. But they come every night now, and not just once. All night I drift in and out of consciousness, slipping from one scene to the next. I'm slipping now, even as Dave calls my name. A memory crawls over my shoulders and settles into my chest. A memory—a dream. From last night? The night before? It doesn't matter. The dream is under my skin now, burrowing deep like a thorn.

* * *

I slump against the woman standing next to me, trying to take some weight off my swollen feet. Her elbow is poking me in the diaphragm, and another woman is puffing warm, stale breath over my face. Both have the worst body odor I've ever encountered.

But I don't care. I don't care about anything but the deep ache in my belly and the excruciating pain in my legs and back.

Not for the first time, I think I would gladly cut off one of my toes for the chance to sit down. But there's no room. There are so many bodies packed into this rolling cage that we are physically unable to do anything but stand upright. I've long since lost any sense of modesty or shame, though I haven't a stitch of clothing and I've fouled myself more than once. I'm not the only one who has.

I close my eyes and let the throbbing in my temples lull me into a state somewhere between sleeping and waking that feels like someplace else. It's dark and unsettling and it makes me feel sick, but it's better than where I was.

* * *

"Sasha? Are you okay?"

I jerk at Dave's hesitant touch on my hand. My neck prickles with heat, shame chasing away the shock of his fingers against my skin. I push my soup away, and it shivers like Jell-O against the sides of the cup. This was a mistake, the whole thing—I'm such an idiot. I should never have said anything. And to *him*, of all people.

"I should go." I stand abruptly and fish a few bills out of my wallet. "I'll see you later."

Dave stands too. "Sasha, wait—"

"I'll see you later."

I lurch out of the booth and nearly bowl over a passing waitress. I mutter an apology, so desperate to leave that I'm not even embarrassed.

"At least let me drive you home," Dave pleads. "Come on, it's late—"

I should answer him, maybe say something reassuring. I don't. My back is already turned, shielding me from his questions—and his pity. I don't need it. I don't need *him*. I just need to go home.

* * *

I walk slowly, not because I want to but because I can't go any faster. My legs tremble so badly I'm afraid I might fall, but my shame and regret urge me on, stinging against my neck and back like a whip. What possessed me to say those things? To say anything?

If the goal was to instill any semblance of trust between us, I failed. Miserably. He probably thinks I'm unstable now—or worse, *fragile*. It's going to make working together even harder. And what if he tells someone?

My breath comes faster. If anyone thought I wasn't—*well*—they might make me see a doctor. And doctors will go for whatever diagnosis makes *them* feel better. They twist your words, the circumstances, anything to shove you into a neat little box for their files. What if they put me in a hospital—shut me away until I give up living, like my mother?

I pause for a moment and close my eyes, willing the air to flow smoothly in and out of my lungs. I'll have to work harder, that's all. I'll even try again with Dave if all else fails. Everything will be fine.

I start walking again, a little more steadily this time. But my heart keeps pounding.

A shriek of sirens splits the air. I flinch and cringe away as the ambulance thunders past. Two police cars follow, and a firetruck after that.

My nose wrinkles in irritation. Why do they call out the firetruck every time an ambulance is called? Does every victim of a medical emergency spontaneously combust?

I rub my temples, grimacing against a headache that's been brewing all night. If only I could sleep, everything else would fall into place—Dave, Swan Lake, my failing body, everything.

I'm just tired. So, so tired.

Instead of fading into the distance, the sirens' wailing cuts off abruptly. I frown. The emergency must be close by, then. My neck prickles. It couldn't be—*no*. No, nothing could have happened to Baba Nadia. I'm just being paranoid.

But I speed up anyway, my purse bouncing against my hip as I break into a jog and then a run.

The firetruck is on my street.

And the ambulance…God, it is. It's in front of our house. Two paramedics are loading a gurney into the back.

"Wait," I pant. "Wait!"

But I'm too far away and too out of breath for anyone to hear. What breath I have left is better spent on my legs. I take the last block at a dead sprint before skidding to a halt just as the ambulance doors slam shut. It rumbles away, leaving me gaping after it. I cast around wildly. There must be someone left. An EMT. A police officer. Something!

"Sasha!"

I spin around and find James dashing toward me. My foot catches on the uneven sidewalk and I lurch forward into James' arms. I clutch at his jacket and pull myself upright.

"What happened?" I gasp. "Is it Emily? Or—"

"It's Nadia," he confirms, his face stricken. "She must have fallen on the stairs. Emily needed to stop by the office after dinner and—we found her."

I swear my heart stops dead in my chest before shuddering back into a full gallop. "She's not—"

"No," James says quickly. "God, no. She's broken her hip and collarbone and who knows what else, but she's alive. Emily went with the ambulance. I just need to finish with the police and then we'll follow." He pulls me into a rough hug. "Just sit tight for a minute, okay? Everything will be alright."

He hurries back inside before I can respond. I sink onto the curb, my head between my shaking hands. My body rocks back and forth with no conscious direction from me, like someone is sitting beside me and pushing, pulling me away into the dark. Pain flares behind my eyes, and my vision goes gray.

"Baby, baby, rock-a-bye," I whisper, "on the edge you mustn't lie."

My throat closes before I can finish the rest of the line: *or the little gray wolf will come and bite you on the side.*

A tiny whimper escapes my lips, and I wrap my arms around myself in a vain attempt to stop shaking. My nails dig into my sides like teeth. The wolf is coming. Something dark, something dangerous has been stalking me from the shadows of sleep, and it's getting closer.

The wolf is coming to drag me away, and this time Baba Nadia won't be there to save me.

25

Pirouette

The drive to the hospital is tense and silent. James makes a few attempts at reassurance and, when that fails, at light conversation. I say nothing and lean my head against the cool window, watching the streetlamps flash by. But the lights make my headache worse, and eventually I close my eyes.

The melody of Baba Nadia's lullaby drifts in and out of my ears, swelling and receding in sickening waves.

"*Bayu, bayushki, bayu,*" I sing softly, hardly aware of the words.

"What's that?" James asks, tilting his head toward me.

"Nothing," I mutter. "Just a song."

"Good idea."

He turns on the radio—Classical FM, of course—and what should be playing but Tchaikovsky's Swan Lake Suite? I bite my lip. If I'd been able to do my job, if I hadn't let my dislike of Dave get in the way of my performance, I would never have been out with him tonight. I would have been at home with Baba Nadia, and none of this would've happened.

I press my face into the window hard enough to bruise my cheek.

Bozhe, please, let this not be real. Let me be dreaming.

My wish is granted…but I'm falling into the dream, not out, and this dream is even worse than what I left behind.

* * *

We stand in a line—all of us, men and women, all naked and shivering in the rain as a man inspects each of us closely, somehow making marks on a leather tablet with a piece of crystal. He looks different from the other guards. He's small and a little chubby. Instead of leather and metal, he wears soft, loose robes in shades of red.

When he gets to me, he smiles widely, chortling with pleasure, and turns me around in a circle. I stare at the ground, unable to muster the energy to be offended.

After the inspection is finished, the man in red says something to the guards and shows them his writing pad before toddling off. I watch him go, glaring sullenly at his back, until a sudden motion at the end of the line catches my attention.

A trio of guards moves down the line, two of them grabbing each captive by the arms while the third does...something. I can't see what's going on.

As the guards come closer, I find out. I look on, helpless, as they take hold of a boy barely into his teens. He's tall, but so skinny the guards' hands circle all the way around his biceps. His face looks like a child's. The third guard presses something into the captive's hip, making the boy's face contort in a silent scream as he thrashes in pain.

When the guards move away, I see an angry red starburst pattern imprinted in the boy's flesh. A puff of wind blows the scent of charred flesh across my nostrils, and my stomach lurches. But I don't move. I don't even tremble: my every muscle is frozen in disgust, pity...but mostly fear.

The next captive, well-muscled and clearly in the prime of his life, stares at the brand in horror. Then he spins, jerking his arms out of the guards' grasps. He shoulders the third guard aside and runs for the woods, his legs pumping frantically.

Go, go, I want to shout, my heart in my throat. But the man doesn't make it ten yards before a spear appears in his lower back as if by magic. He staggers and falls to his knees, hands wrapped around the shaft protruding from his stomach. He stares at it almost curiously, as if he hasn't yet realized what it is or what it means.

My legs ache with the need to run—but toward the dying man or away? To help or to flee? I want to believe I don't know, but I do. And it shames me.

A guard saunters forward, drawing a long, wicked looking knife, and jerks the man's head back by his hair. Now the wounded man knows what's happening. Even impaled upon five feet of wood and metal, he struggles, right up to the moment that the guard slits his throat.

I gag at the sight of dark red blood pouring out onto the ground, but there's nothing in my stomach to come up. The guard turns and shouts something at us in his strange language, pointing at the body repeatedly with his knife. I can't understand his words, but the message is unmistakable: This is what you get. Don't try it.

The guard plants a foot in the dead man's back and jerks his spear free. He drags the body off the road with the help of the other two guards, and then they continue on down the line as if nothing happened.

No one else moves a muscle, not even to cringe away from the branding iron.

No one screams.

When it's my turn, I almost fall to the ground, I'm shaking so badly. But I notice the guard with the branding iron hesitate. He touches the silvery scar bisecting his face and wavers, only for a moment. Then his eyes harden, and he motions to the other two guards to take my arms. I want to faint at the sight of a killer's bloodstained hands gripping my elbows, but no such luck. At least the murderous one isn't wielding the brand.

I close my eyes, hoping that it will make the agony easier to bear; it doesn't. Oh, it doesn't at all. I want to escape the evil thing eating away my flesh, but I can't. I can't move—they'll kill me. I try to scream instead, but no matter how hard my chest heaves, no sound comes out, not even a whimper.

My knees buckle when the guards release me. I sink to the ground and weep silently, forcing air into my lungs through a throat constricted by pain and fear. My teeth chatter. My limbs shake.

Why are they doing this?

Why are they hurting me?

What have I done?

* * *

I return to myself with a gasp, my heart pounding. What have I done?

Oh, I know what I've done. I've been thinking of myself as some tragic heroine burdened by the weight of responsibility, like stupid Henry IV. *Heavy is the head that wears the crown,* my teacher had declaimed just this morning, and I nodded as if I knew exactly what she meant. But I didn't know a damn thing.

I've been acting like a prima donna for months. I see that now. I let myself get distracted by my own feelings: I was resentful and petty, and I dropped the ball. The problem was never Dave. It was me. Even if he was insufferable, a real dancer—a professional—would be able to put that aside and *dance.* I've let my grandmother down, and now she's—she's—

"Sasha," James says, loudly enough that it makes me wonder if it isn't the first time he's said it.

"Sorry, what?" I wedge my hands between my knees to keep them from shaking.

James makes a sound like he's about to say something, then stops himself. After a moment, he says, "We're here. I'll drop you off at the door. Parking can be a nightmare."

James pulls up to the curb, and I'm out and running almost before the car has stopped. I burst into the lobby and whirl around in a panic, squinting against the harsh fluorescent lights and shiny linoleum. Where is Baba Nadia? Who can I even ask? Shouldn't the information desk be front and center? Where the hell is it?

"Sasha!"

I whip around and find Emily striding toward me, her phone in her hand. Her eyes are red, her cheeks pale.

"I'm sorry, I thought you'd be at the main entrance," she says. "Is James coming in?"

"I guess," I say. "Where's Baba Nadia? Is she okay?"

"She's stable," Emily says, which doesn't really answer my question. After a brief hesitation, she adds, "They think she didn't just fall. There's something the matter with her heart—though whether that caused the fall or the other way around, they don't know. They're running tests now. But either way, her injuries aren't helping the situation. It...it doesn't look good."

I stare at her, uncomprehending. "What does that mean? What's going to happen?"

"I don't know, honey," she says gently. "No doubt they'll tell us in the morning. For now, we're going to go home."

"No." I shake my head. "No, I want to stay. I need to see Baba Nadia."

"You can't, sweetheart." She closes her eyes, stricken. "I know you're disappointed. I am too, I—I thought we'd be able to see her. But the doctors said—"

"I don't care," I yell. "I don't care. I need to see her."

"Sasha—" She reaches for me, but I slap her hand away.

"You can't tell me what to do," I snap. "I'm eighteen. I'm an adult."

Her lips tighten, though I can't tell whether it's from grief or stress. Guilt flashes through me and vanishes just as quickly as it came. I don't care if I'm being unreasonable. I don't care if I hurt her. All I care about is my grandmother.

Emily rakes her fingers through her hair and closes her eyes for a moment. When she speaks again, her voice is steady.

"We aren't allowed to see her right now. So we're going home." Her eyes soften and fill with tears. "I know you're an adult, Sasha. But I promised Nadia I would take care of you if anything happened to her, and that's what I'm going to do."

* * *

There's food. They throw a few crusts of stale bread into the cage and laugh as we fight over them. A dirty, stubbled knee smashes into my face as I reach into the melee with one hand and shove aside a frail old woman with the other. My hand closes spasmodically around a scrap of bread but, as I bring the prize to my lips, another girl tries to snatch it from me.

I jerk away and bite her grasping fingers, lips pulled back from my teeth. She glares at me and rubs her hand, like I've done something rude, like she has every right to my food. I glare back and chew as slowly as possible, both to make it last and to rub it in the thief's face. I hope they sell her soon. She's been a steadily growing pain in my ass for weeks now.

I'm not sure what it is that annoys me so much, there's just something about her. Every time I see her stupid, pouting face, I want to slap it. I try to remind myself that I don't know her, she's probably a nice person—and anyway, why shouldn't she pout? We gave up hope of escape long ago. Most of us don't even bother looking beyond the bars of our cage. We're broken, hopeless, wretched scraps of flesh and bone. If ever there was a situation to warrant a good pout, this is it.

It's no use—I hate her. I hate every inch of her, from her stupid blond head to her once no doubt perfectly pedicured toes.

She used to be pretty. But now her long golden hair is no longer gold so much as a dull sand color, almost brown, and it hangs in greasy tangles around her face.

31

Not that I can point fingers. My hair looks—and smells—like something you might find smeared on the bottom of your shoe. Several weeks' worth of grime has crusted on my body and raised angry, putrid rashes in the creases of my elbows, armpits, everywhere skin touches skin.

But at least I'm alive. A few days ago there was rain, and the next morning one of the girls began to cough and shiver. Last night the guards pulled her corpse from the cage and left it by the roadside. Our only response was to take advantage of the extra leg room.

The giddy surge of relief lasted no more than a day. New aches and pains arrived to take the place of old cramps, and now we shove and twist against each other just as violently as before. Another inch or two and I could unbend my knees. Another foot and I could lean against the bars.

We need more space. I consider the pouter, eyeing her emaciated form, and smile as thunder rumbles in the distance.

* * *

I wake, shaking, in a pool of sweat. Each thump of my heart is like a hammer blow to the chest. My breath comes short and fast, making my head swim.

"Ba...Babulya..."

It's like one of those nightmares—almost everyone has had them. The ones where you scream and scream, but you can only whisper with death inches away. Is this what it was like for Baba Nadia as she lay broken and hurting after her fall? Did she call for me, for Emily? Is she trying to call for us now, all alone in the hospital with doctors hovering over her like crows?

The moonlight streaming through the window goes dark as I gasp for breath. Grief and discomfort give way to real fear—*Bozhe,* what is happening to me?

Instinctively, I try to call out for Baba Nadia before I remember that she's in a bed somewhere…dying, just like me.

My throat closes, and for a few awful seconds I really think it's the end. But then my bedroom door bangs open and seems to blow the air back into my lungs. Emily freezes, silhouetted in the doorway, then rushes to my bedside and clicks on the light.

"Oh, honey." She takes my hand and chafes it gently. "Sasha, listen to me. You're going to be fine. You're having a panic attack. Just listen and breathe, okay?"

Emily keeps up a steady stream of quiet reassurance until my breathing eases, then brings me a set of fresh pajamas to change into. I pull them on with shaking hands, the terror of my dream clinging to my mind like a stubborn film of grease. I don't want to go back to sleep. I don't want to dream again.

Thunder booms, rattling the window frame. Sweat springs to my skin once more. But I say nothing as Emily tucks me into bed with a kiss, just like Baba Nadia used to. She hesitates in the doorway, then turns the clicks the light off. I open my mouth to ask her to stay and then close it again. I've already scared her. If I scare her too much, she might not want me anymore. And if she doesn't want me—who will I have left?

My hands begin to tremble as Emily closes the door, leaving me in total darkness. God only knows what I'll see if I close my eyes.

A wisp of melody slides out of the darkness and into my ear, slithering into my head and through my veins, rattling my bones. I burrow deeper into the covers and hum to myself, rocking back and forth, until the shaking stops. I hold my hands to my face, as if I can hide from it all.

But I can't.

I know I can't.

Pas marché

It's almost a week before Easter, the opening night of the Academy's production of Swan Lake. The stage seems ominous and dark, despite the glaring stage lights. I try not to wince as I glide through the crowd of white-clad swans. My step is light, my lines are perfect. I trust my partner completely—recklessly—and I fly.

Baba Nadia would be proud, if only she could see.

But Baba Nadia isn't here, and she doesn't know that my trust in Dave could more accurately be called apathy. I don't care anymore if he drops me. I don't care about anything, really. My world has ended, and I have nothing left to fear.

Baba Nadia is wasting away in hospice care and has been for weeks—not quite ready to go, it seems, but with no way back. I was so relieved when she was released from the ICU. I thought she was just going to stay in the hospital for a little while to convalesce. But Emily isn't one to sugarcoat things, and the doctors were very clear: Baba Nadia is going to die.

Someday soon, I'll be an orphan.

But it hasn't happened yet, and a small, secret part of me hopes for a miracle today. At Easter, we say *Khristos voskres*…Christ is risen.

Millions of people all over the world believe that a man rose from the grave. Is it so far-fetched to believe, then, that Baba Nadia might beat the odds and rise from her deathbed? Well…yeah. It is. I know that. But still, a part of me believes that I'll take my last bow and see Baba Nadia's face in the crowd.

I look out at the audience, and something inside me unravels. My mind hovers over the stage while my body continues to spin far below me. The audience takes over my vision, glowing as if under a spotlight. There are so many faces, all of them staring…

* * *

There's a boy staring at us. He's young, maybe ten, and eating some kind of kabob. I lick my lips, studying the glistening drops of grease on his hands with an intensity that scares me.

A stray breeze blows the smell of roasted meat in our faces; we suck in a collective breath, as if that will let us taste it. My mouth fills with so much saliva that some spills out. I can't even spare a thought to be disgusted with myself, though saliva trickles unchecked down my chin. My every brain cell is trained on the meat.

The boy giggles and skips across to the men's wagon, holding the kabob just out of reach of a sea of outstretched hands. I wish I could feel sorry for them, tell them they're making fools of themselves, but all I can think of is how much I wish I were closer so that maybe I could reach the kabob.

The boy wiggles the stick of meat, taunting his rapt audience in what sounds like the same strange language the guards speak. And then—he wiggles the stick a bit too far, and someone's fingers catch the tip. The kabob topples to the ground and the man who touched it licks his fingers madly. The boy scowls and kicks it aside as a woman, likely his mother, swoops in and shoos him away. I can see her scolding him—for dropping the food, no doubt. No one seems to care about us. They don't even seem to really see us.

I turn my head in disgust and immediately wish I hadn't. There, in the center of the square, the skinny boy, the one who was branded just before I was, is on the auction block. The townspeople look at him with frank, cold appraisal, like he's a mannequin in a store window.

They don't see a person. They don't see a scared, pimply pre-teen. They see a thing; an object. And who knows? Maybe they're right.

* * *

I walk offstage and stagger slightly as someone thrusts a bouquet of roses into my hands. Why—am I done? Did I do it? I don't understand—but James and Emily are pulling me into a joint embrace, hugging me and each other simultaneously.

"You were amazing, Sasha," Emily tells me, her eyes wet. "I'm so proud of you."

"Any notes for me?" I ask James, smiling weakly through my confusion.

I almost hope he does, that he has a laundry list of critiques. Maybe it would help me remember something—anything—from the performance. My fingers creep up to my temple, where my grandmother's crown bites into the tender skin. My head throbs under the crown's suddenly unbearable weight.

"Not a thing," he says with a grin. "Come on, there are some people you should meet."

Before I know it, I'm being passed from hand to hand in a whirl of faces and flashing cameras. Compliments rain down on me, the cacophony of excited voices crashing against my eardrums. I haven't slept through the night in days—weeks—and my body is on the brink of failure. It's all I can do to maintain a faint, polite smile through it all. My murmured responses go mostly unnoticed, until a man with a particularly toothy grin catches my hand.

"Beautiful," he says. "You dance just like your mother."

"I—thank you," I say stiffly, trying to tug my hand away. "You knew her?"

"I met her once," he says. "Lovely woman. Such a shame…"

My lips part to release something gracious and appreciative, but I have no breath. It's as if some vital connection has been severed and my lungs are collapsing in on themselves.

James pulls me away and steers me toward a distinguished looking woman—another trustee of some prestigious school, no doubt—but I duck out from under his arm. My head, already aching from the strain and bright lights, is starting to spin and pound simultaneously. The toothy man's words echo in my ears and on everyone's lips: *just like your mother*.

I push my collection of bouquets into James' arms. "I need to go."

Before he can protest, I slip away through the crowd, dodging admirers' outstretched hands and calls for my attention. My smile has slipped, and I can't seem to get it back. I know I must look ungracious, maybe even haughty, but I can't help it. I have to get out of here before I vomit or pass out or do something else equally shameful. Better to look like a bitch than an invalid.

The dressing rooms backstage don't offer the privacy I hoped for. My fellow dancers lounge on couches or on the floor, leaning against each other in easy camaraderie. Jealousy flashes through me and morphs into a stab of pain that makes me hiss.

"Sasha!" Dave rises to greet me with a huge grin. "My queen, my light. The belle of the ball."

A blond girl whose name I should know sniffs and gives me a wide, fake smile. "Shouldn't you be out there with your adoring fans?"

"I just need a minute," I mutter, and turn to go.

"Wait," Dave calls. "Are you okay?"

"Of course she isn't," the blond girl says. "She's a total fraud. She doesn't deserve to be out there. She doesn't deserve any of this."

I whip around. "Excuse me?"

"What?" The girl frowns at me. "You know it's true. You're *weak*. You're broken. You're going to end up a failure, just like your mother."

"Shut up." My voice is low, almost soundless, like the growl of a dog about to strike. "*Shut up*."

Everyone is staring at me. Dave looks worried—scared, even.

"What?" I ask him belligerently. "You heard what she said."

"Sasha," Dave mutters, "she didn't say anything."

Waves of heat wash over me and then turn to ice, freezing me in place. Why is he lying? But then—what if he isn't? My stomach plunges, and I stagger into the door frame.

Dave leaps to my side and slips an arm behind my back, supporting me. "Let's get some air," he says. "And some water. Sound good?"

"I'm fine," I tell him. "I'm *fine*."

I'm not fine. My legs are shaking so badly my knees knock together. The ground spins beneath me. Saliva rushes into my mouth. I choke and clap a hand over my mouth, breathing hard through my nose. Dave pulls me down the hall and into the bathroom, his arm tight around my waist.

"I'm fine," I say again, but my voice is a ragged thread.

"Of course you are." He blots my face with a damp paper towel. "You're good. You're the best."

I am—it's not arrogant to say so. But is that enough? My mother was the best, too. That didn't stop her from going crazy. It didn't stop her from dying. And how many times have I heard it today?

I'm just like my mother.

* * *

The next day, I begin my hunt for answers. I slip into the office furtively, like a thief, though I have every right to be there. The business is going to be mine, as Emily pointed out, and so will the house once I turn twenty-one. Or maybe thirty. Emily explained the terms of my grandmother's will, but I can't remember any of it. It doesn't matter, though, because everything here is mine by right. My desk, my file cabinets, my everything. But I still don't want anyone to know what I'm doing in here.

I go to the squat wooden cabinet where Baba Nadia keeps the family records and slide open one of the drawers: Birth certificates for my mother and me, social security cards, the deed to the house…not what I'm looking for. The next drawer has a tab labeled "Medical." I pull out a handful of folders and flip through them until I find one labeled "Lara."

I open it, heart pounding. It's filled not only with typed medical reports but whole packets of what must be my grandmother's handwritten notes. My lips move silently as I struggle with the Cyrillic characters. Minutes pass, then hours. Page after page until the letters blur before my eyes and I can't tell anymore if the symptoms I'm reading about are my mother's or my own: Insomnia, nightmares, hallucinations, delusions, weight loss, heart palpitations, panic attacks…it's all there. My story or my mother's, it doesn't matter. It's all one in the end.

And the end is right there on the last page, staring me in the face.

"Lara umerla. Vrachi skazali eto byla anevrizma. Oni ne mogut byt' uvereny. Chto by yeye ne ubilo, yeye bol' zakonchilas. Bozhe, daruy moyemu rebenku pokoy."

Lara is dead. The doctors said it was most likely an aneurysm, but they cannot be sure. Whatever killed her, it ended her suffering. God, grant my child rest.

I rise from the desk slowly, as if I've aged seventy years in the last—how long has it been? The sun was high when I started reading, but now the moon hangs heavy and solemn over the rooftops.

The house is silent; Emily must be out with James. I'm glad. She needs time for herself…and time with James. She'll need him when I'm gone.

My eyes burn. How long will I last? What a cruel irony it would be if Baba Nadia were to outlive me. But we won't be parted for long. There's some comfort in that, at least.

I drag myself up the stairs and stagger into the bathroom, my grandmother's notes still clutched in my fist. The tile floor, usually freezing, seems warm under my chilly feet. I'm so cold all the time, like I've already turned into a ghost. Or a corpse.

"Stop it," I mutter. "Stop."

I turn on the faucet and pour a handful of hot water over the back of my neck, my face. I brace myself against the counter, my head hanging between my shoulders. Then I look, unwillingly, into the mirror.

My bloodshot eyes stare back at me like two flickering embers in a bed of ashes. Deep shadows lie in the hollows of their sockets, emphasizing the harsh redness of the lids. I turn off the light before splashing more water on my face. I don't want to see my reflection—if that's what it is. That…*creature* in the mirror can't be me.

I take the notes again, staring down at the words that hold my fate. I look at them for a long time. Not reading, just looking.

Finally, I stir and move to fish a box of matches out of a drawer, pushing aside my moonstone necklace. I don't want to see it. It's not mine anymore; it belonged to someone else, someone who could live the life Baba Nadia worked so hard to prepare for her.

I'm not that girl.

I set the notes on the tile floor and hesitate for just a moment before striking a match. No one can know what those pages contain. No one. I won't let them send me away to rot in a mental institution for the rest of my life—however long that might be.

I drop the match and watch my future burn.

* * *

Hot water hits my body, making my many cuts and abrasions sting. A rosy-cheeked older lady in an apron sets down her bucket and picks up a sponge. She dips it into a basin of water and quickly wipes away the topmost layer of grime from my body. The water feels heavenly but having someone scrub me all over—and it really is all over—is uncomfortable and intrusive.

When the worst of the grime is gone, the lady leads me to what looks like a small swimming pool. She carefully cleans the cuts adorning my arms and back and then pushes me into the pool.

None too gently, she rubs powdery soap into my hair and pushes my head under. Once my hair is clean and detangled, she gives me another good scrub with a long-handled brush and then goes to work on my hands and feet, trimming and cleaning my nails and rubbing lotion into my cracked skin. Then comes hot wax. Even if I had the courage to protest, I wouldn't. Though excruciatingly painful, it feels like she's tearing away all those weeks of sweat and grime and hunger along with my body hair.

Afterward, she rubs a soothing, lavender-scented balm into my skin and brushes my teeth with a kind of bristly cloth. I feel like a dog at the groomer's, but I don't care. It's wonderful. Being clean is even better than being fed, and being clothed is best of all.

I nearly weep as the woman swaddles me in a soft, supple wrap dress. The creamy white cloth feels comfortably secure against my torso, like a harness. She puts thin white slippers on my feet and I close my eyes, wiggling my toes inside the smooth leather.

Next, the woman brushes out my hair until it's dry—strangely, it only takes a few minutes—and braids a few pieces back to keep it out of my face. She steps back, looking me over with sharp eyes, then nods once and shoos me out into a small garden.

Though my feet keep moving, my mind recoils. There's no auction block, but I just know that the richly clad spectators milling around the lush garden are in fact buyers. My eyes flick to the other girls. They stand in a row beside a long decorative pool, clean and clad in the same white dresses. The row is short; our numbers have dwindled as we meandered through the countryside. Some died, most were sold.

We reached the city—this glittering, dizzying, magnificent city—two days ago. Those of us who are left are young and lovely and strong...at least, strong enough to have survived this long. We are the elite, it seems, the only stock worthy of the city's wealthiest inhabitants.

A man in red shoves me forward, and I take my place—next to Pouter. Of course.

I curl my fingers into my skirt and resist the urge to pull her now-shiny yellow hair. Her hands twitch, perhaps with the same desire. I stare straight ahead, inspecting a garden wall artfully draped with ivy and climbing roses. It comforts me that I can still appreciate beauty after everything that's happened. I hope they never take that from me.

I shiver.

My name is Sasha.

I have to remember. I don't want to become like the blank-eyed slaves who trickle into the garden bearing trays of food and drink. They're like ghosts, impervious and empty, more like cardboard cut-outs than people. The man in red, the one who ordered our branding, roams among us, adjusting a neckline on one girl and smoothing a lock of hair on another.

A tremor runs through my body as I'm reminded of the reason we've been bathed and clothed: Rich people don't want dirty slaves.

Customers appear a short while later and stroll around the garden admiring the sculptures and mosaics—and us, the merchandise. They're certainly a cut above the buyers we saw in the countryside. They glitter with jewels and subtly iridescent cosmetics, men and women both. They wear loose, flowing robes and gowns—layers and layers of rich fabric in all the colors of the rainbow. Everything about them unapologetically screams "wealth."

One of them will buy me.

One of them will own me.

The man in red calls for the crowd's attention and jerks the first girl in line to her feet. The bidding begins. The girl on display is the picture of resignation: bowed head, slumped shoulders, limp hands dangling at her sides. I cast my own eyes to the ground. I know I'll be no different when it's my turn. I'm not stupid; I remember the man who tried to escape.

My eyes flick to the back of the garden, where the grizzled old guard with the scar on his face watches from the shadows. He stares at me with that same strange expression I saw just before he branded me. I plead with my eyes, silently begging him to help me. But he looks away.

* * *

"Babulya?"

I drag myself out of bed and trip over—something. There isn't anything on the floor. Anything but me. My stomach heaves. I pant and force myself to my feet. Where is Baba Nadia? Panic leaks into my chest. Something dark flutters against the edges of memory. Something about my grandmother. Where is she? Where is Emily?

But—why would Emily be here in the house with me? I haven't needed a babysitter in years. Baba Nadia trusts me, she—she's not here. *She's not here.*

I sink back to the floor as the truth washes over me. Baba Nadia isn't here because she's at the hospital, in hospice care. She's dying. She may already be dead. But Emily should be here, I remember that now. She must be here somewhere. I can find her. I can—I *can*...but I don't. My eyes drift shut, and I find someone else instead.

* * *

Our mistress—Ismeni, I remind myself—dismisses us for the afternoon. She sits at her mirror and combs her long auburn hair with a complacent smile, as if she's already forgotten we're there. I turn and follow my fellow slave, Dove—I think her name means 'dove'—into the garden. As always, she sits beside the fountain and stares into the water while I wander the garden paths. It doesn't matter that the flowers I admire today are the same ones I marveled at yesterday. I forget them within hours. I forget a lot of things.

I have to work hard to remember that I haven't always been this dull-witted. Once, I was as bright and vibrant as these flowers, and I think I can be again. I used to be someone else, someone stronger. My mistress has started calling me something, but it's not my name. I don't know what it means. It's just a word.

It's not me.

Or maybe it is—I wouldn't know. I don't know who I am anymore, and I don't like looking in the mirror. I don't like seeing my reflection and feeling no recognition. That girl, that stranger, she's not much to look at, anyway. She's thin and pale, all sharp angles and shadows. Her eyes are empty, soulless, like two windows with a blank wall behind them. They make my chest ache.

I blink, bringing myself back to the present, and let my eyes drift over the garden and up to where a hulking, ominous house of stone perches atop the ravine like a malevolent toad.

It's stark and ugly, nothing like the rest of the beautiful, sprawling villas that run the length of the narrow valley. At the head of the valley lies a truly magnificent palace which seems to cascade down the mountainside right alongside the waterfall. The falls bisect both the palace and the ravine itself and disappear into the ground—or the air. I often wonder about that, but rarely for long. There are other, less confusing things to think about.

I sigh, imagining what it would be like to stand on one of the many bridges connecting the two halves of the palace. How pleasant, how soothing it must be to lean against the rails, to feel the cool mist on my face and listen to the wild rush of water surging past.

The canyon wall surprises me, rising to meet me like a wave out of the ocean. I've come to the edge of the garden, though I don't remember how I got here. I look around at the overgrown rose bushes and decide that I like this place: It looks lost and forgotten, just like me.

A flash of white among the roses draws me further into the thicket. There, illuminated by a shaft of sunlight slanting over the cliff face, is a marble swan. I trace the stone feathers, each one exquisitely detailed. The wings are slightly extended, as if the swan is about to take flight. I frown as knowledge stirs sluggishly under my skin.

My eyes travel over the proud curve of the swan's head, and two flashes of insight blaze in quick succession. First, a word. The word, the one Ismeni uses to call me. I know what it means— swan. She's been calling me Cygnet. That's my name.

Second, denial. My name isn't Cygnet. I know it in my bones. But if Cygnet isn't my name, what is?

Frowning, I back away from the swan statue and turn. Nestled against the rock wall is a small, empty pool surrounded by a beautifully carved wooden rail at waist-height. I lay my hand on it, still troubled by my newfound realizations.

Maybe it's just that unease that makes the carvings under my hand feel wrong. I want the rail to be smooth. But the motion feels natural, more natural than anything I can remember feeling for...I don't know how long. My other hand rises, seemingly of its own volition. I bend sideways and reach over my head. The stretch in my side feels nice. I do the same thing with my other arm.

I do it again, this time bending my knee over flexed toes. I don't know where the motions are coming from. It scares me, but it feels too good to stop. I sink into deep squats with my toes pointed outward. My skirts get in the way, so I pull them up around my waist and use one of my many sashes to keep them there.

Next I rise on my toes and stretch my feet. I bend down over straight knees, feeling the tension at the back of my legs. I reach out with pointed toes to the side, in front, behind, each time rotating my leg from the hip. I sweep each leg across my body and back, dragging my toes along the ground. I touch pointed toes to my knee and stretch my leg out from my body in a perfectly straight line before bringing my toes back to my knee.

Each movement flows into the next, as naturally as one breath follows another. I continue, enthralled, as strange words pass through my head: Plié. Relevé. Passé. Tendu. I don't know what they mean, but I like the shape of them. I turn them over in my mind, examining each syllable. Like the touch of the wooden rail, they feel familiar. But why?

* * *

I come to on the floor in the hallway outside my room. My breaths are short and shallow. My head spins. Images flash through my mind, sharp and painfully clear: An auburn-haired woman beams as she ties a silk ribbon around my wrist and leads me from the line of slaves; sunlight flares as I step out of a litter, then disappears into shadow as the lady leads me into the shadow of a narrow ravine; a tiny, dark haired woman takes my hand and leads me through the halls of an opulent villa.

The visions—or memories—come hard and fast, tumbling over each other. I moan into the carpet and clutch my head, hissing in pain. Is this another panic attack? Emily knows what to do about those. I need to find her—no. No, I need my phone. I remember, now. Emily is at the theater, dealing with some snag in the production.

I lurch first onto my hands and knees, then to my feet. Where is my phone? I wrack my brain, trying to remember the last place I saw it. The kitchen, I think. I take a step toward the stairs, and weakness floods through my legs. I clutch at the banister and make my way one stair at a time. It takes ages, so long that I begin to notice things I never thought about before. Has this scratch in the bannister always been there? Has that step always creaked? And the carpeting—was it always so mottled? It's all different shades of beige and brown. Is that right?

By the time I reach the bottom, I know something is terribly wrong. This isn't my house. I must have left the house while I was—asleep? Unconscious? *Bozhe*, where am I? Whose house have I broken into?

I creep into the kitchen and whimper in relief when I find my phone on the kitchen table. I hadn't imagined that, at least. I snatch it up and navigate to my favorites. My finger hesitates over Emily's name. What am I going to tell her? She's going to freak out. As she should—she didn't sign up for this. She may have agreed to be my guardian, but she's not even thirty. She shouldn't have to deal with this insanity. No. I won't call her.

I scroll down and click on a different name. The phone begins to ring, and I hold my breath.

"Hello?"

"Dave?" My hand shakes as I press the phone to my ear. "Are—are you doing anything right now?"

"I just got home. Don't tell me you want to rehearse again. We have three performances this weekend—"

"It's not that." I close my eyes. "I need—I'm—Can you come get me?"

There's a beat of silence, then, "Where are you?"

My gaze skitters over the tall stools nestled against the counter, the vase of flowers on the windowsill, the bright yellow wallpaper. I don't recognize any of it.

"I don't know." I try to laugh, but it comes out more like a sob. "I don't know where I am."

"Okay—okay, stay calm. Um, look around," he says. "What do you see?"

"I'm in someone's kitchen." My vision goes fuzzy at the edges, but I force myself to focus. "Yellow wallpaper, white curtains. There's a painting of a chef next to the stove. I shouldn't be here. I should leave."

"No," he says sharply. "Stay there—I'm coming. I know where you are."

I scan the room, desperately searching for some spark of recognition. My eyes catch on the refrigerator, and everything else goes dark. Sound—music—replaces vision, shrouding my mind like a mist.

Bayu, bayushki, bayu.

I draw a ragged breath, my chest heaving with the effort, and whisper into the phone.

"Dave—there are pictures on the refrigerator. Pictures of *me*."

"It's okay," he says. "Just hold tight. I'll be there in ten."

Dave stays on the phone with me while he drives, trying to help me stave off the panic attack. I'm too scared to be annoyed at his overly earnest tone. I just huddle on the floor and do as he says, breathing *in* through the nose, and *out* through the mouth until he appears at the kitchen door. I get up immediately and try to push by him.

"Let's go," I gasp. "Hurry—someone might come. I want to go home."

"Sasha." He stops me with his hands on my shoulders. "You *are* home. This is your house."

"What? No. It's not, it's… it's…"

I look around, suddenly unsure. But then a door slams in the hallway. My heart slams once against my chest, then flutters weakly. I turn to Dave, clutching at him with shaking hands.

"Someone's here," I hiss. "We have to go."

"No, Sasha—"

"Sasha?" It's a man's voice. "Is that you? Em?"

"Who…?" I lean away, trying to tug my arm out of Dave's hold.

"It's just James," he says. "It's okay, calm down—"

"Dave?" The man pokes his head into the kitchen. "Oh, good, I thought it was just going to be Sasha. You're here to rehearse?"

I don't say anything. I just stare at him, my whole body shaking. His eyes sharpen and he raises a hand, as if to reach for me. Another man flashes before my eyes, red faced and red robed, laughing as the auburn-haired lady ties the ribbon around my wrist.

"Don't touch me." My voice comes out in a harsh, strangled whisper. The younger man's hand is still on my arm. I wrench away and press my back to the wall. "Get away from me."

The men's eyes flick to each other, then return to me. They move back to a safe distance, but don't look away. The older one pulls out a cell phone as I sink to my knees, my hands plastered against the wall for support.

Dark spots dance in front of my eyes—I feel sick.

"Emily," I hear the man say. "You need to come home. Now."

en Dedans

Ismeni's husband Orean bellows at her, veins popping out in his neck. Her only response is to throw a vase at his head. She does it with only a flick of the wrist—she doesn't lay a finger on the vase, but it somehow flies through the air like a missile. It surprises me every time I see her do something like that, though I'm not sure why. She does it all the time.

While Ismeni and Orean snarl at each other, Dove and I do our best to melt into the wall. Orean likes to hit things, and all too often an unlucky slave is what gets hit.

I'm not totally sure what they're fighting about, but I think it has to do with the dark-haired beauty Orean brought home. I know she's not a slave; I heard her speak. Even if I hadn't, I would have known. No slave ever carried herself with such supreme self-assurance. She confronted the gathered household not like a newcomer under scrutiny but like a lioness observing a herd of gazelles.

No, she's no slave. I think she must be Orean's lover. I can't imagine what else would make Ismeni so angry.

Ismeni hurls a silver goblet next, this time aiming lower. As Orean frantically shields himself, she turns on her heel and sweeps away. Dove and I trail after her. I wonder idly how Ismeni can move so quickly without any appearance of hurry. If it weren't for the telltale flutter of her skirts, you'd think she was floating.

I hope Ismeni isn't too upset to let us into the garden. I need to go back to the wooden rail.

I feel my brow furrow into an unaccustomed expression of anxiety. The muscles of my face feel stiff, as if they've gone unused for too long. My heart pounds, rattling against my rib cage with each beat. The physical sensations scare me. I think I haven't felt this much for a long time. I think I forgot how.

I forget so many things.

* * *

I open my eyes and flinch at the glare of sunlight slanting through the car windshield. Where am I? Who—I squint at the driver and go limp with relief. Emily came. Emily saved me. A whimper slips through my lips, and Emily squeezes my hand. Her fingers are slick with sweat, but her voice is as soothing and steady as always.

"It's okay, baby, we're almost there."

She brushes my hair out of my face haphazardly, her eyes on the road. I moan and twist against the seat belt digging into my hip bones.

"Pull over," I croak. "I'm going to be sick. I—"

* * *

I hurry through the garden, drawn relentlessly to the rail—the barre. I need it. It's like a drug...or like medicine. The more I practice, the more alert I feel.

At first, I thought it was just a byproduct of my growing physical strength, but I've become increasingly certain that it's more than that. My dreams have become more and more vivid, filled with fantastical images and people who seem familiar despite their outlandish clothing. They speak to me in a strange language—and I understand them. But I can never remember what they say.

I'm sure my grasp of my mistress's language is improving much more quickly than it was before I found the barre. I responded appropriately to more than half her commands yesterday, without Dove's help. I even understood her when she said goodnight at the end of the day.

I reach the barre and begin the familiar-not-familiar motions. My muscles stretch and contract smoothly with the occasional twinge as my limbs form new shapes seemingly on their own. I lose myself in it, thinking of nothing but the moment.

"Beautiful."

I spin around, clutching the barre for support. The girl—Orean's lover—approaches and lays a hand on the barre. She imitates me, stretching her leg out behind her in what's actually a pretty good arabesque. *She grins and motions for me to continue, but I back away, my heart pounding. My eyes dart to the path. I wonder if I should make a run for it.*

The girl moves to block me off, holding her hands out. She speaks softly and soothingly, but I catch maybe one word in five. She must see the confusion on my face because she stops chattering and places a hand on her chest and says,

"Sadra."

She looks at me half expectantly, but she must know that I can't answer her. Just in case, I try. Cygnet, I try to say. My name is Cygnet. Nothing comes out, but that's not why I frown. It feels wrong—Cygnet. Definitely wrong.

But if that's wrong, what's right?

"My name is Sadra," she says again. "I've come to help you."

She moves her hand from her chest to mine, and I flinch away. She holds me firmly by the shoulders and looks me in the eye. I get distracted by the unusual color of her eyes, a light honey-cinnamon that contrasts oddly with the smooth brown of her skin. Dark, wild curls tumble over her shoulders and kiss her cheeks. She taps my collarbone to get my attention, and my gaze catches on a swirl of inked roses on her chest, just below the hollow of her throat.

"Understand?" she asks. "I will help you."

Help me? I frown. Help me do what? I don't think I'm doing anything wrong, exactly, though I suspect that Ismeni—and Orean—wouldn't like it. Perhaps she knows what the motions are. Yes, that must be what she means. I return to the barre and continue with my routine. She watches me, her eyes sad. But after a while, she joins me.

She copies my motions, following my lead. It makes me feel good, somehow. Like I know something. She lets me follow her, too. She shows me a short series of movements that incorporate her whole body, even her head and hands. It's lovely. I try to copy her, and she puts a hand over her mouth to hide a smile. She shows me again, more slowly, while I watch and move with her.

This time I get it.

She points to me, raising her eyebrows. I spin, whipping my foot around. Fouetté. As before, the word appears out of nowhere. Or like it was there all along and I never noticed it.

As I turn, my skirt flies up. This time Sadra can't hide her amusement. I smile back sheepishly, wishing I could laugh with her. She seems nice.

I let her come toward me, though I watch her warily. She plucks my sash away, letting my skirts fall.

"Tie them," she says, making the motions with her hands. "Like this."

She points to her own skirts and pulls aside a flap in the front, showing me that they're not skirts at all but very loose trousers. I tie my skirts between my knees to make trousers of my own—sort of. They'll do, anyway. I wish I'd thought of it sooner.

"Again?" Sadra wiggles her finger in a circle and points to me.

I show her the fuetté once more. Her first attempt is no better than mine, which makes me feel better. I can't laugh when she falls on her behind, but she can, and she does. I decide I like her. I'm sorry when I have to leave.

Before I go, she squeezes my arm gently.

"Tomorrow," she says, laying a hand over her mouth and mine. "I won't tell."

* * *

I clap my hand over my mouth as if I can physically force my stomach back into its proper place. The glowing red letters of the emergency room glare down at me through the car window. Emily's already fumbling with my seat belt, unbuckling me like I'm a child. I need to get a hold on myself. Right now.

I know the truth. I know I'm not going to get better. But Emily can never know how bad it really is, not until I'm gone. It'll be quick—for one of us, at least. She won't know. I won't let her suffer the descent with me.

I wave Emily away and step onto the cracked asphalt of the hospital parking lot, breathe in the sharp spring air. The sun hasn't yet set. I'm awake. I'm in control. I'm fine.

* * *

I sit huddled in my chair with my arms and legs crossed, limbs drawn so tightly together I feel like a pretzel. A wrinkled old man in a white coat sits across from me, his eyes twinkling behind thick glasses. His demeanor is friendly and warm. Charming, even.

I want nothing to do with him.

"So, Sasha—"

"Aleksandra." I lift my chin and look him in the eye. I don't smile.

"Sasha!" Emily glares at me; I ignore her.

"Aleksandra, then." The doctor glances at his pad, unperturbed. "I'm Dr. Hadley. I understand you had a bit of a scary moment this afternoon."

I shrug. "Yeah. But I'm fine now."

"Do you want to tell me about it?"

"No."

"Sasha, please," Emily hisses. She looks apologetically at the doctor. "It was a long wait."

I snort. "That's what happens when you go to the emergency room and you're not gushing blood."

Dr. Hadley's mouth twitches before he looks down again. It makes me like him a little better. Or hate him a little less, if it even makes a difference.

I'm mad at him, mad at Emily, mad at myself. This petulant, snotty brat—it isn't me. I'm supposed to be mature and responsible and poised. Once upon a time, I was all of those things and more. But now more than ever I can't let anyone know that I'm sick. That I'm going to die.

"So tell me what's been going on," the doctor says, and I press my lips together.

Emily fills him in instead, glancing from time to time at a little red notebook. My eyes widen in a sort of awed horror. She's been writing down everything that's been happening to me, both physical and—I force myself to acknowledge it—mental. She's been taking notes, just like Baba Nadia did for my mother. Emily tells the doctor everything, even the sleeping pills I'd been sneaking when I thought she didn't notice.

Even the voices I heard after opening night.

Even the nightmares.

"Dave told you." I swallow, blinking back tears. "He had no right."

"He was worried about you," Emily says gently. "We all are."

"It could be side effects from the sleeping pills," Dr. Hadley says. "Do you drink?"

I blink. "What?"

"Alcohol compounds the pills' effects," he says. "It could explain some of your symptoms."

I gape at him, then turn to Emily, waiting for her to laugh.

"It's okay," Emily says quickly. "No one's going to be mad."

My lip trembles. What have I done that she's so ready to think the worst of me? Unless she knows—and she might. She had all those notes. She's clearly noticed more than I thought. A cold knot of fear tightens in my chest. But I clear my throat and answer as if a piece of me hasn't just died.

"I haven't been drinking."

Dr. Hadley frowns. "Can you hop up on the table for me? I'll examine you, and then we'll draw some blood."

I climb onto the table, trying to hide how much effort it takes. But I can't help the flutter in my heart or the rattling wheeze in my chest. Dr. Hadley's face is impassive as prods my abdomen, my neck. I shiver as cold metal slides across my chest and back. I try not to flinch when he shines a light in my eyes. I can't see much around the bright spots in my vision, but I can tell he doesn't like what he sees.

"Well," he says when he's done, "you're dangerously underweight and your heartbeat is irregular. How long have you been restricting your caloric intake?"

I laugh. "Forever. But I give my body what it needs. I have an app that tracks my macros and everything."

There's no need to tell him I've stopped using the app, that I can't remember anymore what I've eaten or when.

"Anorexia nervosa is very common, unfortunately, especially in dancers—"

"That's not what this is," Emily cuts in, her eyes flashing. "Something is wrong with her, and it's *not* anorexia. Or bulimia, or any of that. I've been around dancers my whole life, and I've been teaching teens and pre-teens for the past ten years. Believe me, I know the risks, and I know the signs."

"Perhaps I should speak with Sasha in private?" Dr. Hadley suggests.

"Fine." Emily's voice is pleasant, but her jaw is tight. "I'll want a word with you afterward. In private."

"You didn't have to do that," I say when she's gone. "I wasn't lying."

I rub my hands over my arms, trying to suppress a shiver. Not of cold, but of weakness. I'm so tired. How much longer can I keep this up? A few more minutes, at least. I can do that.

"But there isn't anything else going on?" Dr. Hadley asks. "Anything that you don't want Emily to hear?"

Man, you have no idea.

"Nope," I say aloud. "Nothing at all."

"Well, I'd like to ask you some questions anyway if that's alright."

I shrug and sigh, letting my hands fall into my lap. "Go ahead."

Even though I don't have anything to hide—aside from, you know, going crazy—I'm kind of glad he sent Emily away. Some of the questions, though harmless, are undeniably embarrassing. I guess I can understand the questions about drinking and smoking and sexual history and all that, but what information can he possibly glean from the frequency and appearance of my bowel movements?

By the time he's done, the idea of getting stuck with needles has taken on a certain appeal.

A nurse leads me down the hall to a tiny room stocked with the usual bio-hazard bin and boxes of medical supplies. The only furniture is a chair equipped with a hard, plastic armrest that looks more like a foldable tray. I nod and mumble through the nurse's questions, then sit in the chair with my arm extended.

My skin looks almost gray in the harsh fluorescent lights, the veins running underneath like sickly blue and green rivers. I look away as the nurse ties a strip of latex around my upper arm. Already I can hear a faint ringing in my ears. My face is cold.

"Alright, honey?" the nurse asks. Her voice sounds kind of thick and hollow, like she's in a tunnel—or I am.

I nod weakly, leaning my head into my other hand.

Bayu, bayushki, bayu...

"What a pretty song," the nurse says. Was I humming again? "Okay, make a fist for me. Nice and tight. There you go. Now a little pinch..."

I breathe heavily through my nose, waiting for the needle.

When it comes, I don't feel it. My vision fades, and I lose myself in my lullaby. For a moment, I could swear I feel my grandmother's hand on my cheek.

"All done."

Groggily I look up, squinting at the nurse. She swabs my arm with something cold and wet, then covers the tiny red dot with gauze and a band-aid.

"I heard you're a dancer," the nurse says with a wink.

The bandage is decorated with tiny pink ballerinas. I force a smile as I try to push myself out of the chair. I sit back down immediately, my head swimming.

"Easy there." The nurse glances over but doesn't put down the vials she's holding. "Sit tight for a second, sweetie."

She finishes labeling the vials and then loads them into a tray before handing me a packet of crackers and a tiny juice box.

"Stay here until you feel better. There's no rush."

I sip on my juice, watching her as she arranges my blood samples on a tray. Her hands are slender and graceful, dark like—

"Sadra."

"Hm?" The nurse turns to me. "Sorry, honey, what was that?"

"Oh—nothing," I mutter. "Just, um, thanks. For the juice. I do feel better."

"Good. Give it another few minutes, though, okay?" The nurse takes the tray and moves away. "I'll be right back."

I wait a few more seconds, then get to my feet. This time, I stay upright.

I slip out the door and hurry down the hall. Which exam room was I in? My lips tighten in irritation. Couldn't the nurse have reminded me, or shown me where to go? She just dismissed me. Didn't she? I slow, suddenly unsure. What exactly did she say? I can't remember. But it doesn't matter now. I need to find Emily before someone realizes I'm lost.

I pause outside each curtained cubby and listen until I hear Emily's voice. I start to reach for the curtain, then stop. Emily's voice is agitated but also hushed. Secretive, almost. I take a step back to hide my feet and tilt my head to listen.

"I was only sixteen when she died," Emily says. "I knew she was—unwell—but I never knew the specifics. Nadia kept it all pretty quiet. But my mom remembers a bit and she said—she said even before it got really bad, before they put her in the hospital, Lara didn't sleep. She would get confused, forget things—normal things—but then talk about stuff that never happened. Could…could Sasha have the same thing her mother had?"

"And what did her mother have?"

"I don't know—no one did." Emily sniffs. Is she crying? "That much they told me. The doctors never figured out what was wrong with her. They called it idio—idiopathic. Idiopathic something."

"Well, it's possible Sasha has some kind of hereditary condition," Dr. Hadley says. "Though unlikely. The only thing that comes to mind is Fatal Familial Insomnia, and even that is a huge long shot. But there is a genetic test we can do, just in case."

I shiver and sway, wrapping my arms around myself. A passing nurse frowns at me. With effort, I stop swaying and give her what I hope is a reassuring smile. It must look okay, because she nods and keeps walking. I focus again on what Dr. Hadley is saying.

"Ms. Somers…I know you don't want to hear this, but you might do better to consult a psychiatrist. Schizophrenia has a significant genetic component—"

"I thought of that," Emily interrupts. "But she's too young—doesn't that usually hit people in their twenties or thirties?"

"Usually, but not always. It can affect teenagers, though the symptoms are slightly different. Has there been any indication of visual hallucinations?"

My heart stops, then clenches painfully as Emily starts to cry in earnest.

"I don't know. She hasn't said anything," she chokes. "About anything. She doesn't talk to me anymore. I don't know what to do."

I back away and wander down the hallway until I find the waiting room. The chairs are cold and hard, but I curl up in one anyway and wrap my arms around my knees.

I hum. I rock: The habit is so ingrained I almost don't feel it anymore, and I can't make myself stop, despite the curious looks I draw from other waiting patients. The song has me in its grip now, and it won't let go. I can't tell if the music is in my head or my throat, or both. When I close my eyes, I can barely tell that I'm moving. But I *am* moving.

* * *

I make my way through the garden, torn between excitement and fear. What if Sadra told someone, or what if someone followed her? Or, worst of all, what if she's not there?

The thought makes my stomach twist, though my fears are—I think—unfounded. She was there yesterday and the day before, and the day before that. She smiled at me, laughed with me like we were just two girls. Like we were equals.

And... she's there. She beams at me and gives me a tentative hug. I smile back, my lips trembling. Sadra chatters something at me before turning to grab a pile of clothes hung over the barre. She shakes out a set of trouser-skirts like the ones she wears, displaying them proudly.

"For you," she says, motioning to me.

I discard my skirts and put on the trousers, wiggling excitedly at my newfound freedom of movement. I bend over backward and put my hands on the smooth stones, then bring my legs over. I come upright to see Sadra gaping at me.

"Again," she says eagerly. "Again."

We dance together, exchanging techniques and showing off, but this time Sadra ends each of her demonstrations by pointing out an object and saying its name, or pantomiming an action and giving me the word. At the end, she gives me a word and I point to the object or perform the action. It's not ideal, but it's better than nothing. I wonder why no one else has tried. Why has it not occurred to Ismeni that I could do my job better if she taught me her language?

But then, Ismeni doesn't know I've gotten smarter. I was so slow and stupid before, and I forgot everything so quickly. She probably assumed—rightly—that it would be a waste of time to try to teach me anything beyond fetching and carrying and cleaning.

Maybe there's some way I can tell her that I'm better now. But I don't want to get Sadra in trouble, and I don't want to stop dancing. I bite my lip, wondering what I should do.

Nothing, I decide. Sadra will teach me. She'll help me.

She said so.

* * *

"There you are." Emily looks down at me, her eyes clear. No redness, no puffiness. No sign of her earlier tears. "Sorry it took so long. I had a few questions for Dr. Hadley."

"It's fine," I say, struggling to focus on her face. I take a deep breath and push away the voices and images that keep nibbling on the edges of my consciousness. "Em, I'm—I'm sorry about all this. You have enough to deal with. Baba Nadia, the school—I shouldn't—"

"Oh, sweetie, it's not your fault." Emily sits beside me and slips an arm around my shoulders. "Don't ever think that. And don't worry—we're going to figure this out. It'll be okay."

I nod, but it's only to make her feel better. I hope she can't feel me trembling.

"But…" She stops, her voice shaking. She clears her throat and takes a deep, slow breath. "You need to rest. I talked to James, and he agrees. Christie's going to dance Odette this weekend."

I don't say anything. I knew this was coming. Once, the thought of someone taking my place filled me with rage, dread, shame…but I don't feel anything now. I should say something, reassure her somehow or at least acknowledge her words. But the words won't come. I stare at my hands knotted in my lap.

"You've already had three performances," Emily rushes on, misinterpreting my silence. "And you were amazing. This won't hurt your prospects one bit, and it'll be such a great opportunity for Christie…"

She plows ahead with her little speech, which she must have been practicing while I waited for her. Though rushed, it has a rehearsed feel that isn't at all reassuring. No matter what Emily says, I know what's coming, and it's not going to be okay. But I don't care. It's hard to care about anything these days.

I'm tired.

So, so tired.

en Croix

Easter comes, and with it a sense of mingled dread and opportunity. Everything about the day seems backward and unnatural. For the first time ever, I skip the midnight mass and Sunday service. I can't face it without Baba Nadia, and Emily says I'm not well enough to go, anyway. I don't even bother to argue with her when she suggests we wait until the next day to visit Baba Nadia. I just get in the car and wait.

We ride to the hospital in silence, but I let her help me out of the car and support me as we walk inside because I know it will make her feel better. But by the time we reach the elevator, I'm leaning into her as much for my own sake as for hers. My breath rattles in my chest, and my hands are weak and clammy on Emily's arm.

I glance up, willing the elevator to hurry. The numbers overhead glow and shift, counting down with relentless precision. Already the chilly stillness of the hospital is seeping into my bones, sucking greedily at the few scraps of warmth I have left. Emily squeezes my hand and punches the elevator button again.

Three…two…one.

The elevator doors slide open, revealing a rumpled middle-aged man with bloodshot eyes and dark smudges of stubble on his chin and cheeks. The skin of his face sags with an unhealthy pallor that speaks of long, sleepless nights and unanswered prayers.

I look away as I step aside to let him off the elevator. He brushes past, his eyes blank and unseeing. I watch him go and sing under my breath as the doors close:

"Bayu, bayushki, bayu..."

Emily helps me into the elevator, and I lean against the wall with a grateful sigh. After a few restorative breaths, I check my purse to make sure I have my speakers. We're going to hook them up to my phone and play music for Baba Nadia. Emily suggested it, and I'm glad she did. I don't know if it will help, but it can't hurt and it makes me feel like I'm doing something useful, like I'm not coming apart at the seams.

"Are you sure you're up for this?" Emily asks, her eyes worried. "You should be in bed."

"It's Easter," I say. "She shouldn't be alone."

"Sasha, she'd understand—"

"I'm fine," I mutter, and pretend to fiddle with the speakers.

Emily purses her lips at my blatant lie. I've stopped even pretending to want to eat, and she's had almost as little sleep as I have, up at all hours of the night helping me through the aftermath of my increasingly violent night terrors. We haven't been to see Baba Nadia all week. But today is Easter, a day for family...and for miracles: *Khristos voskres.* Christ is risen. Maybe Baba Nadia will, too.

The elevator dings and the doors slide open. We head for the circulation desk, and the muscles around my spine clench in response to a strange tension in the air. There's something in the faces and gestures of the bustling nurses that makes me unaccountably nervous.

"Name?" the nurse asks without looking up from the forms she's filling out on the counter.

"Emily Somers and Sasha Nikolayeva," Emily says. "Here for Nadia Nikolayeva."

The nurse's head jerks up.

"Ah," she says. "Yes, of course. Could you have a seat, please? The head nurse will be with you shortly."

My fingers tighten on my purse. "Something's happened."

"You don't know that," Emily says softly, but her features are tight.

"I do." The ground tilts beneath my feet. "She's dead."

"Sasha, calm down—"

Whatever expression appears on my face must be pretty alarming because the nurse shoots out from behind her desk. Together, she and Emily guide me to one of the hideously floral chairs that dot the small lobby. I move slowly between them, making a conscious effort to move my legs. My muscles feel heavy and somehow gooey, like they're melting off my bones. The nurse hovers at my shoulder, anxiously wringing her hands as I lower myself into the chair. She's saying something, but the words seem to bounce off my ears without penetrating.

My head sinks into my hands. Two pairs of shoes enter my vision, then a third. Velcro, no laces. How odd. I drag my eyes upward and squint at a round, kindly face framed by steel gray curls and glasses with plain black lenses.

"Donna," Emily says, sounding relieved.

Someone—Donna, I guess—takes my wrist, feeling for the pulse. The gesture snaps me back to myself. I snatch my hand away.

"I'm fine," I mumble. "Fine."

"She is," Donna agrees. "More or less."

Emily sighs.

"Sasha, you remember Donna, don't you?" Her voice is falsely bright. To Donna, she murmurs, "How is Nadia? Is something wrong?"

"I'm sorry," Donna murmurs. "She passed just a few minutes ago. I was about to call you—"

No, no, no. It can't be true—and maybe it isn't. Maybe I'm hearing things again. Hope lances through me, scalding my heart.

"Did she really say that?" I ask Emily. My fingers twitch and spasm on the arms of my chair. "Did you hear her?"

A tear slips down Emily's cheek. "Yes, baby. I heard her."

I close my eyes. "I want to see her, please."

Donna frowns, looking at me sharply. "Perhaps… you should take a moment to prepare yourself."

"No," I say. "I want to see her now. Please."

Emily bites her lip. "Maybe you should wait."

"No."

Donna studies me for a moment, then nods. "Come with me."

"What happened?" Emily asks. "Was she…was anyone with her?"

"I sat with her until the end," Donna assures us. "Nothing happened, it wasn't violent. She was ready to go."

My breath catches and I whisper, "It should have been me."

If Donna hears my whispered recrimination, she ignores it. "Here we are."

Emily lays a gentle hand on my back. "Do you want me to go in with you?"

"No." My hand is already on the door. "Not yet."

"I'll wait down the hall," Emily whispers. "Take as long as you need."

I push the door open and then hesitate, afraid of what I'll find. What does death look like? What if it's ugly or frightening or demeaning? Is that how I'm going to remember Baba Nadia? What if I forget the way her eyes sparkled, or the way she closed them when she danced? What if I forget her strength, the perfect arch of her foot?

I flip the light on and move slowly to the side of the bed. Someone has combed her hair and folded her hands over her stomach. I always thought that when someone dies it would be obvious that the person is gone and what's left is just an empty shell. But when I look at my grandmother now, I don't see a shell. I just see Baba Nadia.

Of course it's her, I think, and reach out with trembling fingers to touch her face. Her cheek is still warm.

She has changed, though. Her descent into death has taken its toll. Her skin is drawn tightly over her bones, and her body is shrunken and skeletal. Even so, she looks like she's sleeping. I even think I see her chest rising and falling. I know it's my brain playing tricks on me, seeing what it expects to see, but it's unnerving.

I pull the blanket up over her shoulders and tuck them in with shaking hands, then sink to my knees. Music pulses in my head, my ears, my chest. For once, I don't resist. I sing without fear and pretend I'm singing her to sleep.

> *"Bayu, bayushki bayu*
> *Nye lozhisya na krayu ..."*

Something rattles out in the hall, jerking my attention away from Baba Nadia's corpse. I spin around on my knees and catch a glimpse of an orderly's enormous shoes as he passes by with a food cart. The cart and footsteps pause, then resume and eventually fade. A relieved breath hisses between my teeth. I'm not ready to share my last moments with my grandmother, not with anyone. Not yet. But Emily might come looking for me soon, and I need to look like I'm keeping it together.

I force myself to rise and gather the little pillows and blankets I'd brought from the house. I reach for the pictures and then decide to come back with a box rather than risk breaking them. They might not mean much to me, but they meant everything to Baba Nadia.

I pick up the portrait of Baba Nadia then, tracing my fingers over the high cheekbones and wide gray eyes, so like her daughter's—and like mine.

"Sasha?"

I jump and almost drop the picture. Donna crosses to me and pulls it gently from my hand, tracing the lines of my grandmother's form. Nadia Nikolayeva had the classic ballet figure: slim, with long legs, an elegant neck, high insteps. Maybe a little taller than average for a ballerina, but her body was fluid, light…and strong. She was famous for her strength, her endurance.

I blink back tears. That endurance has finally run out.

"It's lovely," Donna says as she sets the frame down on the table. "You look just like her."

"I know." I wrap my arms around myself. "Did you want something?"

If my rudeness offends her, she gives no sign of it. "Emily was just wondering if you need a few more minutes or if she can come in."

"No," I say, suddenly desperate to leave. "No, I'm done here. Emily should have a chance to—to say goodbye."

She nods and bustles away. She probably expects me to wait—it's only been a few minutes, after all. Not long enough to say goodbye. But no amount of time would be enough for that, and I can't stand this room a moment longer. Baba Nadia's body draws my gaze like a magnet. Her chest rises and falls, rises and falls. Our lullaby is in my head and in my ears…and on her lips.

The orderly and his food cart roll past once again, sending a wave of onion-scented air into the room. My stomach roils, and I stumble down the hall until I find a bathroom. The door crashes closed behind me just as I collapse over the toilet and heave. My stomach is empty, but my whole body convulses with the need to eject—something. My stomach, my intestines, who knows? My bones, maybe. When the spasms finally ease, I close the lid and prop my elbows on top, my hands over my face.

A muffled laugh slips through my fingers. So much for my Easter miracle. The words of the Acclamation slide over my tongue, smooth and bitter as tears:

"Voistinu voskres."

Truly, he is risen.

* * *

My arms are wrapped around myself as I rock back and forth in the passenger seat, the seat belt locking with rhythmic clicks each time I rock forward. Emily's hands tighten on the steering wheel, but she doesn't say anything. I bite my lip and force myself into stillness.

I meant to try to sleep. I was hoping that a few minutes' rest would help me gather the strength I need to face what's coming. But I gained neither rest nor strength, and now I'm out of time. We're here, passing through a forest of headstones sprouting from the ground like ugly, sinister flowers. Today we come to plant one of our own.

Emily nudges me. "We're here."

I nod without speaking and fiddle with my seat belt as Emily gets out and strides over to the funeral director, no doubt to discuss some small detail that might have been overlooked. Baba Nadia trusted her to execute the will, and Emily has taken the responsibility very seriously. She looks so poised and elegant in a black sheath dress and simple pearl earrings. She glides over the uneven ground, even in heels. My stomach clenches. She looks like Baba Nadia.

"Ready?" James asks from the back seat.

I'm not. But I get out of the car anyway and let him lead me through the orderly rows of headstones. My steps slow as we approach the crowd of mourners, and James slows with me, his eyes worried. I take a steadying breath and force one foot in front of the other until I'm at the edge of the grave, looking into the gaping hole that will house my grandmother's bones.

I hardly notice the murmured condolences and soft pats on my back and shoulders, my gaze fixed on the fresh grave and the mound of dark earth beside it.

Emily takes her place at my side as the priest welcomes the crowd of mourners. I lean into her and rest my head against her shoulder. On my other side, James squeezes my shoulder. I nod in acknowledgement, then close my eyes and do my best to pretend that I'm alone in some dark, safe place. The priest's voice fades into nothing, replaced by the lullaby that has become both a comfort and a torment.

But soon another melody intrudes, and I open my eyes. The pallbearers are approaching, accompanied by an old woman's voice raised in song.

> *"Gori, gori, moya zvezda,*
> *Zvezda lyubvi, privetnaya!*
> *Ty u menya odna zavetnaya,*
> *Drugoy ne budet nikogda."*

"What does it mean?"

I jump, then sigh as I turn and find that it's only Dave. James gives him a disapproving glare, but I shake my head.

"I don't mind."

The pallbearers place my grandmother's coffin beside the grave, their movements perfectly coordinated. Their heads are bowed, but their backs are straight and strong. Dancers, like most of the people here. Nearly all my grandmother's students have come, flying in from all over the country—all over the world—to say goodbye, even with only three days' notice.

They loved her.

One man in the crowd looks different, though, and it's not just the strangely cut leather coat he wears or the pale scar on his face. He carries himself not like a dancer but like a fighter. Despite the lines around his eyes and the gray in his hair, he looks dangerous…and familiar, though I can't think why. I wonder uneasily if I should tell someone, but I don't want to draw attention to him—or to myself. I don't want to add to Emily's worries.

Dave nudges me again, drawing me back to the song. I translate over my shoulder as the song continues, each word dropping like a stone onto my chest.

"Shine, shine on, my star
Shine, friendly star,
You are my only cherished one,
Another there will never be
By the heavenly strength of your beams
My whole life is illuminated
And if I die, over my grave
Shine, shine on, my star."

My voice breaks on the last line, and Emily slips her arm around my waist. I keep talking, trying to contain or at least cover up the overflow of emotion.

"It's a love song, really." My voice is flat and dull. "I think it reminded her of her husband—her first husband."

"Or grandfather, or your mother," Emily murmurs. "Or you. She'd want you to keep shining."

I don't reply. What is there to say? I suppose there's only one thing left, and when they ask me to "say a few words," I'm as ready as I can be.

"Ya tebya lyublyu, Babushka," I whisper, and drop a single, pale rose onto the coffin as it sinks into the ground. *I love you.*

Dozens of roses follow until the casket is completely obscured. I turn away as the true burial begins. The sight of fresh earth scattering across the bed of white makes me want to run and never stop.

I look across the grave instead. The scarred man's eyes find me, and I shrink into myself. There's a depth of grief there that scares me even as it baffles me. I shiver. I don't know who he is, and I think I don't want to find out.

But his eyes catch me again, and once again I'm struck by the feral look in his eyes and the ferocity that emanates from his body, even in stillness. A wild creature, through and through. A lion, maybe…or a wolf.

* * *

There's a wolf—no, a fox. Who brings a fox to dinner? This isn't the first time, either. I've seen them before, the green-eyed man with his little friend. When I accompany Ismeni to the palace for fancy parties, I sometimes see the fox flirting with adoring young ladies and begging for scraps of food while his master lurks uncomfortably in the corner.

And now they're here. Orean and Ismeni are united, for once, as the hosts of some small but very important party. Something to do with Orean's sister, Cimari and I don't know if it's a good thing or not.

I hear Cimari's name on everyone's lips, but she doesn't seem happy or excited. But then, she never does. I've only seen her smile with real pleasure once, and that was when she had a slave whipped for spilling wine.

Dove and I stand against the wall with the other slaves. Most are strangers—I only know Orean's and Cimari's; at least, I recognize them. I suppose I don't know them: As far as I can tell, they don't have names. I feel sorry for them, that their masters don't value them enough to give them that. They don't seem to be valued at all—or even needed. I've never seen either of them do a single thing. I don't understand it. Maybe it's because they're still in the fog, like I was before I found the barre—and Sadra. Maybe they can't do anything.

Orean rises from his cushioned seat and crosses to an open space in the middle of the room. His voice echoes as he addresses his guests, the words winging away into the shadows of the vaulted ceiling. With an expansive wave of his arm, he motions for both Sadra and Ismeni to rise. They do so, wearing identical strained smiles. I watch, mystified, as they move together to the center of the room. And then the music begins.

With only her voice, Ismeni fills the room. It sounds—no, it feels—like there must be a harp, or a flute, or an entire orchestra accompanying her. But it's just her. Despite her skill, Sadra's dancing is overlooked as every eye in the room is drawn to my mistress. Even I can't look away for long, though I've been dying to see Sadra dance to music.

Ismeni, though, is singing to only one of her admirers, a man sitting beside the fox-friend. The man's eyes shine, though they somehow seem sad, too, or maybe just tired. A crown of woven flowers wrought in white and rose gold nestles among thick black curls. My gaze settles on the crown, drawn so completely that, for a moment, I break free of Ismeni's song. I had a crown, once.

My forehead wrinkles in a tiny frown. I had a crown?

Ridiculous.

I watch Ismeni again. She holds the crowned man's gaze throughout the performance, and he beams at her, his face glowing with pride. I glance at Orean and note with relief that he hasn't noticed someone else is playing the role of proud husband. He just seems annoyed that Ismeni has stolen the show from Sadra.

When the song ends, I expect Ismeni to look smug. But she blushes and smiles shyly at the man—her lover?—like a teenager. When she turns to accept an old woman's congratulations, the smile remains, curving on her lips like a secret too delicious to hide. I've never seen her look so beautiful, though her shining auburn hair and luxurious white gown are just as perfectly arranged as usual.

Ismeni and Sadra bow to each other, then to the room, before giving the floor to an older man dressed in thick white robes. He has the look of a powerful man gone to seed: his shoulders are broad, but just the slightest bit rounded. His billowing robes can't completely hide the paunch at his middle. The skin at his neck and jaw sags a bit, lending a petulant cast to the arrogant set of his jaw.

He makes a speech, something about joining families. It's a betrothal, I realize. I don't hear anything about love, I don't think. I haven't learned the word for love, but certainly nothing he says seems to fit. Not that I blame him. Cimari has nice features—shiny black hair, rosy cheeks, a neat figure—but she isn't attractive. She's the opposite of attractive...

Not ugly, though. Repellent, maybe. Yes, that's it. She repels.

The man—Cimari's fiancé, I'm sure of it—finishes his speech and turns to Cimari. He holds his hands out, as if offering something to her. There, trapped between his fingers, is a small bird. The watching guests sit on the edges of their seats, childlike in their excitement. Even Cimari looks almost eager.

The bird begins to glow. The light pulses, growing steadily until it's so intense I have to close my eyes. When I open them, I see that Cimari's fiancé holds a trembling puppy in his hands. He offers it to Cimari, who takes it with a small wrinkle of her nose and immediately passes it off to Orean—who hands it to Sadra. Cimari's magician fiancé doesn't notice; he's too busy accepting the room's applause.

Not everyone is pleased, though. The man with the fox looks furious. I follow his eyes and see a tiny, crumpled form fall from the magician's fingers. The bird—it's dead. Sadra, too, shoots a dark glance at the couple as she soothes the puppy. The poor thing cries piteously in her lap, obviously frightened.

Poor baby, where did he steal you from? Did he take you from your mother, your brothers and sisters? I know how you feel.

I frown, wondering where these thoughts are coming from. How, exactly, do I know what it feels like to be torn away from my family? I've been Ismeni's slave since...I don't know. Forever.

Haven't I?

* * *

My head bounces against the window with a loud *thunk* as the car lurches over uneven ground. I'm in the car again with Emily, driving away from the grave site. Is the service over? I suppose it must be. But where's James?

"Did James leave?" I ask, rubbing a thumb over my necklace.

"He's going to the reception to honor your grandmother. He'll do all the socializing and small talk for us."

"Where—where are we going?"

"Home, honey."

Emily's voice is tremulous but somehow resigned. Have I been forgetting again? How many times have I asked, and how many times has she answered? What has my body been doing without me, while I was—elsewhere?

Emily seems to be out of comforting things to say. I'm too afraid of giving anything more away to risk speaking, so we ride home in silence. Once there, Emily lets me hide in my room for a little while. It isn't long enough. It seems like only a few minutes before she lets herself in and flicks the light on. Night has fallen. I've been sitting in the dark, and I didn't know.

"I've been looking through the file cabinets." Emily sits on my bed and eyes me warily. "Do you know where your mom's medical records are? It would really help if we could find them."

I open my mouth to answer her—to lie—then close it abruptly. My teeth click together. I'm tired of lying. It's too hard. "I burned them."

Emily puts her hands over her face and groans. "Sasha, *why?*"

"I didn't want to see them anymore," I admit, my lip beginning to tremble. "And I didn't want you to know. Please don't make me go to the hospital."

"But they can *help* you—"

"No, they can't," I say flatly. "No one can. I know what's going to happen."

Emily takes my hand and holds it tightly. "And what do you think is going to happen?"

I bite down on the inside of my lip to stop the trembling and look Emily in the eyes. "I'm going to die."

Balancé

"Sasha, it's almost time to go." Emily hovers in the doorway of my room, her eyes downcast. "Are you ready?"

"Almost. I just want to go to the garden and—and the studio. You know, say goodbye."

"Don't talk like that," Emily says, her voice thick. "You're going to be fine. You're going to go to the hospital and they're going to make you better. End of discussion."

When I don't answer, she ducks away. I remain curled like a shrimp on my bed until I hear her bedroom door close. Only then do I rise and pad down the stairs in my bare feet. Baba Nadia used to move around the house in just the same way: silent and slow, like a ghost. I wonder if that's what I am now, a ghost. Just a pale, frightened wisp of what I used to be.

With the shutters closed, the studio is so dark I can barely see. I like it. I don't need light to find my way. I know every inch of the place. The only thing the light would show me is my own reflection, and I don't want to see that.

I move to the barre and lay my hand on the smooth wood. In the dark, it's not my own silhouette I see in the mirror but my grandmother's. She watches me with loving but critical eyes, correcting my form and posture, tapping out a steady beat with the cane she never really needed—until the day she fell.

My arm trembles as I raise it above my head once more. My strength is already fading, though I could swear I've only been dancing for a few minutes. There's a pain in my chest that bodes no good, but there are worse ways to go—wouldn't it be better to die here, with Baba Nadia's voice humming in my ears, than in a hospital bed surrounded by strangers?

For a moment, that's all I want. I want to die here in the dark, dancing for my grandmother one last time. I want to be with her there in the mirror, or in heaven, or in a fresh grave next to hers. It doesn't matter where as long as I can see her again.

But I promised Emily. Last night I promised her that I would try to live, to believe that I can be saved. Baba Nadia wouldn't want me to go back on my word. She always said that you have only one promise to give and if you break it, you can never truly make another one.

I promised Emily I would try.

I lower my arm, letting it fall forward onto the mirror where it meets Baba Nadia's reaching hand.

"*Skora uvidimcya,*" I whisper.

See you soon.

I make my way through the shadowy corridors of the studio, retracing my steps back toward the light. My breath feels thick and sticky, the air pushing in and out of my lungs as if fighting against a barrier each way.

The house and studio are separated by only a small garden, but it might as well be an entire content. Halfway across, the pain in my chest returns and forces me to my knees. With shaking fingers, I brush away a low-hanging lilac blossom that tickles my face as I lean against an artfully placed boulder for support.

"*What is your name?*"

I squint. Sadra stands before me, a determined glint in her eye. I'm standing, too, wondering when and how I got to my feet. But then

Emily calls me, and I'm crouched again in the shadow of the lilac bush. Or are they roses?

* * *

"Give me your name, Cygnet."

I don't like to hear her call me Cygnet. It's not my name. Coming from her, my friend, it hurts. I want to tell her—I can almost remember—I want to say it out loud, but I can't. She knows that.

"What is your name? Tell me."

* * *

"Sasha," I mumble. "I'm Sasha."

"Sasha?" Emily is calling me again. She sounds scared.

* * *

"Cygnet! Pay attention." Sadra holds me by the shoulders, looking deep into my eyes. She's so pretty and strong. I wish I could be like her. "You must tell me your name. You must speak to me."

Why does she keep demanding that I speak, as if I have a choice about it? I have no voice. We both know that. I'm a slave, a nothing. That's just the way it is. How could it be any different?

But a little voice in my head protests. I do have a voice, it says.

I do have a name.

Remember.

Speak.

* * *

I force myself to my feet, but fear makes my legs weak. Emily. I want Emily. I need to tell her that I've changed my mind, that I want to go to the hospital. I want them to fix me.

I don't want to die.

I open my mouth to cry out, to call for Emily, but the words don't come.

My voice is gone.

** * **

"That's it." Sadra squeezes my shoulders. "Yes, that's it. You can do it."

"Ss...Ssaah..." I hiss through my teeth, my face scrunched up with effort. I feel like I'm trying to do something that my brain just doesn't want to do. But I want to do it. I want it so badly it hurts. My fists clench, nails digging into my palms. My body shakes. Speak, I shout inside my head. Speak.

Speak.

II

Act Two: Sotto

"All that we see or seem is but a dream within a dream."

-Edgar Allan Poe

Couru

"Sss...Ssss...Sa-SASHA."

Sadra's eyes go wide. I stare back at her, my mouth hanging open. Then she whoops in excitement, grabbing my hands and swinging me around in a circle. I break away from her and stumble into the barre. I clutch at it, my head spinning.

The wooden carvings under my hand turn into a whirl of images tearing across my eyes: A dead boy, a man with a scar reaching for my necklace and tearing it from my neck. Hunger, cold, fear, despair...and pain. Terrible pain. A woman slapping me then kissing my face—Ismeni. Cimari, Dove...Sadra.

They're memories. *My* memories, yet at the same time completely foreign. They belong to the other girl, the other Sasha.

They belong to Cygnet.

"Sasha," she says. "That's your name?"

"Wh-What? What i-isss..." I don't recognize the words that I force out of my mouth, but I understand them. "How—"

"Sasha and Sadra," she says. She smiles at me and taps her ear. "It sounds nice together, doesn't it?"

I back away from her, dragging myself along the barre. "Y-you did this. You took me. You huhh...huh...hurt me."

"What?" Sadra's face goes blank with shock. "No, Sasha. I'm your friend. I helped you. You were—"

I shake my head, cutting her off, because I already know. I was empty, lost in the fog. I was without thought, drifting through each day, my only emotion a dull sort of cheerfulness. I followed orders placidly, never thinking to question my state, my being.

People poked me, prodded me, slapped me around, and I never lifted a finger to stop them. I never *wanted* to stop them. I just wanted to do better.

A low moan escapes my lips. The weight of my shock, my shame, sends me crashing to the ground. I brace myself on hands and knees, my wrists trembling from the impact. Bile scorches my throat and sinuses, but I don't let it out. The muscles in my neck seize and twist with the strain, making my head and shoulders heave.

As I fight to recover, Sadra rubs my back and murmurs soothing nonsense under her breath. Finally, the pressure subsides, and I let my head hang between my shoulders. After a moment, I push Sadra away and struggle to my feet, wiping my mouth and nose with the back of my hand.

"Stay away," I say. "No more. *No more.*"

"Cygnet—I mean, Sasha—wait!"

But I'm already gone, staggering through the garden paths. I'm confused—I know my way back but not how or why I know, or where I want to go. Sometimes I see the garden of my dreams and sometimes I see my garden at home—or was that the dream?

Dogwood trees merge with rose of Sharon; irises shiver and blink and become day lilies. All around me, colors and shapes swirl together as my brain struggles to make sense of this new reality.

Dove finds me braced against the garden wall; my forehead pressed against the cool stone. I whip around as she approaches, falling into a defensive crouch. Her eyes are almost as frightened as my own. She takes my arm, her fingers digging painfully into the flesh above my elbow as she hauls me roughly upright.

I open my mouth to protest. She slaps it shut.

Holding a hand to my face, I stare at her in shock and start to back away, preparing to run—if I can. She holds a hand up in an easily recognizable message: *Stop*.

I do. I hate how natural it feels, how automatically I obey her command. She breathes deeply in through her nose, motioning upward with her hand. She blows gently, letting the air slip out through rounded lips. I almost laugh. In through the nose, out through the mouth, just like Emily used to say.

When I'm calmer, Dove takes my face between her weathered hands and looks me in the eye, making sure she has my attention. She passes a hand over her face, smoothing away all expression until it forms a familiar, doll-like facade. Then she makes eye contact once again and draws her finger across her throat. Her eyes bore into mine, willing me to understand.

She draws her hand across my face and her finger across my throat. *Pretend*, she is telling me, *or they'll kill you*. I believe her.

* * *

I lie awake.

My heart pounds; saliva floods my mouth. My head and my stomach spin around and around until I think I'm going to be sick. I swing my legs off the narrow cot and put my head in my hands. *In* through the nose, *out* through the mouth.

Don't moan. Don't cry. Just breathe.

I spent all day carefully, almost obsessively, monitoring my expressions, my posture, my every movement. Through it all, I kept waiting, hoping for some secret message, some sign from Sadra that she would keep her promise. I remember, now, how she found me in the garden and tried to make me understand.

I'll help you, she said. But how? When? And, above all, *why*? I doubt very much that she found me by chance, and I doubt even more that she's doing—whatever she's doing—out of simple curiosity or the goodness of her heart.

I should just go to sleep. Even if unconsciousness doesn't transport me back home—and I strongly suspect that it won't, despite the initial surge of hope I felt when the idea first occurred to me—it will at least reduce the amount of time I have to spend waiting for answers.

I don't know how much longer I can take this. Every breath is a struggle against the waves of panic beating against my mind. My feet itch with the need to move, to *do* something. Anxiety ripples up and down my body, making the skin of my back crawl and twitch with nerves.

Every instinct screams at me to run, or fight. But there's no one to fight, and nowhere to run.

I lift my head from my hands and stare at the door, lit by a small strip of moonlight coming in the window. My heartbeat grows louder in my ears as my vision begins to blur and shift. The walls seem to expand and contract with each ragged breath, drawing closer and a closer around me. Panic spills over. I can't do it—I can't wait.

I have to go. *Now.*

I rise, driven by a single, all-consuming thought: Find Sadra. But where does she sleep? In Orean's chamber or in her own? Not that it matters, since I don't know where to find either. But I do know where the garden is, and I know that's where it happened—whatever *it* is. Sadra might realize that it's the only place I would think to go, and that I might be desperate enough to try.

I slip into the night, scurrying down the stairs and through our small courtyard until I come to the garden door. I ease it open and flit from shadow to shadow, every nerve ablaze with fear. The garden looks different at night, the beautiful plants and sculptures transformed by moonlight and shadows into something sinister and grotesque. My legs shake so badly I'm afraid I can't go on. But I do, because I must. I've done a stupid, dangerous thing, and now I have to try to make it worth the risk.

Finally, I creep into my corner of the garden and look around. My heart plummets. The clearing is empty. But I try, just in case.

Softly, I call, "Sadra?" And again, "Sadra, please. *Sadra.*"

She's not here.

Blood drains from my face and seems to pool somewhere around my feet. My head swimming, I lower myself to the ground and crouch among the roses with my arms wrapped around my stomach: Inhale, exhale. Repeat.

For several long minutes, I do nothing but quiver in the shadows. My limbs seem locked into place, paralyzed by fear. But staying here would be even more foolish than leaving my room in the first place, and the longer I stay, the more likely discovery becomes. I have to go.

Shaking, I take one step onto the path. Then another, and another. I block out the little voice that whispers of terrible possibilities and unknowns. If I think about what will happen if I'm caught, I'll be too scared to move.

It takes less than ten minutes to cross the garden, but it seems like several years. When I reach the door, my legs go weak with relief and I have to lean against the ivy-covered wood for a moment.

It's alright, I tell myself. You did it. You're safe.

I reach for the wrought iron handle and pull.

The door doesn't move.

I try again, harder this time. Nothing happens.

Breathing hard, I yank on the handle as hard as I can, putting every muscle I have into the effort. The door doesn't budge, doesn't even creak. Instead, it remains spitefully, unnaturally still.

I turn away and press my hands against my head, desperately

considering my options. Can I climb the wall? No, too high. Can I break the door down somehow? No, too loud—and too stupid. Is there another entrance? No—wait. There is.

I set out once more, making sure to stay in the shadow of the wall. There's a small tree beside the kitchen courtyard that I think I can climb, and the vines covering the walls there are thicker, sturdy enough to hold my weight.

I hope.

The short dash to the kitchen courtyard, though agonizing, passes without incident. I try the door, just in case, but this one too seems to be equipped with the same strange locking mechanism. I find the tree and ascend as silently as I can manage. The top of the wall is just close enough that I can stand on the last sturdy branch and haul myself up, though I scrape my elbows and shins in the process.

I slither over the other side immediately, clinging to the climbing vines and scrabbling for a foothold that isn't there. My stomach lurches as the vines break, sending me tumbling. I hit the ground with a *thump* that knocks the air right out of my lungs. My diaphragm seems to have forgotten how to function, but my ears work just fine: Someone is inside the kitchen.

I drag myself upright and cast around, desperately searching for a place to hide. But there's nothing, nothing! I have to move, at least, away from the tell-tale broken vines.

Oh, I am so dead. So dead and so very, very stupid. But it's too late for that—focus!

The kitchen door swings open, revealing a slim silhouette. When the figure steps out into the courtyard, the light spilling out of the door reveals Cimari's face, alight with curiosity. A glowing orb appears in her hand, seemingly from nowhere, and she holds it up, peering into the shadows. I force my muscles to relax and my eyes to soften into mild neutrality. My only hope now is to play my part as convincingly as I can.

Cimari's eyes find me quickly and immediately narrow in suspicion. "And what are you doing out here, little doll? I wonder."

She studies me for a moment and then nods abruptly, turning on her heel. "Come with me," she calls over her shoulder.

She doesn't wait or even turn to look and make sure I'm following because of course she knows I'll obey. I'm a thrall.

So I trail after her, my movements as smooth and calm as I can make them. While we walk, I wrestle with my body's reaction to this latest disaster. A thrall's heart wouldn't race, nor would a thrall's breath come so fast. A thrall's forehead wouldn't bead with sweat.

If she sees any of it, the game is up, and I don't want to know what happens if I lose.

It's hard, nearly impossible…but only nearly. Though my mind is racing, wondering where we're going and what will happen when we get there, my face and body form a perfect facade of indifference. I am, if nothing else, a performer. *I* control my body, my face. They can't take that from me. If Cimari looks back, she won't see my fear or confusion. All she'll see is a thrall.

Finally, Cimari stops and raps on a door. No one answers.

My heart gives a little lurch in another attempt to start pounding again. While we were walking, my attention was so consumed with maintaining my mask that any notice of my surroundings escaped me completely. Now, I let my eyes flick ever so slightly over the dark corridor. Torchlight illuminates tapestries depicting scenes of violence and domination: hunts, battles, boozing—and women. I look away in disgust. I've never been in this part of the house before, but I have an idea of where we might be. And if I'm right…

I'm right. Cimari knocks again, and this time the door cracks open to reveal Orean's angry face. His expression softens, though, when he sees his sister. The door opens wider, and he leans against the doorframe. His hair is rumpled, and his robe looks as though it was thrown on in haste over…nothing. Ugh.

"What is it, child?" he asks. "You should be asleep. You have your lesson with the Premier in the morning."

"I know," she says, dimpling.

I blink at the sudden change in her demeanor. She seems almost…nice. No, more than nice. Engaging. Charming, even. It unsettles me.

Cimari moves, her hand resting lightly on his arm. "And I wanted your permission to present this thrall to him."

Orean closes his eyes and sighs. "Cimari, no. We've already lost one thrall to this foolishness—a thrall that turned out to be perfectly safe, may I remind you."

"But it was out of its chamber, wandering about," she insists, her gray eyes wide with innocent concern. "My betrothed said—"

"My wife is overly indulgent with her pets," Orean says dismissively. "Nothing more. I will not be embarrassed again, Cimari. Go to bed."

"But—"

"No," Orean says firmly. "I've only just returned from Council, and I am weary. I will tell you once more, sister, and you will obey me without any more tricks—*Go to bed.*"

Cimari blushes. Her lower lip creeps out ever so slightly and I realize with a start that she's no older than I am: Her usual haughty expression and cruel little smile make her seem older. The thought that someone so young could be so cold is unnerving, even in my current state.

"What shall I do with this, then?" she asks, jerking her head in my direction. Her veil of sweetness is gone as suddenly as it came.

"Leave it here," Orean says. "I'll deliver it to my wife in the morning."

Cimari smirks at this. She gives me a long, measuring look and then turns, leaving me alone with Orean. He pulls me into the chamber with a sharp jerk. I stumble and land hard on my hands and knees but get up immediately, resuming a poised, neutral stance.

"My sister has brought us a toy," Orean announces.

"I see that."

My heart stops; I know that voice. I peek through my lashes and see Sadra reclining against the pillows, clad in nothing but bedsheets and the rings on her fingers. Revulsion creeps over me in a slow, clammy ooze as I realize what Orean has in mind.

Sadra rises, wrapping herself in a length of silk, and moves toward us with a sensual sway in her hips. There's a glint in her eye and a wicked little smile on her lips—nothing to suggest she knows me or cares at all about what Orean means to do with me. I force myself to relax as Orean slips my shawl off my shoulders. It puddles on the floor, followed a moment later by the shift I wore to bed.

Don't move, I tell myself. Don't move, don't let him see.

But he *can* see me—all of me. I can feel his gaze traveling over my body like the tip of a nail, scratching a hot, shameful line across my shoulders and down my back.

A weight settles on my neck; my lip trembles. I don't know if it's fear or self-control that keeps me from slapping his hand away, and I hate myself for it.

How far am I willing to take this charade? Orean's hand slides lower, his fingers skimming over my back. Cold washes over me as I realize that it's not a matter of willingness. I don't have a choice, not really.

Bile rises in my throat. No. *No.* I should fight. I *must* fight. I can't just let him—but what would that achieve? He could snap my neck in his hand right now. I wouldn't stand a chance.

"Come," Orean says to Sadra, tickling my collarbone with a lock of my own hair. "Have a closer look. I know the Temple doesn't approve of thralls. Surely you must be curious."

"I can wait for that," Sadra says, and kisses him. "But not for you. The

Council takes up entirely too much of your time—and your energy." She laughs throatily and hands him a cup. "Poor old man," she teases. "I've made you a tonic."

Orean gives an appreciative grunt. "Kind of you."

Orean takes the cup and downs its contents in one gulp. He doesn't see the flicker of satisfaction cross Sadra's face, but I do, and I dare to hope as she insinuates herself between me and Orean, pushing him away and guiding him toward the bed. His movements are strangely fluid; his feet scrape across the floor, and his head bobs weakly on his shoulders.

Sadra dumps him on the bed, where he sprawls motionless among the covers. She studies him for a moment, then gives him a vicious poke in the back of the head and turns away. I stoop and pull on my shift with shaking hands, gasping in little jerks.

"Thanks be," Sadra breathes, putting her arms around me. "Hush, now. You're safe."

"Wh-what—"

She grins wickedly and holds up her hand, flicking at one of the rings with her thumb. The flat blue stone rises, revealing a tiny chamber that must have held some kind of drug. Somehow, I'm not shocked. And I'm not sure if it makes me trust her more or less.

"Sit," she says, pushing me into a plush chair and tucking my shawl around me. "Wait."

I watch, my muscles clenched in misery, as Sadra climbs onto the bed beside Orean. She tucks her hair behind her ear and leans over, whispering into his ear. I wonder a little bit what she's doing, but I can't seem to hold onto the thought long enough to really do a good job of it.

My mind is—not empty, not like a thrall's—but frozen, stuttering and blinking like the screen of an overloaded computer about to crash. Questions tumble over and around each other, filling my mind so that I can't properly think about any of them.

What is Sadra doing here? Why did she save me? If she's trying to help me, why is she with Orean? Why should she care anything about me in the first place? And why in the world does she have poison hidden in her rings? Who needs to keep weapons like that on hand—in bed?

"Sasha." Sadra kneels in front of me, and I blink as she grips my knee. "We have to go."

"Is he dead?" My eyes flick to the figure on the bed. If he's breathing, I can't see it.

"No," Sadra says. "Just asleep. Come, now."

Sadra tows me through the halls, stopping only to drag me into an empty room when the house steward passes on his nightly rounds. Has he reached my room yet? Has he noticed I'm gone? He could be on his way to Ismeni right now. I could be lost.

I should be panicking right now, but I feel curiously calm, like my body and even my thoughts are moving along without me. I follow Sadra without question, too numb to protest her rough treatment or remove her hand from my wrist.

Sadra sighs in relief as we slip into the bedroom I share with Dove. There's no movement from Dove's bed, but that very stillness gives her away. Guilt cracks the ice around my mind, just a little.

Poor Dove. I must be making her crazy. How does she do it? How can she stand to continue like this?

I shake my head in disbelief, then remember the weight of Orean's hand on my neck and the whisper of cloth against my skin as it fell to the floor. I'd do a lot to never feel that again.

I sit on the bed and hold my head in my hands.

"Sasha," Sadra whispers, sitting beside me, "I know you have questions. I will try to answer, but I'm afraid you won't understand. Not yet."

I nod, too miserable to speak.

Sadra hesitates, then says, "There is…a thing I can do. While you sleep. It will help you. Will you let me?"

I don't see that I have a choice about it. This isn't something I can handle by myself. If nothing else, I learned that from tonight's disastrous escapade.

I close my eyes, releasing a long, shuddering breath. "Yes."

Pas de deux

I lie curled on my side with the thin hospital sheets pulled over my head to keep out the light. It hurts my eyes, and the chair in the corner is scaring me. Not the chair object, I mean, but the chair itself. The...the idea of the chair: It used to have two names, and now it has three.

Emily is arguing about it with the doctor, but she doesn't realize that's what they're talking about. I try again to tell her the chair's new name. Nothing comes out. I try harder, straining to pull the words out of my mind and into my mouth.

"There it is again," Emily says. "At first, I thought it was Russian, but I asked someone and he said it wasn't. It doesn't sound like gibberish, though, does it? It sounds like a word."

"Ms. Somers, aphasia can present in many different ways—"

"I know," Emily snaps. "You told me that. But what if it's, I don't know, a name? A place? What if she's trying to tell us something?"

"She probably is," the doctor allows. "But unless we can find some significance in her utterances, our efforts are better spent on her other symptoms."

Symptoms? What symptoms?

Someone else enters the room and starts talking about abuse—Abuse, with a capital "A." They're talking about James—but why? What does he have to do with anything? I wish he were here, though, because Emily is crying, and I can't comfort her. I can't do anything.

* * *

A breeze drifts in from the window and wakes me as it hits my sweat-soaked body. My eyelids twitch, then still. What will I find when I open them? Pale blue walls covered with photographs and dance posters or hard, bare stone? Fear grips my belly in its fist and squeezes.

You know, a voice whispers. You know. Hiding won't change that.

Reluctantly, I sit up. I'm still here, still in this strange world of my nightmares. I shiver as the voices and feelings from my dream come back to me. I didn't know, I didn't remember—I wasn't *me*. Not the me that I am now, anyway. It was like being inside another person's head. Just like *this* world felt when I was on the other side, I realize. But now this feels real—horrifically, terrifyingly real.

But *I* feel real. I feel *good*. My body is strong and healthy, and my mind is clearer than it's been since before Baba Nadia died. What does that mean? Was this real all along and I'm just now waking up? Is the doll now that other Sasha, the other me?

Does that person even exist?

I don't understand. I press the heels of my hands against my temples, automatically suppressing a groan.

Don't speak.

Don't make a sound.

Oddly, it's Sadra's voice rather than my own reminding me to stay silent. As my eyes travel around the room, words pop into my head—words I didn't know before.

For a moment I panic, afraid that these are the only words I have, that I've lost the languages I grew up with. With a guilty glance at Dove's sleeping form, I break my rule and whisper to myself: "Chair. *Stul.* Window. *Okno.* Bed. *Postel.*"

Those words are still there. Other things aren't, though: My toes wiggle freely, unencumbered by the bruises and blisters I've carried with me for nearly ten years, ever since I first began dancing *en pointe*. My grandmother warned me that it was a serious step, that it would hurt and keep hurting. I didn't care. I wore my torn toenails and knobby knuckles like badges of honor and kept dancing. I never tried to hide them—they were just as much a talisman as my necklace was. A charm, a reminder of who I am.

And now they're gone, melted into smooth, clean skin.

My necklace…if I focus, I can call up the image of a figure bending over me, silhouetted against a hazy background of blue-white mist. A scar stands out more clearly than the face behind it; a drop of sweat—or perhaps a tear—falls onto my cheek. Sensations I remember more clearly: warm, rough fingers at my neck; a sharp jerk as the chain breaks; and a rush of grief.

Tears sting my eyes as they have so many times since Sadra pulled me completely into this world. I blink them away. I'll have a lot more to cry about if I get caught.

I close my eyes and school my features into stillness. Smooth, like glass, like the porcelain doll they think I am.

Dove stirs, reminding me that it's time to start the day. There's an empty basin resting on the table between our beds. I take it outside, through the door that leads from our bedroom to a stone balcony. A flight of stairs made from cobbled stone takes me to the small courtyard where Dove and I get our water twice a day from a hand pump.

Outside the courtyard lies the garden. I allow myself one longing glance toward the old wooden door and then hurry inside with the water. It's only a few hours. Half a day, no more, and then Sadra will be able to tell me what the hell is going on.

* * *

Dove and I take turns washing. While I run a wet cloth over my face and body, Dove lays a clean dress on my bed. A shift follows, along with soft leather slippers. It must be a habit from—from before, when I needed her to help me do everything. My mouth pulls sharply downward; I hide it with the shift, pulling the thin fabric over my head. When Dove turns, my mask, like the rest of my clothes, is firmly in place.

I sit patiently while Dove arranges my hair and then her own with quick, sure movements. How can Ismeni not realize that there's a person behind those dark eyes? What Dove does is art—no empty shell could produce such elegance. How can they not know?

We find Ismeni still in bed, sprawled in a tangle of blankets and nightclothes. Somehow, she looks elegant even with her limbs flopping around and her hair in her face. Dove moves about the room, putting away stray pieces of clothing and tidying Ismeni's vanity. I help her, earning myself a long look from Dove but no protest.

"Good morning, my darlings."

Hearing such an endearment from Ismeni's lips sends disgust rippling over my skin like a wave of heat. Ismeni yawns and stretches, oblivious. She smiles at me with genuine fondness, and my heart warms in spite of myself—another reaction from "before." It makes me sick.

By the time Ismeni finishes getting ready, my face is aching with the strain of maintaining a blank expression. Not for the first time, I marvel at Dove's seemingly effortless performance. Practice, I remind myself. It just takes practice and repetition, like anything else, and I know I can do *that*.

The thought comforts me as we follow Ismeni to breakfast. As she takes her place between Orean and Cimari, Dove and I take ours with the other thralls along the wall. Sadra sits at Orean's right hand, nibbling at a piece of cheese. Though she hides it well, I can tell she's tired. There's a sort of hesitation to her movements that I'm all too familiar with. I know the kind of bone-deep exhaustion that makes you weigh every ounce of strength like a miser with his last few coins. Whatever she was doing to help me last night, it took a lot out of her.

A tinkling laugh distracts my attention. Ismeni and Cimari are talking and giggling like schoolgirls. Their conversation moves too quickly for me to catch most of it, but I understand enough to know they're talking about Cimari's wedding. Cimari doesn't seem all that interested, though, and neither am I.

I tune them out…until I realize they're talking about me—or us. The slaves.

"You will dress your thrall in something a *bit* more presentable, I hope."

Ismeni eyes the frayed and ill-fitting gown on Cimari's slave, who stares at her grubby feet with perfect indifference. The muscles in my back clench against an involuntary shiver.

"I suppose so." Cimari grins, nudging Ismeni with her elbow. "You can be in charge of its attire. I know how you enjoy playing pretend."

Ismeni smiles, unperturbed. "There's no shame in wanting to be surrounded by pretty things. Does the Temple not teach us to look for beauty in everything?"

"It's more than that with you," Cimari says. "It's like you think they're your friends."

"But they are." Ismeni smiles at me and Dove, and my jaw aches with the urge to grind my teeth.

"No matter how well you dress them or train them, they're not *people*, Isi." Cimari laughs, genuinely amused, while I breathe through my rage—in through the nose, out through the mouth.

"Oh, hush," Ismeni says tolerantly. "You have your own blind spots. Your fascination with Light is most unseemly in a girl of your station. You're lucky to be marrying someone as silly about it as you are."

"Silly! He's the House Premier!"

"And, anyway, it's not all pretend," Ismeni says. "Thralls can learn quite a lot, if you're willing to teach them. Cygnet has been positively blooming. I have high hopes for her."

"Yes…it has been progressing quite quickly lately, hasn't it," Cimari says, giving me a narrow look.

"Aha," Ismeni says. "So you *have* noticed."

"It's odd," Cimari replies. "So, yes, I noticed. And did you know—"

"Tell us more about the wedding banquet," Sadra says quickly. "Will you sing, Ismeni?"

Ismeni and Cimari both look at her in surprise but aren't stupid enough to be rude to her right in front of Orean. Sadra pulls Orean into the conversation as well, drawing everyone's attention away from the subject of slaves—or thralls, as I suppose we're called. But now and again Cimari's hard black eyes flicker in my direction, gleaming with interest.

Finally, Ismeni rises from the table and beckons to Dove and me. Cimari's eyes narrow, and she flicks one manicured finger in my direction. A sharp pain stings my neck, but I don't cry out or even break my stride as I follow dutifully after my mistress. Cimari will have to do better than that if she wants to break my mask. But despite my bravado, a twist of fear lodges in my spine. I know Cimari *can* do better than that. And I suspect she will, if given the chance.

When Ismeni finally dismisses us for the afternoon, I nearly burst out of my skin trying to stay calm. As soon as I reach the shelter of the garden, I run, darting along the paths until I reach my secluded little nook. The roses are in full bloom, as always, little bursts of color and delicious perfume. They're like tiny stars, filling the shadows with light. And in spite of everything, it soothes me.

"You're here!" Sadra moves forward as if to hug me but then stops, lowering her arms. "I was afraid you wouldn't come."

"I came," I say. "I need to know—what is this place? Why did you bring me here?"

"*I* didn't do anything of the sort. I was sent to help you," Sadra explains. "By people who don't believe the House's lies, who fight to free thralls and heal them. We're called the Bird's Path."

"Heal—I am sick?" My heart flutters. It's been less than a day, in my mind. Though my body is strong and healthy now, I can remember all too clearly what it's like to be ill.

"Perhaps 'heal' isn't the best word," Sadra admits with a sigh. "But I don't know how else to say it—I'm no Lightcrafter."

"Lightcrafter?"

"Light," she says. "Power—what Ismeni uses to move things and create her glamours."

"I don't understand," I say. "What is glamour?"

"How Ismeni changes her appearance at will," Sadra explains. "Perhaps you've never noticed—she's much more subtle about it than many women are."

"I thought it was paint," I say, remembering how I marveled at her skill with cosmetics.

"Some of it is," Sadra admits. "She's very good at it. But Light is—it's—oh, curse it, I don't know how to explain."

"*Magiya,*" I murmur. Magic. Surrounded as I am by ever-blooming roses, I don't question it. "I know what it is. Is that my sickness? This Light?"

"Yes," Sadra says. "Sort of. They told me all about it, but I don't understand it, either—not completely. The people I work with, they told me that thralls *aren't* empty shells, that they're *people* whose minds have been trapped by the House of Light and Shadow."

"What is—who—what are you saying?" I breathe heavily through my nose, frustrated as much by my own inability to form questions as Sadra's shoddy explanations.

"They said this would happen," Sadra mutters, and drops onto an old bench overgrown with vines. "I'm sorry, Sasha. I'm going about this all wrong. I'm supposed to start from the beginning—but where's the beginning?"

"How I am here?" I suggest.

"Alright. Come sit and I'll try to explain."

"Is it safe?" I ask warily, looking back toward the house.

"It's as safe as it's ever been," Sadra replies. "That is to say, not very, but safer than anywhere else."

With another nervous glance at the house, I settle myself on the bench beside her.

With a deep breath, Sadra begins, "You were brought here—to this world, to Kingsgarden—by the House of Light and Shadow to be a vessel for Light. That's what we call the power that some people can use to do extraordinary things. But people think that you were *created,* not stolen from somewhere else. They don't know that thralls are—well, alive. Aware. Or that they could be. Many really aren't aware. Do you remember?"

"Yes." I shiver. "Some. I was empty before."

"Yes, empty," Sadra agrees. "Your mind was being used for something else—for Light. It comes from you, through your brand. It comes from your mind—and your body. If we don't stop it, it will kill you eventually. We call it the Pall."

I touch the scar on my hip. "This? This kills? How long?"

"It could take years—twenty, maybe, or thirty. It depends. I don't know the exact mechanics of it, but the Pall preys on your mind like a leech. Do you know what I mean? It lies on your skin and sucks the blood out." At my nod and wrinkled nose, she continues. "The Pall siphons your energy out of your mind, and the brand on your hip gathers the energy and focuses it into Light so that it can be used by the people around you. That's why Lightcrafters take their thralls everywhere they go—or nearly everywhere. Luckily for us, Ismeni is fairly devout." Seeing my confusion, she adds, "That's where Ismeni goes every day—to the Temple of Graces. Thralls aren't allowed there. Mother Wenla says they're a distraction."

"But I am alive," I remind her. "I am aware. How?"

"You have a strong mind," Sadra says with a smile. "And you made it stronger."

"By dancing," I say.

"For you, yes. It's a matter of focus," she says. "And discipline, or so they tell me."

"Dove does something," I tell her. "She sits at the fountain and stares, every day. She is awake."

"Is she?" Sadra's eyebrows shoot up in surprise. "Are you sure?"

"Yes," I say, forcing myself to look her in the eyes. It goes against the grain, these days. "Will you help her, too?"

"I...I don't know," Sadra starts uncomfortably, "I was only sent for you."

"Why only me?"

"Because you were the only one we knew *could* be saved," she says. "But now...I don't know. Even getting just you out will be terribly dangerous. We'll have to wait and see."

"Cimari knows," I say. "Or she...what is the word?"

"Suspects," Sadra supplies. "Yes, I'm sure she does. But she's been wrong before, and we can use that to our advantage. Still, you'll need to be very, very careful."

"Wrong how?"

"She's betrothed to the House Premier—the head of the House of Light and Shadow," Sadra explains. "I'm sure he's fed her the House's standard and entirely false explanation of awakened thralls: that the 'empty' body of a thrall has been inhabited by a spiritwalker, a person who can cast his soul outside his own body. Orean says Cimari sent one of her thralls to the House for 'inspection'."

"What happened?" I whisper.

"I couldn't say." Avoiding my eyes, she adds softly, "But the thrall didn't come back."

Nausea floods my belly. "What will I do?"

"Nothing," Sadra says, gripping my wrist. "Do nothing—and, above all, *say* nothing. No matter what happens, don't make a sound. The House will stop at nothing to keep their secret safe. If they find out about you, they'll take you away and we won't be able to get you back."

She releases me and chews nervously on her lip.

"There's so much you don't know, and I can't explain a lot of it in a way you'll understand, yet. But I can help you."

"You put words in my mind," I say, frowning. I'm not sure how I feel about Sadra messing around in my head, but I can't deny that it's a useful trick.

"Yes," Sadra admits. "I Whispered them to you while you slept. It's my Gift."

"What is—"

"Tomorrow," Sadra says, shaking her head. "You still have to dance, and Ismeni will be back soon."

Reluctantly, I get up and follow her to the barre. Questions swirl in my mind: What exactly is this Bird's Path? And who within that organization, if that's what it is, sent Sadra to find me? And how did they know I could be saved? Come to that, how *are* they going to save me?

Sadra said something about being healed. What would that entail, exactly? If my mind and body were being used for Light before, am I not producing it anymore? Am I not a source of Light anymore now that my mind is my own? And if I'm not, won't someone notice?

"Focus," Sadra reminds me, seeing my stiff, distracted movements. "Let it go, Sasha. I know you must be frightened, but I promise you:

There are people who want to help you—and we will. We're going to get you out of here. But you have to trust me."

Trust her. It shouldn't be that simple, but it is.

Baba Nadia's lecture on trust comes back to me, as clearly as when she first spoke them to me so many weeks ago: *In the end, it's a choice. You need to choose to believe that your partner will catch you, or you will never fly.*

Sadra, for better or worse, is my partner now, and I have no choice but to place myself entirely in her hands. I don't like it. I don't want to, but I have to. She's my only hope of salvation in this crazy place, so I will trust her.

It doesn't feel much like flying…but it will have to do.

Pas du chat

Emily is singing to me, stumbling over the words. She never did have an ear for Russian.

"Bayu bayushki bayu
Seedit kotik na kriyu
On ne bedin ne bahat...
Oo nyevo..oonye vo..."

Emily stops and laughs a little, shaking her head.

I'd laugh too if I could. Her accent is terrible, even after practically living with Baba Nadia and me for over ten years. We always laughed about it, just like we laughed when she helped me learn English so the other preschoolers wouldn't make fun of me. I would give anything to laugh with her again.

"Sorry, bug," Emily says. "How about this one? You liked it when you were little, remember?"

"I see the moon, the moon sees me
The moon sees somebody I would like to see
God bless the moon, and God bless me
God bless somebody I would like to see.
God bless somebody I would like to see."

Emily stops and looks into her lap. Her jaw and throat tighten; she swallows several times and lets out a ragged breath.

I stay quiet. I don't want to make any sound; I know all that will come *out is a sharp grunt or, if I'm lucky, a kind of animal moan. It scares her, so I don't try anymore.*

Emily looks at the ceiling, at the door, anywhere but me. I keep my eyes fixed on her face, as if I can force her to look at me.

"Oh, God, Nadia, I wish you were here," Emily whispers, wiping the tears from her eyes. She takes several more breaths before finally looking at me. "I'm sorry, sweetie. Ignore me. Where was I?

"Do you believe in lovin', honey?

Mm, you bet I do.

I believe in lovin', honey,

When I'm lovin' you..."

* * *

I wake with tears pooling against my eyelids. I want to go home so badly it's like a physical ache throughout my whole body.

Emily, poor Emily.

Her name runs after itself through my mind, repeating in an endless loop. I hate myself for putting her through this; I hate Sadra for doing whatever she did to pull me into this world, even if it was to win my freedom and ultimately save my life.

Better that I had died, in this world or at home, or both. Anything to keep Emily from suffering this way.

A cool hand wipes the tears from my cheeks and comes to rest on my forehead; I look up to find Dove standing over me, her eyes full of compassion. I wonder if she had someone to comfort her when she woke to find herself trapped in a nightmare. What kind of strength must it take to face each day alone?

Dove pats my cheek gently and motions for me to get up. With a sigh, I throw back the covers and obey. Whatever I might be feeling right now, there's work to do—if not for Ismeni, for me. My task for the day remains the same: don't screw up. Don't make *any* noise, don't draw attention to myself in any way. Trust Sadra.

It's been nearly a week now, and it's getting easier—trusting, at least. I haven't been killed or dragged away by the House of Light and Shadow, after all. And I find that I like Sadra, that my affection for her before I woke up was real. She's capable, confident, and wickedly funny. Though she can't be much older than I am, she reminds me a little of Emily: Some days that similarity eases the ache of missing home; sometimes it makes things worse.

But there are still questions that need answers, and today I plan to insist that Sadra give them to me as best she can, regardless of the language barrier that makes things so difficult. I just need to make it through this morning until I can escape to the garden.

Ismeni isn't making it easy, though. She mopes, she whines, she sighs. She composes poetry out loud for her "dear Miocostin," whoever that is. Her lover, I suppose. She puts us through our paces as if we're trained dogs, for no other reason than boredom. Through it all, I maintain the serene, vacant countenance of a thrall. I keep my bitterness and shame and disgust buried deep inside, where no one can see it or even guess at its presence. But it's hard. It's so hard.

At midday, Ismeni leaves for the Temple and Dove and I let ourselves into the garden. Dove takes her usual place at the fountain. Not for the first time, I wonder what she does. Perhaps it's a kind of meditation, a way to keep her mind strong like Sadra said. But I don't wonder long; I have many more immediate concerns to address.

"Hello, friend," Sadra says cheerfully when I reach her. "Shall we dance?"

"Not yet," I say firmly. "I have questions."

She shakes her head and unfolds from a deep stretch.

"Sasha, it's so difficult to explain—"

"Try anyway," I say. "And I will try to understand."

Sadra sighs. "Alright. What do you want to know?"

"You say you're here to help me," I say, "and I believe you. But why do you—why are you with Orean? He's…he's bad. Very bad."

"Because that was the easiest way to gain access to the house—to you," Sadra says promptly, looking pleased to be able to answer so easily.

I frown. "No one thought it was strange?"

"What was strange?" Sadra asks, puzzled.

"He's married," I point out. "He has a wife—but he has you, too."

Sadra looks at me, seemingly baffled. "Why should it matter? Temple initiates are forbidden to bear children or inherit property. That's what marriage is for, after all, and the only reason anyone cares who sleeps with whom. Ismeni does seem a little annoyed, I grant you, but she knows I do his household great honor by accepting Orean's patronage."

Seeing my skeptical look, she insists, "It is often done. Households provide initiates of all disciplines with funding and facilities and in return, we add luster to the house's reputation and standing. We share our talents and also our bodies, if we choose. Occasionally our hearts."

I trail my hand over the wooden rail as I process what she's told me. "I don't understand. Ismeni is not of the Temple, and she has a…I don't know how to say it." I purse my lips, groping for the right words. "A man, a—"

"A lover," Sadra supplies. "You're right, that is a bit confusing. Ordinarily, Orean would be well within his rights to flog her for her infidelity, but her case is rather different. Her lover is King Miocostin, you see."

I grit my teeth. Of course "dear Miocostin" is not just some guy but the king of this horrible place. Figures.

Sadra continues, "Orean can't make a fuss about it, even if he wanted to—and I don't think he does. I'm almost positive Orean is using Ismeni to feed the king false information, and his marriage to Ismeni is nothing more than a business arrangement, anyway. He has the standing, but she has the money… Had, I should say. Orean gained control of all of it when they wed. And he uses every bit of it to further his own ambitions, the pig."

She makes a face and adds, "Orean certainly isn't someone I would choose for my own purposes, but…well, it was the only way to gain the necessary access and mobility within such a high-ranked household. Only the king holds more power than a Councilman like Orean."

I shoot her a look out of the corner of my eye, my nose wrinkling in distaste even as my brow furrows with unease and guilt. I don't like the thought that I've put her in such a position. But she doesn't seem to mind it too much, which is itself so strange I don't know how to respond. I bend into a stretch to hide my confusion, and Sadra chuckles.

"I haven't had to actually bed him but once or twice," she says. "Being a Dreamwhisper has its advantages."

"A what?" I ask, glad to be distracted from her previous revelations.

"A Dreamwhisper," she repeats. "It's my Gift. It's how I've been helping you. I put the words into your mind while you sleep. I do the same with Orean—I Whisper to him of all the pleasures he didn't *technically* enjoy, though as far as he's concerned, he enjoyed them very much. It's only to his benefit, really. I doubt what I have to offer would be as exciting in truth."

She grins at me, inviting me to share in the joke, but I ignore it in favor of a more pressing question. "Does the Gift come from Light? Are you using me like they do?"

Sadra's eyes widen. "Stars, no. My Gift is mine and mine alone. Everyone is born with a Gift, and everyone's is slightly different, though they generally fall within one of several broad categories.

"The Lady Ismeni is a Catchsong, for instance. You've heard her sing, haven't you? It's hard not to listen—impossible, sometimes. Orean is likely some kind of Truthseer. I'm not positive, but I've noticed that he has an uncanny knack for guessing people's weaknesses."

"What is Cimari?" I ask, though I have an idea.

"I *think* she's a Honeytongue," Sadra says, frowning. "Or a very weak Heartstouch. It's odd, because usually your Gift aligns with your personality. You know, Ironarms and Swifts like to exert themselves, Greenloves like to be outside, Beastspeakers love animals, and so on. And most Honeytongues and Heartstouches are friendly, outgoing, warm...but I've seen enough of Cimari when she's not trying to get something from someone to know that she is none of those things. She's cold, driven...and, I think, very angry."

Sadra shrugs. "But I don't know. It's hard to tell with Orean and Cimari. Not everyone's Gift is readily definable or well developed, especially among the wealthy, who tend to prefer Light... Cimari certainly does! It takes less effort and energy—of their own, that is. They use yours instead. The Pall takes all the energy that should be going to feed your Gift and your mind, and your brand converts it into Light for others to use. That's why thralls are so...blank. Empty."

"But I am not empty." Relief at this truth shivers through me. "I am awake."

"Yes," Sadra agrees, but her face is troubled. "And now that your mind is your own again, the Pall is taking the energy from your body. Which means that we are operating on a much tighter timetable now. I don't mean to scare you, but I think you have a right to know. What would have taken decades could now use you up in as little two years."

"Then why?" I ask angrily. "Why did you not just leave me?"

"Because we're trying to save you," Sadra cries. "Were you happy, wherever you were? Were you well? If you were, if you want to go back to that, I'll crave your pardon and leave you to it. Stop dancing, stop fighting the Pall, and all will be as it was."

I open my mouth, then close it. When I do speak, it's in a much lower tone. "No. I was not well. I was sick. Very sick. When you heal the Pall, will it make me well? Will I go back?"

"I…I don't know." When I take a breath to argue she cuts me off with a gesture and says, "Truly, Sasha, I don't. There are many things the Path elders haven't told me."

She joins me at our makeshift barre and rests her hand over mine. "Let's dance now. Please."

I stare at her, my jaw set in a mulish expression. I want to ask her about the visions of my other self in the hospital. What do they mean? Are they real? Am I someone else now or am I truly in two places, one soul in two bodies? And, most importantly, what will happen to me if one of those bodies dies?

But I don't have the words yet to ask her these things. So I bite my tongue and join her at the barre to dance. As terrified and confused as I am here, what waits for me in my old life is even worse, at least until I can be cured of this Pall. Until then I have to fight it, however I can.

My mind settles slightly as I join Sadra at our makeshift barre, and I fall into the calm focus that she tells me keeps my mind strong against the Pall.

For a blessed thirty minutes or so, I let my worries go and think of nothing at all. But when I leave Sadra and make my way back to Dove, even more questions plague me, crowding my mind until there's room for nothing else.

I'm so preoccupied I don't see Dove's penetrating stare of warning until it's too late.

A voice cries, "Oh!" A foot comes down hard on my foot; a trail of jam drips down the front of my dress and onto the ground, where a broken pastry sticks out of the dirt like a tombstone. I keep my eyes on it, afraid to look up.

Please, no. Don't let it be her. Please.

"Oh, dear, what *have* you done?"

Cimari stands before me, her face arranged in an exaggerated expression of outrage. "Guard," she calls, her voice now rippling with astonished dismay.

Guard? Since when do guards hang around the garden? She must have been waiting for me—she *wanted* this to happen. She knows—*Bozhe,* what am I going to do?

I stare at her, my jaw locked shut. I don't even have to try to hide—I'm frozen.

"My lady?"

A household guard appears, his brow furrowed with concern. Cimari fusses over her stained skirts, twittering like a little bird about how the gown was a special gift from her beloved brother and, oh, how *can* Ismeni abide such wildness in her thralls.

"They're beasts, my lady," the guardsman says, eager to help. "And beasts need discipline. Training, see."

A tiny, almost imperceptible smile of anticipation flickers on Cimari's lips, then disappears as quickly and completely as if it were never there.

"You're right, of course," Cimari replies tearfully. "I suppose…yes, I think we must."

She covers her face with a trembling hand, as if she can't bear to watch what will happen next. But I know she's likely hiding a smirk as she whispers, "Guardsman, fetch a whip."

Fouetté

My knees hit the gravel hard.

Though I know the sickening crunch is nothing but the loose stone shifting beneath me, I can't help imagining my kneecaps crumbling to dust. Pain radiates through my bones, making my breath come fast and my muscles contract. Cimari grips me by the hair as she rips my dress right off my back. The tattered rags hang from my waist, exposing my torso to the guard's speculative gaze.

Tears of shame spring to my eyes but don't fall as I fight against the instinct to cover myself with my hands. A thrall has no modesty. A thrall doesn't care. A *thrall* has no sense of ownership over its own body, and so it can't be violated.

"Strike," Cimari says.

A line of fire snakes down my back. The urge to cry out is—almost—overwhelming. I grit my teeth, letting my head fall forward between my elbows. Cimari jerks it back up, her hand twisted in my braids. Sweat beads along my hairline, on my lip, the small of my back. I want to fall forward, onto the ground, but Cimari still has hold of my hair; if I don't support my own weight, she'll tear it out.

"Strike."

My breath whistles through airways constricted by fear and pain; my head swims. No sound. No sound. No struggle. Nothing. Do *nothing.*

"Strike."

I don't know how long it goes on. I thought I knew pain. And I do—every dancer does. But this is something else, something infinitely more debilitating. No one has ever *hurt* me before. It's the intention, the desire to cause pain, that makes it so disturbing. I've never encountered such malice. It makes so little sense to me that I start to believe that there must be some reason, some purpose behind it.

I must deserve this, somehow, because why else would it be happening?

"Strike."

Bile rises in my throat and forces its way into my mouth. *No.* I clamp my lips and teeth tighter together. I can't let it out. Vomit surges upward into my sinuses and drips from my nose instead, blocking my airways.

I can't breathe—I can't see.

Sweat streams down my face and gets in my eyes, making them water and sting. The guard continues his work, oblivious to my internal struggle—a struggle I lose with the next fall of the lash. I choke as the contents of my stomach bubble out of my mouth and over my chin. And still, Cimari doesn't let go.

"Str—"

"*Stop.*"

Gasping for breath, I turn my head ever so slightly and peek behind me. The guard lowers his whip. His face is flecked with blood—my blood.

Ismeni stands in the doorway of the garden, white-faced with rage. She stalks forward and grabs the whip out of the guard's hand. For a moment, I think she's going to attack him with it. But she throws the whip aside and rounds instead on Cimari, eyes blazing.

"How dare you." Ismeni's hand lands with a sharp crack, leaving a lurid red print on Cimari's cheek. "How dare you lay hands on Cygnet?"

Cimari holds a hand to her face once more, her eyes wide with what I think might actually be real shock. "Isi—"

"What reason could you possibly have to interfere with *my* thrall?" Ismeni demands.

"I—it—look at my dress!" Cimari wails, tears leaking from her eyes. "It's so wild, Isi, I was only trying to help—"

"Help!" Ismeni cries. "Look at what you've done!"

"I'm sorry, Isi," Cimari says. "I am, I just—"

"Leave me," Ismeni snaps disgustedly, then turns to the guard. "You as well. You should know better than to indulge a foolish girl's whim. My husband will hear of this, I assure you."

"Isi, I—"

"Just go, Cimari. We will speak of this later."

I've never seen Ismeni so angry, not even when Orean brought Sadra home. Her whole body shakes, as if physically struggling to contain her fury. Despite myself, I find comfort in her anger and the tenderness with which she wipes my face clean. For a moment I let myself believe that she cares for me, that she's outraged by the abuse of an innocent rather than the damage of her property.

Once Cimari is out of earshot, Ismeni turns and calls, "Help me."

"Oh, my stars…"

Sadra appears at Ismeni's side. I blink, wondering if the pain is making me see things.

With no more than a wary glance at each other, they help me to my feet and tow me inside, not to my room, I notice, but to Ismeni's.

Every step is agony. Even the slight impact of my footstep makes my back burn and throb. They hold me upright by my arms, trying to avoid the bleeding gashes on my back and ribs.

Ismeni lays me face-down on her bed. I watch Sadra out of the corner of my eye as she sets a jug of water on a nearby table and then flits from the room. Ismeni dabs at my back with a soft cloth. Though her touch is gentle, I can't help cringing away, my eyes squeezed shut against the sting.

The door opens, and I hear Sadra's voice: "Here—and I brought more cloths."

"That will be all," Ismeni says curtly.

Sadra's footsteps retreat; the door opens once more.

"Wait…Sadra." Ismeni pauses in her ministrations. "Thank you."

I crack open one eye and see Sadra nod, then close the door quietly behind her. Ismeni sits beside me, tears dripping from her lashes. Her mouth quivers as she dips a new cloth into the water and applies it to my back. I twitch, closing my eye again.

"I'm sorry," Ismeni murmurs. "I know it hurts. Sleep now, sweet girl. Everything's going to be alright.

> *"Hush, sleep little one*
> *The moon is on her way*
> *Sailing for the morning*
> *To meet the golden sun."*

I've never been able to resist Ismeni's voice for long, even at my best—and I'm definitely not at my best now. Something feels different, though. There's a strange pulsing in the air, a glow, a shining that I feel more than see. Confusion breaks through a wave of nausea. I can't be seeing anything at all; my eyes are closed. Or are they? I can't tell. But how do you feel something shining without heat?

I don't know. But it seems like only moments before I hear Ismeni's voice again, this time ringing with authority but no longer singing.

"Enter."

I stir at the sharp tone in Ismeni's voice, automatically moving to do her bidding, whatever it might be. The swollen, lacerated flesh on my back burns and aches, sharp and dull at the same time. I clutch at the sheets; blood falls from my bitten lip, smearing the pristine sheets with red. I squint at the stain and try to imagine that it's only ink, that I haven't shed even more blood for Cimari's malice.

"You sent for me, Isi?"

Cimari's voice. Cimari is *here*. I writhe once against the sheets, then force myself into stillness. Ismeni is at my side in an instant. I want to close my eyes, but I'm too afraid. I watch them both through my lashes, hardly daring to breathe.

"Easy," Ismeni whispers, then turns to Cimari with a face of stone. "I would like to know why you saw fit to flog Cygnet for something that was, by all accounts, your own fault. You were just looking for an excuse, weren't you? Cimari, this spiritwalker nonsense must stop."

"But, Isi, I really thought—"

"You *really thought* your last thrall was compromised as well," Ismeni snaps. "And you were wrong. I thought the experience might have taught you some humility, but evidently I was mistaken."

"But it's been acting so strangely," Cimari insists, wide-eyed. "I didn't tell you —I found it wandering about the other night. It was in the kitchens! Why would it go there?"

Ismeni throws up her hands. "Obviously, she was looking for food! How many times has that puppy of yours done the same thing?"

"But the evidence—"

"The evidence suggests I need to give Cygnet a bigger meal before bed, nothing more," Ismeni says. "I'm sorry, Cimari, I must ask my husband to speak to your betrothed. This is getting out of hand."

"No!" Cimari cries. "No—Isi, please. I'm sorry, I made a mistake."

"*I'm sorry* isn't good enough," Ismeni says sternly. "Not this time. Cygnet is not a toy. She is a living, breathing creature under my care and entitled to my protection. Leave me, Cimari, and don't let me see you anywhere near Cygnet *or* Dove."

"That girl needs something else to occupy her time," Ismeni mutters when Cimari is safely gone. With a sigh, she adds, "I worry about her. If only she would take an interest in something other than Light! There are plenty of other suitable pastimes for a girl of her age and station.

"She could serve in the Temple or with the House sanctuaries in the City, if she prefers. She could certainly stand to improve her dancing. How many times have I offered to find her a tutor? Or I would tutor her myself if she would rather sing. But no! She wants to be a High Lightcrafter. She chooses the *one* path that is closed to her, the poor dear..."

Yes, I think darkly. Things must be so *difficult* for her.

The poor dear.

* * *

"What do you mean, Master Doran isn't coming?"

I lift my head weakly from the bedclothes, straining to hear what's going on outside the door. Orean rarely ever enters the women's wing. I hope Ismeni doesn't let him in here. It doesn't look like she will; I can see her through the partially open door, her posture stiff and forbidding. She won't let him in. She can't. Sweat breaks out on my forehead as I recall with awful clarity the feeling of Orean's hands on my shoulders and my clothes slipping to the floor.

"I told him his services were not required," Orean says. "It's a completely frivolous expense and an embarrassment to us all. Calling a Lighthealer to attend a *thrall*—we'd be a laughingstock."

"How can you be so cruel?" Ismeni cries. "Cygnet is in pain, she's suffering—"

"Don't be so dramatic, my dear," Orean says, his tone dismissive. "It's just a few cuts. Besides, you have a spare. Use your other thrall—the old one."

I wish I could see Ismeni's face. Her shoulders are rigid, her back stiff and straight. But her voice, when she speaks again, is studiously calm.

"Her name is Dove," Ismeni says. "And she's too frail to accompany me outside the Terrace. Even more so since she saw what happened to Cygnet."

"Ismeni, you must abandon these ridiculous fancies," Orean snaps. "You and Cimari both. It's a *thrall*, for beauty's sake. While I highly doubt it's a spiritwalker waiting to murder us in our beds, I doubt even more that it suffers as you or I might.

"I have taken Cimari to task for her presumption, and she has expressed her regret and contrition. Let that be the end of it." A beat of silence, then, "Very good. Now, Sadra would like a word."

Sadra? Perking up hopefully, I wait with bated breath until Ismeni steps back to let Sadra into the room.

"Do sit down," Ismeni says stiffly. "How can I help you?"

"When I heard what happened with Cimari, I thought I might be able to help," Sadra says.

I shift slightly to get a better view and see that she's cradling something in her arms. When she holds it out to Ismeni, I see that it's the puppy Cimari received as her betrothal gift.

"I thought you might want her. Poor thing, I really don't have the time to do right by her, though I've been doing my best," Sadra says. "I was going to ask Lucoran to take her and raise her with his foxes, but maybe she'll do better here. I've heard that sick animals can benefit from company. Perhaps it's the same for thralls."

"Oh!" Ismeni blinks in surprise. "I—what a kind thought."

What is Sadra playing at? I need a doctor, not a puppy... It'll probably drool on me.

I narrow my eyes at the puppy as Sadra places her carefully at my side. I've never had any pets of my own—Baba Nadia firmly believed that animals belong outside, working for their keep.

But I have to admit, it—she—looks sweet with her fluffy ears and silky pale fur. Even her weirdly long legs and pointy nose are cute in a gangly, dorky sort of way. When she snuggles against my side, I do actually feel a tiny bit better. She's so warm—it's like having a little heated pillow, if that pillow were to snuffle around the hollow of my neck and lick my ear. But it's not as gross as I imagined. In fact, it's kind of nice to be shown some genuine affection, even if it's from a dog.

But I can't let the puppy distract me. My gaze drifts up to Ismeni's face, soft and unfocused. I hate it, but it's my own—my only—kind of magic. I can see her, but she can't, or maybe just *won't*, see me.

"She's precious," Ismeni says with a reluctant smile. But when she turns her gaze toward Sadra, her eyes grow sharp and suspicious. "However, I do hope you had something more in mind for Cygnet."

"I think I can get you a healer," Sadra says. "Not a Lighthealer—but a Gifted one."

"Oh? Who?"

"Mother Wenla."

"The Temple Mother!" Ismeni's eyebrows shoot up in surprise. "She would do that for you?"

"I think so. She all but raised me," Sadra says, and grins. "But it wouldn't hurt if you promised to spend some time teaching at the Temple. Songs Mistress recently retired to the cloister and her replacement hasn't arrived yet. I know Mother Wenla would appreciate the help."

"Of course," Ismeni says dismissively. "But Cygnet—I don't want to leave her alone more than I have to. Cimari said she would behave, but..."

"I could take her," Sadra offers. "Perhaps we'll explore the markets.

I wouldn't mind spending a few hours every week spending Orean's money."

I glance at Ismeni, worried that Sadra has gone too far, but Ismeni merely smirks. After a moment, however, her smile fades.

"Why are you doing this?"

Sadra doesn't answer right away. What can she say to that? Surely not the truth?

"Because I know the feel of a whip on my back," Sadra says softly. "No one should have to endure that, not even a thrall." At Ismeni's questioning look, she continues, "I was born in a tavern. My mother died, and my father left. The tavern keeper let me sleep in the cellar in exchange for what small labor a child could perform. Mother Wenla brought me to Temple when I was six."

"I see," Ismeni says. "And Orean—"

Sadra shrugs. "You need fear nothing from me. My vows prohibit me from marrying or bearing children. Even if I could, I wouldn't."

"Then why are you here?" Surprisingly, Ismeni seems merely cautious and curious rather than angry. "Any household on the King's Terrace would be wild to host a Temple initiate of your caliber."

"I have my reasons," Sadra says. "And love is not one of them, I assure you. I may share Orean's bed on occasion, but my heart is given elsewhere."

Ismeni looks her over with sharp eyes. "Are you a spy, then?"

"Nothing so official," Sadra replies. "My only allegiance is to the Temple. If your husband's opponents on the Council know his secrets, they didn't get them from me."

"In truth, I don't know that I would care if they did," Ismeni says. "I must assume your presence here has something to do with these 'Council meetings' that seem to take place so frequently of late. Council meetings that are most certainly not sanctioned by the king.

"My husband believes I am silly and soft and completely oblivious, that I can't tell when he's planting 'evidence' against this or that lord. He is a fool, and it is my fervent hope that you are here to cause trouble for him."

Sadra smiles.

"I suppose you can't say one way or the other. No matter." A chair scrapes as Ismeni gets to her feet. "I haven't been to prayer since Cimari…I don't suppose you would stay with Cygnet for a little while?"

"Certainly," Sadra says. "I'll speak with Mother Wenla this evening if you like."

"I thank you," Ismeni says, inclining her head in a formal-looking gesture. "I won't forget your kindness."

Sadra smiles again. "That, as I'm sure you realize, is the idea."

Ismeni smiles too, wryly. "Yes, I suppose it is, isn't it? Very well, I acknowledge the debt."

Sadra and Ismeni share a nod of guarded respect as Ismeni leaves for prayer. As soon as she's gone, I allow myself a whimper of pain.

"Where were you?" I whisper, my voice raspy. "Ismeni keeps making me sleep. How long has it been?"

"Two days." Sadra comes to sit by my side, scratching the now sleeping puppy behind its ears. "How do you feel?"

"Bad."

"Not as bad as you look, I hope," Sadra says.

"Worse," I grunt. "This Mother Wenla—she will help?"

"She will." Sadra brushes a lock of hair from my cheek. "I promise. She'll heal you as best she can, and she'll help you get out of here. She's one of the Bird's Path elders."

"Is it true, what you told Ismeni?"

"It is."

"Is that why you help me?"

"Partly." Sadra smiles. "But also because it's the right thing to do, and because you're my friend."

"I can't be," I tell her, and blink away tears. "I'm not really here. I'm…I don't know the word. My head is sick."

"You're not crazy," Sadra says firmly. "And you're as real as I am. Imaginary people don't hurt as much as you do, I'll wager." She shakes her head. "I don't know how you did it, Sasha. You were amazing."

I frown. The idea of being admired for submitting to a beating makes me feel dirty.

"You brought Ismeni," I say instead. "How did you know?"

"Dove found me," Sadra says. "She didn't speak, but she made her meaning clear. You were right about her."

"Will you help her?"

"It's not my decision," Sadra says gently. "Now, listen, since you can't dance, I have some mental exercises for you to do…"

I follow Sadra's instructions, doing my best to clear my mind. But try as I might, I can't ignore the distractions piling up in my mind: I'm worried about Emily; I'm worried about Dove; my back is on fire, and where it doesn't hurt, it itches; I'm thirsty; I'm hungry—but nauseous; there's a crick in my neck from lying on my stomach for two days; and, of course, I don't know if any of this is real.

But I do my best to do as Sadra says, and finally she lets me fall into a fitful sleep.

As always, I dream.

* * *

"Hi, Sasha."

My eyes move slowly, laboriously, but I keep trying until they rest on James' face. There are lines there that I don't remember. His mouth hooks down, pulling his gaze along with it. I wonder what he's doing here without Emily, but I'm glad to see him.

"Emily misses you," he says. "We all do. I'm sorry it's been so long. There were some...complications that we had to sort out. Some Social Services peon seemed to think—but you don't need to worry about that.

"Anyway, I have something I thought you might like. I dug up some footage of your grandmother performing and digitized it. Emily gave me your tablet so I could bring it to you."

James props the tablet up on the little table next to my bed. I watch, enthralled, as a young Nadia Nikolayeva floats across the stage, first in black and white and then, later, in color. She was magnificent. Once, I aspired to that level of skill and grace. And I could have done it; after the Swan Lake performance, offers came flooding in.

But everything has changed. Even if I get out of here, I'll never be what I was. I don't know what kind of life is waiting for me when or if I leave the hospital.

Whatever it is...I'm not sure I want it.

Arabesque

"Are you *sure* you need to keep her overnight?" Ismeni hovers at the litter's curtain, looking up at Sadra with an expression equal parts worry and suspicion. I sit in shadow, trying to ignore both the pain in my back and the four thralls holding the litter on their shoulders. Though Ismeni put some kind of—according to Orean—hideously expensive salve on my back, the burning ache is only just bearable.

"Don't worry," Sadra says. "We'll take good care of her. The Healing will go better if she can rest after. I'll have her home first thing in the morning."

Ismeni purses her lips. "See that you do."

I wince as the litter begins to move, catching me off guard. My hips ache from the strain of holding my spine perfectly straight; I can't slump against the pillows as I so badly want to. The slightest relaxing of my posture makes the scabbed cuts on my back twist and pull. A trickle of blood is already creeping between my shoulder blades.

Each bump and jerk of the litter opens new rivulets as we make our way through the city. I grit my teeth and endure it silently, as a thrall would. Sadra sits across from me, her lips twisting in helpless sympathy. She doesn't say anything, until a particularly sharp swoop of the litter makes me hiss in pain.

"Not much longer now," she promises. "We're almost there. It'll stop hurting soon."

I let out a skeptical grunt. Even though I've seen Ismeni use Light, I have trouble believing that my hurts will magically disappear—or rather improve, as Sadra so carefully qualified. A Lighthealer can make injuries vanish as if they'd never been; a Gifted one can only speed up the natural healing process.

The litter jerks as one of the thralls stumbles beneath us. I close my eyes against the flare of pain in my back and the sharp crack of a guard's whip outside the litter. When I open my eyes, I focus on the sights and sounds beyond the litter's drapes. The City of Roses really is beautiful, and I only rarely get to see it.

Everywhere I look there are elegant archways and delicately curved rooftops, all in pale pinkish stone. Flowers and vines spill from windowsills, and it seems like every other block we pass through is a courtyard decorated with marble statues and fountains.

People bustle about in colorful costumes, conducting business and laughing with friends. There are street performers everywhere. There's dancing, singing, acrobatics—there's even a puppet show.

A puff of cool, crisp air ruffles the veil draped over my head and shoulders. It feels like September. October, maybe? But, no, it was spring when I crossed over. It was warmer back home, that's all.

When the litter finally stops, Sadra leaps down with the kind of thoughtless exuberance I once had and took for granted. I climb out of the litter after her and try not to see the scarred backs and shaved heads of the thralls who carried us. I shiver, wondering what might have become of me if I hadn't been young enough or pretty enough to serve on the Terrace. The thought of considering myself lucky makes me sick, and yet I know it's the truth.

We enter the Temple through a small side door, as far away from prying eyes as we can manage. Even so, we don't entirely escape notice.

"Sadra!"

I shrink into the shadows as a short, round figure appears seemingly out of nowhere and throws herself at Sadra. Accustomed as I am to Ismeni's calm complacency, the girl's exuberance is a little alarming. How nice it must be, to live so…loudly.

"Hello, Feli," Sadra says with a laugh, returning the girl's hug. "How are you?"

"Tired," the girl says. "I've been preparing night and day for my Trials. I don't know what I'll do if I don't win my Mark. If I have to stay cooped up in here for another year, I'll go mad."

A flicker of interest distracts me from my thoughts. Trials? Mark? I glance at Sadra's tattoo, a scrolling rune intertwined with a rose. Perhaps it isn't just decoration, as I always assumed. I'll have to ask her later, if there's time. I can't ask now—I can't say anything. I'm a thrall.

My curiosity dissolves into longing as I take in the easy familiarity between Sadra and Feli. What would it be like to join in their conversation, to be just another girl?

"I'm sure you'll be fine," Sadra says. "But you might just find you miss Temple life when you're out on your own. I know I do."

"But you live in the King's Terrace," Feli protests. "You get to go to parties and wear pretty dresses and meet people—you've met the king!"

"It's not always fun. It's work, just like you do here." Sadra grins. "Well. Maybe not *just* like."

Feli giggles but then stops, noticing me for the first time. Her eyes go wide. "What are you doing with a *thrall*? What will Mother Wenla say?"

"The thrall isn't mine, obviously, and it's Mother Wenla I'm here to see," Sadra says. "Go let her know I'm here, will you? I'll be in the old practice rooms. And, Feli—keep it quiet."

Feli nods seriously and runs off, her golden curls bouncing on her shoulders.

"This way," Sadra murmurs. Once we're safely away, she slips a hand under my elbow for support. "Just a little farther and you can rest."

Sadra and I make our way slowly down a deserted corridor until we come to a room that I recognize instantly, though I've never set foot in the place. The floor is made of smooth, polished wood. No clutter, no furniture except for a chair tucked away in one corner. All it needs is mirrors and a barre.

"I thought you'd be more comfortable here," Sadra says with a slight smile. "Wait a moment."

Beside the chair sits a large harp and, beside that, a door. Sadra opens it to reveal a small but neat closet and pulls out several pillows. She lays them out on the floor, and, at her urging, I lay myself carefully on top of them with a grateful sigh. Just as carefully, Sadra opens the back of my dress and applies more salve. The cold sting makes my flesh twitch, but it helps.

"It's safe now," Sadra says. "You don't have to pretend."

"Yes I do," I whisper. "I'll always have to pretend."

"No," she says. "Not with me. You can cry. Or curse, or yell, or whatever you want to do."

"I don't want to cry," I say. "And I don't know any curses."

"Well, I know plenty," Sadra says cheerfully. "I can teach you."

By the time Mother Wenla arrives, the fire in my back has receded to a throbbing ache and I've added a wealth of filthy words to my still growing vocabulary. But as soon as the door opens, Sadra leaps to her feet, her face burning a little.

"The sun shines on you, Mother."

I twist my neck, trying to look at her without moving too much: Sadra's mentor is tall and imposing, with piercing blue eyes and sleek blond hair faded in places to a buttery white. She carries herself like a queen. But when she smiles, I see the warmth inside her and understand Sadra's faith in her. Something about Mother Wenla immediately inspires confidence.

I begin to hope.

"As it shines on you both, children," Mother Wenla says with a gracious nod. "Let us begin."

"Wait," I protest. "I have so many questions—"

"I'm sure you do," Mother Wenla says gently. "But they must wait until you are well enough to ask them. Sadra, if you would?"

Sadra settles herself at the harp and begins to play a simple, repetitive pattern that I'm not sure can really be called a tune.

"Try to relax." Mother Wenla lowers herself gracefully to the floor and touches cool fingers to my skin, making me shiver. "Focus on the music, not on me."

It's surprisingly easy to do as she says. The harp's notes are hypnotic, lulling me into a state of hazy half-sleep where pain seems like something separate from myself, something distant and pale and small. Warmth replaces pain, enveloping me in a soft, colorless glow that nevertheless puts me in mind of honey and lavender, or perhaps chamomile. Wherever I am, I want to stay here forever. I don't want to go back to the pain and fear and helplessness.

But I do go back, however reluctantly. Mother Wenla's voice guides me back into my body, and I find that the pain I expected to be waiting for me is gone, or nearly so.

I roll over and sit up, holding my dress to my front with one hand and reaching over my shoulder with the other to feel the soft, new skin.

"You'll have a scar, here," Mother Wenla says, touching my back. "The other marks will soon fade, but this one was too deep."

"What did you do?" I ask. "Not just about the cuts. There was something else. I feel…different."

Mother Wenla smiled. "You feel healthy. You've been affected by the Pall for so long you don't remember what it feels like to be completely well. I simply…gave you a boost."

"Thank you." I swallow against the sudden tightness in my throat. "I… I don't know what else to say."

"Nothing else is necessary," she assures me. She rises and helps me to my feet. "Move around a bit—work the muscles. It will help."

"Will you show us your bal-lay?" Sadra asks, pronouncing the unfamiliar syllables carefully. "I've been so hoping to see what it really looks like."

I hesitate. Who brought me to the Temple's attention, and why? How do they plan to remove the shadow on my mind—the Pall, as Sadra and Mother Wenla call it? And, most importantly, when can I leave Ismeni's household?

I want answers…but I want to dance more.

"Will you play for me?" I ask.

"I will play," Mother Wenla says, and raises an eyebrow at Sadra. "Sadra's fingers are not as practiced as they should be."

Sadra blushes and moves to let Mother Wenla take her place at the harp. I toss her the pillows on the floor and, after a moment's hesitation, slip my gown off my shoulders. The heavy fabric will tangle around my legs until I can't move, much less dance. I kick it aside and tie the fine linen of my shift between my knees. Much better.

Mother Wenla begins to play a gentle tune a bit like an allemande. I move carefully at first, warming and stretching my muscles until they can carry me safely. As the music shifts, so do I, falling into the unfamiliar tonalities and strange, uneven meters. It feels different, challenging, but not unpleasantly so.

Though my eyes are closed, my whole body—my whole

being—reaches for the music pulsing around me. Drops of sound like liquid gold ripple from Mother Wenla's harp, and Sadra has unearthed a small drum from somewhere. Each beat settles into my chest and lower back, anchoring me as my toes stretch up to the ceiling or flick lightly along the floor. I dip, I spin. I fly, arms and legs outstretched like a bird's wings.

I come to rest with the music, letting my arms fall slowly to my sides as the last note fades. A fine sheen of sweat glistens on my skin; I haven't worked this hard in months. I dab at my face with the skirt of my discarded gown and peek shyly at Sadra and Mother Wenla. My shoulders relax at the broad grin on Sadra's face and the more subtle smile of approval on Mother Wenla's. Their respect, their acknowledgment of my art, means more than I thought it would. I wasn't aware of how badly I needed someone to look at me without pity.

The glow of satisfaction doesn't last long. A low, rough chuckle from somewhere behind me sends me scuttling across the room before I've even registered what the sound was. When I've regained control of my limbs, I move cautiously out of Sadra's shadow to stand at her side.

There's a man standing just inside the doorway, his scarred, weathered face lit by a beam of sunlight that slants through the room's high windows. A scar—a *scar*—I know this man. At least, I recognize him.

"My thanks," the man says. "It's been a long time since I last saw a ballerina dance."

I instantly forget whatever it was I was going to say. Instead, I ask, "And where...where did you last see a ballerina dance?"

"The Bolshoi," he says softly. "In Moscow."

I gasp and move forward, holding my hand out as if in supplication. "*Vy Russkiy?*"

After a slight hesitation, he replies, *"Niet...ya Bolgarin."*

Disappointment makes my chest seem to deflate. Bulgarian, not Russian...but it doesn't matter. What matters is that he's like me. He understands what it is to be a thrall. And he escaped, he—I frown suddenly and narrow my eyes.

"You stole my necklace," I say, with only half a thought to spare for how natural it feels to slip back into the language of Kingsgarden.

"Borrowed," he corrects me. "I borrowed your necklace. For safekeeping."

My heart leaps. "You still have it?"

"I do," he says. "But perhaps this isn't the best place for that conversation. It will be a long one."

"Indeed," Mother Wenla says. "Sasha, Sadra will show you where to clean up. You can join us in my study when you're ready."

"I'm ready now," I say quickly. "Please—"

"It will be a long night," Mother Wenla says, shaking her head. "Take some time and refresh yourself before we begin."

Reluctantly, I let Sadra tow me away to the Temple's bathing chambers, where I hastily wash and dress in the clean gown Sadra provides. As I smooth the fabric over my hips, I marvel at the change in my reflection. The gown, though simple, is lovely. The color is entrancing—a rich, vibrant burgundy that would never be found on a thrall.

Look at me, it says. *I am someone. I am real.*

"It's a little big on you." Sadra purses her lips, looking me over critically. "But it'll do. Just bring it in some here, tie this a bit tighter—" I gasp as she yanks a sash into place around my waist. "Lovely. But what to do with your hair?"

I huff impatiently. "Who cares about my hair?"

"You should, if you don't want to be recognized," Sadra says sharply. She lifts a lock of my hair and twines it through her fingers. "Hm.

Blond, I think, but more honey than wheat. Yes, that will work."

Sadra rummages in a cabinet and emerges with a wig, already styled in a mass of loops and braids. She settles it on my head, tucking my own hair firmly underneath.

"Give it a shake," she says a few seconds later, and I tilt my head from side to side. The wig stays in place. "Good."

She crosses to the door and looks back at me expectantly. I hesitate, fingering a shiny braid.

"Will this work?"

Sadra nods. "It's worked before—repeatedly. The citizens of the City have no reason to think a laughing, talking woman is anything but what she appears to be. Now, if anyone asks, you're meeting with Mother Wenla because you're considering taking your vows."

I follow Sadra through the Temple, trembling with eagerness and the after-effects of exertion.

Despite my impatience, I can't help but admire the architecture. Though everything is made of stone, nothing seems heavy. Light streams in through windows and open courtyards, illuminating every inch of the place right up into the vaulted ceilings. Delicate, subtle carvings decorate pillars and arches, and potted plants dot the hallways. Everything about the Temple whispers of clean lines and serenity.

A wistful sigh escapes my lips. Perhaps I could stay, hide here until they can get me away to wherever they plan to take me. The waiting wouldn't be so terrible in a place like this.

"Sadra!"

It's the chubby blond, the one who accosted us not two hours before. She gives me a bright smile and holds her hand to her heart, dipping her head in greeting. At Sadra's nudge, I return the gesture.

"My name is Feli," the girl says. "Are you a new initiate? What's your name?"

"This is my friend Calla," Sadra says without missing a beat. "She's considering taking her vows."

"Was that your thrall I saw earlier?" Feli asks me. "They're not normally allowed in the Temple, you know. You'll have to give it up."

"I know," I mutter. "I—um—"

"We've taken care of it," Sadra says smoothly. "It's stashed in a storage room."

"Are you a musician or a dancer?" Feli asks next, squinting at me. "You don't look like a sculptor, or even a painter. Not with those hands."

What's wrong with my hands? I resist the urge to look.

"I'm a dancer."

Warmth fills my belly after I speak. *I am a dancer.* They haven't taken that from me.

Yet.

"Well, I hope you join us," Feli says. "You'd love it here. We all do."

"I hope so, too," I murmur.

After a few more pleasantries, Feli skips away, leaving me to stare after her in disbelief.

"She had no idea," I say wonderingly. "And she looked right at me. *Both* times."

"People see what they expect to see," Sadra says with a shrug. More softly, she adds, "Your mask is…very good."

I wince. It is good. Dove trained me well. When people look at me, their eyes slide over my face without seeing it. I'm like a chair, or a boring painting—just part of the background.

"Come on." Sadra takes my elbow and gives it a squeeze. "We have somewhere to be."

We hurry now to avoid any more interruptions. Of course Mother Wenla's study is on the opposite side of the Temple and up three flights of stairs. By the time we arrive, I'm flushed and breathing a bit hard, but perhaps that's more from anxiety than effort.

The scarred man stands at the window with his head bowed and his hands linked behind his back. When we enter, he turns. The moment his gaze falls on me, it sharpens, lingering on my face and hair.

I look away, unsettled by the attention.

"We're sorry for the delay," Sadra says. "It couldn't be avoided…we ran into Feli again, and you know what she's like."

Mother Wenla's brows lift. "And did she…"

"She had no idea," Sadra said smugly. "I think when the time comes, we needn't be too worried about Sasha being recognized."

"When the time comes for what?" I ask. "Please, somebody tell me what's going on. I've waited long enough."

"You're right, you have," the scarred man says. "You're called Sasha?"

"Yes," I say. "It's short for Aleksandra."

Something strange passes over his face, but it's gone so quickly I think I must have imagined it.

"I guess you know that already." I bite my lip, wondering if I offended him, or if maybe he doesn't like to be reminded of home. "And, um, what's your name?"

"I am called Bard."

"Bard?" My brows draw together in puzzlement. "That's your name?"

"No," Bard says, his voice suddenly sharp. "Never mind my name. That man died long ago. I… I have something for you."

After the briefest of hesitations, he takes my hand and places in it a coiled silver chain pooled around two silver swans. I feel the breath leave my lungs like a trapped bird making for the sky. I sink into a nearby chair, my free hand pressed hard against my chest as if to hold my heart in place.

"You don't know what this means to me," I say softly. It's an effort to speak—my throat has closed so tightly I can barely breathe. "I thought

I'd never see it again."

"If someone else had gotten to you first, you wouldn't have seen it again," Bard says. "And we might never have seen *you* again, if that someone knew what it meant. It was the necklace that let me know you had the potential to overcome the Pall. That you brought something with you from the other side indicates an uncommonly strong…essence, I suppose you could say. It's not just the strength of your mind, though of course that's of at least equal importance. When I saw the necklace, I knew you could be saved."

"What do you mean, 'the other side'?" I ask. "What is this place? Is it another world? Is it even real?"

Bard sighs. "It feels real, does it not? Your fear is real. Your pain is real. The danger, I promise you, is very real. Reality isn't something you can measure objectively, Sasha. For our purposes, I think it's not an important distinction to make."

He has a point. There's no way to answer that particular question, so I move on to the next, my voice tight and sharp as I ask, "Who are you? Why are you helping me? I remember you—you were with *them*. You put me in a cage. You branded me."

"I did what I could for you without compromising my position," he says calmly. "I have worked to free many before you, and I hope to free many more, with the Temple's help. I can't do that if I am discovered."

"You sent Sadra to find me."

"No." He shakes his head. "Mother Wenla did. I knew you would be on the King's Terrace, but I didn't know in which household. The Temple knows everything that goes on in the Terrace, and in much of the city."

I look at Mother Wenla. "So you knew about…all this?"

She nods. "My man and I founded the network we call the Bird's Path. Together we recruited allies among the Temple initiates, and some select civilians, Truthseers and Healers, mostly, who already suspected something was amiss. My man—"

"Do you mean your husband?" I ask, confused by her phrasing.

She shakes her head. "Temple initiates take no husbands and have no children. But I loved him…and he died. He withered away under the Pall, and I could do nothing to save him. After I lost him, I continued our work, identifying awakened thralls and spiriting them out of the Cities, into the countryside where they could spend the rest of their lives in freedom and relative safety. I found Bard in a gutter some thirty years ago. He was drunk, raving—"

"But she listened," Bard interrupted. "She believed me when I told her that I had found the Apostate."

"The—the what?" I look at Sadra, but she looks as confused as I feel.

"The Apostate," Bard repeats. "Once one of the highest-ranking members of the House, and one of the best Lightcrafters in the kingdom. He was poised to become the youngest Premier in a century at least. But when he discovered the truth about thralls, he rejected everything and disappeared. No one knew where, and only a few knew the real cause of his desertion. But there were rumors…"

"And you followed them," Sadra prompts when he falls silent.

"Yes. It took me five years, but I found him. He lifted the Pall from me," Bard says. "As he will from you, if we can get you there in one piece."

"And where is 'there', exactly?" Sadra asks.

"Never you mind," Bard says, scowling. "We've already shared more than we should. If you fell into the House's hands…"

"Exactly," Sadra insists. "You always say 'no one knows more than they need to,' so why—"

"Sadra," Mother Wenla interrupts softly and shoots a glance at me. But I'm still absorbing Bard's words.

"Bard. If you're still here…" I lose my breath as the implications crash over me. It takes several moments to find my voice again. "There's no way back, is there? Even if the Pall is taken away, I'll be trapped here forever."

"Not…. not necessarily," Bard says slowly. "I chose to remain here rather than take the risk. Time moves strangely between the worlds. What I saw—years had passed, maybe even decades. My wife had married another man, thinking I was dead. My family was gone. There was nothing left for me there."

"How did you know that?" My necklace bites into my palm as my hand tightens into a fist. "Did you—did you see things in your sleep? Were you…back there?"

Again, that odd hesitation. "At first, yes. But the dreams became more infrequent as I gained greater control over my mind and body. After the Pall was lifted, the dreams stopped almost completely."

"*Almost* completely?" I press. "What did you—"

"Forgive me." Bard lifts a hand to silence me. "They are painful memories, and private. I'd rather not discuss it further."

I open my mouth to argue, then settle back in my chair and ask instead, "What do you mean, you chose not to take the risk? *Is* there a chance I could go home?"

"I can't say," Bard answers. "It's—complicated."

"Well, try," Sadra says, giving him a hard look. "I'm sure we can keep up."

Bard shakes his head. "It's too soon. I won't burden Sasha with that knowledge. The two of you need to focus on making sure Sasha stays out of the House's dungeons."

A chill washes over me. If the House of Light and Shadow has dungeons, it must have the authority to put people in them. But how? Kingsgarden is a monarchy. I would have thought the power to incarcerate people lay with the king and his representatives. I've been thinking of the House as a private—and shady—business venture, but maybe its influence is more pervasive than I thought.

"How much power does the House have in Kingsgarden?" I ask. "Is it a part of the King's government?"

"Not officially," Mother Wenla says, pursing her lips. "But I cannot deny that it's influential. Here in the City of Roses, we have a saying about the king's crown. Have you seen it?" I nod, remembering the wreath of golden flowers glinting against the king's dark curls. "We say the crown's blooms have three thorns: The Council, the House of Light and Shadow, and the Temple of Graces."

"So…a lot of power," I say, my voice faint.

Dread coils in my belly like a cold chain. I press a fist into my middle and concentrate on keeping my breath even.

Bard hesitates, then takes my free hand. "We will protect you, Sasha. You mustn't waste your strength on fear. You'll need all of it to fight the Pall until we can leave."

I swallow and try to smile. When I can't manage that, I squeeze his hand and whisper, "When?"

"Not for some time, I'm afraid," Bard says. "The journey will require extensive preparation. Certain arrangements must be made, and they won't be complete before winter closes the eastern passes."

"So… how long?" My voice is stronger now. "A few weeks? A month?"

"More than that," Bard says gently. "The end of next spring, at the earliest."

I close my eyes. So long… but how long, exactly? I open my eyes and look at Sadra.

"What…what season is it?"

Sadra shoots me a look of mingled alarm and confusion that quickly shifts to understanding…and pity.

"It's autumn." She squeezes my hand. As I grapple with this new information, she turns her attention to Bard and Mother Wenla. "Nine months. Eight, if we're lucky. What in the name of all that's beautiful are we supposed to do until then? We can't just go on as we have, not for that long. Orean will sense my Whispering eventually, and Sasha—you can't expect her to live like this for three more seasons! This is all wrong—why did you even—"

"*Sadra.*" Mother Wenla's voice lashes out like a whip, silencing Sadra's outburst.

"Can't I stay here?" I ask at the same time, horrified by the thought of living under Orean's roof for so long. "I could—"

"No," Mother Wenla says gently. "The risk is too great. If you should be discovered, we would lose everything."

"There's no place in the City—or a village somewhere—"

"The more times you move, the greater the danger," Bard says. "Right now the safest place for you is with Lady Ismeni. If that changes, we will of course re-evaluate our options. But for now, you'll have to endure it."

"Safe!" Sadra explodes. She turns to Mother Wenla. "You saw what Cimari did to her!"

"I did, and I commend Sasha for her bravery," Mother Wenla says. "Sasha, you've convinced the Lady Cimari that she was mistaken, that you are an ordinary thrall. But do you not think it would renew her suspicion if you disappeared now?"

Sadra and I share a sullen glance. Mother Wenla is right. And so tomorrow I'll return to Ismeni's service and live for the better part of a year as a soulless, mindless nothing, condemned to live in fear but forbidden to show it.

I shake the thought out of my head. I still have one more question to ask.

"What about Dove?"

At Bard's look of confusion, Sadra says, "The other thrall—the other woman—serving Ismeni. I told you about her."

"Ah." Bard looks at me with pity in his eyes and I know what he's going to say. "I'm sorry."

"Why?" I ask softly. "She's awake, I know it. If I can be saved, why can't she?"

"She probably could be," Bard admits, "if she survived the journey. But I'm afraid that she very likely would not. From what Sadra has told us, it's a miracle that she's survived the Pall's effects as long as she has."

"Ismeni herself doesn't expect Dove to live through winter," Mother Wenla adds. "You were meant to replace her."

A small sound slips through my lips, part groan and part gasp. "H-how do you know this? Why—"

"Lady Ismeni told me so," Mother Wenla says. "While we were making the arrangements for your visit. I know it must be difficult to hear, but you must put Dove out of your mind, at least in regard to our plans. *You* are our priority, Sasha. I hope we can trust you not to take that responsibility lightly."

"But why?" I ask. "Why am I your priority? What's so special about *me*?"

Bard and Mother Wenla exchange a long look.

"Every life we are able to save is special," Mother Wenla says finally. "Unfortunately, Dove's is not one of them. I'm sorry."

I take a breath and stand up. "I think I'd like to go to bed."

"I'll show you where." Sadra stands too and takes my hand. "Goodnight, Mother."

"Goodnight, my dears," Mother Wenla says. "Rest well and try not to worry. Tomorrow won't look so bleak in the sunlight."

"Thank you for your help," I murmur, avoiding her eyes.

"It is our honor," Bard says. "It was…a pleasure to meet you, Sasha."

I nod and follow Sadra out of Mother Wenla's study, but I only make it a few steps before I sag against the wall. I lean my head against the cool stone, closing my eyes tightly against the tears that strain against my lids. Nine months! I'll never make it. I can't—Sadra pinches my arm and pulls me upright, a hard gleam in her eye.

"No time for that," she says. "Follow me."

"What? Where?" I ask, confused by her urgency. "Aren't we going to bed?"

"Oh, no," she says grimly. "We're not going to bed. We're going out."

Chassé

"This is so stupid," I hiss, my feet dangling several feet above an uncomfortably narrow stone wall. "We're going to get caught, or I'm going to break a leg—or both."

"We *will* get caught if you don't stop whining and get down here." Sadra perches on the wall easily, staring up at me with her hands on her hips. "Just let go."

Just let go... As if it's that easy. As if one mistake, one misstep couldn't cost me my freedom and my life. But I've been afraid for too long. Obedient for too long. I've been a *thrall* for too long.

I screw my eyes shut with a growl and then open them as I release the tree branch I was clinging to. I land on the wall without so much as a wobble and release a slow, steady breath. Sadra smirks at me but nods in approval. I make a broad *after you* gesture. She rolls her eyes and sets off along the wall, keeping low.

"Are you going to tell me what we're doing out here?" I ask as I follow.

"He's broken nearly every rule Mother Wenla taught me," Sadra says. "The Birds have never operated on the Terrace, and we never try to awaken thralls until just before the extraction is to occur, to prevent exactly what they're asking of you. It's cruel—barbaric—to expect a fully conscious, sentient being to endure life as a thrall for so long. And did you see the two of them just before we left? There is something different about you, something special, and I want to know what it is. We won't get anything more out of Mother Wenla or Bard, but I think I know someone who can give us some answers."

"Who?" I ask, trying not to trip over my skirts as we scurry along the wall.

"A fledgling named Maro," Sadra says.

"A what?"

"We call newly freed thralls fledglings," Sadra explains. She shoots me a swift grin. "You're a nestling. As fledglings settle and find their places in the world or within the Bird's Path, they take on new titles. The Path's guides are called peregrines, infiltrators like Bard are owls, informants and eyes in the Cities are sparrows. You get the idea. Most fledglings are happy to aid the cause however they can, but some are…not as helpful. Maro falls firmly into the latter category, though I'm hoping that will work to our advantage tonight. He may be more forthcoming with information than a good little Bird would be."

We travel in silence for some time, our attention fully occupied by the tricky path of the stone wall. After a time, we use a conveniently placed torch sconce to swing down into a deserted alleyway. I shake some clinging debris off my skirts and look around eagerly. Despite the danger, a little prickle of excitement dances across the nape of my neck. For a few hours, at least, I can almost pretend that I'm free.

"This way," Sadra whispers, and sets off down the alley. "Stay close to me. Oh, and take this. Stick it in your hair." She hands me a jeweled pin plucked from her own braids, and I slide it into mine. "But be careful—it's poison. It won't kill you, but it will hurt more than anything you can imagine and freeze your muscles."

I wonder if she'll let me keep it when I return to my life of servitude. How useful it would be to have a weapon like this to protect myself from Orean and Cimari. If either of them touches me again…but no.

Even if I had a weapon, I could never use it. I would expose myself, and I would be lost. My only defense is compliance and invisibility.

"You'd better take one of these, too," Sadra says, pulling off one of her rings. "Flick the catch with your thumb—like so—and blow the powder into your attacker's face to blind and choke him."

"How likely is it that I'll need these?" I ask nervously. My back prickles, remembering the lashes, and I shudder. I'm not at all eager for another encounter with physical violence.

"Middling odds," Sadra says with a shrug. "This isn't the safest area."

I let out a sharp breath through my nose and shoot a hard look at Sadra's back. Frustrated though I am with Bard and Mother Wenla's cryptic explanations, I'm not sure my need for answers is so great that I'm willing to take another beating for them. Whatever answers we get from this fledgling Maro had better be worth the risk.

"Why do you have all these?" I ask as we hurry through the dimly lit streets.

"All Temple initiates are provided with basic training and tools necessary to protect themselves," Sadra says. "Initiates of my occupation are given more to ensure unsavory characters don't take advantage. It's no secret that Temple Companions are both beautiful and deadly. It adds to the prestige."

Not for the first time, a surge of mingled jealousy and admiration rises in my chest. Sadra is everything I'm not and can never be in my current state: free, capable, strong. But I know now that there's hope. I will walk the Bird's Path and one day I'll be all those things…if I survive.

I look around uneasily at the dark corners and eerie shadows of the City, struck again by the risk we're taking. Raucous noise emanates from some buildings, ominous silence from others. The few City dwellers we come across move with hurried, furtive gaits, reinforcing Sadra's warnings. Though the streets are clean—much cleaner, in fact, than many city streets I've seen back home—there's still a whiff of something sour in the air.

"In here," Sadra says, pulling me through a dilapidated wooden door.

I blink and wrinkle my nose against the smoky haze of the tavern. Torches line the wall, their flickering light an unsettling change after the steady illumination provided by globes of Light on the Terrace. The sounds and scents—and bodies—of rough men press against me as Sadra and I push our way through the crowd. I shift my shoulders, uncomfortably aware of the eyes following us across the room. There are times the invisibility of thralldom could be a blessing.

I follow so close on Sadra's heels that I run right into her when she stops.

"Maro," Sadra purrs, sliding into the lap of a greasy, bewhiskered pile of ale-soaked rags and tangled gray hair. "It's been too long."

"You," the lump growls. "What do you want?"

"I want you to order a glass of wine for me and my friend here and take us upstairs." She giggles, leaning in close to murmur, "Do as I say or you'll wake in the morning with festering boils on your arse, you spineless little worm."

Maro gives her a look of deep dislike but lurches to his feet, calling loudly for wine and a room. At Sadra's nod, I let him sling an arm around my shoulders and we stagger through the tavern amid a flurry of cat calls and howls of approval. When we reach the base of the stairs Maro turns and bows extravagantly to general applause and then pulls us into the shadowy stairwell.

"Up there," he says gruffly, giving us both a shove.

Sadra motions for me to go first, placing herself between me and Maro. At the top of the stairs, I find a single door. Beyond it lies a dark, shabby room filled with even shabbier furniture. I enter and place myself against the wall, both out of habit and a reluctance to sit, as the only options are the bed and a rickety, moldy looking chair. Maro immediately flops backward onto the bed and throws an arm over his eyes. Sadra glances at the chair and then joins me against the wall.

"So," she says, crossing her arms. "I have some questions for you."

Maro grunts, belches, and lifts his head to peer at us through his hair. Despite his general sloppiness, his gaze is sharp.

"You? Or your nestling, there?"

I step forward to answer before Sadra can say anything. "The nestling. I need your help."

He grunts again. "What are you doing out and about, anyway? The peregrines must have left months ago."

"That's why we're here," Sadra says, giving me a warning look. "Our current case is…unique. Sasha can't go back to her nest without some answers, and we're not getting them from Bard."

"Ah, yes, our dear savior himself," Maro sneers. "Anything to poke a stick in his eye. What do you want to know?"

"Do you have any idea why Bard would have me wake Sasha so soon? Why would he take that risk?"

"Perhaps he thought the risk of waiting was greater," Maro says with a shrug.

"The risk of what?" I ask, stepping forward.

"Not all nestlings take flight," he says. "If left too long, some never wake up. Not that that ever seemed to bother him before."

"So why would it bother him now?" Sadra wonders, glancing at me. I shrug, just as baffled as she is.

"As to that, I couldn't say." Maro leers at me. "Your nestling's a mighty pretty girl, though. Could be Bard's finally developed a taste for something more than duty and honor and all that."

"Doubtful," Sadra says. "There must be something…"

"Might be her Gift he's after, then." Maro squints at me. "Any sign of it yet, girl?"

"I—I don't think so." I never considered that I had a Gift.

"Well, it's not likely 'til the Pall is lifted," he says. "Still, though, I can't think what else he might be interested in. Lives and breathes for the Bird's Path and the Apostate, that one."

"Can you tell me about the Apostate?" I ask. "Where is he, how do we get there, what happens when the Pall—"

"Slow down, nestling," Maro growls. "You'll find the Apostate on an island in the South Sea."

"The South Sea," Sadra cries. "But that's on the other side of the Crown's Teeth!"

"The what?" I ask.

"The mountains that ring Kingsgarden," Sadra explains. "Untamable, unconquerable, filled with all sorts of man-eating beasts—both human and animal."

Maro snorts. "The Forest Folk don't eat people, dolt. They just don't like outsiders. But they like Lightcrafting even less and tolerate Bard's little enterprise on account of it. They think Light's unnatural, see. An abomination."

"Who is the Apostate?" I ask. "Does he have a name?"

"Sure he does," Maro says. "I think it's Porr. Parr? Somethin' like that. Never cared much, myself. And he don't care about us, neither, not unless we're willing to lay our lives down for him. If'n you won't be one of his damned Birds they just cut you loose to starve or die in the streets."

"Oh, have mercy." Sadra snorts, rolling her eyes. "You were given a more than generous allowance to get you started. It's not the Path's fault you drank it up in weeks. You could have—"

"I could have what?" he snarls. "My Gift is weaker than a newborn rat and useless to boot. I was a bookkeeper in my old life. I can't hunt, can't fight, I don't know nothin' about farming. And I can't keep books here, can I, not knowing the runes and all? All I'm fit for in this world is what I'm doing—cleaning the gutters and drinking myself into an early grave. This isn't my place. I don't belong here." His eyes cut to me. "You listen, nestling, when you get the chance, you think hard on what you choose."

"Choose?" I repeat, my heart pounding. "What do you mean? Is it possible to go back?"

"Ah, he hasn't told you, has he?" Maro gives an unpleasant smile. "Well. Boils or no boils, I think I've said enough."

His smile widens, revealing a mouthful of yellowed, rotting teeth. He laughs and looks me right in the eyes. "Yes, I think I've said more than enough."

* * *

"Well," Sadra says as we slip out of the tavern. "That conversation wasn't *unfruitful*."

"Why wouldn't he tell us what happens when the Pall is lifted?" I wonder fretfully. "It must be something terrible."

"Not necessarily," Sadra says, though she sounds uneasy. "It could just be Maro being Maro. He'd think it a great joke to give you a fright over nothing. Though he'll find it less funny when he wakes tomorrow with those boils."

"Can you really do that?" I wonder.

"I can and I will," she says darkly as we turn a corner. "And it'll serve him right, the filthy little—"

She cuts herself off and slows, taking hold of my arm. Six men lounge against a low wall some ten yards away, watching us with the lazy interest of sleepy lions surveying a couple of stray zebras.

"If it comes to trouble, stay behind me and get your back against a wall," Sadra mutters to me. To the men, she says, "A fine evening to you, gentlemen."

Her voice is firm and friendly, betraying no trace of fear or even concern. I try to mimic her confident stride, but I'm afraid I'm doing a poor job of it. The men seem to think so, too: One of them grins wolfishly at me and nudges the man next to him.

"It'll be finer still in but a moment," he says. "Once you hand over them pretty jewels and whatever coin you got. Them dresses ain't too shabby, neither. Better give us those, too."

The man's companions guffaw, slapping him on the back and praising his wit in gleeful hoots.

"I think not," Sadra says politely. "A daughter of the Temple of Graces can't be seen walking the streets naked, now can she?"

The man falters at that, but quickly rallies even as the others begin to mutter.

"What would a Temple initiate be doing in the lower city at this time of night, eh?" he demands, giving one of his friends a shove. "She ain't nothin' but a lying bitch what needs t'be taught a lesson—in the name of the Temple's honor, like. It's a killin' offense to impersonate an initiate, girlie, you know that? But we's fair and merciful types, ain't we, lads? We'll leave you your life and take your coin—and whatever else you have to offer in the way of compensation. Seems only right."

"Yes, quite," Sadra says. "And I shall certainly extend you the same courtesy, for you must know that it is also a killing offense to attack a Temple initiate." She tugs down the neck of her gown to reveal her Mark. A couple of the men blanche, but their leader only sneers.

"Enough," he snarls. "Get 'em, lads!"

Sadra pushes me back until I hit the wall of what looks like an abandoned tavern on the opposite side of the street. The men fan out as they approach, flipping knives from hand to hand and cracking their knuckles.

Sadra produces a curved blade seemingly from nowhere which she holds with a firm, easy grip. I pull the pin out of my hair with shaking hands, silently cursing everyone and everything that led us to this point. I take a breath and force my hand to steady. At least one of these apes is going to feel its sting.

Steeling myself, I step forward. But Sadra dispatches the leader before I can even blink, knocking his blade away as it passes from one hand to the other and sweeping her own across his throat. The others pause as he slumps to the ground, then approach more cautiously. Their rough laughter and banter are gone, replaced by cold, calculating malice. Sadra falls into a defensive crouch and hisses at them to get on with it. I copy her stance, my fingers tight on my hair pin.

The remaining five burst into motion all at once, three attacking Sadra head on and two circling around to get to me. I focus on my attackers, knowing I can do nothing for Sadra. They're hard, ugly brutes with rotten teeth and lank, greasy hair. But, ugly as they are, they each have six inches and at least seventy pounds on me. I can't count on them being slow, either, as they look to be all muscle.

I flick my thumb against my ring and raise my hand to my lips, blowing just as my first assailant reaches for me. A cloud of grayish powder catches him full in the face and he stumbles away, choking and wheezing. I dart past him and plunge my hair pin into the arm of the second man. He lets out a wild shriek of pain and falls to the ground, convulsing.

I back away and turn to see Sadra fending off the last two thieves with vicious swipes of her knife. My stomach turns over. She gave her most valuable weapons to me—that knife is all she has! I look at the pin in my hand, wondering if it's only good for one use and if I can get it into one of the thieves without getting in Sadra's way. Probably not. But what can I do? I can see that Sadra is tiring, and so can the thieves. They taunt her now, using words so filthy I don't know what they mean.

The one I hit with tear-powder seems to be recovering. Before he can get his hands under him to push himself off the ground, I lean over and slam his head into the ground. He lies still.

Sadra is still fighting, but with a hint of desperation now. Cuts adorn her hands and arms, and she's breathing heavily. I hover uncertainly until the second of Sadra's opponents notices me. I see it in his eyes when he decides that I'd make an easier target. I lift my skirts and run.

Panting and silently cursing the skirts, I dash up a street which I *think* leads to the Temple. Heavy footsteps pound behind me, drawing closer. A cold sweat breaks out along my back and shoulders. I'm not going to make it—he's going to catch me. Without stopping to think, I skid to a halt and turn in the same motion, screaming as loud as I can right in my attackers face. It's enough to make him hesitate—only for a moment, but a moment is all I need to plunge my hairpin into his left eye. He shrieks and staggers away, clutching his face. One of his flailing arms catches me in the chest. I stumble backward and catch the hem of my skirt under my heel.

A pair of strong arms catch me as I fall, winding around my waist and pressing me back against a hard, muscled, very male torso. I twist away, thinking it's another thug, but it's only a dark-haired young man with his hands up in a deliberately non-threatening pose. Though his face is in shadow, something about his broad-shouldered, lanky form seems familiar.

My gaze falls to the fox sitting at his feet, and my memory flashes on the scene of Cimari's betrothal. He was there! The man with the fox—he was angry that the Premier had killed a little bird to summon Pretty Girl. And now he's here, staring down at me with bewilderment and concern.

I back away and blurt the first thing that comes to mind. "What are *you* doing here?"

The man raises his eyebrows, his green eyes sparking in the light of a lantern. "Have we met?"

Crap. What can I say to that? Nothing that isn't dangerous or stupid or both.

"I need help," I say instead. "Those thieves—there are more of them. Please, my friend is—"

"Show me where," the man says, and runs with me back to where I left Sadra.

The street is empty. My gaze skitters frantically over the bloody cobblestones as I search for Sadra.

"No," I breathe. "She was here, she was—"

"Shh," my companion says, laying his hand on the small of my back. "Listen."

It's hard to hear anything over the noise of my own harsh breathing. But after a moment, I make out the sound of men jeering and laughing. I bolt in that direction with the fox and his master hard on my heels. We find Sadra cornered in an alley by three men. Reinforcements, or maybe they just wanted in on the fun. My blood boils. But I don't know what I can do. My last weapon is stuck in an eyeball somewhere.

The dark-haired man doesn't hesitate. He draws two knives at once and wades into the fray, plunging his blades into his first opponent before the man even realizes he's there. The fox leaps for the throat of the second but gets a hand instead. The fox's victim yelps and whips the fox around, trying to dislodge him. The last of the thieves faces off with my new friend, leaving Sadra free to slump to the ground in exhaustion. I edge around the violence and drop to my knees beside her.

"Are you alright?" I ask, wringing my hands as I scan her body for injuries.

"Fine," she pants. "Who—oh, no. *Lucoran?*"

"So that's his name," I mutter. "I'm sorry. He just showed up, and I didn't know what else to do."

Sadra rubs a hand across her forehead, leaving a streak of blood. "You were right, Sasha. This was a stupid—*watch out.*"

I spin, crouching protectively over Sadra as the fox's victim lumbers toward us. The fox himself lies some feet away, shaking his head dazedly.

Something nudges my hand; I take it, trying to hold the knife the way Sadra did, but it feels clumsy and foreign in my hand. Though he has no weapons, the thief grins, sensing my lack of skill. He approaches with eager steps.

"Don't hesitate," Sadra whispers.

Terror sets my nerves ablaze, its fire driving me forward in a swift, silent rush. I drive my knife straight toward the thief's belly, but he twists, seizing my wrist with one enormous hand and forcing me to the ground with the other. He squeezes my wrist and the knife clatters to the ground, out of my reach. Frozen with horror, I stare up at his toothless grin.

Then the fox is there, snapping at the man's face. In his shock, he lets my wrist go and falls backward. I'm on my feet before he hits the ground. Without hesitation, I stomp on his lower belly with all my strength. The thief goes white, clutching himself in almost comically exaggerated agony.

"Well done," a voice says in my ear.

I whirl around, my hands curling instinctively into claws. But it's only the dark-haired man, Lucoran, Sadra called him.

"See to your friend," he suggests. "I'll clean up."

I take his advice and help Sadra to her feet, trying very hard not to hear the sound of a sudden wet gurgling behind me. Sadra hugs me, her arms tight around my shoulders.

"Can you ever forgive me?" she asks.

"You were right, we never should have left the Temple. You could have been killed."

"*I* could have been killed?" I ask incredulously. "What about you?"

She smiles weakly. "Oh, those rats never had a chance."

Despite her brave words, I can tell she's shaken. There's an almost imperceptible tremor in her hands that tells me just how close she came to losing the fight—and her life. Very deliberately, I set aside the rest of that thought and look around for Lucoran. He's finished with the last of our attackers and is fastidiously wiping the blood off his knives.

"Blessed Sister," he greets Sadra, eying her curiously. "What an unexpected pleasure to see you in the Lower City, of all places. Shouldn't you be at the palace?"

"I could ask the same of you," Sadra replies. Her tone is light, but she moves to place herself between me and Lucoran. "But I won't tell if you won't."

"Fair." Lucoran grins. He steps around Sadra and nods to me, placing his hand over his heart in the City's gesture of greeting. "I'm afraid I didn't get a chance to introduce myself properly. My name is Lucoran. Luca, to my friends."

"And are we your friends?"

I raise my eyebrows, trying to ignore the flush rising in my cheeks. My mind and body are both buzzing with fear and relief, my emotions so scrambled that I can't tell if I'm blushing from nerves or attraction or both.

"Oh, definitely," he says with a crooked smile. "There's nothing like a little bloodshed to seal a friendship."

"Quite right," Sadra agrees, then nudges me toward the mouth of the alleyway before turning back to Luca. "Truly, we are in your debt. But you must let us go and forget you ever saw us. I swear on my talisman, our lives depend on your silence. Can we trust you?"

For a moment he looks like he wants to argue, but in the end he nods and steps back. The fox leaps into Luca's arms and stares at us with an unsettlingly keen gaze, as if he, too, is wondering just what we're up to. I lower my eyes and follow Sadra.

At the mouth of the alley, I half turn, looking back at Luca. Our eyes meet one last time, and then Sadra pulls me away into the darkness.

Soutenu

I can hear music. It feels familiar and foreign all at once, filling my chest with an ache I don't understand. A name tickles my mind and then slips away, leaving me reaching vainly after it. But it comes back again and again, each time inching a little closer to my grasping fingers until I catch it and hold it to myself-Tchaikovsky. I'm not sure what it means or why it's so important, but I know that it is.

I see faces. An old woman sits beside a child's bed, humming a lullaby. A young woman sits beside a sleeping girl, whispering strange words. Another woman, slightly older, sits beside a hospital bed, weeping.

I whimper, pained by the conflicting realities, until they coalesce into one.

Emily doesn't notice when I open my eyes; her face is pressed into the sheets of the hospital bed, her hands clasped over her head. Her shoulders shake with the violence of her grief. I want to comfort her, but when I reach for her my arm jerks against the padded cuff around my wrist.

I can still hear the lullaby weaving in and out of the music coming from the speakers next to my bed—my cage. But the lullaby isn't coming from Emily, or from the girl who stands behind her, watching me with wide, honey-colored eyes set in a dark face. Recognition flickers, then dies. If I knew her once, I've forgotten.

I focus on the lullaby, trying to hum along: All that comes out is a low, tuneless moan.

Emily raises her head, revealing a look of misery so intense it makes me *cringe back into my pillows. The girl behind her reaches tentatively over Emily's shoulder, holding her hand out to touch my face. I twist away with a sharp squeal, thrashing against my restraints. Something is wrong—the dark girl isn't supposed to be here.*

I look back at Emily, hoping she'll make the dark girl go away. But Emily is gone. In her place is a woman—a woman whose face terrifies me in its familiarity. It isn't just her eyes or her mouth or the shape of her face, though they look just like my own—like Baba Nadia's. It isn't that. It's the wild blankness that hides behind her eyes, even on good days. I thought I had forgotten. I thought I'd lost all memories of this woman. And yet, here she is.

I scream.

The dark girl withdraws her hand hastily and backs away into the corner. Her eyes dart around the room. Her shoulders quiver with tension. She's afraid. She's not supposed to be here.

A high-pitched sound, almost a whistle, escapes from my lips. The woman's hands are on my shoulders, pushing me into the pillows. She calls for help. The dark girl hugs herself as nurses rush in to sedate me. Something sharp pricks my arm.

The music takes me back.

Bayu, bayushki, bayu.

* * *

"Sasha?"

I open my eyes slowly, afraid, as I so often am, of what I'll find. I close them again after meeting Sadra's gaze. Even in the pale pre-dawn light, I can see the pity and horror written all over her face.

"I'm sorry," Sadra says softly. "I've never—it's not supposed to work like that."

I should ease her worry, tell her it's alright, but it isn't alright. I feel exposed, dirty, like a snail without its shell. When she looks at me now, she'll see a raving, drooling beast. She'll see something lower even than the mindless drone that the citizens of Kingsgarden think I am.

"Sasha, was that…"

"Yes." I look away. "That was me—on the other side."

Sadra frowns. "Sasha, if that's what's waiting for you…do you really want to go back?"

"It's not—that's not how it's supposed to be." I look down and pick at the blanket covering my legs. "It wasn't always like that. It's the Pall somehow, I know it is. Once it's off, maybe…"

"Maybe what?"

"I don't know," I lower myself back onto the pillows and stare at the ceiling. "I don't know."

"And who—" Sadra cuts herself off with a sharp jerk of her head. "Forgive me. It's not my place."

"It's alright," I say dully. "You're wondering who the others were."

Sadra nods and scoots closer on the bed. "The one who changed. I assumed she was your Emily. But then she became…someone else."

"My mother," I whisper, and lower my eyes.

"You told me she died," Sadra presses, her face intent. "You said she had a disease of the mind."

"Yes."

"But haven't you thought what that means?" Sadra's voice is urgent now. "If what's happening to you also happened to *her*…what if she wasn't mad? What if she's *here*?"

"So what if she is?" I turn away, unable to look her in the eye. "What can I do about it?"

Sadra sucks in a sharp breath. "You can find her! After you're free of the Pall—"

"*If* I can be freed from the Pall, I'm going home," I snap. "What proof do we have that she's here? And what if she is? She'll have been here nearly fourteen years. You said thralls rarely last more than ten."

"Bard says time flows differently here," Sadra argues, her voice rising. "It might not have been that long. She might have been freed. We can at least *ask*—"

"No!"

Sadra flinches at the anger in my tone and then stares at me, shaking her head in disbelief. "Sasha, it's your *mother*." She tries to reach for my hand, but I slap it away.

"Emily is my mother." Grief and longing squeeze my throat like a noose. "My mother...Lara...she died when I was four, and she *was* mad in that world. My grandmother had to explain to her who I was every time we visited the hospital. She didn't know me. She didn't love me. Emily does. She raised me, she and Baba Nadia. I have to go back to her if I can. I have to."

I put my hands over my face, fighting to contain the tide of despair and frustration surging through me.

"Alright," Sadra says after a minute and touches my shoulder. "I'm sorry, Sasha. Hush, now. It's alright. I'll say no more about it."

I can see her through my fingers. I can tell there's more she wants to say on the subject, but she doesn't. Instead, she drops her eyes and holds her hands out, palms up, in a formal-looking gesture of supplication.

"I owe you another apology, Sasha. What happened last night—it was stupid and reckless and entirely my fault. I'm so sorry. Can you forgive me?"

It takes me a moment to respond. It *was* stupid and reckless...but it wasn't entirely her fault. I didn't want to go in the first place, and I'm not convinced that Maro's information was worth the risk, but she can't take all the blame. I could have said no. I could have obeyed Mother Wenla and gone to bed. But I didn't.

"It's not your fault," I say, but it sounds a little stiff even to me.

"Not entirely convincing, but I'll take what I can get," she says wryly, then sighs. "Lucoran's presence complicates things."

"Who is he, exactly?" I ask. "I've seen him at the palace—and at Ismeni's, too, I think."

"He's the king's bastard brother and the captain of the royal guard," Sadra says. "He's very close to King Miocostin and their sister, the Princess Arismendi. He's not terribly active politically or socially, but there's a good chance your paths will cross on the Terrace. I just pray that when they do, he doesn't recognize you."

"He won't," I say firmly. "My mask will hold."

Sadra nods. "It *must* hold. And Sasha…I saw the way you looked at him. I know his attention must have felt good after so long with only my poor self to keep you company." She smiles, but her eyes are dark with concern. "Some small part of you may want to let him see the truth. You can't. You must stay strong and stay hidden. Believe me, I know what it's like to live each day lying to someone you love. I don't want that for you."

Heat rushes to my face. It's a bit rich, I think, for her to lecture me after all the trouble she got us into. I was grateful for Luca's help, of course—who wouldn't be? And if, much later in the evening, after we were safe in bed, I remembered his hands on my waist or his quirky, crooked smile and gallows humor, I was able to push all that aside. Because I know—I *know*—that it wouldn't matter, not if he knew the truth.

She's wrong: I *don't* want him to see the real me. Would he touch me like that again, would he still smile at me, if he knew what I am?

I know the answer already, and I don't appreciate being reminded. And I certainly don't need her flaunting her own freedom to love and be loved in the same breath.

"He won't see me," I say evenly. I lie back and close my eyes. "I'm tired. I need to sleep more."

Sadra pats my knee and sighs. "So you do. I told Mother Wenla you were too upset to sleep last night. She'll be along to give you another boost, and then we have to go. We're already late, and Ismeni isn't going to be happy about it."

I nod silently, my face turned toward the wall. I don't hear her get up, only the soft tap of the door closing behind her.

My lashes tremble against my cheeks, but no tear escapes.

My lip lifts in a silent snarl as my fist hits the wall with a dull, empty thump.

Go back? How can I, after tasting freedom for the first time in months? I can't, I *can't*…but I will, not because I have no choice but because I want to live long enough to make my choice count. This isn't my moment, not yet. When it comes, I'll know, and I'll act. But for now, all I need to do is nothing at all.

Dessous

"Dove's not doing too well."

I try to keep my tone mild. Sadra and I are in the garden, playing with Pretty Girl, the puppy, but we've been tense and awkward with each other in the weeks since our botched rebellion.

We don't talk about Bard's plans for my escape, because that could all too easily lead to the many questions we failed to answer that night and the dangers that resulted. While I believe I have in fact forgiven her, I don't want to dwell on it, either. She's my only friend here, the one person in this world I really trust. I can't afford to push her away.

So we content ourselves with dancing and teaching Pretty Girl nonverbal commands—or trying to. I've never tried to train a dog before. Hell, before Pretty Girl I could count on one hand the number of times I'd even touched a dog. Even so, she has won me over completely in the weeks since Sadra brought her to me. I'd never experienced such unthinking, limitless devotion before. I didn't know how healing it could be. I'm lucky to have her.

"Can't we do anything for her?" I ask, looking up from rubbing Pretty Girl's belly. "Dove, I mean."

"Like what?" Sadra asks. "I don't mean to be callous, Sasha, but there isn't anything to be done."

"There aren't medicines to make it easier? She's in pain."

My throat constricts. Though she hides it well, I see the way Dove's features tighten when she gets out of bed in the morning. No matter how skilled an actress she is, she can't conceal the pallor that creeps into her face by the end of the day or the way the air whistles in her chest after climbing the stairs to our room.

Sadra frowns. "There are, but under the medicine's influence, she'd be of little use to Ismeni. Orean…he doesn't keep anything that isn't useful."

"He would kill her?"

"Or let the House take care of it," Sadra says. "Ismeni might argue, and she might win…but I don't want to take that chance. Do you?"

"I wish she would speak to me," I say, tugging a stick out of Pretty Girl's mouth. "She could if she wanted to, I'm sure of it."

"But she doesn't want to," Sadra reminds me. "If she wants our help, I think she knows by now that we would give it."

"Yes," I sigh and get up, dusting off my skirts. "I should get back."

Sadra nods. "Be careful."

I signal Pretty Girl with a subtle flick of my hand, and for once she moves immediately to my side and follows as I weave through the garden paths. Dove is seated, as usual, on the lip of the fountain. I stand quietly at her side until she finally gets to her feet. Though her lips are pinched and white, I know better than to offer her any assistance. I keep my face smooth and blank, as she taught me to do. The ability to hide in plain sight is our only defense in a house full of enemies.

Dove may soon die, but I won't let that moment come any sooner by revealing our secret.

The threat of discovery haunts me day and night. Sometimes, in that hazy place between sleeping and waking, I feel again the flesh of my back parting beneath the whip. I feel the blood trickle down my rib cage and pool in the small of my back.

Other times, I feel strong arms around my waist and a flutter of warm breath on my cheek. I've learned to savor those moments, those memories, in the seconds before I'm reminded of the danger they represent. Though there's been no sign of Luca, I know it's only a matter of time until we cross paths again, either here or at the palace. But my mask will be perfect. I will be still. I will be silent. His eyes will pass over me.

He won't see.

* * *

"Please, just tell me what's going on," Emily begs. I can barely hear her through the door to my room.

"I honestly don't know what's going on," another woman says. "I wish I could tell you."

"But you know something," Emily argues. "I can tell. You have to tell me what it is."

"I don't—I think I know something, but even if I'm right, I don't know what it means," the other voice stammers. "I don't know what's wrong with her."

"Tell me anyway," Emily pleads. "I have to know. Please, Carmen."

"Emily..."

"What, do you think I'm going to sue you if you're wrong? You should know better by now."

"I know you wouldn't, but Emily...I really don't know how it will help."

"But it won't hurt," Emily insists. "Carmen, you said you consider me a friend. If you really meant it—"

"Of course I did," the other voice—Carmen, whoever she is—says quickly. "Okay. If I'm right...it looks like Sasha's not always conscious."

"Well, obviously," Emily says with a huff. "She hasn't been herself since—"

"I don't mean lucid," Carmen cuts in. "I mean conscious—as opposed

to unconscious, as if she were under anesthesia, or if she were brain dead. Even when she's awake, she's not completely here. It's like she's flickering in and out, but too quickly for us to see just by looking at her. I think that's what's causing her neurological symptoms, but I don't know why, and I can't prove that it's even happening. I'm sorry."

I stop paying attention.

If I'm not always here, where am I?

* * *

I open my eyes, my body buzzing with awareness. I don't need Pretty Girl's soft growl to tell me that there's a stranger in our room. Before I can do more than shift under the covers, a hard, calloused hand closes over my mouth. An arm like a steel band circles my waist, jerking me out of the bed. Pretty Girl barks once and then yelps before subsiding into silence.

"Don't make a sound," a voice whispers in my ear. His grip tightens on my jaw. "You will come with me, and you will do so quietly, or I will kill you."

This is it—the House has found me—but how? My mask was perfect, I know it was. And why now, weeks after Cimari's attempt to expose me? Come to that, why snatch me from my bed in the middle of the night? The House of Light and Shadow is more than powerful enough to take me by less dramatic means. What is going on?

My attacker half-drags, half-carries me backward out of the room, down the stairs, and through the gardens without giving me a chance to find my feet, much less struggle. He stays in the shadows—easily done, as very little moonlight makes it into the ravine. As we approach the wall of the mountain, I tense, thinking he'll finally stop. He doesn't. He ducks under a bush and pulls me after him. I close my eyes against the stabbing branches and leaves of the bush and wince as my feet and calves scrape against cold, wet stone.

When I open my eyes, I panic. What did he do to me? He's blinded me somehow! I can't see a thing, not even the faintest suggestion of form. Suddenly the air seems thicker, almost solid, and too big to enter my lungs. I tug frantically at the hand on my mouth. It only tightens in response.

"I'll let you go in a moment," my captor growls. "Don't try to run. You'll only hurt yourself in these tunnels. I think you won't scream—you have more to lose than I do. Nod if you understand."

I nod jerkily, straining against the weight of his hand, and gasp as my lips come free. I cough against the sudden influx of air. In my terror, it doesn't occur to me to pretend. I have to speak.

"Who—who are you?"

"You wound me," the voice says in a normal tone, and now I recognize it. "I thought I'd made more of an impression."

"Luca." How did he find me? How—and what—does he know about me? I could swear I haven't seen him since the night in the alley. "Please, you don't understand—"

"You're cursed right, I don't understand," Luca snaps. "And you'd best have an *excellent* explanation, because right now the only reason I can see for posing as a thrall in a Terrace household is to get close to a Council member—or the king."

"You don't understand," I say again. "I *am* a thrall."

"You must think I'm very stupid," Luca says with a snort. "Or perhaps you're not that bright yourself. May I remind you that thralls *can't speak?*"

"No—you don't—thralls aren't what you think they are." I clutch at my head. How can I explain—and how can I make him believe? "They didn't make me. They stole me. Please—*please*—don't let them find me. They'll take me away—they'll hurt me."

"Who?" Luca demands. "What are you babbling about?"

I take a breath and let it out slowly, willing myself to be calm. "The House of Light and Shadow. They've convinced everyone that they made thralls—created them, like dolls—but they *lied*. Do you hear me? *They lied.*"

"Well," Luca says after a pause. "I have to commend your imagination, at least. That is the most—"

He cuts off abruptly at the sound of small rocks tumbling against each other. A voice—Sadra's!—curses, softly at first and then more loudly. A soft yip that sounds like a laugh answers her.

"Kirit," Luca growls. "It took you long enough."

Something small and soft passes around my ankles. I jump and trip over a loose stone. Only Luca's tight grip on my arm keeps me upright.

"Sasha?"

"Here!" I cry. "I'm over here—with Luca."

Luca sighs irritably but doesn't relax his hold on me. Finally, Sadra's groping hands find me and—after poking me in the eye—settle on my shoulders.

"Lucoran," she says. "*What* are you doing creeping around and abducting people in the middle of the night?"

"What are *you* doing aiding a spy and possible assassin?" he retorts. "I let you go, and I didn't question you. And *this* is what you've been up to?"

"What we're up to has nothing to do with you," Sadra says. "And Sasha is nothing of the sort, as I'm sure she's told you by now."

"I did," I confirm. "He doesn't believe me."

"Understandable, though disappointing." Sadra pats my shoulder. To Luca, she says, "You're a Lightcrafter, aren't you? Can't you feel the Light coming off her?"

A pause.

"It must be coming from an amulet," Luca says, but there's the slightest hint of uncertainty in his voice.

"You had your hands all over me," I huff. "Where do you think I'm hiding it? Up my—"

Sadra raises her voice, drowning me out. "There is no amulet."

"You can't seriously be asking me to believe this nonsense," Luca cries. "I don't know how a Temple initiate got caught up in this, but—"

"I didn't get caught up in anything," she says. "The Temple recruited me for this. Would you believe Mother Wenla's word over mine? It could be arranged, though I doubt she'd be pleased to be woken at this hour."

"The *Temple Mother*—"

"We need Bard," I murmur to Sadra. "He's not going to believe anything we say until he sees proof."

Sadra sighs. "I think you're right." To Luca, she says, "Would you consent to take a walk with us or are you going to ruin everything we've worked so hard to achieve?"

"Take a walk where?" Luca asks suspiciously.

"To see someone who can give you proof that what Sasha says is true," Sadra says. "Will you come?"

"Please," I add softly, shivering against the fears that seem so much closer in the dark.

At first, he doesn't say anything. I hold my breath, only letting it out when I hear him release his. The fox yips, as if answering a question I can't hear.

"Alright," he says. "But if I'm not completely satisfied that you're telling the truth, I go straight to the king and then to the House Premier."

"That won't be necessary, I assure you," Sadra says. "Sasha, you should go back to bed before you're missed."

"No." Luca's hand tightens on my arm. "She comes with us."

"That's really not a good idea," Sadra argues. "If they notice she's gone—"

"I don't care," Luca snaps. "Neither of you is leaving my sight until I'm sure you're not going to run off and kill someone to cover your tracks."

"Charming," Sadra mutters to me. "I can see why you were so taken with him."

My voice gets stuck on a lump in my throat that has nothing to do with fear. Don't be a baby, I tell myself. I should have known to expect this sort of reaction.

Of course he doesn't believe me. And his assumption is a logical one. But he'll see. He'll see I'm telling the truth, and then—I stop myself. And then what? He'll carry me off into the sunset? No. The best I can hope for is that he won't turn me over to the House of Light and Shadow.

Luca jerks on my arm and I stumble forward, tripping on the uneven floor of the tunnel. I was stupid, so stupid, to build up this vision of him in my head, an exaggerated image of chivalry and safety based on one kind act. I hadn't thought it would do any harm. I thought it was nothing more than a story to comfort myself at night. But now, confronted with the hard and downright hostile reality of my fairy tale prince, I see how a dream can hurt.

* * *

We stumble through the darkness, Luca dragging on my right arm and Sadra clinging to my left. Every so often the fox—Kirit, Luca called him—brushes by, tripping me up or nearly stopping my heart, or both. At any moment, Ismeni could discover my empty bed and ruin everything. The minute the news reaches Cimari's ears, she'll know that she was right about me and she'll hunt me down—and then what?

Sadra always refuses to talk about what exactly the House does with "defective" thralls, but the look that invariably appears on her face when I bring it up is enough to discourage further questions.

But now all the questions I never asked seem to spill out of my head and into my belly, where they writhe like angry snakes. It's worse, I think, to be frightened without knowing what to be frightened *of*.

By the time the first sliver of light appears, my whole body aches with physical and mental strain.

"Wait," Sadra says as we approach a thin crack in the tunnel wall. "I'll fetch him here."

"I told you, neither of you is—"

"What do you think will happen if you drag us both out there like this?" Sadra snaps. "Even at this hour of the night, there are folk who will ask questions. We don't have time for questions. You keep Sasha with you, and I'll bring Bard. Where are we?"

"Near the guildhall, in the courtyard of a private home."

"Your private home, I presume," Sadra says. She doesn't wait for him to reply. "Bard's quarters aren't far from here. I'll be back before the next bell."

Sadra moves around me and trips, cursing as she falls onto her hands and knees. Luca lets me go, as if by reflex, and I kneel to help her. As I crouch beside her, she slips something hard and cold into my hand and whispers in my ear, almost too quickly for me to understand–"If I'm not back in time, or if he tries to move you, stick him with that and run for the Temple."

I curl my fingers carefully around the—I hope—freshly poisoned hairpin and help Sadra to her feet before curling my arms around myself to hide my hands.

"I'll see you soon." Sadra hugs me briefly. To Luca, she says, "Don't do anything stupid."

"I'll give you the same advice," Luca says, a bite to his tone. "And a chaperone to make sure you follow it. Kirit will accompany you."

A sliver of light illuminates Sadra's wry smile as she bends to offer the fox her fingers to sniff. "I welcome the company, if not the sentiment."

Darkness envelops us once more as Sadra slips through the crack, her body filling the space completely. She grunts softly as she wiggles through, and I wonder how Luca manages to fit. I reach out with cautious fingers and find the wall, following it down until I hit the floor. I settle myself on the uneven ground and draw my knees to my chest. The stone is hard and cold, but I sigh anyway, tipping my head back.

My eyes drift shut of their own accord, as if my body is simply unwilling to expend any more energy on worry or fear. It's a peculiar feeling—depressing, certainly, but at the same time oddly pleasant. It strikes me that perhaps dying might feel a little like this—like release.

That wouldn't be so bad. The thought so disturbs me that I pinch myself awake and climb back to my feet.

"How did you find me?" I ask, more from a desire to break the silence than out of real curiosity.

"Kirit," he replies. "You can hide your face, but you can't hide your scent."

"Can you…can you talk to him?" I ask incredulously.

"Of course," he replies, sounding surprised and a little annoyed, like it's something obvious. "I'm a Beastspeaker."

I glare at him. "I liked you a lot better when you weren't being a horse's ass."

"Well, I liked you a lot better when you weren't an assassin," he retorts.

"I'm *not*," I cry. "I've told you what I am, and Sadra has confirmed it. I know you don't honestly think I'm an assassin, or you wouldn't be here."

Luca makes a noise of frustration. "I want to believe you. Of course I want to believe I didn't make a mistake—that I didn't commit treason—by letting you go that night. But it's ludicrous, what you're telling me."

"Is it?" I ask softly. "Is it really so hard to believe? Thralls breathe, like you. We eat, like you. We bleed, like you. Most of us can't speak, but plenty of people can't, whether from illness or injury. Is the thought that thralls suffer a kind of illness so outlandish?" I shake my head. "No, not an illness, an…an affliction. Because it didn't just happen, Luca. It was *done to us.*"

I hesitate, then reach out and take his hand. Blushing at my boldness, I guide his fingers beneath the edge of my nightdress and onto the rough, lumpy scar tissue at my hip. His hand jerks slightly in surprise, then settles, his fingertips exploring the edges of the brand. I tense, though his touch is in no way sexual or even aggressive. It's just that I avoid touching the brand or even looking at it if I can, and exposing it to Luca's examination, even in the dark, makes my stomach turn.

"Do you think it's a fake?" I ask. "Do you think I did that to myself?"

"I don't know what to think," Luca says.

I release his hand and turn away.

"No," I say bitterly. "You don't *want* to think. It's staring you right in the face and you just don't want to see it."

He doesn't answer, and I don't press him. If he's not going to say something along the lines of *I'm sorry, I'm a huge idiot, of course you're right,* I don't want him to say anything. I wish I could tell myself that we only met once, that he doesn't owe me anything—but he does, just like every other person in this stupid city. They all owe it to me to open their damn eyes and *see* me.

It's a relief when the opening in the rock goes dark once more, signaling Sadra and Bard's arrival. Sadra sidles up to me immediately, her body tense.

"Bard's angry," she murmurs. "I had to tell him about that night. He wants to send me back to the Temple."

"He can't," I whisper, aghast. "Can he?"

"No," she says. "There's no way they can place someone else in the household at this point without raising suspicions. But he's absolutely furious with both of us."

"Sasha," Bard says sharply, interrupting our whispered conference. "Get back to bed. I'll deal with the two of you later."

Luca protests, "She's not going anywhere until—"

"She's going," Bard says, his voice hard. "Right now. Every minute of delay increases the danger you've put them in. Are you so confident in your conclusions that you would risk having their blood on your hands? If there is even the slightest doubt in your mind, you must let them go."

I see the silhouette of Luca's head jerk downward in a stiff, unwilling nod.

"Very well," he says. "Kirit, show them the way and then wait for me."

Kirit nips my ankle, making me jump, and yips for us to follow. We comply readily, eager to escape Bard's disapproval. Stubbed toes and scraped knees are a small price to pay to delay whatever punishment Bard has in mind.

When we finally slither out from under the bushes in Ismeni's garden, I half expect to be seized by a mob of House mages. But there's nothing. The garden is as still and silent as ever, sleeping in the shadow of the mountain. We leave Kirit crouched amid the branches and flit through pools of darkness like wraiths, fear keeping our steps light and quick. When we part ways in the garden, Sadra opens her mouth to speak, then shakes her head and squeezes my shoulder before disappearing into the dark.

Pretty Girl is waiting at the door, as if she knew I was coming—or as if she's been waiting there the whole time I was gone. I bend to greet her before she can start whining, then straighten and ease the door closed. Dove's gaze spears me as I turn back, her eyes glittering in a sliver of moonlight. For once, I stare back instead of lowering my lashes in deference.

Say something, I urge her silently. Scold me, yell at me. Tell me how stupid and careless and immature I was to put my own desires ahead of our safety. But she merely rolls over to face the wall, turning her back on me and my foolishness.

Effacé

I run through the darkened garden, dodging the shadows that reach for me with clawed hands. Climbing roses leap from their trellises and wind around my ankles, their thorns digging into my skin and tearing it away as they drag me down. I writhe in the loose gravel of the path, stones and thorns alike cutting me open.

Footsteps crunch somewhere behind me, filling my chest with a wild, blind horror. I lunge against my bonds, heedless of the threads of blood streaming down my body. But the roses hold me fast, pinning me to the ground.

I watch with helpless terror as Cimari approaches with slow, measured steps.

"I see you," she whispers. "I see you."

Cimari pulls something from behind her and I lose what little air is left in my lungs, thinking it's a whip. But it's not—it's worse than that. It's a blade, silver and shining in the moonlight. The tip glitters unnaturally as Cimari lays it against my abdomen. I suck in my belly, cringing away from the bite of metal as I hadn't bothered to do with the thorns, but I can't escape it.

Cimari presses gently, drawing a single drop of blood. She moves the tip and draws another. And another.

Then she looks at me.

"I see you," she says... and slides the blade between my ribs.

* * *

I wake, gasping for breath, in a cold sweat made even colder by a slight breeze drifting from the open window. I draw my blanket closer around me and focus on the warmth of Pretty Girl's weight across my knees.

A dream. It was just a dream.

The thought gives me comfort, but only briefly. It really *was* just a dream, wasn't it? When was the last time I had one of those? When was the last time I closed my eyes and saw anything but cold metal instruments and pitying faces around my bed? I'm not sure I ever have, not since my arrival here. What could it mean?

I reach down and drag Pretty Girl's growing bulk into my arms, ignoring her grunt of protest. But despite Pretty Girl's heat against my chest and the blanket around my shoulders, I can't seem to get warm. I spend the rest of the night shivering, my eyes wide open against the dark things that wait for me—both in this world and the other.

* * *

"The sun shines on you."

Sadra's smile is tentative as she greets Ismeni at the breakfast table, but it widens at Ismeni's cordial response. She and Ismeni have developed, if not a friendship, at least a fragile bond rooted in mutual disgust for Orean's brutish ways. Sadra takes pains to keep Ismeni under the impression that she's spying on Orean for the Temple, and Ismeni doesn't pry. In fact, she seems to enjoy the idea that someone's pulling one over on him, even if it isn't her. She knows—everyone knows—that Orean is aware of her affair with the king, and I think it annoys her that her husband couldn't care less.

"Will you be joining us at the palace this evening, Sadra?" Ismeni asks, leaning around Orean, who continues to eat his breakfast in silence.

"Yes and no," Sadra replies. "I'll be performing for the king's equinox celebrations."

"How lovely." Ismeni beckons a nearby thrall. "Tea, husband?"

"Thank you, no," Orean says, politely enough. But he ruins it by adding, "You will attend me in my chambers when I return from Council. I will expect you at midday, no later. And remember to review the menu for tomorrow evening's banquet with the cook, if you please."

His tone chills me. Not that it's malicious—it's anything but, in fact. He might as well be talking about a cow or a pig...or me. That's how he sees Ismeni: livestock. He needs her only to produce an heir, and, in spite of my circumstances, I sometimes worry for my mistress.

As soon as Orean leaves, I let my eyes drift slowly to Ismeni's pale, stiff face. Sadra told me—and I believe her—that Orean doesn't keep anything that isn't useful to him. What will happen to Ismeni if she doesn't give Orean his heir soon?

An anguished yelp distracts me from my thoughts. I keep my gaze soft and unfocused but watch out of the corner of my eye as Cimari steadies herself with a hand on the back of her chair.

"Overgrown rat," she mutters before kicking Pretty Girl out of her way.

Anger burns under my skin as Pretty Girl rushes to me, limping slightly on the foot that Cimari stepped on. She cowers against my legs, whimpering, staring up at me with begging eyes. My stomach twists with the desire to give Pretty Girl the comfort she needs and pain at my inability to do so. The weight of my servitude presses on me like a physical force beating down on my shoulders. I've never felt so helpless—or so useless—in all my time here.

"Cimari!" Ismeni cries, her eyes wide with shock.

"Forgive me, Ismeni," Cimari says, instantly contrite. "I just—"

For once, Ismeni doesn't fall for Cimari's charm. "She's just a baby," she says angrily. "She doesn't know any better, but *you* should. I can't think what has gotten into you lately. First Cygnet, now this!"

Sadra stays silent throughout the exchange, keeping her eyes on her plate and trying to remain unobtrusive. Getting involved would only draw attention, and the last thing we want is Cimari wondering why her brother's bedmate would care about a dog or a thrall. And she *would* wonder, for it wouldn't occur to Cimari that caring is something that comes naturally to many people.

"Cygnet, pick her up and take her to your chamber," Ismeni says. "Then come help me dress."

With a last, withering look at Cimari, she sweeps from the room. I gather Pretty Girl in my arms and follow with Pretty Girl's legs and tail dangling awkwardly. She'll be too big to carry soon. My arms tighten around her reflexively, as if in denial.

I find Dove sitting in bed with a pile of mending. She flicks a glance at me, then down at the bed beside her. I settle Pretty Girl on the bed with Dove and turn to leave, but Pretty Girl's soft whine makes me hesitate. She doesn't understand why I sometimes can't play with her or pet her or even acknowledge her, and when I can't, it hurts her. It hurts me. But I leave anyway.

Cimari is in Ismeni's rooms when I get there, pacing like a caged animal. I hide my surprise and drift to Ismeni's bed. As I set the coverings straight and fluff the pillows, I keep half my attention on my work and half on the ladies' conversation.

"You don't understand, Isi," Cimari is saying, "The Premier, he—"

"Oh?" Ismeni raises an eyebrow. "Let me guess. He was different, before you were betrothed. Kinder. More caring."

"I never needed coddling," Cimari protests, wrinkling her nose.

"But yes, he was different. He taught me. He confided in me. He—I thought—respected me. I thought we would be partners. But it's been weeks since my last lesson. All his time is taken up with 'matters of state'—matters he seems to think are far beyond the mental capacities of a mere *woman*." Cimari's voice is thick with bitterness. "Why could I not have been born a man? Why are women barred from serving the House directly or progressing to the highest levels of mastery? It's not fair!"

I have to turn my head away to hide my disgust at her hypocrisy. Poor Cimari, unable to pursue her chosen career. She has to stay at home with her jewels and perfumes and slaves instead.

"Life often isn't," Ismeni says dryly. "I understand your frustration, Cimari, but I can't condone your behavior these past weeks. Truly, my dear, it's been appalling, and I'm not the only one to notice. People are beginning to talk. You must control yourself. Is that not what your precious House teaches? Control?"

Cimari's lips press together, then release as she sighs. "You're right. I will do better."

"See that you do," Ismeni says. "I will not tolerate further abuse of *any* creature in my care. If you cannot value Cygnet and Pretty Girl and Dove for their own sakes, you will at least respect my claim on them. They are not yours to discipline. They belong to *me*. Is that understood?"

"Of course," Cimari agrees. "I *am* sorry, Isi."

"Don't be sorry. Be better."

Ismeni's words are stern, but a smile takes the sting out of them and Cimari leaves in good spirits. It takes all I have to keep my resentment from showing on my face or in my movements. Of course Cimari finds it easier to understand ownership than empathy, but it hurts that Ismeni would resort to the same logic. I shouldn't be surprised, but so often it seems like she and Cimari are two entirely different species.

What I resent even more, though it disgusts me to admit it even to myself, is Ismeni's very real affection for Cimari, a sociopath capable of feeling sorry only for herself and her own problems. And, despite everything, I think that Cimari's desire for Ismeni's regard is genuine. Their relationship is, if not healthy or profound, at least mutual.

It's a relief when Ismeni finally releases me into the garden for the day. I pass Dove's fountain with a pang of worry; Dove has stopped coming to the garden and rests in bed instead. She seems to grow weaker by the day. How much longer can she last like this?

* * *

I wake once again with a hand covering my mouth. This time, though, the hand is accompanied by a musky-smelling weight on my chest and an anxious whisper in my ear as I jerk in panic.

"It's just me." Luca removes his hand, and Kirit sticks his nose in my face instead. Luca scoops him away, depositing him on the floor with Pretty Girl. "Sorry. I didn't know if you would scream. Bard sent me."

"Where's Sadra?" I ask suspiciously, sitting up. "I'm not going anywhere without her."

"I went to her first," he says. "She's waiting for us in the tunnels."

"Let's go, then."

"Wait." He puts a hand out as if to take hold of my arm, then pulls it back. "I owe you an apology."

"Do it outside," I say with a pointed glance at Dove's bed. "She needs to rest."

"Oh—of course."

I tell Pretty Girl to stay. Luca moves toward the door, his shoulders stiff. Kirit scampers ahead of him, slipping into the night and pausing on the stairwell. His ears twitch to and fro, and after a moment he looks back at us before disappearing down the stairs. The wind, crisp and sharp, blows through the open door as if in invitation. I step forward to peer apprehensively into the dark, shivering at the soft hiss of rustling leaves outside. Who knows what eyes could be watching us from those shadows?

"Follow Kirit," Luca whispers in my ear. "Stop when he does. He'll see us safe."

We make our way carefully through the garden—much more carefully than we—*he*—did last night, that's for sure. The muscles in my back clench painfully at the thought of what would have happened if we had been seen. I shoot a resentful glance at Luca over my shoulder. His apology had better be a damn good one.

"The entrance is just through there," Luca says finally. He points at a riot of bushes hugging the canyon wall. "But first…can I try to explain?"

I shift uncomfortably. Suddenly I'm not so keen on the apology. "We should go—Sadra's waiting, and so is Bard."

"It will only take a moment," Luca says. "Please, just listen."

"Like you listened to me?" I snap, surprising both of us with my anger. "The longer we're out here, the longer Sadra and I are both at risk. If you're going to help us, *help*. Don't make things more dangerous for us."

Luca nods, his eyes lowered. "This way."

He holds the branches back as best he can and points me toward the small crack in the cavern wall. I duck through and find Sadra clutching a torch. She hugs me tightly, holding the torch out to the side.

"Stars, but it's scary in here," she whispers. "Even with a torch. Every shadow looks like a rock worm about to swallow you whole."

I open my mouth to ask what a rock worm is, then decide I probably don't want to know. I have more than enough material to fuel my nightmares. No need to add more.

"At least then we wouldn't have to face Bard," I say. "He must be furious."

Sadra smiles at the half-hearted joke, then makes a face. "Let's get on with it, then. Keeping him waiting won't do anything to sweeten his temper."

Luca clears his throat awkwardly and gestures for us to follow him.

Tonight's journey through the tunnels is only slightly less uncomfortable than the last. The silence is thick enough to cut with a knife, smothering us like a heavy, scratchy wool blanket. Shadows leap toward us and away, seeming to taunt us as we pass. Torchlight catches the occasional reflection from the stones of the tunnel, winking like tiny eyes and appearing and disappearing at random. I'm so relieved when it's over I almost forget to be afraid.

The tunnel's exit is an uneven hole at about chest level. Through it, I can just make out an overgrown garden path and the bottom of a door beyond. Luca offers his hand, but I ignore it, hoisting myself up and through with a bit of scrambling.

A damp, cold breeze makes me shiver as I step aside to let Sadra climb out after me. Luca and Kirit follow, showing no sign of discomfort or surprise at the cold. They must not spend very much time in the Terrace, where the seasons never change.

"Welcome to my home," he says with an ironic little bow. "Won't you come in?"

I give him a dark look and push past him, making for the door that already stands open. Bard waits for us in its shadow, his face hard as granite. My steps slow, then resume their steady progress; I square my shoulders as best I can. I did a stupid thing. I have to pay for it, and cowering won't make it any easier.

"Upstairs," Bard says curtly. He jerks his head at us to follow and disappears into the house.

Sadra hands me the torch and we follow in silence. Luca bolts the door behind us and catches up in a few long steps. Another step and he's past us and at Bard's side, directing him into a room at the top of the stairs.

Sadra and I pause on the last step. We exchange a look, then enter the room.

"Sit," Bard says. He points to two chairs settled close together. "Both of you."

We sit.

"I thought you knew the danger surrounding you," Bard says after several long, uncomfortable seconds. "Evidently, I was mistaken. I am more than disappointed—I am disgusted. You each should know better."

He turns to look at me, and I wince.

"Sasha, you have felt the pain of the whip on your back. I thought you would pay it more heed. I thought you were intelligent enough to realize that the House is capable of far worse.

"And you, Sadra, you *know* what they are capable of, for I have shown you. As it appears that you have forgotten, you will share in Sasha's lesson regarding exactly what kind of treatment you may expect from the House of Light and Shadow if you are caught."

Bard lowers his head, but not fast enough to hide the spasm of emotion that crosses his face. Cold creeps into my bones. I don't believe he means to beat me, but I have this awful feeling that whatever he is going to do might be worse.

"Give me your hands," Bard says softly.

I place a trembling hand in one of his; Sadra puts hers in the other. A heartbeat later, another hand settles over mine. I look up, startled, and meet Luca's gaze. His apology is there in his eyes, and I find that it is a good one after all. His words are for Bard, but his eyes stay with me.

"Give me your lesson also."

"So be it," Bard says. "Sasha. Do you know what a House amulet is?"

"It…it holds Light," I say uncertainly, tearing my eyes away from Luca's. "Like a thrall, but not as much, and it doesn't last as long."

"Yes. I'm going to show you how an amulet is made." He looks at me, his eyes sad. *"Prosti menya."*

Forgive me.

"Close your eyes," Bard says, and we do.

* * *

They're here. Bodies lie scattered amid the dead leaves, still and silent as death itself. But they're not dead—not all of them, not yet. Most will live to be transported and sold. But the others…

One day, I will bring an end to this atrocity. I will end it, or I will die trying. No more will suffer as I have suffered—I, who was one of the lucky ones.

There are children stirring. Dread roils in my belly, threatening to tip over into panic. The children—those who live—are never sold. It's a poor investment, a House brother once told me. Even if a child should live to be sold, it won't fetch much of a price. The Pall uses a body up in ten years, maybe twenty. A young child wastes half that time or more growing into something useful.

"Attend, guardsman." A small man in House robes sweeps by me, disappearing into the mists of the Deadwood. His voice floats back to me like a wraith. "Bring the small ones."

Sweat breaks out on my forehead. I can't. I can't do it. I can't stand by and watch evil men perform evil deeds before my eyes and do nothing.

But no, not nothing. Bile rises in my throat. Not nothing. I lead the lambs to slaughter myself. I deliver them with my own hands.

I see seven tiny bodies. Of those seven, four tiny chests rise and fall with movements so slight as to be nearly imperceptible. Three are still as stone. I lean over one, a tow-headed boy of about seven. His lashes flutter and he looks up at me with cloudy blue eyes that make my chest constrict with a familiar pain. My mouth firms in a split-second decision. I cannot save all of them, but that doesn't mean I can't at least attempt to save one of them.

I kneel over the boy and bend close to his face as if listening for his breath.

"Wait. Be quiet. Then run." I repeat the simple instructions in as many languages as I can, then move on to the next body.

A spasm of self-loathing wracks my bones. What a truly sad and unworthy savior I am, unable to offer more than a few words that will more than likely amount to nothing more than a slow death by exposure or starvation.

And yet. It's a better death than that which awaits him at the hands of the House mages. My heart turns to ash in my chest as I take the next body into my arms. I want to look away, but I force myself to take note of her red hair, her freckles, the milky pallor of her skin. I will remember you, I tell her silently. All of you.

When the last child has been collected, the ritual begins. Three small forms are suspended above a smooth marble basin as long as a man is tall. The writhing bodies of the children are held with bands of Light twined around their wrists, their ankles, their ribs, and their foreheads. The Light shines without heat, without sight.

Look away, my rational mind pleads. I will not, my heart replies.

Chanting fills the air, low and sickening in its rhythm. The Light binding the children pulses in time. My blood thrums in my veins, drawn unwillingly into the pattern. Pressure builds and throbs in my joints and behind my eyes. Sweat pours down my back, soaking through the shirt I wear under my leathers.

At the pressure's peak, just when I fear my skin might burst with it, a robed mage steps forward and opens a cut along each child's wrist. The pressure eases. I hate myself for the flush of relief that takes its place.

Blood drips steadily, tracing the swirling marble with red.

Another cut, another release.

The blood pools like ink, spreading across the length of the basin. The chanting grows louder, more insistent, drawing Light into the basin to mingle and fuse with the children's lifeblood.

After far too long, the steady drip of red slows, then stops. The children are gone, their lives emptied into a pool of swiftly congealing blood cradled in marble. Soon the blood will be as hard and brittle as bone, ready to be crushed and beaten and re-molded into amulets: Three innocents reduced to commodities for sale.

I turn away. I hate the hooded men—but I hate myself more.

* * *

Bard releases my hand and steps away. My fingers twitch, spasming, and latch onto the remaining hand—Luca's. He grips mine just as fiercely, his knuckles white. My other hand flies to my mouth as I gag, bending over double in my chair. Sadra swallows and reaches over to squeeze my shoulder with a clammy, shaking hand.

"My Gift is memory," Bard says bitterly. "I have seen many things: Vile, evil, hateful things, and they will never fade. They will never leave me. Remember that I carry this burden for *you*, child, and for those who will come after you. Do not disappoint me again."

He leaves us, and we watch him go in silence. Then we too make our way into the night, guided by the light of a single torch too small to keep the darkness at bay.

Fondu

That night, my visions return. I don't feel glad, but I don't feel frightened, either. *I don't feel anything, because I'm not me. I'm* her—*the other Sasha.*

✳ ✳ ✳

A man sits beside me, his large hand folded gently over mine. My fingers twitch and flex into claws, then spasm under the force of an invisible string pulling them outward, then flex again in an endless, erratic cycle. But the man doesn't seem to mind. He has a name. I knew it once, but not anymore.

"I have to ask you something, Sasha," he says, and when he says my name, I know his. James. He's James.

"I know you can't answer, but I still have to ask. You know how much I love Emily. She's...she's my whole world. When I look at her, it's like seeing my own soul walking beside me, and it gives me more hope and—and peace than anything ever has. Because she's so pure and strong and beautiful and good, and if she loves me, there must be something beautiful and good in me, too.

"I'm going to ask her to be my wife, and I've come to ask for your blessing. I don't know if you can hear me, or understand me, and even if you do, I know you can't answer." When he laughs, it sounds more like a sob. "I guess I was hoping for, I don't know, a sign or something. Pretty stupid,

huh? But I brought the ring to show you. I think she'll like it—she's been dropping hints about a princess cut..."

My eyes roll toward a sparkling stone set in velvet. It seems to flicker in and out of sight, overshadowed by other images.

Someone is crying, someone buried deep inside me.

Yes, the voice weeps. Take care of her. Love her, since I can't.

I don't like the crying. It plucks at the stitches holding me together, threatening to pull me apart, and so much of me has already unraveled. I don't like it. I want it to go away.

The man is talking to me again.

"Don't give up," he says. "Please. Come on, kid. There's so much left for you to live for. Come back to us."

* * *

"I'm trying."

My eyes are open, my lips parted, but I can't tell if I spoke aloud.

Beside me, Kirit yawns and stretches, his paws rumpling the blankets. He cocks his head at me, little more than a black silhouette against the slightly lighter darkness of pre-dawn. On my other side, Pretty Girl slumbers on, a heavy weight pressed against my back. My eyes flick to Dove's bed, but she too is fast asleep. It makes me worry: There was a time when the slightest sound or misstep would earn me a sharp glance or a pinch on my arm. But now she lies still and silent as the grave, insensible to my mistakes and the danger they pose.

I can do better. I *must* do better, or risk losing my chance to go home. I'll never see Emily get married. I'll never play with her children and teach them to dance. I'll never thank her for doing the same for me.

Fighting the urge to weep, I raise a hand and scratch Kirit behind the ears. He leans into my hand, offering his chin and neck, and soon my fingers are covered in tufts of fur. By this time Pretty Girl has woken up enough to get jealous of the attention, and she paws at my hand with a whine. Smiling, I pull Pretty Girl closer and kiss her head. Kirit doesn't protest but curls up in my lap with a small huff.

I suppose Luca must have sent him to keep an eye on me—probably at Bard's request. But maybe not. Maybe Kirit's here because he wants to be. Maybe he's a friend.

And maybe Luca is my friend, too. He said he was, the first time we met, and he seems sincere in his desire to help. I nod to myself. I think I can count him among my friends, which brings my total up to four—two of those four are furred, but still.

I fall back to sleep thinking of Luca.

In the morning, Kirit is gone, with only a faint musky scent and a dusting of fur across my blanket to give away his visit. I study the fuzz worriedly but then decide that Kirit's hairs blend in well enough with those left by Pretty Girl. Just to be safe, I shake the blanket out and sneeze as the cloud of fur hits my nose.

I slip out as quietly as I can to get water from the cistern and let Pretty Girl do her business. When I return, I lay out Dove's clothes and set her laundry aside with mine. I'll do both later. Next I sweep the floor, clean the mirror, and pull out the creams and perfumes Ismeni likes us to wear. I wait until the last possible minute to wake Dove, nudging her awake only after I've triple checked that there's nothing else that I can do for her.

The bones of her shoulder feel frail and almost hollow under my hand, like those of a bird's wing. I give her the tiniest shake, half afraid that she'll crumble into dust at my touch. Her eyelids rise slowly, as if even that tiny movement is a hardship. But after a moment, the rest of her follows just as gracefully as ever and I could almost believe that everything is as it was.

My old life feels distant and pale, like a picture on the wall. I mean my *real* life, not the mockery of existence that my life has become in the hospital. It takes genuine effort these days to remember that I used to go to school and dance with my friends and talk with Baba Nadia and Emily to plan for my future. Some days I wonder if any of it was real. Perhaps I really am crazy, and it was that other world that was the dream.

But no. Baba Nadia was real, I know it. How could she not be? No one could dream up a woman like her, so full of love and strength and everything good that I aspire to. And I'm not alone—Bard is from my world, and he's real. So I'm real, too.

I breathe heavily through my nose, fed up with my circular, anxiety-fueled thoughts. Yes. I'm real, Bard's real, everyone's real. Everything there and everything here, and everything sucks anyway, so who cares?

Trying not to stomp, I leave Dove with her needle and thread and make my way to Ismeni's chambers. Pretty Girl trots at my heels, ready to start a new day. I envy her innocence and especially her optimism. It's like she's incapable of thinking "today" will be anything but wonderful. I hope that never changes for her.

I pause outside Ismeni's door when I hear raised voices. Ismeni's I recognize right away, but it takes a minute to realize that the other is Orean's. What is he doing here? He almost never comes to Ismeni's rooms. If he wants her, he has someone fetch her to him like he's ordering room service.

A thrall wouldn't be put off by yelling—lacking any kind of understanding or social skills—so I can't be, either. I ease the door open and sidle through as unobtrusively as I know how, keeping close to the wall and pretending I'm not there. It works. Neither Ismeni nor Orean even glances in my direction.

"Barren!" Orean is apoplectic with rage, his bugging eyes shot with red. They look like they're about to pop out of his face, which is flushed to a truly alarming shade of purple. "And I had to hear it from the Bloodseer! You thought to keep it from me? I'll have you flogged for this, you—"

"I didn't even know, you fool," Ismeni shouts back. "He obviously thought you have more right to the information than I do. Or perhaps he thought the news would be less painful coming from my loving husband. More fool he, if so."

"Silence," Orean roars, and deals her a vicious backhanded blow to the face that knocks her clean off her feet. "You will let it be known that you have grown weary of the city and wish to live a quiet life on my country estate. You will get rid of that ridiculous dog and deliver the thrall—the old one—to the House for disposal. The other will be sold. You have two weeks."

Orean slams out of the room, leaving Ismeni crumpled on the floor.

She blinks dazedly and raises a trembling hand to her face. Pretty Girl rushes to Ismeni, her ears pinned anxiously against her head. Her tail wags so hard it makes her whole body wriggle. A pang of jealousy stings my belly as Ismeni gathers my puppy into her arms, but it fades quickly. I can't begrudge her whatever comfort Pretty Girl might provide. She looks like she needs it, and I think it's helping. Some color has returned to Ismeni's face, and her eyes have regained their focus.

"Hush, sweet girl," Ismeni croons, but an undercurrent of steel runs through her voice. "That oaf thinks we're disposable, all of us. And he thinks I'm stupid, or blind, or both. He can believe as he likes—but I'll be making my own arrangements."

* * *

Ismeni wastes no time in her preparations. That very night, at a banquet held in honor of Princess Arismendi's eighteenth birthday, my mistress slips away into the labyrinthine corridors of the palace. I follow as closely and silently as her shadow, wondering just what she has in mind.

She leads me into an unfamiliar wing of the palace where everything looks…no less grand, but maybe more lived in. In spite of my unease at the situation, my skin prickles with curiosity. I've only ever been in the public wing with its grand entrance and lavish banquet halls and, once, in the deserted rooms where the king and Ismeni like to spend *quality time* with each other.

Ismeni's pace slows when we reach a door with two guards posted outside. One of them steps into her path with his hand held up for her to stop.

"I must ask you to return to the festivities, my lady," he says.

"Certainly," Ismeni says with a smile. "But first I must speak with the king." She sidesteps him neatly and knocks on the door before either guard can stop her.

"My lady," they both protest, shocked, but she only smiles her most charming smile and knocks again.

The door opens.

"Lady Ismeni."

He doesn't seem happy. In fact, the king looks ready to throttle her. A muscle tics in his jaw and his lips are compressed into a thin white line. But his voice remains cool and light, as if her sudden appearance isn't anything out of the ordinary. My heart beats faster: Orean speaks softly, too—right before he strikes. What kind of man is the king?

"My king, I'm sorry, I—"

Miocostin cuts off the guard's babbling with a smooth gesture. "It's quite alright. I *was* expecting the lady, but it slipped my mind. My mistake. Please, my lady, join me."

He steps aside for Ismeni to enter, and she sweeps grandly through with me bobbing in her wake like an acorn in a stream. Miocostin closes the door behind us and turns to Ismeni, his face thunderous.

"What are you doing here?" he hisses. "Are you mad?"

"You're not even a little bit pleased to see me?" she asks, her smile trembling.

If I could, I'd roll my eyes. Or maybe not. Underneath her charm and bravado, she must be terrified. I would be, in her place.

Miocostin pinches the bridge of his nose and sighs. "Of course I am always happy to see you, my dear. But to come openly to my chambers this way—what were you thinking?"

"I'm sorry," Ismeni whispers. "It couldn't be helped. My husband plans to exile me to his country estate. I'm barren, you see."

Miocostin's face softens at the wobble in her voice.

"Oh, my love." He crosses to her in two long strides and takes her into his arms. "I'm sorry."

"I don't care about that," she says with a snort. "As a lady of my acquaintance once said, no one deserves to die childless more than he does. But I think—I am certain—he means me to die out there so he can marry again. And I will die, I will—I can't live without you. I won't."

"Peace," Miocostin murmurs, stroking her hair. "Of course I won't allow you to be sent away. You will remain in the palace as my companion. If he can have no heir from you, he has no grounds to deny me. I only wish..."

"What, my love?" Ismeni looks up at him, her face shining with adoration and relief. "We will be together—what more is there to wish for?"

Miocostin looks away, almost shyly. "I wish I could give you the position you deserve. I wish you could take your place as my consort—my wife."

Ismeni's eyes widen, then fill with tears. "Oh, my darling," she whispers, shaking her head. "I don't need any of that. I only need to be with you."

My heart squeezes. Will I ever look at someone the way she looks at him? Will anyone ever look at me that way in return? Probably not, especially now that I'm about to be sold. But does the universe have to rub it in my face by forcing me to see exactly what I'm missing?

He kisses her forehead. "And so you shall be, my heart. Don't be afraid. All will be well, I swear it."

A sharp knock comes from the door.

"My king?" one of the guards calls. "It's time."

With a sudden, charming grin, he bows and offers his arm. "Will you allow me to escort you, my lady?" At her confused look, he adds, "I mean to make the announcement tonight. Why wait?"

Ismeni bites her lip, then shakes her head. "We can't, my love. Not yet. I must see Cygnet and Dove safely settled first. They belong to Orean, not to me. If I leave their sale to him, they'll end up as toys in a brothel, I know it."

"So sell them to me," he suggests.

"And possibly give away our plans?" She shakes her head again. "No. I have a buyer already who will take them both and treat them kindly. The transaction is nearly complete. We need only wait another two days, three at the most."

That's news. Alarm and resentment flare simultaneously. I should be grateful that she cares enough to hand pick a buyer, but the fact remains that I'm hers to sell. The knowledge burns in my chest with an intensity that will never, ever fade.

"Your kindness does you credit, my love," Miocostin says, kissing her swiftly. He sighs and smiles down at her. "But I must admit, I am most impatient for your business to be concluded. To have you here, always at my side…I never thought it would be possible. It pains me more than I can say that you will never know the joy of motherhood—of course—but what a stroke of luck!"

"I don't care," she says again. "It's a price I would pay a hundred times over to be with you."

"You must send word as soon as the sale is complete," he says. "I want you here with me."

"Of course," she promises. "But for now, you must go. Your sister will be wondering where you are."

"Bother my sister," he says, bending to kiss Ismeni again.

Ismeni laughs and steps away. "Go. You don't want to hurt her feelings. It's her birthday."

Reluctantly, Miocostin lets her push him out the door. Ismeni waits several long minutes, then beckons for me to follow her and we return to the party. She mingles with the crowd, smiling and chatting as if she had never left, while I hover in her shadow. My thoughts are boiling with questions: Who is this buyer and what will this mean for my plans with the Bird's Path? Will they still be able to rescue me or am I doomed to remain a thrall forever? Will I ever see Sadra again?

The thought of being sold tortures me all through the evening and into the night. I'm wild to talk to Sadra, desperately hoping she'll be able to provide some reassurance but also dreading her answer. I imagine her face filling with pity as she tells me there's nothing to be done, that it's over. Or, at best, that I'll have to wait another season, or perhaps another year, while Bard makes new plans for my extraction. I imagine it over and over, running through every scenario I can think of.

But when I finally find her in the garden, I'm not at all prepared for her response to my torrent of questions.

"Oh, that." She grins, her golden eyes crinkling at the corners. "It's us."

"What?"

"The buyer," she explains. "She's with the Bird's Path. Silly—you didn't think we'd pass up an opportunity like this, did you? You're going to Mother Wenla's counterpart in the City of Lilies. An old lady with old money. Very irritable, I'm told, but very passionate about our work. She finances and facilitates all the—er, activities—in the City of Lilies."

"Isn't the City of Lilies very far away?" I ask, confused. "How did you manage to set this up so quickly?"

"Her agent happened to be in the City of Roses," Sadra says. "Good thing, too, or we'd have been in real trouble even if the lady were here herself. Women can't make business agreements on their own, you know."

I shake my head but don't comment on the Garden's pervasive misogyny. I already knew this world was cruel and unfair. "And is the agent...one of us?"

"Yes," Sadra says. "But more like you than like me, if you catch my meaning."

Excitement stirs. Another escaped thrall! Maybe he'll be more forthcoming about his past than Bard is. Though I understand now, at least a little bit, why Bard doesn't like to talk about his experiences, I still want to know more about how I came to be here and what others before me have gone through.

I shake my head again, this time to clear it of the almost painful haze of excitement. Freedom! No more Ismeni, no more petty orders, no more fear, no more...my excitement evaporates as quickly as it came.

"What about Dove?"

Sadra squeezes my hand. "Ismeni sold you both. But, Sasha...we can't save her. The best we can do is make her last days as comfortable as we can."

"It's better than handing her over to the House," I say firmly.

No matter how unfair it all is, it's not Sadra's fault, and in the past few weeks I've accepted the truth. Dove is practically on her deathbed already. She'd never make it.

"But what about you?" I ask Sadra. "Are you...?"

Her hand tightens as she shakes her head. "I have to stay," she says. "It would look strange if I left too. But I'll see you again."

"You shouldn't make promises you don't know you can keep," I say softly, my eyes stinging. "You have obligations here. Responsibilities...and loved ones."

There's nothing she can say to that, so she doesn't try.

I leave the garden with a storm of conflicting emotions swirling under my skin. Foremost among them is an ache that I don't have a name for: There's relief, hope, joy, yearning...and yet the ache is none of these. There are no words, and perhaps none are necessary. But the other feelings...I know their names: grief and guilt, for Dove; anger, for the society that has collectively refused to see the truth; fear, for my future...and envy.

Jealousy spreads prickles over my skin like a rash, bringing with it a surge of irrational hatred for the faceless man who holds Sadra's heart. Now that the moment is almost upon me, I can't imagine leaving this place—not without Sadra. I've relied on her entirely, leaned on her every step of the way. Losing a limb would be less debilitating.

I can't do it.

But I'll have to, because I'm not the only one who has a claim on Sadra. Still a tiny, shrill voice in the back of my head whines that it's not right, not *fair*, that I need her more than some faceless man. I'll beg her to come with me, or I'll refuse to go. I'll—

I stop in the shade of a willow tree, look around, duck beneath the willow's branches...and slap myself. Hard. I scrub my hands over my face. Take a breath. Slap myself again. It's too bad Sadra took back her poisoned hairpin, because I could use a shot of mind-numbing pain right about now.

I am far from composed, but I'm out of time. I arrange my features as best I can and emerge from the willow with my limbs shaking and a desperate prayer running through my head. It's the same one that has followed me for months, though I've almost forgotten it was there:

Don't screw up.

Battement

I spend the rest of the day nearly jumping out of my own skin, terrified that I'll let something slip. Ironically, Ismeni seems to fear the same—and with good reason. If Orean finds out what she has planned, he might find a way to ship her off to the hinterlands before the king can step in to prevent it. And, while I'm sure Miocostin would waste no time in retrieving her, who knows what "accident" might befall Ismeni in the meantime?

It almost makes me feel guilty, or at least sorry for Ismeni, as it's my fault she's staying. But then, it's only fitting that she won't get her freedom until I get mine—and that she's suffering for it right along with me.

It takes me a long time to fall asleep that night. Every time I close my eyes, fearful thoughts crowd my mind, clamoring for attention. So many things could go wrong… What if this "agent" is caught by the House of Light and Shadow? Or what if he falls and breaks his leg and doesn't get here in time to take me away from all this and Orean gives us to a brothel or to the House instead? What if, what if… Sadra was right. No good comes from "what if."

It's a relief when Pretty Girl's bark jerks me out of my fretful dreams. I bolt upright and scramble out of bed almost before I realize what I'm doing. Pretty Girl sits on the floor next to Dove's bed, her nose resting just close enough to touch Dove's hand. I drop to my knees beside her, my hands fluttering over Dove's body just as they did once before—but that was a different life, a different body. Baba Nadia is dead…and Dove, I think, isn't far behind.

I lunge backward as a terrible sound is ripped from Dove's throat. My heart pounds. I've never heard a sound like that from anyone, much less from Dove. Something awful must be happening for her to throw away her mask like that: She's dying.

What can I do? If Ismeni knew, would she send for a Healer? I don't have to ask myself if it's too dangerous to try to communicate with her, even nonverbally. And Bard would go absolutely out of his mind if he knew I was even considering it. But I can't just stand by and watch Dove die.

I grab Dove's walking stick and head for Ismeni's rooms, fully aware that I'm about to do something monumentally stupid.

"What—what—" Ismeni shoots upright and flails about in a panic when I shake her awake. "Cygnet! What are you—"

I shove the walking stick into her hands and wait with my heart in my throat. Thank goodness, she grasps the essentials immediately and jumps out of bed, dragging me along behind her. She dashes for the door without even bothering with a shawl.

When we reach Dove, we find her gasping, her breath rattling in her throat. Pretty Girl whines piteously at her feet, pawing at the blanket and nosing Dove's hand. Ismeni strides across the room and throws a ball of light against the wall, where it clings like a glowing lump of dough. I stand as close as I can manage without blowing my already mostly blown cover.

Bozhe, I hope this was worth it.

"Hold on just a little longer, my Dove," Ismeni whispers, rubbing Dove's hand. "Don't go. We still need you, little Cygnet and I. Dove. Dove? Look at me."

"*Pa—Pahhhh.*"

Ismeni freezes, her eyes wide and fixed on Dove's mouth.

My feet carry me forward almost against my will. I drop to my knees next to my mistress, putting my hand over hers and Dove's. I don't dare look at Ismeni, but I feel her gaze on me. With an effort I can feel through my fingers, Dove raises her eyes to mine.

"*Pater noster, qui es..in caelis...*"

Ismeni gasps and wrenches her hand away, scrambling backward. I lean closer to Dove.

"*Sanctificetur...Nomen Tuum...*"

The language is unfamiliar, but the rhythm of the prayer tugs at some of my earliest memories. *Otche Nash, suschey na nebesakh...Our Father, who art in Heaven...*

The words come readily to my lips, and I open my mouth to release them. But I stop myself, pinned by Dove's suddenly blazing eyes. Her fingers brush against my wrist in an echo of her old pinches.

And then she's gone.

I take a shuddering breath, trying not to let it turn into a sob. A barely audible whimper escapes and I dart a glance at Ismeni. If she heard, she gives no sign of it. She stares at Dove with a mixture of grief and terror so intense it transforms her whole face. She doesn't move. She barely breathes.

The door slams open. Ismeni jerks and lurches gracelessly to her feet as Cimari hurries in, accompanied by her brother and her betrothed, the Premier. I rise too and drift backward until my back is against the wall. Sweat springs to my skin, cold and clammy.

Don't notice me. Please don't notice me.

"It's dead?" Orean asks. He doesn't even look at Dove.

Ismeni nods dazedly. The Premier moves forward and lifts his hands over Dove's body. He holds that pose for a moment, and I get the feeling he's searching for something. Whatever it is, he doesn't seem to find it. When he turns around, Dove turns with him, floating in the air. Her arms and legs dangle carelessly, like those of a discarded doll. One of her feet drags along the floor.

Heat builds, slowly replacing the cold pit in my belly. But I don't dare turn away or show any sign that it bothers me. Instead, I try to focus on Pretty Girl's warm weight against my leg and the firm coolness of the wall at my back. Anything but the scene before me.

"Was there anything…unusual?" the Premier asks. "About the thrall's death?"

At this, Ismeni looks sharply at her sister-in-law and visibly pulls herself together. "No, nothing," she says smoothly. "She passed quietly, thanks be."

"And how did you happen to be present for the event?" the Premier asks next.

"She was old," Ismeni says, "and very unwell. I've been monitoring her closely."

"My sister cares deeply for her thralls," Cimari explains with the barest hint of a smirk.

"Don't, Cimari," Ismeni says, closing her eyes. "Not now."

"There was nothing at all out of the ordinary?" the Premier presses. "Think carefully. The passing of a thrall can be…dangerous."

"There was nothing."

"What about the other one?" Cimari asks eagerly and I force myself to keep my eyes fixed on the opposite wall.

"Nothing," Ismeni says firmly. "Are you quite finished? I'm very tired."

"The other must be cleansed, good lady," the Premier says.

My heart pounds. Cleansed? I don't know what that means, but it can't be anything good—not if Cimari is gunning for it.

"Out of the question," Ismeni says. "Cygnet stays with me."

"My dear," Orean says, attempting a conciliatory tone. "The taint—"

"No."

Orean's fists clench, but the Premier lays a hand on his arm and bows slightly. "I see no immediate danger," he says. "However, you must be vigilant. Do not hesitate to call upon me at the slightest indication of…"

"Of what, exactly?" Ismeni asks, her eyes flashing.

"Anything out of the ordinary, my lady," the Premier finishes blandly.

"Certainly," Ismeni says, then gestures to the door with a motion that's just a hair less graceful than usual. "But for now, it's past time we were all in bed."

Ismeni kicks everyone out, somehow contriving to seem gracious and elegant while she does it. After closing the door on Cimari's suspicious, discontented face, she turns and leans against the wall with closed eyes.

I don't move. My legs feel rubbery, and my heart hammers against my ribcage like it's trying to escape. I wonder frantically if I should just come clean and beg her not to tell-Cimari's not through with us, I know it.

"Good night, Cygnet," Ismeni sighs and turns without looking at me. "Try to get some sleep."

And then she leaves.

My knees give out and I slump to the floor, shaking. I can't breathe. My head spins. I feel like I'm dying. What the hell just happened? Why is Ismeni covering for me? Maybe she's not covering—maybe she's in shock and has already repressed the whole thing? Or maybe she'll wake up in the morning and tell Cimari what really happened.

Quivering, I push myself to my feet. I have to find Sadra. I have to tell her what happened so she can get word to Bard. He'd want to know about this, I'm sure of it. I stagger toward the door only to find it swinging toward my face; I reel backward, my legs collapsing under me.

"Sorry, sorry!" Sadra helps me to my feet and guides me to the bed. "I've been lurking around the corner waiting for everyone to clear out."

"How did you know?" I ask.

"Orean," she says, shrugging. Then she looks down. "I'm so sorry about Dove, Sasha, truly."

"It's worse than that," I say grimly, and tell her everything.

"Shadow and blight," Sadra curses. "You—"

A sound, slight but distinct, makes us both freeze. I grab hold of Sadra's hand and hiss, "Hide!"

"Where?" she asks, her fingers tight on mine.

"Under the bed," I whisper. "There isn't anywhere else."

Sadra drops immediately and slithers under the bed, twitching the end of her shawl out of sight just in time. I stand by the bed, my eyes focused on nothing. For once, it takes no effort. Though I can hear the door open and shut, I can't see anything—the hall lights have been extinguished.

Light blossoms suddenly, blinding me. Tears gather in my eyes, and I blink furiously in reflex. But I don't let my gaze focus on the figure before me. I know who it is and why she's here and I'm not going to give myself away. I'm not going to give her a damned thing.

"Speak," she coos, moving closer. "I won't hurt you."

Bullshit. I don't react but thank every lucky star in the sky that it's Cimari in front of me and not Ismeni. If it were my mistress, I might be tempted. But Cimari is such a snake I probably wouldn't believe her even if she were telling the truth.

"I suspect that you're…special," Cimari says, her voice warmer than I've ever heard it. "I can't be sure unless you tell me, of course. I'm betrothed to a very powerful man who can help you, but he won't unless I can show him that you're—different. Speak, please. Let me help you."

She stands very close, her face just inches from mine. My teeth grind against each other. My hands begin to shake. I hide them in the skirts of my nightdress. This unnatural sweetness won't last, I know. Given a choice between the carrot and the stick, Cimari has a well-documented preference for the latter, at least in my case.

Though I saw it coming, the sting of her hand connecting with my face is shocking. My head snaps to the side, and I stagger slightly. My heart races, and so does my mind. I don't know what to do—what a thrall would do. Stand and wait for another blow? Cringe away? I've only ever seen Orean hit thralls, and they just picked themselves up and continued with whatever task they weren't completing to Orean's satisfaction. But I have no task.

Cimari saves me from having to make a decision by yanking me back by the hair. She hits me again, this time in the gut. I double over, my mouth opening and closing uselessly. All the air in my lungs is gone, and my paralyzed diaphragm can't replace it. While I choke, Cimari shoves me to the ground and kicks me squarely in the ribs, sending a bolt of blinding pain shooting through my body. It almost makes me grateful that she's already knocked the wind out of me—if I had any breath, I'm sure I would scream.

A tiny snarl drags me out of my cloud of pain. Pretty Girl stands at my head, growling and snapping at Cimari. I raise a hand and try to pull her back, but the pain in my ribs is excruciating. I try again, and this time I manage to get my fingers around Pretty Girl's collar. Cimari's eyes lock on my hand, her eyes narrowing, and I know I've made a terrible mistake.

"I wonder..." Cimari hums and taps a finger against her lips. "I suppose I already knew your own pain wouldn't be sufficient inducement...yes, I do wonder."

Before I can wrap my mind around her meaning, Cimari's foot lashes out and catches Pretty Girl under the belly, sending her sprawling and spinning across the floor. Pretty Girl wails, a hair-raisingly human sound of fear and pain. Every atom of my being screams at me to get up, save her, shield her from the evil creature that's hurting her. But I don't. And, like Bard, I hate myself for it.

But it's not only my life that hangs in the balance. Sadra, Bard, Mother Wenla…all of them depend on my silence, and if I betray them, I also betray the imprisoned souls who need their help.

Cimari stamps her foot. "I'm right about you, I know I am. They all think I'm just a stupid little girl, but I'm *right.*"

The world seems to tilt as Cimari strides after Pretty Girl and places a small, dainty foot on her neck. My eyes close in denial, but I force them open again and look into Pretty Girl's eyes as she cries and struggles to break free.

"Speak," Cimari says. "One word, and she lives. Surely you can manage that much?"

For a moment, I think I will. I think I'm lost. But a hard, invisible band closes around my throat. In the end, it's not the desire to protect my friends that catches the words in my chest, but the desire to save my own skin. It's natural, I suppose. It's primal…it's disgusting. And it's ironic—that this need to survive should make me want nothing more than to die.

With a dull crunch and a *crack* like the snap of a dry branch, Pretty Girl's neck breaks under Cimari's foot. Pretty Girl spasms once, then lies still, her gangly little legs limp and disarrayed. With barely a glance at the crumpled form under her feet, Cimari steps over Pretty Girl's body and returns to my side.

"I know what you are," Cimari snarls, jerking my head back by the hair. "Abomination. Don't think this is over."

My head slams into the ground and explodes with pain. I don't see her leave, but Cimari must be gone because now Sadra is kneeling beside me. Her hands flit from my arm to my head to my hip and back again. Longing for my grandmother's gentle touch blazes almost as hot as the agony in my head and ribs.

"Babulya…" I whisper dazedly. *"Bol'no."*

It hurts.

"What? What are you saying? Sasha?"

It takes me a minute to find the right words. "My…the bones, there…I think they're broken."

"Your ribs," Sadra whispers. "They could be. But you have to get up. We have to go."

"Go?" I ask. "But…what about…Bard…the buyer…"

"Never mind that," Sadra says, getting her hands under my shoulders. "Up, now." I bite back a cry. "I know, love, I'm so sorry. But you have to. It's going to hurt a lot worse if Cimari gets you alone again. Come on, push with your legs…"

With Sadra's help, I lurch to my feet. I'm afraid I might throw up. But I can't, because I think it would kill me. Cottony pressure builds in my ears. Sadra is urging me along, but her words are drowned out by an ominous ringing. My head feels heavy. Everything hurts so badly. I want to stop and sit down, but that would hurt too. It might even hurt more.

I don't know how we get out of the house. I can't think of anything but putting one foot in front of the other. I'm only vaguely aware of Sadra guiding me along, keeping up a steady flow of encouraging nonsense. Everything in the world seems to have disappeared—everything except for the pain. It's only the slightest lessening of agony that tells me we've stopped. We're in the garden, just outside the tunnel's entrance. I stare back at the house and blink once, twice, three times.

"She'll never touch you again," Sadra says, misinterpreting the look. "Never."

"No," I agree. "And if she tries…"

I meet Sadra's eyes, my head suddenly perfectly clear.
"I'll kill her."

III

Act Three: Rallentando

*"It's a wild place, and very unsafe. And where are we,
really—there or here?"*

-Richard Adams

Assemblé

"*Sasha! Spokoyno, Sashka. Ty v bezopasnosti.*"

I swim through the darkness, casting around for the voice calling to me. The voice tells me I'm safe, but I don't know. I don't feel safe.

"*Baba Nadia?*" *I ask uncertainly.* "*Gde ty?*"

Where is she? Why can't I find her? Something plucks at my memory—something important—but terrible—something about Baba Nadia. She's gone, she's...

She's dead.

* * *

"*Niet!*"

"Hush, Sasha." I flinch away from the figure standing over me, silhouetted in the lamplight. "It's alright now. You're alright."

"Bard," I breathe. "What happened—how did I—"

"Kirit found you after Sadra left you in the tunnel," Bard says. "He fetched Lucoran. You're in his house."

"I don't hurt anymore. I'm—" I freeze under the sheet covering me, suddenly noticing the way it slides over my skin. "I'm naked."

"You were wounded," Bard explains. "It was necessary. But the Healer was female, if that's any consolation. And I've brought you some clothes." He gestures to a pile of neatly folded cloth beside the bed.

"What do you mean, I was wounded?" I ask. "Was it my head? I don't remember anything after—after Cimari."

"You did indeed sustain a head injury in addition to several broken ribs," Bard says gravely. "But I was referring to the wound on your hip."

"A wound." I blink, nonplussed. "But what…?"

"Sadra cut out your brand," he explains. "So that you couldn't be tracked by the House of Light and Shadow or recognized as a thrall."

"I don't understand." I clutch the blankets to my bare chest and squirm upright so I can look him in the face. "How does cutting out my brand help? Is it the brand that holds the Pall?"

"You recall that your brand serves as the focal point for your energy, gathering and concentrating it so that it can be used by others." At my nod, he continues, "Without that brand, your energy is released in a form too diffuse to be recognized or used by a Lightcrafter."

"But the Pall is still on me." I look at him for confirmation. "It's still stealing my life away and just—leaking it out into the world?"

"Essentially, yes," he says. "And you should know that after Sadra cut out your brand, we had to further disguise the area with—with hot oil."

I yank the covers up to expose my left leg and hip, and my heart leaps—the brand, the symbol of my enslavement, is gone. But in its place is a vast, rippling sea of scar tissue that spreads from my hip all the way down my thigh and onto my knee. I twist my leg back and forth and feel the scar pull with a sharp twinge of pain. If shifting from side to side hurts, what will happen when I walk? When I dance? I look up at Bard, alarmed.

"Will the scar go away?"

Bard closes his eyes, looking a little ill, but quickly recovers himself.

"Some of the scarring may yet fade in time, but it will remain fairly extensive," he says. "I'm sorry, Sasha. We did the best we could. It shouldn't affect your ability to dance as long as you treat the area to keep the skin supple."

I let out a tiny sigh of relief and pull the blankets down. "How long has it been?"

"Two days," Bard says. "Going on three. It's just after midnight. Lucoran is sleeping downstairs."

"And Sadra?" I ask. "Where is she?"

"Mother Wenla thought it best that she distance herself for a time," Bard says, a little stiffly. "Sadra will remain in the Temple cloisters until it's safe."

"But it wasn't her fault," I protest. "She was just trying to help me—"

"No one thinks it's her fault," Bard says. "Indeed, we owe her a great debt. Because of Sadra's Dreamwhispering, Ismeni thinks you died as a result of Cimari's assault. Sadra handled a difficult situation with commendable finesse. However, Mother Wenla feels—and I agree—that Sadra has allowed herself to become too emotionally entangled and would do better in the cloisters."

"She's my friend," I protest, my throat tightening. "My only friend. How can you punish her for that?"

"It's not a punishment," Bard says patiently. "No one is angry with her—or you, for that matter. We only want to keep you both safe."

"And how are you going to do that?" I ask. "What happens to me now?"

"You will stay here with Lucoran," Bard replies, "as his Companion. When the passes open in the spring, we'll—"

I hold up a finger. "Companion?"

Sadra has explained a Companion's role repeatedly, insisting that it's not the same as a prostitute, that sleeping with influential people in return for gifts and privileges is a perfectly respectable thing to do.

She doesn't understand my distaste for prostitution, either, since the City's prostitutes aren't prey to the same dangers faced by prostitutes in my world. They're protected by a guild and can apparently make quite a good living. We've spent a truly silly amount of time arguing about it—to no avail, it seems. Revulsion twists my features as I stare incredulously at Bard.

"Yes, Companion," he says, his voice firm. "Don't look at me like that. Obviously, you aren't expected to provide any actual, er—"

"Companionship?"

"Yes." His gaze softens. "I know how it must seem to you, Sasha. I really do—we come from the same world, you and I. But this isn't that world. To host a Temple Companion in one's home is a great honor, one that will increase his status and yours. No one will question your presence here, and no one will wonder if he seems…protective. You have been sheltered and secluded in the Terrace these many months, and there is much you don't know. Lucoran will be able to guide you and protect you until it's time for you to leave."

"And no one else can do that?" Heat rushes to my face at the thought of sharing living quarters with Luca. "Why can't I stay at the Temple?"

"Too many people," Bard says, shaking his head. "Too many relationships. Do you think you're a good enough liar to hide the truth from all of them?"

I sigh. I think I could, actually—but I don't want to. I don't want to exchange one mask for another.

"This truly is your best option." Bard pats my hand, his face sympathetic. "The arrangement with Lucoran will give you mobility, respectability, even autonomy, though certain boundaries must be observed to ensure your safety. You won't find that anywhere else, not even the Temple."

Resentment creeps into my chest. Is this really the best cover they could come up with? I'm supposed to let people think I'm sleeping my way to the top? That I'm some kind of *pet*? An ornament for a lord's household? It's not that different than thralldom, in that regard. But if there is a better option, I don't know enough about this world to find it. Not yet, anyway.

"What does Luca think about all this?" I ask.

"He agrees it is the most practical solution," Bard says. "And of course he understands that you are to be his Companion in name only."

"Oh, good," I mutter.

"You should rest," Bard says after a moment and moves to get up.

"Wait." I reach out and seize his wrist. "I need you to tell me—what do the visions mean? And…and what does it mean if they stop?"

"Visions?"

"When I sleep," I say urgently. "I'm back—back there. I'm in a hospital and I'm sick. I think I'm dying. Or I was. They started to go away, like you said. And now you tell me I've been asleep for nearly three days and there was *nothing*. What does it mean? Is it because there's nothing to see? Am I…am I dead there?"

"I can't tell you, Sasha." He shrugs and spreads his hands in a helpless gesture. "I don't know."

"Yes, you do," I insist. "You know more than I do. You must know *something*—it happened to you, didn't it?"

"I experienced something like what you describe," he acknowledges. "And, like you, I wondered what it meant. But I came to realize that it was pointless to speculate. Perhaps I died, perhaps not. It makes no practical difference here and now."

"It does to *me*, if I might be able to go back one day. I know there's something you're not telling me about what happens when the Pall is lifted. But maybe you're right," I say bitterly. "Maybe it doesn't matter if I can't go back. I don't deserve to go home. I let Pretty Girl die. She was just a baby, and I let her die because I wanted to live… I hope I *am* dead."

"Stop it," Bard says, his voice sharp. "I wish I could give you answers, Sasha. But I can't, because I don't know them. I wish even more that I could give you absolution. I can't, because there is none. You were forced to make a terrible choice, and now you must find a way to live with it. I can't tell you how."

"How do *you* do it?" I press, growing desperate. "How do you live with what you've done?"

He spreads his hands, helpless. "I don't know. I just keep trying."

He reaches out as if to touch my face, then pulls his hand back and crosses to the door.

"Get some sleep," he suggests, and closes the door behind him.

I glare at the door, my vision blurred by tears.

A soft whine sounds from somewhere below me, and I lean over to see Kirit crawl out from under the bed. He jumps up beside me and lays his snout on my shoulder. I run my hand gently over his head and play with the fluff around his ears and cheeks, my breath catching at the memory of Pretty Girl's feathery wisps of fur. My poor, sweet baby. She didn't deserve to die.

What would Emily say if she knew what I'd done, what I'd become? Even if somehow I make it home, how could I ever face her? But how can I not? If I give up now, Pretty Girl's death will count for nothing. I will have committed an atrocity of selfishness for no purpose at all.

Kirit lifts his chin from my shoulder, and a second later there's a knock on my door.

"Sasha?" Luca calls. "Can I come in?"

I hesitate. The blanket feels suddenly much too fragile against my bare skin. Practically transparent. But hiding from Luca now will only make things more awkward later. I force myself to speak.

"Yes." It comes out as a strangled whisper. But as I clear my throat to try again, Kirit yaps once and Luca lets himself in. I look sharply at Kirit, then at Luca.

"Can he understand me?" I ask. "I thought only a Beastspeaker…"

"He can understand you if you keep it simple," Luca says. "It's quite extraordinary, really."

"Clever boy," I murmur, stroking Kirit's head again.

"He is," Luca agrees. "But it's not so much that he's more intelligent than other animals. It's more a matter of opportunity and interest. He's fascinated by us, and through me he's been able to learn not only how we speak but how we think and reason, at least to a certain extent."

"And you've learned from him, too?" I guess.

"Oh, yes. The world looks indescribably different through his eyes." He looks down, suddenly uncomfortable. "Kirit doesn't really understand—or maybe it's more accurate to say he doesn't always accept—certain human concepts. Concepts like politeness or privacy, for instance."

"Oh?" I blink at him, wondering where he's going with this.

Luca grimaces a little. "He was listening to your conversation with Bard and relaying it to me, even though I told him I didn't want to hear. He thought I should know—mostly so I could explain it to him." He shrugs, his cheeks flushed pink. "He's very curious, and not at all tactful about it, I'm afraid."

"Oh," I say again and drop my eyes.

"I didn't mean to eavesdrop," Luca says hurriedly. "But I wanted you to know…Bard told me how it was for you, living as a thrall. I'd wager a finger at least that the king's best soldiers don't have your self-discipline, or your courage. But I know you might be lonely without Sadra, and I thought—I mean, I hope …"

In spite of everything, I smile at his flustered earnestness. He smiles back, his teeth flashing white in the dim.

"I'm doing a poor job of explaining myself, aren't I?" he says wryly.

"I just want you to know that I'll be your friend, if you want, not just your bodyguard. It would be my honor."

A hint of warmth seeps through the icy crust of bitterness and grief.

"I'd like that," I tell him, a lump rising in my throat.

He grins, suddenly boyish. "I'm glad."

Changement de pieds

I finger the strands of my hair, now a light rust-color thanks to the harsh dye Luca delivered to me this morning. The difference, though subtle, is startling. I barely recognize the person staring back at me in the mirror. But then, it's been so long since I really looked in a mirror that I might have simply forgotten what to expect.

I hold the mirror out and step into the patch of light coming in the window, studying my face carefully. No, I decide. It is different. *I'm* different.

It's not just my hair. My face has lost the last of its childish roundness, revealing the hard, elegant lines of my bones. My skin, hidden from the sun for months on end, is as pale as milk. My lips, though full and generous, have lost their sweetness, making the firm line of my jaw seem brittle without a smile to soften it. My eyes, once cloudy with dreams, are cold and sharp. The hint of red in my hair makes them seem bluer and brighter, like chips of ice.

I nod in satisfaction. I don't look like me, but I don't look like the thrall Cygnet, either.

I lean the mirror against the window and use it to arrange my hair into a series of loops and braids. That done, I put on the soft wrap dress Luca brought me, pulling the cloth snug around my torso and shaking the skirts out to fall in heavy folds to my ankles. I stroke the fabric, my eyes roaming greedily over the deep blue and the creamy, pristine embroidery on the cuffs and hem. The dress is simple, but indisputably the garb of a citizen—and a high-status citizen at that.

A tiny sparkle catches my eye, drawing my gaze to the floor. My moonstone necklace winks at me like a long-lost friend turned up unexpectedly on my doorstep. I stoop and pick it up, cradling it in my hands. I stare at it for a long time before finally fastening the chain around my neck. I face myself once more in the mirror.

I'm not a thrall anymore.

I hike up my skirt and twist, staring down at the mess of scar tissue on my left hip. The brand is gone, just like Bard said. The whole area looks awful—a ruin of puckered, melted flesh stretching from the crest of my hipbone down to my thigh. But the starburst insignia of the House is gone.

"Sasha?" Luca taps on the door. "Are you ready? Mother Wenla is expecting us."

"Yes, I'm ready."

Luca's eyes widen when I open the door.

"You look lovely," he says. "But different."

"That's the idea," I remind him with a slight smile.

"Come on, then," he says, offering me his arm. "We shouldn't keep the Temple Mother waiting."

He tucks my hand into his elbow and leads me out into the busy streets. Kirit trots cheerfully at our heels, and Luca's stride is relaxed and easy. I hurry along beside him, trying not to slink or creep. It's only with great effort that I resist the urge to cringe into his side. After the tranquility and quiet of the Terrace, the chaos of the City is terrifying.

But it's exhilarating, too, with a crisp wind blowing out of the autumn sky. How many times have I wished I could be a part of these crowds? How many times have I imagined myself strolling along these streets on an errand of my own choosing? And now here I am, free to meet the gaze of passers-by and smile at a little girl who waves at me from her father's shoulders.

"I'm sorry," Luca says as we make our way toward the Temple.

"For what?" I ask, looking up at him in surprise.

"For that." He nods toward my hip. "I helped Bard with the, ah, process."

"Oh." I twist my hands into my skirts, fingers clenching, then look up at him. "It's alright. I don't remember it. And I'd rather have a scar than—than what was there before."

We walk the rest of the way in silence. I can't tell, really, whether the silence is comfortable or not. I imagine it would be, if the rest of the world were silent too. The crowds and their noise still make me jumpy. Kirit, perhaps sensing my unease, yips and gives me a wide, panting smile. I can't help but smile back. I scoop him into my arms and cuddle him as we walk, finding comfort in his weight and warmth.

I breathe a sigh of relief when we reach the sanctuary of the Temple. The soft murmur of conversation and prayer mingles with wandering strains of music, ebbing and flowing like breath in the lungs. Despite the ambient noise—or perhaps because of it—the Temple is permeated with a sense of purpose and serenity that calls to mind my grandmother's studio. I close my eyes, imagining that the chatter all around me is that of students and parents. The music is Tchaikovsky, Prokofiev, not the strange melodies and rhythms of Kingsgarden.

"Sasha." Luca touches my elbow. "This way."

Reluctantly, I leave the music behind and follow him into the upper stories of the Temple where Mother Wenla waits in her study. She rises gracefully from her desk and greets me with a warm embrace. I study her through my lashes, looking for some sign of anger at our lateness. There is none. My muscles relax.

"The sun shines on you, my child." She lays a hand on my forehead, frowning. "Sit. You need a boost."

"Shall I leave you, Mother?" Luca asks, hovering awkwardly near the door.

Mother Wenla gives him a stately nod. "Return at the evening bell, if you please."

Luca bows his head, then winks at me as he and Kirit back away.

Mother Wenla nudges me toward a cushioned bench when the door closes. We sit, my hands clasped in hers. She closes her eyes, and I wonder if I should close mine. But I don't. I watch her instead, my gaze tracing the soft lines around her mouth and eyes. I see laughter and joy, but also hardship and grief. Was it the strength of her character or the strength of her love for her unnamed man that led her to found the Bird's Path?

A little shock runs up my spine as I recognize in her the same hidden iron that my grandmother possessed. For once, the thought of Baba Nadia doesn't stab into my belly, but instead wraps around me like a warm blanket. The warmth doesn't fade but grows, filling my body with a steady flow of energy and strength that I didn't realize I'd been missing. This must be the "boost" Mother Wenla was talking about.

"Thank you." Her eyes open, and I squeeze her hand. "Truly."

"Of course, my child."

Mother Wenla pats my cheek in response and returns to her desk, pulling out a small packet from underneath. At her nod, I approach and take it from her. Inside I find a spread of seemingly random objects: a thin, flexible wire; a series of rings and lockets; a dagger so slim it seems little more than a needle; soft straps of various sizes and lengths; a wrought-silver comb; and a set of hairpins. It's the hairpins that make it all click—these are the tools of my new trade: A Companion's weapons.

"You will come to me each week for counsel and instruction,"

Mother Wenla informs me. "The Bird's Path is well able to protect its nestlings in the ordinary course of things. However, your situation is far from ordinary, and you must be able to protect yourself. Lucoran will teach you the fundamentals of unarmed combat. You and I will practice…alternate methods."

A thrill of vicious pleasure ripples through me at these words. I told Sadra I would kill Cimari if she ever touched me again, and I meant it. I'd tear her throat out with my teeth if I had to. But it would certainly be easier with the training and tools offered to me now. I think of Sadra's skill with her poisons and daggers. Will I ever be that good?

"I'm sure you're very busy," I say, looking at the floor. "Couldn't Sadra teach me?"

"Sadra is unavailable, as I'm sure you've been told." Mother Wenla fixes me with a stern gaze. "I expect you to work hard and without complaint, Sasha. Your safety and that of the Bird's Path depend on it."

I nod, chastened. At her raised eyebrows, I add, "Yes, Mother."

"Very well," she says. "You will be Marked with the insignia of the City of Orchids. It's far enough away that people won't think it strange if you're a bit backward."

"But…I heard that it's illegal to impersonate a Temple initiate," I say. "I heard that it's punishable by death."

Mother Wenla smiles. "So it is. But you *are* an initiate, Sasha. You may call your Temples by a different name in your world, but I believe you share our faith."

Yes, we do call our "Temples" by a different name. We call them conservatories…or studios, or Academies.

"Are you ready to receive your Mark?" Mother Wenla asks.

I stand, the packet of weapons clutched to my chest. "I'm ready."

* * *

Mother Wenla leads me into a tidy, well-lit chamber behind her office. A high padded table stands in the center of the room. The walls are lined with cabinets and shelves, but everything is so neatly arranged that there's plenty of room to maneuver.

"This is where I perform more complicated Healing," she explains. "It will do for your Marking."

"Will you be Marking me?" I ask.

She surprises me with a merry laugh. "Certainly not. My talents lie firmly in the musical realm, I'm afraid. No, you'll be Marked by the best, a dedicant named Calan."

At Mother Wenla's direction, I perch on the table. We don't wait long before a soft knock signals Calan's arrival. Mother Wenla opens the door and ushers in the biggest man I've ever seen. I blink at his hulking shoulders and shaved head, which seem at odds with his twinkling black eyes and rosy cheeks. He bows his head, then gives me a warm smile.

"The sun shines on you."

"And on you," I reply, smiling in return.

"I'm afraid I must leave you for now," Mother Wenla says. "Take your time, my dears."

"Is this your first time under the needle?" he asks as he unloads his tools from a worn leather case.

"Yes," I say, eyeing the steadily growing array of needles and ink pots on the counter.

"I won't lie," he says. "It will be painful. Just do your best to breathe and remember that the beauty will remain long after the sting fades."

I soon find that the needle does hurt, but it isn't as bad as I thought it would be. It's unpleasant, certainly, but manageable. Even so, I take his advice and concentrate on my breathing rather than the burn of the needle.

Soon I fall into a kind of trance and realize this must be very like what Sadra tried to get me to do when I couldn't dance. Time is meaningless, and so is pain. Nothing exists but the steady rise and fall of my chest and the cool air sliding into my lungs. It comes as a shock when Calan taps me on the shoulder and tells me he's finished.

"Already?" I blink up at him, groggy and confused, as if I've just woken from a deep sleep.

He smiles and hands me a small mirror: There, just under the dip between my collarbones, is a swirling rune surrounded by delicate orchids inked in soft blues that offset the stark black of the rune. I frown. As beautiful as it is and for all the honor and prestige it will supposedly bring me, I'm not sure I like exchanging one brand for another.

"What's wrong?" Calan asks, his black eyes sharp on my face.

I hand him back the mirror and do my best to smile. "Nothing. I'm sorry. It's—it's lovely."

"You can speak freely," he says. "I know what you are. And what I am."

My breath hitches in surprise. "You're—you were—"

"A thrall," he confirms. "Yes."

"Then you know what it is to be…to be *claimed*," I say. "To have it burned—or Marked—on your skin."

"I do," he says softly. "That's why I marked my own claim."

He pulls up his shirt and hooks a thumb into the waistband of his trousers, flashing a swift smile of reassurance at my embarrassed twitch. But the instinctive protest dies on my lips as I see the bold splashes of color spilling across his hip and up onto his side. More importantly, I see the scar underneath where his brand was cut.

I look up at him, hardly daring to speak the words. "Can I…I mean, will you…"

"Yes," he says. "If you wish it."

"I wish it," I breathe.

Now that I know the trick of it, it's easier to slip into my trance. I rest contentedly in my own mind, aware of the needle's burn but not bothered by it. Some time later—minutes or hours, I can't tell—Calan taps me once more. I blink groggily as I come out of my trance and twist, trying to get a good look at his handiwork. Did he get it right? I tried my best to describe what I wanted, but now all my explanations seem like so much meaningless babble.

"Wait," Calan says, and disappears through the door.

He returns moments later with a long mirror and props it against the wall. I climb down from the table and hike up my skirts, my heart thumping.

"Oh, Calan," I whisper when I see it. "It's perfect."

The awful mess of my scar has been replaced by a swirling, delicate design composed of tiny vines and symbols. Each shape is independent of the others, but they come together to form a larger design suggestive of a bird surging into flight. Not just any bird—a swan.

"These runes are for strength," Calan explains quietly. "This one for stillness and serenity. And this…" He taps the rune at the swan's heart. "This is for freedom. It's yours, Sasha. Forever."

* * *

Luca returns soon after to collect me. As we make our way back toward the Temple gates, I try not to pick at the salve-slick Mark on my chest and consider my situation.

Calan was right. I *am* free, Marked or not. But I'm also arguably in greater danger than I was before. Who really knows how or when the Bird's Path will make good on its promise to remove the Pall? Before Cimari, I was content to follow Bard's orders because I had no other choice. But now…I wonder.

"Luca," I say, wincing as a troupe of musicians bursts into raucous song on a nearby street corner. "Your brother is the king."

"He is," Luca agrees. He looks down at me quizzically. "So?"

"Does that make you a prince?" I ask. "You're his brother."

"Half-brother," Luca corrects. "And born out of wedlock to a woman whose name my father never told me. We don't have the same stigma against such alliances as you do in your world, but it does mean I'm not in line for the throne."

"It doesn't bother you?" I ask, curious.

"Stars, no." He chuckles. "It's a miserable, thankless job, as far as I can tell. The world on your shoulders and everyone telling you what you should be doing differently and never a moment of privacy. No, it doesn't bother me. I wouldn't take Costi's place for anything. He wears it well, but the crown is a great burden to him. As it should be," he adds, serious now. "Our father always said ruling is a duty and a sacrifice, not a privilege."

"Heavy is the head that wears the crown," I murmur.

"Yes, exactly." His grins, his eyes twinkling down at me. "I had no idea you were a poet as well as a dancer."

My smile in return is bittersweet. "It *is* poetry, but it isn't mine. It's from a play in verse, written by a man named Shakespeare. I was studying his work when I got sick—when I was taken."

"Ah."

Luca opens his mouth and then bites his lip, as if he doesn't know what to say, and we fall into silence. After a few moments, I reach out hesitantly and lay a hand on his arm.

"Luca, if your brother knew...could he help? *Would* he help?"

"I don't know." Luca sighs, his face troubled. "If Costi learned the truth...I don't know if it would make a difference. The entire infrastructure of our City, our whole civilization, depends on Light. Without thralls, everything would fall apart. What the House is doing is wrong—of course it's wrong, and my brother would see that, but my brother is also the king. He's responsible for the welfare of the whole kingdom. Weighed against the collapse of the world as we know it, he might see thralls as the lesser of two evils."

I push away a surge of bitterness. "So the Bird's Path is my only hope."

"I didn't say that." Luca shoots me a measuring sort of look. "Maybe I'm underestimating my brother. But until we can be sure, I think we'd do best to play by Mother Wenla's rules."

"We?" I meet his gaze with raised eyebrows.

"Yes, *we*. You're my friend, aren't you? I'm happy to help the Bird's Path as long as they're helping you, but I know where my loyalties lie." Luca studies me with sharp eyes. "You don't trust them?"

"Not completely, no." I press my lips together against the sudden tremble brought on by Luca's declaration. "They hold some secrets tight in one fist and dangle others in front of my face with the other. I don't know…maybe I'm not being fair. They've done a lot to help me—or Sadra has, anyway. But I *know* Bard is hiding something from me, and now he's gone for who knows how long."

Luca takes my hand to help me over a rough patch in the street, his brows furrowed in thought.

"What?" I squeeze his hand and look up at him. "You can tell me if I'm being—if you think I'm wrong. I hardly know myself what I'm thinking these days."

"It's not that." Luca stops for a moment and seems to struggle with himself. Then he says, "I don't think you're wrong."

My hand tightens around his. "What makes you say that?"

"Here," he says, pulling me off the street and through the gates of the City's famed gardens. "Let's find a place to sit."

We hurry along the garden paths, twisting and turning among ferns and flowers I never imagined could exist, much less bloom in autumn.

Each section of the garden represents a region of the kingdom, or so I've been told, and every inch of the place is meticulously maintained by an army of both House mages and Greenloves—citizens Gifted with an affinity for plants.

Finally, we find a secluded bench nestled among a thicket of flowering bushes—the City of Camellias, I suppose. We sit, our heads so close I can feel his hair tickle my ear. Anticipation makes my heart race—but is the anticipation for his words, or just his lips? I push the thought away, disgusted with myself. I have to focus.

"When Bard showed me his memories," Luca begins, "the first time, I mean, it was memories of your world. Most of it was awful, terrifying—smoke and filth, noise, machines like I've never seen. There were good things, too. Music and dancing and carts that pulled themselves, people laughing together…

"But there was one memory that I think he didn't mean to share, and I couldn't tell whether it was from this world or the old one. It was a girl—a young woman. I thought it was you, at first. It wasn't, but…Sasha, she looked an awful lot like you. I can't think what it means, except that you must be right. Bard *is* hiding something from you."

I don't say anything for several long moments. My head is spinning, and the gentle breeze is suddenly freezing on my sweat-slicked neck. I swallow several times, trying to suppress a surge of bile. I wish he hadn't told me that. I wish I didn't know.

But I do, now, and I can't hide from the knowledge or what it means.

"Sadra was right," I mutter, my voice faint and breathless. "She'll be so pleased."

"Sasha?" Luca lays a warm, steadying hand on my back. "Are you alright?"

"Mostly." I look up and try to smile. "There are some things I need to tell you."

Kirit, sensing my distress, climbs into my lap and tucks his nose into the crook of my elbow as I wrap my arms around him. Luca's hand moves up and down slowly—tentatively, as if he's not quite sure how or if he should comfort me. I give him what I hope is a reassuring smile and then tell him everything; I leave nothing and no one out. Not my mother, not even Dave.

Bozhe, I barely remember Dave. I wish I'd gotten the chance to thank him—or even say one nice thing to him. It's just one more mistake to add to my steadily growing list of regrets.

"Stars…your *mother*?" Luca says when I've finished. "You think she may have been suffering from the Pall."

"My grandmother kept records," I say. "Her symptoms were almost exactly like mine. It seems too close to be coincidence. Bard has gone to such great lengths and broken so many rules for me, and I've been trying to figure out why…maybe this is the answer."

Luca frowns. "Yes. If he knows her…"

"Or knew her," I say. "We know time moves differently here and there. Who knows how long she's been here, or if she was freed, or even if she survived to be sold in the first place? A lot of us didn't."

I remember the emaciated, wax-white bodies in the Cage and shiver, cuddling Kirit closer.

"Do you think Bard knows?" Luca asks. "That she could be here?"

"I have no idea." My lips twist into a grim smile as an idea occurs to me. "I hope he doesn't. He knows far more than he's willing to tell me. If I had something to bargain with…"

Luca frowns. "That's what you're worried about? Don't you want to find your mother?"

"No," I say shortly. "I don't."

His brows shoot up at that, but he doesn't inquire further. "Well, whatever you want to do, it'll have to wait. He left this morning with a House caravan."

My stomach drops, then settles with surprising ease. Though I hate to admit it, even to myself, it's something of a relief to have this particular choice taken out of my hands. The thought of confronting Bard makes my hands sweat. But is my uneasiness tied to Bard himself, or what he might say?

I stand, shaking off a web of uncomfortable thoughts. I've survived this long. Whatever Bard has to say, I'll survive that too. When the time comes, I'll get my answers, and then *I* will choose what to do with them. I'm free. I can't forget that.

Luca tucks my hand into the crook of his elbow to lead me out of the garden, but I stop him with a gentle tug.

"Wait." I blush as I meet his eyes but don't look away. "We're quite near the Terrace, aren't we?"

"Somewhat near," Luca allows. "But I wouldn't worry. Your chances of being recognized are very, very slim."

"Good. I want to see it."

Luca frowns. "I'm not sure that's a good idea, Sasha. It's unlikely that you'd be recognized, but not impossible. Why take the risk?"

"I'm not sure I can explain," I admit, and this time I do look away. "It's just something I need to do."

Luca studies me for a moment, then nods and leads me down a different path. We walk in silence, but not an uncomfortable one. Kirit frolics in the flowers and bushes, and Luca's arm is warm and steady under my hand. Maybe its wishful thinking, but I feel that he understands my need to see the place where I was enslaved, to stand at its gates as a free woman.

Luca slows as we exit the garden and approach a towering cliff face. But as we get closer, the seemingly solid stone resolves into three dimensions. Behind the cliff's jutting stones lies a narrow passage, one that I remember with painful clarity from my first days in the City. Luca looks down at me, concern pressing a tiny crease between his brows.

"Are you sure?" he asks. "There's no harm—and no shame—in staying away."

I shiver and tighten my grip on his arm. "I'm sure."

We move closer, passing into the cliff's shadow, and round the rocky outcropping that hides the passage.

There it is: the Terrace Gate. Little more than a gash in the rock, the Gate earns its name—and its fame—by virtue of the exquisite carvings etched into the surrounding stone. Dancing maidens seem to leap from the mountainside; young lovers embrace, twining together amid flowering vines. A little girl laughs, clapping, as her mother plays a flute.

One carving in particular catches my eye: an old woman holding a baby. Her stone features are nothing like Baba Nadia's, but the artist, whoever she was, managed to capture something of the perfect tenderness and wisdom that maybe all grandmothers possess.

The carvings go on, I know, all the way into the Terrace itself. They represent all the facets of human love, human beauty…but I wasn't human, then. Not to them.

My throat closes, and it takes me a moment to draw the moisture back into my mouth. But I manage it in the end. I spit at the base of the cliff and turn my back on all the beauty that was never meant to be mine.

Divertissement

The next morning, Luca meets me on the stairs with a wide smile that matches Kirit's.

"I brought you presents," he says.

I pause mid-yawn. "What kind of presents?"

Luca reaches for my hand and tugs me gently down the last few steps. He pulls a small dagger out of his belt and hands it to me.

"I want you to keep this in your hand for the rest of the day," he says. "Don't draw it. Just hold onto it and get used to the way it feels. Can you do that?"

I nod, taking the dagger from him with a strange mix of eagerness and apprehension. The only blades I ever held were meant for cutting vegetables, not people. But my fingers tighten on the dagger's hilt, Cimari's face flashing before my eyes. I study my white knuckles and breathe hard against a surge of sick certainty.

I'll never take another beating lying down.

Never.

"You needn't grasp it quite so tightly," Luca says, his lips twitching. "It won't jump out of your hand."

Still breathing harder than I should, I force my hand to relax. "You said presents. Are there more?"

With a courtly flourish, Luca hands me a vial of perfume. "For you, my lady."

He blushes. "I thought—well. I just thought you might like it."

I take the vial, fighting down an answering blush. He's just playing his role and helping me with mine. But the softness in his eyes, the warmth of his fingers as they brush against my own—it feels real.

Luca steps back and clears his throat. "We should go out. If you're ready, I mean. It's a good idea to be seen together. But if you don't want to—"

"No, I do," I say. "Can—can we go somewhere with food? But quiet?"

He thinks for a moment and says, "I think we can do that. Not many eating houses will be quiet at this hour, but we can get food and take it to the gardens. A bit unconventional for the morning meal, but very romantic."

I smile and try to stifle a thrill of pleasure. "That sounds perfect."

* * *

Luca maintains a steady stream of chatter as he leads me through the winding streets. He doesn't make it obvious, but I know he's chosen a route that bypasses the busiest districts. His consideration warms me and, when he offers me his arm upon entering the crowded marketplace, I take it without hesitation.

"What shall we have?" he asks, scanning the many food carts on display.

"You pick," I say, too hungry and anxious to navigate the overwhelming variety of offerings.

"Well, in that case," Luca says with a grin, and leads me to a stall selling spicy sausages cooked with onions and peppers. "I love spicy food in the morning. Gets the blood moving, you know."

I nod and give him a tremulous smile. As soon as he turns to order, I inch closer and hunch my shoulders against the chaos that surrounds us. Vendors hawk their wares at the top of their lungs, often waving samples or their hands in the air. Carts and tents alike are painted in bright colors and hung with scarves or bells. Musicians take advantage of the large crowds and play for tips, competing with both each other and the crowd itself to be heard. Will I ever get used to this?

Maybe. Especially if it means getting food like this. I lick my lips greedily as the vendor slices open a thick loaf of bread, stuffs it with the sausages, and ladles sauce into every nook and cranny. After a measuring sort of glance at me, Luca orders another. Smart boy. Grateful though I am for his kindness, I'm in no mood to share.

With food in my hands, the noise and bustle of the marketplace falls away. I apply myself to my meal with a single-minded focus that seems to both amuse and disturb Luca. I finish before we get anywhere near the gardens and have to borrow Luca's handkerchief to clean sauce from my face and hands. By some miracle, nothing got on my clothes. I don't think so, anyway. I don't look too hard at the spot of red on my sleeve, which may or may not be part of the cuff's pattern.

"Mmm," I sigh. "That was good."

I sigh again as we turn onto a tree-lined street lit by floating globes of Light. The leaves are almost brighter than the globes, all red and gold and blazing orange. Autumn is in full swing, but seasons in the City seem to be sort of optional, at least as far as the foliage goes. As we round a corner, dogwoods and cherry blossoms rain petals down on our heads.

"I'm glad you liked it," Luca says, eying his now-filthy handkerchief with an expression halfway between dismay and amusement.

My cheeks flush with embarrassment, and I shoot him an irritated glance. "I'd be prepared to bet that you've never gone more than a day or two without a good meal. You don't know what it's like, so don't mock me."

"I would never mock you," Luca says softly. After a moment, he asks, "Didn't they feed you when you were…"

"Oh, they fed us." I shiver as the phantom bars of the Cage rise around me. "A crust of bread every few days. A rotten piece of fruit if we were lucky. On the Terrace it was better. I ate regularly, at least. But it wasn't—it wasn't real food. I never ate a true meal, just ingredients. Boiled oats, for the most part. Sometimes she fed us shaved carrots mixed with unseasoned meat and a bit of rice, all together in a bowl. Like you'd give to a dog."

I meet his eyes. "That's how she saw me, you know. I was her pet."

My fingers drift to the Mark at my throat. Luca takes my hand and holds it in both of his.

"You are no one's pet," he says, his voice low. "Never forget that."

* * *

When we return to the house, I escape to the back garden to do my barre exercises. It's as necessary now as it ever was, but it's not the same without Sadra. The exercises settle me, as they always do, but the resulting calm is tinged with loss.

Luca finds me before I can enter the house. He shoos me back into the garden and tows me all the way through until we reach a flat, grassy area just before the high garden wall. There he lies down on his back and says,

"Get on top of me."

I gape at him. Bard made it very clear to Luca that I was a Companion in name only, and Luca made it very clear to me that he understood this fact. But even if he hadn't, his request now strikes me as a very odd one. Luca grins at my confusion.

"You wanted to learn how to defend yourself, didn't you?"

I raise my eyebrows. "Is that what we're doing?"

"What else?" Luca replies, much too innocently. "I'm going to teach you how to escape if someone pins you down. Come, get on top and pretend you're choking me."

Fighting a blush, I straddle his hips and put my hands on his throat. His skin is warm under my hands, and strangely soft. I'm suddenly seized by the urge to run my hand over the dark stubble on his cheeks and jaw for comparison.

Before I can move—thank God—he surges up and sideways, flipping me onto my back so quickly I have time only to gasp in surprise before it's over. He grins at me, his face inches from mine. Kirit yaps excitedly and bounds over to lick Luca's face, then mine. Luca laughs and sits up, wiping his face. Kirit sniffs industriously around my shoulders and hips, perhaps to assure himself that I'm unharmed. Luca rolls off me and resumes his position on the grass, looking pleased with himself. I rise to my knees and look down at him, half annoyed and half eager.

"How did you do that?" I demand, my hands on my hips.

Luca grins. "Hop on and I'll show you."

I climb on top of him again, and Kirit retreats to a sunny stone to watch.

Luca taps my right arm. "I'm going to trap your arm—here, above the elbow—and your foot. My foot goes on the outside of your ankle, see? This way you won't be able to stabilize yourself when I roll you over...like this."

Luca thrusts his hips up and his shoulders sideways. With my elbow and foot trapped on that side, I have no leverage to resist him, even though he's moving slowly this time.

"Once you're on top, use your elbow—go for the nose, the throat, the belly."

He demonstrates with such precision and restrained power that it makes me shiver. Then he grins at me, and warmth rushes back into my body. Heat flares and settles at each point of contact between his body and my own—and there is a *lot* of contact. I look away, flustered, and push him off me.

"Let me try."

Luca guides me through the motions, correcting my form and modifying my grip until he's satisfied. At first, he moves with me, providing just enough resistance to let me feel the shifts in his weight. But as my confidence grows, he adds more and more force to his own movements until I'm grunting with effort.

"You should rest," he says at last, and helps me to my feet. "That was excellent, Sasha. Truly."

"You were holding back, though," I pant.

"Yes," he allows, and a crisp breeze blows a lock of dark hair across his forehead. "But not as much as you think. I knew what you were going to do and how to fight it. But if I were a common thug, stumbling drunk and thinking you were helpless? I would have been on my back and bleeding long before now."

I examine his face, looking for any sign of teasing, but I find none. The expression in his sharp green eyes is deadly serious.

"You're strong, Sasha," he says softly. "You're powerful. You don't look it, but you are. You can use that—and everything Mother Wenla and I are going to teach you—to make anyone who crosses you very, *very* sorry."

Épaulement

As autumn progresses, our days fall into a pattern: Kirit wakes me just before dawn, and I exercise at the barre Luca has constructed for me in the back garden. I eat a hearty breakfast and then go to the Temple of Graces to attend a service and work with Mother Wenla, who teaches me not only herb craft but sleight of hand and a Companion's combat techniques. She replenishes my energy before and after our lessons each day, and on some days I feel almost as if the Pall has been lifted.

Luca has arranged some sort of half-sabbatical from his duties as captain of the guard, and he's at the house by the time I get home every afternoon. He drills me in defense maneuvers until I can break his holds even at full force, and we move on to kicks, blows, and throws.

Working with him is more satisfying than I could ever have imagined. He pushes me mercilessly, but always with compassion and humor. Each new skill feels like a stitch in a wound somewhere deep inside. Cimari and the House of Light and Shadow still stalk my dreams like the monsters they are, but now—in my dreams, at least—I fight back.

One afternoon, however, I find Luca in the parlor rather than the garden. Kirit is curled before the hearth, glowing like an ember in the firelight. Perhaps it's not so surprising: the day is wet and chilly, the sort of day that lets the cold seep into your very bones. The prospect of rolling around in icy mud is not an appealing one.

As if reading my mind, Luca says, "I think we ought to have a rest today."

I lower my damp hood and join Kirit at the fire, frowning. "Can I afford to take a day off?"

"Yes," Luca says firmly. "You've been working hard, and it's time to rest. If you injure yourself, you'll lose more than one afternoon of practice."

"Maybe…"

I bite my lip, torn between relief at the unexpected respite and my instinctive disapproval of slacking off. But now the abstract fear of failure is eclipsed by the very real fear of capture, torture, and death.

"Let me put it this way." Luca flashes me his most charming grin. "*I'm* taking a day off. You can thrash around in the rain by yourself, if you like."

I wrinkle my nose at him but can't help smiling back. "Fine, then. What are we going to do instead?"

Luca's grin widens. "So glad you asked. The Chalice Carnival is less than a moon away, and I would like to buy you something pretty to wear."

"Is that really necessary?" I ask, heat flooding my cheeks.

"I think it is, actually." Luca shrugs. "It would look strange if I didn't. But, anyway, I want to."

I don't know what to say to this, so I ask, "What's the Chalice Carnival?"

"It's the City's midwinter festival," Luca explains. "Everyone gets dressed up in their best clothes—but not something you bought yourself. The whole night, you're not supposed to buy anything for yourself. Total strangers treat each other to food, wine, gifts, everything. People sing and dance all evening. At midnight, every light in the City goes out and everything goes silent." He grins. "Silent by comparison, anyway."

"Well, that's good," I say somewhat sourly, though in theory the whole thing sounds heart-warming. "Since I have no money to buy myself anything, anyway."

"Sure you do," Luca says cheerfully. "What's mine is yours, Companion of my heart."

I turn to the fire to hide my face. Something about his offer makes me feel uneasy. Dirty, even, though I can't think why. He's provided me with shelter, clothes, food—lots of food, and prepared by the best eating houses, to boot. A good thing, too, since neither of us knows how to cook. And I didn't mind. Until now, I hadn't thought much about it. But now that he's said it out loud—what's his is mine—it feels different, as does his desire to buy me something pretty.

Would Luca's support feel less like charity if I really were a Companion? Would it feel like due compensation or would it feel like prostitution? But then, if I'd been brought up in the Temple, I would have no concept of prostitution as I know it. Maybe I would bask in the gifts showered upon me, secure in my own worth and the honor due my position.

"Have I said something wrong?" Luca moves to my side and rests a hand on my back. "If I did, I'm sorry."

"It's nothing," I say, trying to smile at him.

Luca smiles back, though he still looks concerned. There's a little wrinkle between his brows that just begs to be smoothed out, perhaps with a thumb—or a kiss. Warmth floods me once more, and my smile feels more sincere.

"Really, I'm fine," I say. "Let's go shopping."

With a delighted grin, Luca whisks me out of the house and into the cold, wet streets of the City. The rain has abated somewhat, but a chilly mist hangs in the air, gathering in tiny pearls on the wool of our cloaks and clinging to Kirit's fur. But the weather has kept most shoppers indoors, and the City is as quiet as I've ever seen it.

We visit at least six dressmakers' shops before Luca finds something he deems worthy of me. But that dress, as it turns out, is too heavy to allow for dancing. The gauzy fabric of the next won't stand up to the chill of a winter night. And so on. After the fifth, Luca scowls at me in only half-joking annoyance.

"You need to express an opinion," he says sternly. "This is for you to wear, after all."

I shrug a little stiffly and pull Kirit away from a pair of shoes he's examining with a bit too much interest. "You're the one paying."

"That's not how this works." He rolls his eyes. "I'm buying a present for my lady love, not dressing up a doll."

My face goes cold, and I realize that this is what has been bothering me. I'm not Luca's lady love and never will be…but I have been a doll. Ismeni would put me in dress after dress until she found one that she liked. Sometimes she would even dress me up in her own clothes and laugh at how much like a "real lady" I looked.

Kirit paws at my leg, whining to be picked up. I oblige, and his warmth thaws the ice in my chest. Luca winces and takes my hand.

"Someone needs to solder my teeth shut," he mutters, and Kirit huffs as if in agreement. "Let's try a different store."

I nod silently and follow him back into the cold. The mist has condensed into an icy drizzle; each droplet stings where it falls, so cold it almost feels hot. An image of Luca's parlor with its cozy blankets and thick rugs swims before my eyes. I nod to myself, suddenly and completely certain that I do not want or need a new dress, carnival or no carnival. Luca, busy rescuing Kirit from an ornery cat, is shivering as well.

"Luca," I begin, but my eye is caught by an approaching litter.

The litter is simple by Terrace standards—or at least by Ismeni's standards—and born aloft by gaunt, shivering men clad only in loincloths. Even from the other side of the street, I can see that their lips and fingers are tinged blue. They must be cold enough to risk hypothermia, but not one of them makes any move to warm himself once the litter stops. Their eyes are blank and empty, like glass.

They're thralls.

"Luca," I whisper, closing my own eyes against a wave of nausea and impotent rage. "Help."

"What?" Luca turns and moves immediately to my side. "What's wrong? Where does it hurt?"

"Not me," I snap, though my stomach lurches. "The thralls. We need to help them."

He doesn't answer right away, and for a moment I almost hate him for the pity in his eyes.

"I know we can't swoop in and rescue them," I say. "But you're a Lightcrafter, aren't you? Isn't there anything you can do?"

"You want me to use Light?" he asks softly.

"Someone will use it." My voice is harsh. "Let it be you. Let their Light benefit them, for once."

Luca nods and pulls me in front of him. "Stand here and look amorous."

Before I can ask him what exactly amorous looks like, he bends his lips to my ear and whispers something I don't catch. One of his hands curves around my waist; the other moves against my back, hidden by my hair. I want to ask him what he's doing—and if it's working—but what if I break his concentration? Whoever is riding in the litter could decide to leave at any moment, and we could miss our chance.

I lean into Luca and tuck my face against his shoulder. That should look suitably amorous. It's the best I can manage, anyway. And it's warm. But I wish I knew—

"It's done." Luca gives me a brief squeeze and steps away. "I just hope it's enough."

I turn just as the thralls lift the litter and set off once more. Perhaps I'm imagining it, but their movements seem just the slightest bit stronger.

"What did you do?"

"I returned the warmth to their cores and sealed it in," he explains. "It should last for a few hours, at least."

"Thank you," I whisper.

He shakes his head. "I wish I could have done more."

I bite my lip, staring after the thralls' retreating backs. Against my will, my eyes lift to the cliffs overlooking the Terrace and the City. On the southern cliff, the Temple cloisters perch, tidy and elegant as a dove. In stark contrast, the House of Light and Shadow squats like a dark, poisonous toad on the northern cliff.

"It will fall someday," Luca says, following my gaze. "I swear it, Sasha."

Maybe it will, but I won't be here to see it happen.

"Let's go," I say. "It's cold out here."

* * *

The next morning, Mother Wenla ushers me into her office with only a tiny frown for the grass stains on my trousers.

"You have been practicing, I see. On your own? Lucoran is with the king this morning, is he not?"

"Yes, Mother," I say, clasping my hands in front of me. "We didn't practice yesterday, so I wanted to make up for it."

"I see." She studies me for a moment longer, her frown deepening, then she motions to the spread of pots and vials on her desk. "Let us see what progress you have made in your other studies. Identify the contents—by scent alone."

Obediently, I wave each container under my nose and concentrate on separating the interwoven strands of poppy, valerian, belladonna, and foxglove. Herb craft hasn't come as naturally to me as the more physical aspects of my training, but I've been practicing diligently with a book of illustrations and tiny packets of the different plants. I can't afford to neglect anything that might help me stay alive and free of the House of Light and Shadow.

The memory of those corpse-like thralls kept me up most of the night, and what little sleep I did get was plagued by nightmares. Even now, my hands shake as I set the final vial—lemon balm, mint, and fennel—down on Mother Wenla's desk.

"Well done," Mother Wenla says approvingly. "Now, show me how you would prepare a sedative to be mixed into a goblet of wine."

The lesson continues until, finally, Mother Wenla returns our materials to their respective cabinets. She sits behind her desk once more and gives me a nod of dismissal. When I don't move, she raises her eyebrows.

"Is there something you wish to tell me, child?"

I tuck my hands into the folds of my pants. "Yes, Mother."

"Speak, then." Mother Wenla rises and beckons me closer. "Come, sit here."

I join her on a low couch and wring my hands, suddenly unsure of what I want to say. Mother Wenla waits beside me, serene as always. Though she says nothing, the warmth of her Gift washes over me and eases the tension in my shoulders.

"I saw something yesterday," I say finally.

"Something troubling?"

"Very." The story of the abused thralls spills out of me, the words tumbling over each other in my hurry. When I'm done, I meet Mother Wenla's eyes. "I know you're doing everything you can, but what about me? Can't I do something to help? I'm just waiting around, eating Luca's food and sleeping in his bed and spending his money. Shouldn't I—"

"No." The word is quiet, but definitive. Mother Wenla takes my hands and squeezes them almost too hard for comfort. "Listen to me, Sasha. You aren't just 'waiting around,' as you put it. You are working extremely hard—perhaps even too hard—to regain your strength. You'll need that strength if you are to survive the Pall long enough to see it removed."

I look down. "I just feel so useless. Everyone is doing things for me, and I can't do anything for anyone."

"You don't have to," she says bluntly. "Not yet. Your task right now is to keep yourself healthy and to prepare yourself for what is to come. Until the Pall is removed, that is your *only* task. There will be plenty of time and plenty of ways to contribute to our efforts once you are free of the Pall." She smiles, deepening the laugh lines around her eyes. "I am confident that you will prove an asset to the Bird's Path."

I smile back, but, inwardly, I flinch. She knows I'm going home, doesn't she? For me, there will be no 'after.' I'm going home to Emily and James and the life I was meant for. I have to believe that.

And I do believe it…but that trust suddenly isn't as comforting as it should be. Sadra's face flashes before my eyes, then Luca's and Kirit's, and, finally, the empty, gaunt faces of thralls shivering in the rain. But I can't think of them now. Mother Wenla is right: I need to keep my eyes on the prize.

I'm going home.

Retiré

The day of the Chalice Festival dawns bright and clear. According to Luca, the City of Roses rarely sees snow, despite the mountainous terrain, but in winter a frigid wind cuts through the alleys and steals the very breath from the lips of unwary pedestrians. To save me from that fate, Luca wakes me up at dawn with a huge smile and an even huger pile of clothes, which he dumps unceremoniously on the bed.

"You're supposed to wrap Chalice presents," he says. "Or hide them, sometimes. But I'm terrible at both, so...here."

I take the proffered bundle and gasp as I shake out the butter-soft fabric. I'm not sure if it's a very long tunic or a shorter dress, but, either way, I love it. The top is simple—just a thin tracery of gold embroidery around the cuffs—but the fabric is a rich, dark blue like a deepening night sky. It flows through my fingers like water, so finely woven I can't see the threads.

"These go with it," Luca says, holding up a pair of matching trousers. When he lowers them, I can see the anxious wrinkle between his brows. "I took the measurements from your other clothes, but the seamstress is ready to make any adjustments in time for the celebrations tonight. There are other colors and options here, too, and warm layers to go underneath. You pick out whatever you like, and if you don't like any of them, we can—"

I stop him with a firm kiss on his cheek. "I love it. Thank you, Luca."

He blushes, and so do I. He really is the sweetest man. Which reminds me…

"I have a present for you, too," I tell him. "I've been working on it for weeks."

His smile lights up his whole face. "Oh? What is it?"

"It's a secret," I say, and push him from the bed with my foot. "Go look for it while I get dressed."

Kirit hops off the bed and trots to the door, his tail swishing in excitement behind him.

"No cheating," I call after them as they disappear.

I reach for my clothes and yank them on. There's no way I'm letting Kirit ruin my surprise by sniffing it out too quickly. I spent weeks learning how to cook using the brick oven in the kitchen, and all afternoon yesterday making the little jam-filled cakes Luca loves. They might be a little lumpy and the jam will probably spill out on the first bite, but I think they'll still taste alright.

Downstairs, I find Luca and Kirit seated at and under the table, respectively, with identical too-innocent expressions on their faces. My shoulders slump.

"You found them," I say glumly.

"I don't know what you're talking about," Luca declares, his mouth twitching.

I give him a sour look and cross to the cupboard to extract the cakes, which I'd hidden behind a sack of oats. The icing has solidified into a nice crust, hopefully protecting the dough from drying out too much. I replace the bowl I'd been using to cover the plate and turn slowly, suddenly shy. Luca has given me safety, shelter, friendship…and these lumpy, possibly dry cakes are the best I have to offer him in return.

I mean to say something heartfelt and deep, something that could give him some pale hint at how much I appreciate *him*, not just everything he's done for me, but all that comes out is,

"I tried."

I shove the platter into his hands and busy myself with the kettle. Luca's better at the delicate art of making tea—it's one of his only culinary skills—but my gift to him seems suddenly silly and small and completely inadequate. Not that tea will do much to change that, but I can't bear to look at him just now.

"Sasha."

I don't turn. There's something in his voice that makes my stomach twist. Is it pity? Amusement at my sad, childish attempt at impressing him?

"Sasha, look at me. Please."

"The tea," I mumble, pretending to fuss over the leaves.

A strong arm snakes around my waist, and I find myself pulled back against Luca's body. A few sticky crumbs fall onto my shoulder as Luca leans down to press his cheek against mine.

"I love it. Thank you, Sasha."

I smile to hear my own words offered back to me and turn in his arms.

"Really? I thought they came out alright, but—"

"Really," he says with a smile. "They're delicious. Have one."

He holds a cake to my lips. If it weren't for the little glob of jam clinging to his nose, the gesture would be unbearably romantic.

Thank God for that blob of jam. Instead of melting into a puddle of desire, I have to laugh. I take a bite of the cake but also take a rag and scrub it over his face.

"Oh!" I cover my mouth to hide a jam-toothed smile. "It *is* good!"

"I told you," Luca said with a grin. "Now, come on. It's time to celebrate."

* * *

The City, always bursting at the seams with color and music even on an ordinary day, is positively frothing with festivity. The moment we walk out the door, Luca and I are bombarded with showers of coin and small gifts. We respond in kind, tossing coins and toys from our own collection to the swarms of small children dashing up and down the streets. Revelers spill out of taverns, embracing anyone who stands still long enough and dragging unsuspecting passers-by inside for a drink. Luca, thankfully, shields me from any physical interference and fields the many invitations with astonishing grace and diplomacy.

Or perhaps not so astonishing. Luca is the son of a king, after all, though he rarely acts like it. This new version of Luca is unfamiliar and more than a little odd—but also attractive.

Most days, I remember that Luca is and can only ever be my friend, that it would be not only stupid but unfair to both of us to let our friendship grow into anything more. But today isn't most days. Today garlands of bells and ribbon stretch from balcony to balcony. Music flows through the streets like a river, turning whole city blocks into choirs.

I sing every song, laugh at every joke, eat and drink everything that crosses my path. And I dance. I dance with the blushing city guard in the Temple courtyard, with a little girl in the square, by myself atop a tavern table…I dance with Luca, pressed against his body in the city gardens.

The setting sun casts long, cold shadows across the grassy paths and streaks of pale gold across Luca's face. For once, I allow myself to really *look* at him. His lashes are the thickest I've ever seen on anyone, much less a man. They're not effeminate—they simply emphasize the mischievous glint that I've seen there so many times before. But now, I find that I can't look away.

I don't know why I should be so captivated. Though not ugly by any means, Luca isn't exactly handsome. His is a beauty born of warmth and energy and good humor, a beauty of the spirit rather than of the flesh. His features are angular, almost feral, too sharp for beauty in the traditional sense, and the animal-like directness of his gaze is so often at odds with the gentleness of his smile. The contradictions in his face and his manner are unsettling, entrancing...and dangerous.

"Luca," I whisper. "I..."

His lips quirk. "Yes?"

"I...I don't know." I give a small, breathless laugh and lower my eyes. "I don't know what to say—how to thank you. For this dance, for today, for everything."

"Don't thank me yet," he says, his grin widening. "We still have all night. Speaking of which, we need to get back to the house."

If I shiver, it's because the sun has gathered up its last scraps of warmth and disappeared behind the cliffs. The warmth in my belly has nothing to do with vague, heated ideas of what we might get up to in the dark confines of his—our—house. Nothing at all.

I clear my throat. "The way everyone's been acting, I would have thought the party would go on all night."

"Oh, it will. But first there's the Contemplation." He takes my hand and calls for Kirit, who has been chasing something small and squeaky through the bushes. "Come on."

No matter how much I pester him, Luca refuses to say anything more as he leads me back to the house. The streets are dark, lit only by the occasional candle glowing in a window. We're not the only ones hurrying home. The same revelers that were reeling and dancing just an hour before now march along as if on a mission, their faces still joyful but calm, almost somber.

Intrigued, I tug on Luca's sleeve. "Luca, what is going on?"

"You'll see," he says. "I don't want to spoil the surprise."

When we reach the house, Luca waves me toward the kitchen and disappears upstairs. From the sound of it, he's taking the stairs two or three at a time. Shaking my head, I light a fire in the hearth and set a kettle to boil. Above me, Luca's progress is marked by an occasional thump accompanied by a muffled curse. The Contemplation, if that's what he's doing, doesn't sound very contemplative.

The tea has gone cold by the time Luca returns, but he doesn't seem to mind. He slurps it down and makes another pot while I play with Kirit on the floor.

"So, are you going to tell me what this is all about?" I ask. "Or is it traditional to torture outsiders with suspense?"

"I just want to make it special," Luca says, giving me a wounded look. "It's your first time."

I throw my hands up in exasperation. "First time for *what*?"

"The Contemplation lasts from sundown to midnight," Luca explains. "It's a time to step back from the light and noise of celebration and reflect on what we're truly celebrating."

"Which is?" I prompt. "The Chalice is something more than a drinking vessel, I presume."

"It is," Luca says seriously. "But that's part of the surprise."

I groan.

Three hours later, after numerous attempts to wheedle, trick, or physically force the information out of him, Luca finally relents. My heartbeat quickens in anticipation as he leads me up the stairs by the light of a single candle. Where are we going? Surely not to the bedroom—*that* certainly doesn't seem appropriate for Contemplation.

Or maybe it does. I've certainly contemplated what we might do in a bedroom often enough.

But Luca bypasses the bedroom and opens a trap door in the ceiling, catching a folding ladder as it slides downward.

"The surprise is in the attic?" I ask, peering up into the darkness.

"On the roof," he corrects me.

At the top of the ladder, Luca blows out the candle and puts his hands over my eyes. As he guides me into a gust of cold air, I'm suddenly aware of how very warm and broad Luca's chest is. The surprise, whatever it is, can go hang. I'd rather stay right here in Luca's arms.

But then Luca tilts my head back and releases his hands, revealing a sea of diamonds so impossibly bright, they take my breath away. I blink, so dazzled that I don't realize at first that the diamonds are stars. Raised in the suburbs as I was, I grew up accustomed to seeing a few scattered stars peeking through the haze of streetlamps. It wasn't much different in the City, where light—and Light—covered the stars nearly as thoroughly. I never gave them a second thought, never knew what I was missing. Until now, when every light in the City has gone out.

"*Bozhe*," I whisper.

"Come on." Luca pulls me toward a pile of furs and blankets arranged in a sort of nest. Kirit is already there, snuggled so deeply among the folds, all I can see is the glitter of his eyes. "Lie down."

I lower myself onto the pile and wrap myself in a blanket. "So this is the Contemplation?"

"Well, the star gazing is optional, I suppose," Luca says, lying down beside me. "But since this is your first Chalice festival, I thought we should." He points, his cheek so close to mine I can feel his whiskers. "Look there. That's the Chalice."

I follow Luca's finger to a cloudy formation that puts me in mind of pictures I've seen of the Milky Way. But instead of a long ribbon, the Chalice looks like an overflowing cup.

"The legends say that in the earliest days, we lived and died in darkness and despair." Luca's voice tickles my ear, and, though he drops his hand, he stays close. "Farmers toiled in the fields without respite, never tasting the fruits of their labor. Blacksmiths forged tools and weapons, never toys or lovers' trinkets. Housewives gave birth to children who grew too quickly into adulthood, never knowing laughter. Soldiers killed and were killed without mercy—without knowing why, even. But for all their toiling and striving, they were pale, listless, fearful beings. There was no beauty or courage in the world, only survival. Only hardship.

"But one day, a young blacksmith dreamed of something better. He dreamed of the three Graces: Joy, Passion…and, shining like a beacon, her arms around the other two, Beauty. When the blacksmith awoke, he wept, for now he knew all that his life lacked. He wept a lifetime of tears that had never been shed, and, when his tears ran dry, he fell to his knees and prayed.

"When the blacksmith rose, he went to his forge and fashioned a chalice from gold—a soft, silly metal that served no useful purpose. So he had been told, and so he had believed until he dreamed of Beauty. When the chalice was completed, he went to the vineyards, where the vintner made vinegar to preserve food, clean wounds, quench thirst—useful, practical, necessary tasks, of course. But the blacksmith told the vintner of his dream and showed him the golden chalice, and the vintner in turn showed him what he had discovered: His casks of vinegar, if opened early, produced a liquid with a pleasant taste and even more pleasant warmth.

"The blacksmith and the vintner filled the chalice with wine and offered it to the villagers, who began to laugh and then to sing. When the chief's suspicious soldiers came to investigate, they, too, drank the wine. One soldier after another faltered in the march, and they began to dance.

"And so the chalice performed its miracles, passing from hand to hand, intoxicating the people not only with drink but with joy and wonder. 'There is beauty in the world,' one villager would say. 'Drink deep.' 'Life is sweet,' the next might say. 'Drink deep.' The villagers drank deep from the chalice and began to expect more from life than mere survival. As they sought out beauty and amusement and love, they also found genius and passion for good works, for excellence, for innovation. They found their Gifts.

"The villagers transformed their huts into houses, then villas. The villages grew into towns, then cities, then a kingdom. To this day we gather in the Temple of Graces to seek out the beauty in the world and in ourselves, and every year we celebrate the blacksmith and his Chalice of Gifts."

Luca falls silent. I blink, still entranced by his story and dazzled by the stars. Finally, I look at him and feel a smile spread across my face.

"I love it," I tell him, and it feels like something more, something like… I love *you*.

But that can't be true. I can't love him, just like I can't love this City with all its beauty and songs and stories. This City may be full of beauty, but it's full of monsters, too.

"What happened to the Chalice?" I ask, tearing my eyes away from him.

"No one knows," Luca says. "Though it appears in various legends, usually in a time of great need, amplifying the Gifts of those who drink from it. The legends say that first king of the Garden united the Cities under his rule with the aid of the Chalice."

"And Light?" I ask, and the starshine dims as I remember my place in this world. "Where do the legends say Light comes from?"

Luca shifts beside me, but I don't look at him.

"Sasha—"

His voice is full of tenderness and understanding, everything I could want from him—and everything I can't accept.

"I have to go." I shove the furs—and Kirit—aside and struggle to my feet. "I'm sorry."

I nearly break my neck in my headlong plunge down the ladder, and again tripping over something in the darkness of the attic. The house is little better with the candles unlit and the hearth fire dead. I burst onto the street in a flurry of mussed hair and disheveled clothes. I'm not the only one. It seems the Contemplation can be of a more physical nature after all.

I straighten my clothes with trembling hands, then draw my hood up. A soft yap draws my attention downward. Kirit grins up at me, his teeth glinting in the starlight. I sigh. As chaperones go, it could be worse. I don't even know what I would say to Luca. My stomach is still roiling with a sickening mix of embarrassment, grief, anger…Luca doesn't deserve any of it, but I can't get rid of it. The best I can do is get rid of me.

"Let's go," I tell Kirit, and start walking.

* * *

An hour later, guilt wins out. I slurp down the last of my tea, thank the tea house's proprietor, and head back into the cold. Luca must be worried sick. Or maybe not. He could just as easily be angry with me. Disgusted, even, or just tired of dealing with me and my drama.

My musing doesn't last long. Kirit yips and shoots ahead, throwing himself at a cloaked figure coming around the corner. Luca. I blanch, drawing back momentarily, then force myself forward. Luca strides forward without hesitation, his steps quick and almost eager.

"Luca," I say. "About earlier—"

"Never mind that," he says, taking my hand. "Bard's back."

"What?" I blink, then realize what he said. "Bard! When—how do you know?"

"It was pure luck." Luca shakes his head, his lips quirking upward in the shadow of his hood. "I was looking for you, and I found him. Singing."

"Bard?" I gape at him, too astonished to remember to be awkward with him. "*Singing?*"

"Singing," he confirms. "In a tavern. I didn't recognize him at first without a scowl on his face. But it was him, alright. I suppose he must earn a living somehow when he's not with a caravan. There won't be any more until spring."

"Well, then." I wipe my suddenly damp palms on my skirts, both pleased and frightened at this development. "It's time we got our answers."

The tavern is a surprise. I was expecting something dark and dingy, the Kingsgarden equivalent of a dive bar, but this establishment is open and airy and spotlessly clean. Hardly the kind of place I'd expect to find the perpetually dour-faced Bard.

The tavern keeper greets us with a deep bow and cheery grin, but his smile fades as he takes in our tense expressions.

"A lover's quarrel, eh? No matter, a little wine, a little music, the right atmosphere—everything will come right, you'll see."

He leads us to a table in the corner, where shadows and gauzy cloths hang in thick folds to create a cozy little bower lit by the soft glow of candles. I let out a sharp breath through my nose and resist the urge to roll my eyes. Romance and candlelight is the last thing I need right now.

The tavern keeper leaves us with a last bow and a murmured, "Drink deep."

Luca gives an embarrassed cough as we settle onto the cushioned bench. Something in his breath makes me think he's trying to say something, but I have little attention for him. My eyes are fixed on Bard.

He looks uncharacteristically serene, dressed in white robes with his hair braided in a smooth plait. His face is clean shaven for once and set in an expression of peaceful concentration as he pulls a rippling melody from the harp on his knee. I wouldn't have recognized him if not for the livid scar across his face.

"It's a love song, you know," Luca says. "Not just a tune."

"Mm." I nod, but I'm not really listening.

When Luca tilts his head toward mine, however, I tuck my head against his to hear him sing.

"Leaves turn, snow falls
Green on the ground, sun in the sky.
In each turn of the seasons, I turn to you.
Do you think of me? I think of you.
Every sun, every moon
Every star in the sky shines for you.
I can see the morning breaking in your eyes.
Do you think of me? I think of you."

I pull away so I can look into his eyes. "Luca…"

His lips part, and for one terrifying breath I think he's going to kiss me. I freeze, torn between fear and desire. All it would take is a tilt of my head, one way or the other. I could look away and pretend nothing happened…or I could lean forward just the slightest bit and—a chair scrapes, making us both jump. Bard drops into the chair, glowering at us from under his shaggy brows.

"Hello, Bard."

Luca squeezes my hand and stands to clasp Bard's forearm. Reluctantly, I stand too and return Bard's formal gesture of greeting with a hand over my heart. It takes all my willpower to meet his eyes with squared shoulders and a polite smile, but I get it done. Baba Nadia always said bad manners are never helpful.

"So," Bard says as we all take our seats. He gives me a beady-eyed look. "You seem to be settling in well."

"Well enough," I say stiffly.

We stare at each other for a long moment, seemingly all at a loss for anything else to say. Finally, Luca pushes a tankard of ale in Bard's direction.

"Drink deep," he says. "You've got a lot of talking to do. The lady has questions, and you're going to answer them."

Bard sighs. "Sasha—"

"No," I say, shaking off the last of my doubt—and my distraction. "You know more than you've told me, and I don't believe you don't have answers. You said yourself you already broke the rules to make sure I could be saved, and I want to know why. I'm not leaving until you tell me, and I won't work with you or the Bird's Path, either. I'll take my chances with Luca and the king."

If Luca is perturbed at the idea of being volunteered to blow a nationwide conspiracy open, he gives no sign of it. He nods seriously, his arms crossed over his chest.

Bard snorts. "Don't be ridiculous, Sasha. You need our protection, our resources. You need Mother Wenla's skill as a Healer."

"Luca can protect me," I say, and I'm surprised to find that I actually do believe that. "And Mother Wenla isn't the only Healer in the City. I won't work with people I can't trust."

Bard sighs.

"Ask your questions, then," he says, draining his tankard.

"Tell me about my mother."

Bard's expression goes so completely and abruptly blank that for a moment I'm afraid he's had a stroke or has gone into shock. But then he's back, his brow furrowed. "What about her? She died. I saw you at her burial."

I gape at him. "You saw *what?*"

"I saw you," Bard insists. "It was the first vision I'd had since the Pall was lifted from me thirty years ago. You weren't much younger than you are now. You wore a black dress…and my necklace. *Bozhe*, you looked—you look—just like her."

Cold creeps up my spine when I ask, "Like who?"

"Like your mother," he says, his eyes tight with pain. "Like Nadia. My wife."

I almost don't feel it when Luca takes my hand. For a moment I'm floating above the table, looking down at my body as if it's someone else's. I must have misheard him. He can't have said—

"My wife," he repeats.

"You're Aleksandr," I say numbly. "Aleksandr Nikolaev."

"Yes." He nods, closing his eyes. When he opens them, I see that they're filled with sorrow. "And you are my daughter."

I shake my head.

"You must be," he insists, misinterpreting my denial. "It cannot be coincidence that you find yourself here. The Apostate has theorized that perhaps susceptibility to the Beckoning is inherited, but still…I never thought…"

"The Beckoning?" Luca asks, his fingers tight on my own.

"There is some force, some…thing that pulls the mind from one world to the other," Bard explains. "We *think* that it calls to everyone—but not everyone hears. And not everyone who hears succumbs to it. Only those whose bonds to their own world have been weakened in some way, through madness or grief, or sometimes illness. I suppose it was your mother's death that made you vulnerable."

Luca and I exchange a glance. I feel almost sorry for Bard, and reluctant to tell him the truth. But I have to, if I expect any degree of honesty in return.

"You don't understand," I say, my throat tight. "I'm not your daughter."

"You are," he says gently.

I shake my head, holding his eyes. "I'm not. Nadia was my grandmother."

For a moment, all is silent as Bard's face convulses into a mask of denial and then abruptly clears into an expression of blank, helpless sorrow.

"Your grandmother," Bard breathes, so softly I can barely hear him.

"Yes," I whisper.

An icy fist closes around my heart as I remember something he said to me, the first time I met him. *'My wife had married another man, thinking I was dead...'* But when—and where—did that marriage take place? Sadra told me that time moves differently between the worlds. How much time passed in my world while Bard has been in this one?

"What..." I lick my lips. "What happened to you that you were taken by the—the Beckoning? And when?"

Bard shakes his head. "You don't want to hear about that, *kotik*."

"Don't call me that." I lean forward, my hands clenched into fists. "Tell me! Why did you go mad?"

"Sasha, I—very well." Bard covers his face with his hands and heaves an unsteady breath. He emerges after several long moments, looking desperately unhappy. "It was late in the year of 1977. We were in Paris. Nadia was doing well enough—how could she not? She was an enormously talented dancer in the very birthplace of ballet. But I—I was just another immigrant, trying and failing to find work. And then *he* came."

"Robert Chantry," I whisper.

"He was American," Bard continues. "Wealthy, charming, handsome. He filled her head with talk of New York, San Francisco...but she was married to me. She would never break her vows, *kotik*, you mustn't think that. But I knew she was unhappy. I knew she regretted making those vows. Of course she did! I was her husband, and I could barely manage to put a roof over our heads. I would never be able to take her to America, and he could. She wanted to go. She loved him."

"She didn't." I feel sick. "I saw her face when she spoke of him, and when she spoke of you. She didn't love him."

Bard slumps forward in his chair, like someone punched him in the gut. He covers his eyes with his hand.

"I should have gone back," he chokes. "I've always known it. I made a mistake—I should have gone to her, married or not. Oh, my Nadia…"

"Is it possible?" I grab his arm and shake it. "Can we go back?"

"We can't talk about that here," Bard says, collecting himself. "The risk—"

"*Ya ne zabochus,*" I hiss, then continue in Russian, "I don't care. *You* put everyone in danger by breaking the rules for my sake, so don't lecture me about being reckless. *Tell me.*"

"I can't tell you, because I don't know," he snaps. "Not for sure. When the Pall was lifted from me, I saw…everything. I was both here and there…and somewhere else. I don't know where it was, it was simply—elsewhere. I saw the Apostate tending to my body. I saw the olive groves and the waves on the shore. I saw…other things." He shudders.

"And I saw Nadia. She had Robert's ring on her finger and a child running before her, laughing. So I came back here, to Kingsgarden." He pauses, scowling ferociously into his ale. "It felt like a choice, but I don't know. Perhaps I would have awoken on the Apostate's island in any case. But others I have met said that they too were presented with a choice. The ones who lived, anyway."

"The ones who lived," I echo, feeling faint.

"I told you it was dangerous," Bard says, his eyes hard. "Perhaps the ones who died simply made a different choice—to go home. But there's no way to know for sure. They can't come back to tell us, after all."

"You're saying I'll never go home."

My voice comes out hollow and tinny—or perhaps it only sounds like that to me. My ears feel like they're packed with cotton. Luca is squeezing my hand, demanding to know what's wrong, but I can barely hear him over the pounding of my heart.

"That's not what I'm saying." Bard slams his hand down on the table. "*Listen* to what I'm telling you: I'm saying I don't know."

I don't say anything but lean forward and clutch at my spinning head.

"Sasha. *Sasha.*" Luca pulls me upright and cups my face. He glares at Bard. "What did you say to her?"

"Only the truth," Bard says, now in the Common tongue of Kingsgarden.

"I'm fine," I mumble. "Luca, I'm alright."

But I'm not. I have to force the words out with a tongue gone heavy and clumsy. I take Luca's hands away from my face and take a deep breath.

"What's wrong?" he asks. "What did he tell you?"

"I can't—" I stand abruptly, nearly knocking over my chair. "No. Let me go."

"Wait." Bard stands too and holds a hand out to stop me. "Sasha—"

"No."

I push my way through the crowd and stumble out onto the street. Luca is just seconds behind me, worry and frustration written in every line of his face. He grabs my arm to steady me as I stumble on the uneven cobblestone. The ground seems to shift beneath me so that I can't find my feet. My head spins and spins until I lose all sense of direction: Up is down, down is up, and left and right are somewhere around the corner. I sag in Luca's grip, but he doesn't let me fall.

"What do you need?" Luca asks, his lips close to my ear.

That's a good question. I brace myself against his arms and press my forehead against his chest in a vain attempt to still the whirlwind in my mind. Tentatively, he strokes my hair with one hand and presses the other into the small of my back.

Inside, the tavern has gone eerily silent. Not a single mutter or clattering spoon can be heard. The very air seems to pause, waiting, until—

"Gori, gori, moya zvezda,
Gori zvezda, privetnaya..."

'*Shine, shine on, my star.*' Bard's voice rises to fill the silence, strong and smooth and full of desperate longing. I shiver in Luca's arms and turn my head so that his heart beats against my ear. It almost drowns out the sound of Bard's pain—but not quite.

I know what I want. What I *need*. A respite from the numbness inside me, something to overwhelm me and carry me away from my questions and doubts and, most of all, from the knowledge I chased for so long and now wish I didn't have. Luca could give me that, I know…but I won't use him that way. I step out of his arms, away from his warmth and the unspoken promise of safety.

"Sasha," he murmurs, and the tenderness in his voice and hands is nearly my undoing. "What can I do?"

I shake my head and step away once more.

"Nothing," I tell him. "There's nothing you can do."

Pas de trois

Mother Wenla stands in the center of the Temple's vast, round chapel. Her arms are raised, her eyes closed, like Luca's, like everyone's—except mine. Well, mine and Kirit's, but no one's going to blame him. I don't particularly like coming to these services, but Luca insists that at least occasional attendance is essential to our cover.

It isn't the content or form that I object to. Quite the opposite: each service is more like a yoga class, or sometimes a choir rehearsal, than a religious exercise. I've never been one for spirituality, but, if the circumstances were different, I could see myself on the path of Graces.

No, it isn't the service itself that raises my hackles. It's the company. Every time I see Mother Wenla, I'm reminded that I no longer have a solid path forward, that Luca and I may need to forge our own way ahead.

"In beauty there is kindness, honesty, and excellence," Mother Wenla intones. "May you find beauty in all that you are, and all that you do."

"So shall it be," the congregation chants back, and a beat later the calm breaks as we all climb to our feet and gather our things.

Honesty. I want to snort at Mother Wenla's hypocrisy, but the fizzle of anger in my chest has grown small and stale after so long.

Kirit stretches and yawns, his ears pinned flat against his head.

Smiling, I sling him over my shoulder as Luca and I join the river of dedicants flowing toward the gates. But as we leave, I catch a glimpse of Mother Wenla staring after us.

Luca and I have spent weeks—months—since Bard's confession debating and speculating and wondering if the Bird's Path is really my best hope for freedom. Once, they were my only option. I had no choice but to go along with their evasions and half-truths. But Luca is brother to the king, and so another path is open to me. It has been all along, but I was too scared to take it. That path, though still frightening, started to look a lot more attractive after Bard's damning revelations. I don't know if I'm looking at it through a lens of courage or spite, but the road leading to the Terrace and the king positively glows in my mind, begging me to walk—run—away from Bard and all he represents.

"It's the right thing to do, isn't it?" I ask Luca. "Breaking with Bard and the Bird's Path?"

"If you think so, I trust you," Luca says, but his reassuring smile doesn't reach his eyes. "It's your decision."

I purse my lips, irritation and disappointment pinching my belly. That night, the night of terrible truths, Luca and I came so close to speaking our own truths, things that must remain unspoken for both our sakes. Though the words remained unsaid, we crossed a line, and somehow we haven't been able to find our way back. We tiptoe around each other as though what lies between us is a bomb that might explode if one of us gets too close. It was easier before, when we could pretend we were nothing more than friends…and I miss him, because now we're not even that.

"It isn't just my decision," I argue, ignoring the silent alarm bells that ring in my chest. "It affects you—it affects everyone—if we bring this to your brother."

"You needn't worry on my account," Luca says, his voice flat. "You know I hate lying to him. Keeping it a secret…it's treason."

"But do you think—"

"Curse it," Luca mutters, and nods toward the Temple gates. "Speak of rain, and the clouds roll in."

Bard marches through the courtyard, his dark expression and aura of contained ferocity parting the crowd before him like the Red Sea. My stomach drops. Bard is the very last person I want to see right now—or ever, if I could have my way about it. I pull Kirit more securely into my arms and hide my face in his fur.

"Sasha," Bard says, planting himself right in front of me, "I must speak with you."

I can't think of anything to say that's both reasonable and honest, so I settle for honest, my voice muffled by Kirit's fur. "I don't want to."

"You are acting like a child," Bard says, his eyes narrowing. "I gave you what you asked for, and you don't like it. But it's time to set aside your anger."

Shame floods my body and spills over into a deep blush. He's not wrong, but his self-righteous patronizing sets my teeth on edge.

"I have good reason to be angry. How long would you have kept your secrets if I hadn't forced your hand?" I snap, looking up. "Would you have told me at all?"

Bard looks at me steadily for a moment, then says, "I don't know. I thought I was doing the right thing. I thought I was protecting you."

"Well, it wasn't, and you weren't."

"Evidently." Bard spreads his hands. "I was wrong, and I must beg your pardon. You can trust me, Sasha. I swear it on Nadia's grave. There are no more secrets for me to keep."

I glare at him with baleful eyes. Despite everything, I do believe him. But the weight of his lies—and his truths—drag on me, cut me, and bruise me like shackles. I'll forgive him, or at least work with him.

But first I want to hurt him, make him carry the weight with me. It's childish, even cruel, a desire born of fear and frustration and my own pain. Baba Nadia would be ashamed of me, I know, but the words burst out of me before I can rein them in.

"You told me my grandmother would never break her vows to you, but has it occurred to you that she must have married immediately after your death—and that the baby was born six months later? But then, I suppose you'd have no way of knowing. You never knew your daughter's birth date. You never knew *her*."

Bard stares at me expressionlessly, his face and body utterly still. Kirit whines and presses his nose into the hollow of my throat, as if to stem the flow of words. Luca stares at the ground. Perhaps he can't bear to look at me. I wouldn't, in his place. But I press on ruthlessly, unable to contain the fear and spite burning like acid on my tongue.

"Why would Robert Chantry marry a pregnant woman he had known for only a few months—unless he had reason to believe the child was his?"

"Perhaps he was simply a decent man," Bard says softly. "Or perhaps he loved her."

I snort derisively. "I envy your faith."

"You should share my faith," Bard says, his jaw tightening. "But instead you insult my wife, your own blood, for no reason but that you're angry and frightened. You must be stronger than that, Sasha, if you are to survive this. And you must *listen* to me."

I can feel the weight of his gaze as he turns his eyes pointedly to the moonstone resting just under the hollow of my throat, right in the center of my Mark. Guilt wars with anger at his accusations, both spoken and unspoken. The righteous edge to my anger fades, leaving me feeling small and silly and stupid. Because he's right—I know Baba Nadia loved him. Hadn't I said as much the night he confessed? I didn't mean what I said. I just wanted to hurt him, and now I'm angry at both of us and ashamed of myself to boot.

"It doesn't matter," I say, my voice harsh. "My survival isn't your problem. Not anymore."

Bard gives me a sharp look. "What are you saying?"

"I'm saying I don't want or need anything from you. You lied to me, jerked me around like a puppet on a string. You're not the only one who can help me."

"You're going to the king." Bard pinches the bridge of his nose and sighs. "Sasha, please, don't do anything rash. I know how hard it is to wait, but you won't have to wait much longer. I swear it."

"How can you expect me to trust you?" I cry. "You—"

"Protected and sheltered you to the best of my ability," Bard snaps. "And you are alive today because of it. Wait just a few hours longer. That's all I ask. If you still want to petition the king after you've heard what I have to say, I won't try to stop you."

I waver, curiosity and doubt warring with mistrust. Finally, I nod.

Bard's face softens. "Thank you. I will call on you at the sound of the first bell. Be ready." He turns on his heel and stalks away.

Luca and I stand for a moment in silence. He opens his mouth, then shuts it again and shakes his head.

"What?" I ask, my eyes narrowing.

Luca's face closes like a shuttered window. "I didn't say anything."

"You think I—"

"I think I'd better go," he says quietly. "Costi is expecting me."

His kiss on my cheek is light and dry. At the very moment his lips leave my skin, he leaves me in just the same way: quickly and without a backward glance.

Kirit whines, his little head twitching back and forth as he looks from me to Luca's retreating form and back again. I cuddle him closer and take a breath to calm myself; stopping tears before they rise is second nature to me now.

The sunny spring day seems suddenly colder and dimmer. Still holding onto Kirit both for warmth and comfort, I travel the now-familiar route back to Luca's house. For a while, I thought that I might eventually come to think of the place as something like a home, but that hope evaporated weeks ago.

I never did tell Luca exactly what Bard said about my chances of returning to my own world, and he never asked. Maybe he was trying to be considerate, or supportive. Our...association, or whatever it is we have, has grown so fragile and brittle that he probably feels he doesn't have the right to pry. If so, he'd have a point.

But I hate it, and I'm beginning to suspect he hates me. I wish I could tell him I never wanted this—the silence, the distance. I wish I could tell him what I *do* want. But what I want is exactly what I can't have. I'm leaving, one way or another. When the Pall is lifted, I'll either be a world away or dead. What kind of monster would I be if I asked for his love or offered him mine, knowing that it can't last?

The house seems cold and empty when I reach it, and even a roaring fire in the hearth can't dissipate the chill. I sit at the kitchen table and fiddle with potions and poisons, but my heart isn't in it. I give up after an hour and take myself to bed, where my heavy heart drags me into a fitful sleep.

When I wake, I find Luca waiting in the kitchen, mending what looks like a leather harness of some kind. When I sit, he slides a bowl of fruit and nuts in my direction without looking at me.

I ignore the fruit. Food is the last thing I want right now. My stomach is roiling, and my lungs feel as though they're tied in a knot. The knot tightens as the minutes tick past in uncomfortable silence. I stare at my hands, my knees, the flickering fire—anywhere but at him. I open my mouth several times to say something —anything—but the words stick in my throat. Finally, Luca speaks.

"The eastern passes will be open in a matter of weeks," he says, his voice bland. "I suppose Bard wants to take you to the Apostate as planned."

"Probably." I keep my voice light despite the tightness in my throat. "What will you—"

I cut myself off, and he doesn't press. It's none of my business what he does after I'm gone—or if I'm gone. If he still wants to take his information to the king, he can. I believe Mother Wenla would support him. She doesn't seem the type to be content with operating in the shadows, treating the symptoms instead of the disease, not if there's a choice about it. A thrill of fear lances through my bones at the thought of Luca fighting openly against the House of Light and Shadow. But the reaction, though visceral and immediate, is hastily suppressed. It's not my place to worry for him.

It's almost a relief when Bard arrives, grim-faced and determined. He shoves right by Luca and into the study where he gave us our "lesson" so many months ago. It seems like an age has gone by since he showed us the gruesome images of child sacrifice, but I can remember every detail with painful clarity.

Luca and I follow and take our seats. I cross my arms to suppress a shiver.

"So. What do you want?"

"What I've always wanted, Sasha," Bard says. "I want to see you safe and freed from the Pall."

"By taking me to the Apostate." I swallow, suddenly overcome by a rush of sorrow. "Yes, we guessed as much."

"Actually, no."

Luca and I exchange a glance and then stare at Bard.

"No?" Luca leans forward, his hands clasped loosely between his knees. "Is there an alternative you haven't shared with us? I was under the impression that the Apostate is the only one with the both the ability and inclination to safely remove the Pall."

"He is," Bard says. "But the Apostate is coming *here*."

My eyes widen. "Why?"

"For you," Bard says simply. "And for the kingdom. I sent word months ago informing him of Lucoran's offer of aid, and my departure from our established procedures. He is most eager to meet with both of you."

"Why are you telling us now?" Luca asks, eyes narrowing.

"Mother Wenla has received word from the Terrace that Councilman Orean has been arrested for treason," Bard says. "The announcement will be made in three days. Orean was the driving force behind the House's influence on the Council. Without him, their position will be greatly weakened. I believe this may be the opportunity we've been waiting for. With the House's primary line of influence severed, and with the king's own brother willing to speak for our cause—"

"We bring our case to the king and his council. I tell my brother I've been lying to him for months and then ask him to upend life as we know it...well, good. I'm tired of keeping secrets." Luca's eyes flicker to mine, then return to Bard. "What of Sasha?"

"I have arranged to meet the Apostate in a village some distance from the City," Bard says, looking at me. "From there we can find a safe place, away from prying eyes. He will lift the Pall from you, Sasha. You will be free."

Fear freezes my throat. Yes, I'll be free. But free to rebuild my life in the world of my birth, free to build a new life in this world...or free to give myself over to death? I shiver as I realize the option that should scare me the most has a certain appeal in its simplicity.

"Will you come?" Bard presses, his eyes boring into mine.

I look at Luca for help, but he only shrugs. Here is an option that gives us both what we want. I can think of no reason to reject Bard's offer other than fear and stupid, pigheaded stubbornness. So I don't.

The study feels suddenly empty and yet much too crowded after Bard leaves. I turn to Luca and find I can't meet his eyes.

"I...I need to see Sadra." My voice comes out hollow and faint. "I need to say goodbye. Can you help me?"

"Yes," he says, brushing his thumb across my cheek. "I'll help you."

* * *

It takes Luca two days to arrange, but he does succeed in getting a message to Sadra. The evening of the third day sees us descending into the tunnels for the first time since my escape. I hesitate at the dark hole in Luca's courtyard, remembering the last time I entered these tunnels. My breath catches in my throat as a surge of remembered pain bursts in my ribs and head. I shudder and shift my shoulders to shake off the memory. Kirit crouches under a nearby bush, sulking at being ordered to stay.

Luca calls to me gruffly, his voice echoing through the inky blot of the tunnel's entrance. "Come on, then. Do you want to see Sadra or not?"

"Of course I do," I reply, and let him help me as I lower myself into the ground.

"This way."

He keeps hold of my hand as he leads me forward, guided by the flickering light of a torch.

"Be careful," he says when I trip. "If you break your leg, I might not be able to get you out."

I can't think of anything to say to that. In silence, we pass through tunnels and caverns filled with stalactites and stalagmites until we come to a passage that's hardly more than a crack in the rock. At Luca's direction, I climb in. I fit, but only barely. I look back at Luca with raised eyebrows.

"You'll never make it," I say flatly. "There's no way."

"Hah," he says, a glimmer of humor entering his voice as he passes me the torch. "Watch me."

Luca carefully inserts himself into the crack and, with some acrobatic wiggling from him and a lot of tugging from me, manages to squeeze through.

"I was a lot smaller the last time I came through here," he puffs, laughing a little at his torn and grimy clothing.

He takes the torch back and sets off. I follow happily enough. I'm just relieved that he seems to want to talk to me again. We've barely spoken since Bard's visit.

"How long has it been?" I ask.

"Ten years," Luca says, his voice strained. "I was eleven. The king—the old king, that is, my father—was dying. I was so sure that if only the Healers' Gifts were stronger, they'd be able to save him. I had this mad idea that the King's Chalice was hidden in the tunnels somewhere."

He climbs down a small ledge and lifts me down after him. "Costi came looking for me. He was the only one who had a hope of finding me in here back then. Ari—our sister—she probably could, now, but she was only a little girl at the time. Costi was mad as a boar with a bee-sting when I slipped through that crack. He couldn't fit, and I wasn't coming out for anything. They could probably hear him shouting at me all the way back at the palace with the way everything echoed.

"I searched for the Chalice for hours. I didn't find it, of course. But I did find my way to the cloister's wine cellars." He laughs again. "I scared two drunk initiates out of their skins. I wouldn't tell them how I got there—and Costi didn't, either. I suppose he wanted to keep the secret of the tunnels in the family. They were happy enough to keep our secret if we kept theirs."

"Will your brother be angry that I know about the tunnels?"

Luca snorts. "He'll have a lot more than that to be angry about by the time we're through with him."

"I suppose he will," I murmur.

We continue on in silence broken only by my panting as the climb grows steeper. Not for the first time, I curse the Pall. Even with Mother Wenla's weekly "boosts," I tire much more quickly than I should. I've had to work twice as hard for half the results in my workouts with Luca, and I'm still nowhere near my former level of conditioning. My weakness is an inescapable reminder of the Pall, the House, and the fate that might still be waiting for me.

Two years, Sadra told me. Maybe less. But months have passed since that conversation. Who knows how long I really have, now? I shiver and keep walking.

By the time we reach the cloister cellars, I'm gasping. My legs are shaking so hard that Luca has to pull me bodily out of the tunnel. I sprawl on the floor, my back propped against the wall.

"Here." Luca tucks a flask into my hand. "Drink."

I sip from the flask, careful not to drink too much or too quickly. My hand jerks as the door creaks open—but it's only Sadra. Joy and relief give me the strength to push myself off the wall and stagger forward. I fall into her arms with a cry, my face buried in her neck.

"*Bozhe,* I missed you," I sigh.

She gives me a squeeze in response and steps back, still gripping my shoulders.

"You have no notion how glad I am to see you," Sadra says, looking me over. "Are you alright? I hated myself for leaving you after Cimari hurt you like that, but I had to. You understand, don't you?"

"Of course I do," I assure her. "Bard told me what you did. It was brilliant. But what about you? Is it really terrible here?"

"Not terrible, exactly," Sadra says. "Just painfully, numbingly boring. We're here to contemplate the abstract and intangible: We study movement, but we don't dance. We study the theory of sound, but never sing. We—never mind. I take it back. Yes, it is terrible. Stars, I can't stand it!" She laughs. "But enough of that. Tell me everything!"

We settle ourselves among the crates and potato sacks, getting as comfortable as we can. Luca and I tell her everything we can think of, from Bard's slip with Luca to the confrontation in the tavern to Bard's shocking proposal. Sadra listens intently. I can see emotions flickering across her face, but she doesn't interrupt. When we finish, she sits back, shaking her head dazedly.

"Stars above," she says. "Your grandfather!"

"Only technically." I shift uneasily. I can't bring myself to call him Aleksandr, even in my head, much less think of him as my grandfather. "I hardly know him."

"But now you can!" Sadra says eagerly. "Imagine!"

"I'd rather not," I mutter.

"I don't understand you, Sasha." She wrinkles her nose and gives a frustrated huff. "First your mother, now—but wait! Your mother—does he know?"

I look away. "I don't think so. I—we had other things to discuss."

"But you have to tell him!" Sadra cries. "If there's a chance he could find his daughter…"

"I'll tell him before I go," I promise. "You're right. He—he has a right to know."

"Before you go." Sadra blinks several times and swallows. "So it's true, then? You can go home?"

For the first time, I understand Bard's reluctance to answer that question. I can't say yes, but I can't say no, either. Luca's eyes are on me, burning a hole in the top of my head. I look up and meet his eyes, my throat constricting into a tight knot.

"Bard says he was given a choice when the Pall was removed," I say, my voice strained and ragged. "To come back to Kingsgarden or go home. He chose to come back. He said the same thing happened to every fledgling—at least, all those who lived to tell him about it. They think that the ones who didn't survive chose to go back to their own world."

Sadra and Luca both stare at me, aghast.

I look away. "I have to go home. If there's even the slightest chance, I have to take it."

After a long pause, Sadra says, "You can't be serious."

"I have to try," I whisper.

"Try to do what, exactly?" Sadra is on her feet now, her fists clenched. "All you know is that you can choose to live or die. You want to choose death and—what, hope it doesn't stick? I refuse to believe you're that stupid."

"What do you want me to do?" I demand. "You said it yourself. The Pall could kill me in as little as two years, and I've lived with it for nearly six months. At least this way, I have a chance at going home."

"Bard said you could choose," Luca says softly. "You could choose to stay."

"You think I should just forget about Emily?" I ask, but the question comes out sounding more curious than pointed. "You think I should give up on everything and everyone I left behind?"

Luca doesn't flinch or avoid the question. He looks at me steadily and says, "Yes. At least, I think you should let them go. You don't know what you'd be going back to. There's a very good chance that they've moved on. They've grieved for you, and they've let you go—but we haven't. I'm not saying your old life isn't important or that it isn't worth fighting for, but...you *have* fought, Sasha. You tried. You kept your promise. Your Emily wouldn't want you to take such a stupid risk."

My hands tighten into fists. "You don't even know her. How can you possibly know what she'd want?"

"Because it's what *we* want," Luca says, his eyes snapping. But he continues calmly, "We want you to be safe—we want you to *live*. If we knew for sure you could make it back, if we had more to go on than a very flimsy 'maybe'…but we don't, Sasha."

"And what kind of life will I have here, if I stay?" I demand. "Will I spend the rest of my days living in fear, looking over my shoulder for the House of Light and Shadow and pretending to be something I'm not?"

"That's not how it will be," Luca says. "My brother will listen to us. I know he will."

"So what if he does?" I give him a withering look. "You think the House will just step aside?"

"No, of course not," Sadra jumps in. "But you're underestimating the individuals who make up the House. Only a very small, select minority actually knows the truth about thralls. The House teaches that strength is the pinnacle of beauty, but it doesn't always create power hungry monsters—quite the opposite, in fact. There's a veritable army of Lightcrafters right here in the City dedicated to protecting and providing for those who can't do for themselves. I can't believe that they would just stand by if they knew. It will be hard, I won't deny that. But you could have a life here, Sasha, a good one."

"I—no. It doesn't matter." I shake my head, my hands over my ears. "You don't understand! Emily—"

"*Stop it.*" Luca wrenches me to my feet so that his face is inches from my own. "We do understand—better than you do, I'll wager. Emily isn't the only one who cares about you, Sasha. She isn't the only one who has made sacrifices for you. And hers is not the only heart that will break if you die."

"Isn't there anything here worth living for?" Sadra asks softly. "Do

I mean nothing to you? Does Luca?"

"Of course not." I reach for her and take her hands. "Never think that. But how can I stay, knowing what I've left behind? Would you do what you're asking of me? When I thought I was leaving for the City of Lilies, I was so close to falling on my knees and begging you to come with me. But I didn't, because I knew there was someone you couldn't abandon. I would never ask you to."

Tears shimmer in Sadra's eyes. "That's not fair, Sasha."

"Of course it isn't." My throat is so swollen and tight that I can barely force the words out. "But life isn't fair, is it? I know that better than most."

"But it's not the same thing at all," Sadra insists, her voice stronger now. "How can I not ask you—beg you—to choose us when the alternative is death?"

"Bard might be wrong," I whisper. "The choice might not be a choice at all. I don't know what's going to happen. But I don't want to go knowing that you hate me."

Sadra pulls me into a tight hug. "I don't hate you, idiot."

"Thank you, Sadra." I squeeze my eyes closed, locking the tears safe inside. "For everything."

"Goodbye," Sadra whispers, and lets me go.

Luca says nothing when I turn to face him. His shoulders and jaw remain tight and stiff as he helps me back into the tunnel and stalks away, leaving me to scramble after him as best I can. Even if Sadra doesn't hate me, he surely does.

Well, he's not the only one. I hate myself for putting him through this, and for lying to him for so long. At the same time, the thought of leaving him steals the very breath from my lungs. I imagine waking up each day, knowing that I'll never see him or even speak of him again, and my belly fills with shards of glass.

Luca stops so suddenly I crash into his back and bounce off. He steadies me with a hand clamped around my upper arm and indicates a narrow passage that I didn't notice on the way up to the cloisters.

"I want to show you something," he says. "I found it the first time I came through here, but I've never spoken of it to anyone. We have to leave the torch here. Hold onto me."

I nod silently and hook my fingers into his belt.

We move into the dark, groping with hands and feet over the uneven stone. The blackness is all-consuming, almost solid. I feel as though I should be able to scoop it away with my hands.

"There," Luca finally says, and pulls me through a narrow gap between the stones.

I blink, trying to make sense of the cold drops of silver and white before my eyes. Slowly, my vision adjusts, and I gasp in wonder. It's a lake, smooth and clear as glass, and in its center lies a reflection of the moon and stars contained in a near perfect circle.

We stand for several minutes without speaking or touching. Just looking—and listening, but to what, I don't know. Finally, Luca breaks the silence.

"I think this is—or was—a holy place," he says softly.

"Yes. Yes, I think so, too." I look up at him, but all I can see is his silhouette. "Luca, why are we here?"

"Because I have something to tell you," he says. "And I thought that here, in this place…I don't know. Perhaps it's only that I'm a coward, and I'm afraid to see your face."

"Tell me," I whisper.

Luca's hands settle on my shoulders. Involuntarily, I find myself leaning into his warmth.

"I want you to stay," he says. "I should have told you sooner. I told myself I was respecting your wishes, that I shouldn't burden you with my own desires, but the truth is that I simply didn't have the courage. I want you to stay…not just in Kingsgarden, but with me. I love you,

Sasha."

I rest my forehead against his chest, my eyes closed. I think I can hear my heart breaking open—but no, it's only the rattle of one loose stone against another. My whole body aches with the need to weep. But the tears don't come, and neither does the promise Luca is no doubt hoping for. I can't tell him I'll stay, that he means more to me than Emily does. But I won't lie to him, either. So I tell him the truth.

"I love you."

I know it's not enough, but it's all I have.

* * *

Luca and I stand shoulder to shoulder at the lip of a soaring cliff, looking down into the valley. The City of Roses, true to its name, glows red in the sunset. The sun's dying rays wash over the expanse of white marble and pink sandstone, the towers shot with gleaming sparks of gold.

I don't know if I'll return. If I do, will I be any more whole than I am now? I'll be free of the Pall but burdened by grief and broken promises. I'll be embroiled in a political struggle with not just moral but mortal consequences. The House will know my name, my face.

But I'll have Luca. I'll have Sadra. And they'll have me, for whatever that's worth. I'll be there to share in the struggle.

If I leave, they'll keep fighting for freedom and justice while I return to my own world—and do what? Will I go back to dancing from dawn to dusk, always chasing the next role and competing with a hundred other girls with the same dream? Will that even be an option, or will I wake to find myself years, maybe even decades older and buried under a mountain of medical debt?

Will I wake up at all?

"Sasha," Luca says quietly. "We need to keep moving."

"Tell Bard I'm coming," I say. "I just…need a minute."

Luca nods and moves off as silently as the fox pacing at his side. I turn back to the City, my eyes crawling over every line, every spire until, finally, my gaze comes to rest on the shadowy pocket of the Terrace.

Such things I've seen, such terrible, terrible beauty. I wonder if that's what it means to grow up—to see the terror in beauty, the shadow behind the light. If it is, I've grown up and then some. I feel old, now. Old and confused and scared of what lies on the other side of death.

Wind whips through my hair, stinging my eyes. I begin to hum, then to sing.

"Bayu, bayushki, bayu."

Jeté

Luca lies on his side, tracing the lines of my tattoo with a fingertip. I shiver as his palm flattens over the swan on my hip, his hand warm and rough and far more familiar than I ever thought possible. After our confession in the tunnels, I meant to shut him out. I meant to protect him.

But I didn't. I couldn't. We spent the night tangled together in the dark, too desperate and too drunk with desire to let each other go. If my love was all I had to give, I wanted him to have all of it. All of me. So I gave myself to him, that night and every night since. He'll have me every night that I live and breathe in this world.

I watch him through my lashes, my eyes half closed. There's a curious expression on his face, half-tender and half-pained. It's a familiar expression by now, and I'm sure the same look has appeared on my own face this last week.

Sometimes I come around a corner or look up suddenly and catch a glimpse of his face, unguarded, and feel something inside me come loose, as if whatever was holding me together suddenly isn't. Then he smiles at me and I come together again, but something is subtly, unaccountably different. The fabric that holds me together has changed, just a little bit. Every time this happens a little shiver runs up my spine. I never can tell if the shiver is one of fear or pleasure.

"What are you thinking?" Luca asks, his hand coming to rest on my cheek.

"That you're changing me," I say without thinking.

Luca draws back in surprise. "How so?"

"I'm not sure," I reply. "But I don't think it's a bad thing."

He opens his mouth, then shuts it. But I see the sudden surge of hope flash across his face and feel an answering thrill in my own heart. It dissipates almost as quickly as it came, replaced by guilt—and confusion. I don't even know anymore what to feel guilty about or who I'm going to hurt when the Apostate finally arrives.

If he arrives.

We traveled for nearly a week, only to find ourselves holed up for the last two days in a hay loft, the only accommodation available in the tiny mountain village of Twin Oaks. Bard is camped somewhere out in the hills in hopes of meeting the Apostate on his way into the village. Ornery as he is, I imagine he's happier out there away from the cheerful bustling of the villagers.

"Let's go," Luca says, blowing the straw dust from my hair. "Petal will be waiting for his feed."

As if in answer, a high-pitched neigh sounds from the stall below us, accompanied by the thump of a plate-sized hoof striking wood. I squirm over to the edge of the loft and look down at Luca's gargantuan war horse. I've never seen anything that looks less like a flower. 'Petal,' if that is, in fact, his real name and Luca isn't just teasing me, stands higher than my head at the shoulder, a massive gray mountain of flesh. He's positively monstrous, and I'm half afraid that if I were to fall out of the loft he'd try to eat me, herbivore or not.

I wait until Petal is safely occupied with his breakfast before I dress and follow Luca down the ladder. Luca laughs as I skirt around the edges of the stall, giving Petal a wide berth.

"Come here," he says, hooking an arm around my waist. "Acting like a mouse won't help. It makes him nervous to know that you're nervous."

"How do you know? Can you understand him like you understand Kirit?" I shuffle sideways so that Luca is between me and Petal.

"No, but you don't have to be a Beastspeaker to know that about horses." Luca frowns, staring at Petal. "It's odd, though. Normally I don't have much of a feel at all for grass-eaters. But this morning I could have sworn I *heard* him before I heard him, if you know what I mean."

"Oh, yes," I say dryly. "That's perfectly clear."

"Come on," he says, ruffling my hair. "Let's go eat."

We duck out of the barn and stroll among the massive oaks for which the town was named. Their gnarled trunks and branches tower protectively over the shingle rooftops, dappling every surface in swirling patterns of dark and light. It's a beautiful place, Twin Oaks, but that's not why I love it here. I love this village because there's not a single Lightcrafter and not a single thrall. The village is living proof that life can be made beautiful with one's own gifts. The kingdom doesn't *need* thralls to survive. It can work. It will…but will I be here to see it?

Kirit is already at the tavern, begging scraps from a young girl as she clears the tables. He doesn't have to work that hard—the tavern keeper's eldest daughter was smitten within moments of meeting him. I smile as she dangles a chicken bone over his head, giggling. Kirit plays along, snapping and jumping. He's fast enough to snatch the morsel whenever he chooses, but he likes children.

Luca and I share a hearty breakfast and then go our separate ways for the day, he to assist with the training of a shepherd dog and I to mind the tavern keeper's youngest children while his wife is helping in the kitchen. The tavern keeper wouldn't let us pay as he didn't have a room for us, but we insisted on doing what we can to help out. The whole village is teeming with visitors come to celebrate a spring festival of some kind, and there's plenty of work to be done.

Kirit and I have a wonderful time singing and playing games with the children. Changing the baby's nappies is less wonderful, as I am also responsible for rinsing the soiled ones, but I get it done. The work is simple and sweet, just like the girls, and I'm almost sorry to hand them over to their mother after the dinner rush.

"You'll be wanting to join in the festivities," she says, tucking the baby against her shoulder. "Go on with you, and your young man, too."

I look over my shoulder and see Luca waiting for me near the door. He watches me with an odd look on his face, something almost like hunger. Then I realize he's looking not just at me but at the toddler in my arms. With a quick smile at the tavern mistress, I set down the little girl and go to Luca, who brushes my cheek with a kiss.

"Luca." I push him away so I can see his face. "I've never asked—how old are you?"

He looks at me in surprise. "Twenty. Why?"

I bite my lip. In my world, he could be in college. But here in Kingsgarden, many men are fathers at his age. I'm nineteen by now, I think. Many girls are mothers at my age, too. A wave of some unnamed emotion washes over me, half fear and half longing. I can see it so clearly: a little girl with high, wide cheekbones and green eyes. I wait for the instinctive denial that must surely follow…but it doesn't. The image hangs in my mind as if waiting for me to reach out and take it.

I take Luca's hand instead and we join the river of people outside. Some have candles, but most carry small, makeshift torches woven from dried grass. They move slowly, singing something haunting and solemn in unison. It must be some country dialect, for I can only catch a few words.

The crowd carries us to the center of town, where a huge bonfire roars like a hungry dragon in the courtyard. Even out here in the hills, the center square is beautifully decorated. Instead of marble statues, trees have been trained to grow in spirals and starbursts. Vines cover the walls and houses surrounding the courtyard. It's like a little pocket of forest in the middle of town.

"This is beautiful," I murmur in Luca's ear. The singing has died away, replaced with an expectant silence. "What festival is this again?"

"The Festival of Lights," he whispers back. "To mark the birth of spring."

"Is that a holiday in the City?" I ask with a frown.

"Yes, but it's not a big celebration like it is in the country," Luca tells me. "Households usually just make small offerings, say a special prayer, that kind of thing. The changing of the seasons doesn't mean as much to them."

"What happens now?" I ask.

"Wait and see."

Suddenly there's a cheer as musicians buried in the crowd begin to play. A space clears in the center of the courtyard and a group of young men and young women face off, each side joining hands and holding them high above their heads as they begin to move. I watch the dance, mesmerized, my feet aching with the need to join in. I look at Luca.

"Can we?" I ask, pointing at the dancers.

He grins and moves forward, pulling me after him. We wiggle our way through the crowd until we pop out in the center circle just in time to catch the tail of the girls' line as it passes by. Luca gives me a little shove and I snatch the hand of the last girl in line. I stumble through the first couple of steps until I get the footwork down and then lift my head, smiling at the girl next to me. She smiles back and squeezes my hand. The other girls laugh and hoot, seemingly delighted with my nerve in joining the dance.

I gasp in surprise as the leader of the men's line leaps into the air, supported and propelled by the one next to him, and spins. He lands lightly in a crouch like a cat and slaps the ground before coming up to cheers and trilling shouts from the crowd.

As if it's a signal, the girls vary the dance and I have to scramble again until I find the new pattern. But it's fun. It's so, so much fun. It's nothing like the precise, carefully crafted dances in the City where every step is planned and rehearsed ahead of time. Everyone takes turns leading the line and adding her own ornamentation to the dance while the other dancers follow along. When it's my turn, I feel like I'm a little kid at my first recital. My heart pounding, I add a twist and spin, dropping down to slap the ground as the men had done. The crowd shouts with glee at that. My eyes pass over the crowd until I find Luca beaming with pride as he elbows the man beside him and points at me. Kirit darts forward and prances along at my heels, yapping excitedly as I drop to the back of the line.

I crane my neck as the line travels around the circle, looking for Luca again, and instead find myself staring into familiar green eyes set in an unfamiliar face. A girl's face. Her skin and hair are fair where Luca's are dark, and there's an arrogant tilt to her chin that I've never seen in Luca, but she has the same tall, rangy form and angled cheekbones. It can only be Arismendi, Luca's sister. Her eyes, Luca's eyes, are fixed on my face with an expression of such horror and fear it's like she's wearing a mask. She stands completely still, locked in place against the rhythmic sway of the crowd.

And then she's gone, hidden by the soaring flames of the bonfire.

Luca calls out to me, beckoning, and I break away from the line of dancers. I move swiftly to his side, suddenly uneasy. She can't have known what I am, though I suppose it's not impossible that she might have guessed *who* I am—in general terms, at least. It's common knowledge in the City that the king's brother has won the favor of a

Companion. That by itself, however, wouldn't explain the strangeness of her reaction. I pull Luca's head down so I can speak directly into his ear.

"I think I saw your sister," I say, almost shouting.

"What, here?" He straightens up so he can scan the crowd, an uneasy frown pulling down the corners of his mouth. "Are you sure?"

"No," I admit. "But she looked just like you. Tall, with blond hair and green eyes."

"Where did you see her?"

"She was on the other side of the bonfire." I curl my fingers around his. "But, Luca…I think she's not there anymore. I think something's wrong."

In a rush, I tell him what I saw. I study his face carefully, looking for reassurance. A smile, a laugh, some sign to tell me that what I saw wasn't worth worrying over. I want him to tell me that there's a simple explanation for his sister's presence here and that all is well.

But he doesn't tell me that. A cloud seems to pass over Luca's face as he listens, and with every word I speak, my hopes sink a little lower.

"Come," he says, taking my hand. "We should go."

"Go where?" I ask, following close on his heels as we push our way through the crowd.

"Away from here," he replies. "Out of the village."

"But where—"

"Just move, Sasha."

Alarmed by his tone, I shut my mouth and elbow a fat, jolly-looking man out of my way. I wind my fingers through Luca's belt and hold on tight as he plunges through the mass of bodies. No one protests beyond a few dirty looks; everyone's energy and attention are focused on the music and dancing and the sparks of the bonfire flying upward into the night. But the music has gone sour in my ears, and the silhouettes of the dancers against the flames now seem sinister and foreboding. The spinning, leaping fairies have turned into ghouls, demons cavorting in the flames of hell.

Finally, we escape into an empty street and break into a run, back toward the barn that houses Petal. Luca saddles him with brisk efficiency and leads him outside while I collect our things. He takes the pack from my trembling hands and vaults onto the horse's back, pulling me up after him. Kirit trots ahead, leading us out of the town under the bright silver light of a full moon.

"What about Bard?" I ask.

"He'll find us," Luca assures me. "Or we'll find him."

"But this isn't how we came," I observe tentatively.

Instead of taking the road back to the City, we're heading deeper into the hills. Petal doesn't seem to mind, at least. He surges up the rocky path with self-satisfied snorts, as if to say, *Puny humans, where would you be without me?*

"No," Luca agrees. "We'll return to the City by another route. I'm sorry to drag you out of there like that. I have an inkling of what happened, but until we find out exactly what Ari knows—or what she thinks she knows—I'd rather be overly careful."

"What do you mean?" I ask. "How could she know anything?"

"Ari is Gifted with foresight," Luca explains. "But her premonitions don't come as visions, or even clear information. They're more like very strong hunches. It must have been a very strong one to send her after us all the way out here."

"And what do you think her hunch could have been?"

"As to that, I couldn't say." His voice is calm, but I can feel the tension in his back and shoulders, hard and taut against my own body. "Not the truth—at least, not the whole truth, or she wouldn't have run."

"We should have gone after her," I say unhappily.

"No," Luca replies. "Ari always travels with at least one House mage as part of her guard. She might not know what you are, but, depending on the exact nature of her premonition and what she's told them, the mages might guess." Luca shakes his head, releasing a sharp breath of frustration. "Shadow and blight! Of all the times for her Gift to make itself known."

"Doesn't it usually?"

Luca shakes his head; I wish I could see his face.

"No. It's happened only twice before. Once before our father died, and once before an earthquake."

"Oh," I say, my voice very small.

It doesn't take much effort to imagine what Ari might have seen: death, destruction, political unrest. Civil war, even.

I press my forehead against Luca's spine. It seemed so simple: leave the City, meet with the Apostate. Could this latest complication have been prevented, somehow, or is it just bad luck? Luca knew about his sister's Gift, after all. But, curiously, I feel no anger or blame. It all feels inevitable somehow. If anything, I feel a vague sense of release, as if I'd been teetering back and forth on the edge of a precipice, just waiting to fall, and now someone has come up behind me and pushed me off.

I feel strangely calm. Numb, almost. Fear will no doubt find me, but it hasn't yet. The magnitude of what's coming is too great. I can't comprehend it, so I can't fear it. But I will, I know, because nothing approaches forever. At some point, it *arrives*. And then, I know, I will be afraid.

* * *

A cold wetness presses against my cheek. I jerk, scrambling away until I recognize Kirit's dim outline. The space beside me under the rocky overhang where we made our bed is empty and cold. I crawl

293

out from under the overhang and squint at the shadowy silhouettes of the trees. Clouds have drifted over the moon while I slept, turning silver to black and white to gray. A breeze creeps over my skin and lifts my hair gently from my ears and neck, flicking over and around my body like cold, curious fingers.

Where is Petal? More importantly, where is Luca? I shiver and suppress the impulse to cry out. He wouldn't leave me without good reason, and I can only imagine the good reason is something that won't be helped by giving away our hiding place. No, the best thing I can do is wait. I hunker down in a dip between two rocks. Kirit crouches motionless at my side, his eyes bright even in the gloom.

Our vigil doesn't last long. Luca appears at my side without a sound and motions for me to follow him up the rocky outcropping. I do, stepping where he steps and trying my best to move as he moves. Even so, I make twice as much noise as he does. He seems to float over the fallen leaves and needles and loose rocks without even touching them. It reminds me, oddly, of how Ismeni used to sweep around the halls of her villa as if on soundless, invisible wheels. Even though I'm a dancer, it's a kind of grace entirely foreign to me.

At the top of the outcropping, Luca pulls me into the shadow of a boulder and leans close to whisper in my ear.

"There are dozens of House mages and rangers heading our way," he says. "I sent Petal away to lay a false trail, but they never wavered. Ari must have given them something of mine for a casting to find me."

"But how did so many get here so quickly?" I ask, baffled.

"With Light," Luca says. "It's a filthy, barbaric practice. I knew that much even before I knew the truth about Light. One body takes the place of another—destroying it in the process."

"I saw it happen once," I say, suddenly remembering. "You—you were there. The Premier summoned Pretty Girl—a puppy—for Cimari. A little bird died."

Luca stares at me with wide eyes. "I...yes, I remember. Blight, how many times must I have seen you and had no idea? How much time have I wasted?"

He kisses me hard. I cling to him, desperation and fear writhing together in my chest. But he steps back, leaving me trembling and wide-eyed.

"Kirit will be able to find Bard. Get back to the City and claim sanctuary at the Temple. I'll find you there."

"What about you?" I protest, gripping his wrists as he moves to lower his hands from my face. "What are you going to do?"

"I'll lead them as far away from you as I can," he says bleakly. "Don't worry about me. I'll come for you, whatever happens. Do you believe me?"

I nod jerkily and release him, then freeze as the distant cry of a baying hound reaches our ears. The hair on the back of my neck stands on end.

"They're coming," I breathe, fear washing over me like a stream of icy water.

"Go, Sasha!" Luca hisses, pushing me away from him. "Now—run!"

I stumble backward and trip over a loose rock. By the time I find my feet, Luca is gone.

The hounds' baying is louder now, and maybe it's just my imagination, but it seems to have taken on a note of urgency and excitement. A tremor runs through my body. It's happening. *Bozhe.* It's finally happening. They've found me.

But that doesn't mean they'll catch me.

I follow Kirit down the other side of the hill, moving as quickly as I can without losing my footing. As soon as I reach level ground, I run. But the ground doesn't stay level for long. Despite my long hours of training, I'm wheezing and stumbling after the fifth hill. Or is it the sixth?

"Kirit," I gasp. "Stop. I need to stop."

I clasp my hands behind my head and grimace with the effort of staying upright. Kirit whines and paws at my leg, urging me to go on. I can't—I can't! My legs and back are shaking so violently I'm afraid I'll break apart, my head is spinning, and I could lose the contents of my stomach at any moment, but I have to keep going. Memory surfaces: a man running for his life, a spear—and blood. So much blood.

"That won't be me," I pant, and force myself into motion.

Every breath burns in my lungs, but I breathe. Every step makes my very bones ache, but I run. Better to run until my heart bursts than to let them take me again. I won't let them take me, hurt me, bleed me dry like those poor children.

With a rush of energy born of pure terror, I burst over the crest of yet another hill—and promptly tumble into nothingness. The world flies apart around me as I slide and somersault down the unexpectedly steep slope on the other side, every rock and bush I meet just shy of big enough to halt my headlong descent.

When I finally roll to a stop, all I can do is lie still while the now-visible stars wheel and spin above me. Every inch of me is battered and scraped raw, and an alarming amount of blood runs down the side of my face. When I try to stand, the ground shifts under me like a waking giant. I stumble, gasping as I catch myself on shredded palms.

"That was quite the fall," a voice observes. "Acrobatic, almost."

Slowly, I raise my throbbing head and squint at the gangling teenager in front of me. He stares back with bulging, frog-like eyes, a slight smile on his pale face. He turns his face up to the moon, now freed of the clouds, and then looks back at me again with that creepy smile.

"I thought you'd look different," he muses. "More…impressive, somehow. The elders preach to us about the dangers of spirit-walkers from the day we enter the Academy. I expected horns, scales…a wart, at least. But you're quite pretty." He studies me closely. "I suppose it was a silly notion, anyway. Spirit walkers look like everyone else—they can be anyone, thrall or citizen. That's what makes them so dangerous, isn't it? But still. This is just—well, it's disappointing is what it is."

He sighs dramatically, and it suddenly hits me just how young he is. He can't be any older than I am.

Something about him—the swagger, the drama, maybe even the sprinkle of acne—reminds me of Dave. Loathsome Dave, who turned out not to be so loathsome under the veneer of arrogance. Is there more to this House minion? Some semblance of kindness under his gloating cruelty?

"Please," I croak. "You don't understand. I'm not a spirit-walker. They lied to you, they—"

"Silence!"

He strikes an impressive pose, but the line of his shoulders is smudged by self-consciousness and doubt. Hope trembles in my chest.

"You're not supposed to be here, are you?" I ask.

"Silence," he says again, with much less bravado. But it only takes him a moment to regain his cocky little smile. He taps a finger against his pimpled chin. "No, I'm not. I have a Gift for finding things. The elders don't put much store in the old ways, it's true. But I think in this case they'll be pleased nonetheless."

"They're *liars*."

I close my eyes, overcome by the sheer unfairness of it all—everything, from the atrocities the House has committed to the lies they've propagated to cover them up, right down to the fact that I'm now forced to beg this obnoxious, arrogant little cretin for my life. My eyes snap open. No. I will not do that. I will not beg.

Though I can't see him, I know Kirit is somewhere nearby, and I know his ears are sharper than anything I can imagine.

"Kirit," I whisper. *"Hurt him."*

"What's that?" The boy's eyes narrow. "What did you say?"

I don't wait to see where Kirit strikes. As soon as he breaks cover, I bolt sideways along the base of the slope. One of my legs drags, slowing me down. I don't think it's broken, but something is definitely wrong. There's a deep, fierce ache that burns in my knee like a hot coal.

A rushing sound fills my ears. At first, I think it's my own harsh breathing. But then a cold mist touches my face, and the stone beneath my feet grows slick. I skid to a stop at the edge of a roaring waterfall and teeter for a moment, my heart in my throat. I throw myself backward just in time to avoid an enormous chunk of ice as it crashes against the stony bank and hurtles over the edge. I inch forward and watch it disappear into the mist far, *far* below. What lies beyond that mist? A river, rushing angry and white over the rocks? Or a lake, rippling silver under the light of a full moon?

"There's nowhere left to run. Come with me now."

He's found me. Faces flicker before my eyes: Emily, Luca, Baba Nadia, Sadra, Bard, Mother Wenla…so many things I never got to say and never will. All my love for them, and theirs for me, comes to nothing. My own words echo back to me through time and whatever else separates this world and the other.

It's about freedom, not love.

I answer the young man with my back turned and my eyes closed. "No."

And I jump.

IV

Act Four: Con Fuoco

"It is only through mystery and madness that the soul is revealed."

-Thomas Moore

Porté

I wake to the sound of dripping water and the chattering of my own teeth. I'm damp, but not soaked, and lying on hard, cold stone. Did I make it? Have I by some miracle washed up on the rocky shore of the river? For several minutes I cling to this hope, not daring to open my eyes, until a small, rhythmic thumping reaches my ears—footsteps.

No, no, *no.* I squeeze my eyes even more tightly shut, as if I can change the truth of where I am if only I deny it hard enough. I can't be here, I *can't.* I jumped. I made my peace with death—but not this. Not the House of Light and Shadow.

"I knew it," a voice whispers. "I *knew* it."

My eyes fly open. I know that voice. It's haunted my nightmares for months.

"Cimari," I breathe.

She peers down at me through a small window. Traces of light creep under the door and around her face, illuminating only my immediate surroundings: stone walls, stone floor. Nothing else.

"Please—listen to me." I speak in a low, urgent voice. Ismeni cared about this girl. There must be a reason. There must be something good or fair or at least reasonable in her character. "I'm not what you think I am."

"Actually, I know exactly what you are," Cimari says. A trace of pride colors her voice. "My husband trusts me. He told me the truth weeks ago."

"You know," I repeat, dumbfounded. "Then why—"

"Why don't I free you?" Cimari says, tilting her head. "Because without you, there is no Light."

She says it as if it's simple. And I suppose it is. She wants power and doesn't care where it comes from.

"Besides," she goes on. "You're not a *person*." She waves off my protest. "I know you probably believe you are. But you're just an echo, really. Memory made flesh. The real entity, whoever she was, is long gone."

Her words take my breath away. In just a few words, she's confirmed my every fear. But she's wrong. She has to be wrong.

"That's not true," I say unsteadily. "I have a life. I have a family."

"You *had* a life," Cimari corrects me. "You had a family. But no longer. You forgot them once. You'll forget them again."

"Never," I swear.

Cimari shrugs. "We'll see."

She slides a panel over the window, leaving me in complete darkness. I back slowly into the corner and hug my knees. Spasms of cold and shock wrack my body until my muscles simply lock, clenching and clenching with no release. But I have no thought for my body—this body. Cimari's right about that, at least. Though in nearly every physical particular it's exactly the same, this isn't the body I was born with—it was created, somehow. So what does that make me?

"No," I whisper. "*No.*"

I thump my head against the wall hard enough to see stars and—almost—hard enough to shake that thought right out of my head.

I am real. I am Aleksandra. Sasha. A real girl with real thoughts and passions and emotions. I feel pain and fear and joy—and love.

Once I admitted it to myself, I never once doubted Luca's love for me, nor mine for him. And I won't start now. Luca loves me, and he'll find me. He'll come for me, like he said. All I have to do is wait.

And so I wait. I work diligently at an imaginary barre, filling the hours with calm, smooth motion and the soothing stretch and release of my muscles. But as the hours turn into days, my limbs begin to falter. I've received no food and little water. Much as it did during those first days in the Cage, my mind weakens with my body.

I begin to forget. Little things at first, like the exact words Cimari used to torment me during her latest visit or which corner I used to relieve myself. Then I forget her name. I forget that I ever tried to confine my business to one corner. I forget that someone is coming to find me and take me away from this place. I forget that I was ever outside these walls. And I forget how to dance.

When I sleep, I hear things: Voices calling to me, begging me to wake up. Voices carrying on one-sided conversations that I don't understand. Voices singing, voices sobbing. Sometimes, I hear music. Beautiful, otherworldly music that makes me want to do...something. I'm not sure what it is I want to do, but the desire is so strong it wakes me up.

Often, it takes me several minutes to determine if I'm awake or asleep. I can't remember the last time I saw anything but black. There was a light once, I think. Just a little. It came through the cracks between the rough bits. But there hasn't been any for a long time. I think it's been a long time, but I don't know.

I don't know anything.

* * *

"Sasha," a voice whispers. "I don't know if you can hear me. They say you might. But they say a lot of things."

For a moment I can't hear anything but heavy breathing. I feel warmth...somewhere. My hand? My face? I don't know. My body hasn't moved in so long that I can't remember what lies where.

"Everyone's doing alright. James came by earlier, do you remember? He said to remind you that we're all praying for you. He'd be here with me now, but it's bad luck to see the bride before the wedding. I'm getting married tonight, can you believe it? I wish you could be there, honey. I wish that more than anything."

"I want you to know I love you," the voice goes on. "And that I'm sorry. I'm so sorry. I tried to take care of you. I did my best. And you did yours, baby. It's okay if you're tired. It's okay if you want to stop. But if you can, if you have anything left...keep trying. Come back to me, please. You can't be gone, not yet. Please, Sasha."

* * *

The voice fades away as I swim back to consciousness. I blink. Something is different. The voices are different. And they're angry. One voice in particular stands out. I focus on it, my brows furrowed in concentration. The voice makes me feel strange—warm, and a bit floaty. Odd.

Light flares, sending me scurrying like a rat into a corner where I cower, shielding my watering eyes. The light hurts almost beyond bearing. I whimper and press myself against the stone. I want it to go away—all of it: the light, the noise, everything. But now there are hands on my shoulders, pulling me away from the wall.

"Sasha. Come on, Sasha, you're alright."

It's *that* voice. I don't know why it pulls at me so. The words mean nothing to me. *Am* I alright? I don't know—probably not. *Speak to me,* the voice seems to beg. But what should I say? I'm not sure I can speak now, or if I ever could.

"Hold on," the voice says. "I've got you."

I freeze as I find myself suddenly hoisted into the air and held against something hard and warm. A soft puff of air ruffles my matted hair.

I look around wildly, trying to make sense of the shifting, shadowy forms moving around me. Slowly, my eyes stop watering and I can see that the corridor outside my cell is crowded with men. Some wear robes, some wear swords. All of them are shouting.

"You have no authority here," one of the robed men blusters, puffing up like a rooster.

"As I'm sure you've been informed, I'm here by order of the king," the warm voice says somewhere above me. "Are you challenging *his* authority?"

"The king cannot know the danger this creature poses," the robed man objects. "My lord Premier is with him at this moment, explaining matters. I must insist that you leave that—*thing* where you found it and return to the palace. You're not needed here."

"On the contrary, I believe I am needed here," the warm voice says politely. "But if you'll step aside, I would be more than happy to return to the palace, as you say. The Premier is not the only mage with explanations for my brother. Perhaps you've heard of a man named Porr?"

"Apostate," the robed man hisses, drawing back in shock. But he quickly rallies. "You cannot—"

"Step. Aside." The warm voice has gone steely. "I am leaving, and I'm taking this girl with me. If you try to stop me, there will be bloodshed. I trained as a Lightcrafter in this very facility, as did every one of my guards. Do you really think you can stop us?"

With a flash of light and steel, we sweep past the gaggle of robed men. The man holding me leads us unerringly through a maze of corridors and cavernous rooms until we emerge onto a narrow ledge.

Not three feet from where we stand, the ground drops away into the narrow valley of the Terrace.

I frown. *The Terrace.* I don't know where the name came from or what it means, exactly, but I know that's what the valley is called. I must have been there before. But when? And why? As far, far up as we are, I can still see the perfectly manicured gardens and fancy houses lining the valley. What would someone like me be doing in a place like that?

The arms around me tighten as we make our way down the mountainside. I press my face into the smooth leather jerkin under my cheek, but not out of fear. Both the garment and the body beneath it feel familiar, safe. The heartbeat under my ear tickles my memory like a half-forgotten but beloved song. *You knew me once,* it seems to say. *Know me again. Remember.*

I want to remember. My head aches with trying. But something stands in the way, pliable and formless but solid, like a blanket with no end and no beginning. Has it always been there? Maybe—I can't tell. I'm so confused. What is wrong with me? I know I'm not supposed to feel like this, but I don't know why. I close my eyes and listen to the voices in my head. Maybe they can tell me.

* * *

I drift, floating through something that's neither air nor water. I want to go to the voices that have become my familiar companions these eternities past, but a new voice intrudes, pulling me away toward something that fills me with both dread and longing.

"Remember who you are," the new voice whispers. "Remember that day in the garden? You spoke to me. You told me your name. You're Sasha and I'm Sadra. Remember what I said? Sasha and Sadra—it sounds good

together, doesn't it? Remember. We danced together. You taught me your art and I taught you mine.

"You're my friend—my best friend. My sister. Remember.

"You were in a cage, but you flew away. You fell in love. He's a good man. His name is Luca. Remember..."

The old voices become fainter. Dimmer, somehow. I can't catch the words anymore. But I still hear the desperation, the grief. Guilt gnaws at me, pushing me away and pulling at me at the same time. Which way do I go? Forward or back? Up or down? But which is which?

And does it matter?

"Don't leave me," the voice whispers. "Remember..."

The voice whispers ceaselessly, giving me the story of my life—or part of it. When she—it feels like a she—whispers to me, I find myself nodding along, thinking, yes, that's true, that's how it was. But then I hear the old voices, the sad voices, and they feel true, too.

I don't know what to think.

And so I retreat until, finally, I can't hide anymore.

* * *

Music pulls me out of the darkness and into a bright, airy room filled with simple but elegant furnishings. A green-eyed man and a girl with golden eyes sit beside my bed. She plucks a small harp, her fingers rippling smoothly across the strings. He balances a narrow instrument like a violin on his knee, drawing a familiar melody out of the tiny piece of wood.

I rest my gaze on his face, admiring the hard lines of his jaw and cheekbones and the dark smudge of his lashes. I look at the girl next. I inspect her smoky curls and elegantly arched eyebrows. Their names tantalize me, like a raft bobbing just out of reach in the middle of a storm: so close, but far enough away to leave me drowning.

The green-eyed man begins to sing. His voice is a rough but pleasant baritone that sends every question and doubt winging out of my mind. I watch him, enthralled, my eyes fixed on his lips.

> *"Leaves turn, snow falls*
> *Green on the ground, sun in the sky.*
> *In each turn of the seasons, I turn to you*
> *Do you think of me? I think of you."*

The golden-eyed girl joins him, her voice flowing over and around his like honey.

> *"Every sun, every moon*
> *Every star in the sky shines for you.*
> *I can see the morning breaking in your eyes.*
> *Do you think of me? I think of you."*

The green-eyed man lays down his instrument and kneels beside me, taking my hand carefully in his. For several moments he simply looks at me while the girl continues playing. Then he brings my hand to his lips and places a soft kiss on my fingers.

"Can you tell me your name?" he asks.

I frown. I want to, but I'm not sure I can. My frown deepens. What if I can't and he lets go of my hand? I don't want that.

"Tell me," he says, his hand tightening on my fingers. "Please."

When I open my mouth to tell him something, anything, nothing comes out.

"Tell me your name," he says. "You can do it. I know you can."

His eyes bore into mine, willing me to speak with an intensity that borders on desperation. I open my mouth again and again, hanging onto both his hands as I rock back and forth. My name, *my name*—what is it? I know I've heard it—repeatedly and recently. Why won't it come to me now?

At last, I sit back with a dejected sigh and release Luca's hands reluctantly—and then I bolt upright, my eyes widening in excitement. *Luca!*

I take a deep breath and force out a hoarse grunt. I try again: "L-lu…luuu…"

"Yes." Luca grips my shoulders with trembling hands. "That's it, love, keep going."

"Luc—*Kirit!*"

I laugh at the furry bundle that suddenly appears, wiggling, in my lap. Kirit squeaks as I wrap my arms around him and squeeze, burying my face in his fur. When at last I look up, tears quiver in the corners of my eyes. I reach out and touch Luca's face.

"Luca," I say, my voice broken and gravelly. I turn to the golden-eyed girl, who stares at me with a sort of wistful excitement. "Sadra."

Sadra sets her harp aside and sits at the foot of my bed, her hand resting lightly on my knee.

"And you?" she asks gently. "Who are you?"

"Sasha," I whisper.

My heart and lungs seem to constrict, making me gasp with the pain of it. Luca holds me tightly against his chest, his lips pressed against my hair. Sadra rubs my back with one hand and catches my groping fingers with the other. I cling to them both, shaking uncontrollably.

I came so close to losing them. Now that I know what it feels like, I know I can't do it again. I can't leave them. The realization brings on a fresh wave of grief as I finally accept what I've known for some time: I'll never get my old life back, even if I somehow return to that world. Too much has changed.

"What?" Sadra asks, leaning close. "What did you say?"

I didn't realize I was mumbling. I lift my face and take a deep, shuddering breath, pushing them both away so I can look at them.

"I want to stay," I say.

Kirit yips joyfully and jumps up to lick my face, his tail whipping back and forth. Luca swallows and closes his eyes. I fend off Kirit with one hand and slip the other into Luca's. He presses my knuckles against his lips, then takes a deep breath and opens his eyes. My heart flips at the joy and love I see there, wild and tender and fierce, all at once. I could get lost in those eyes and never even want to find my way back.

"Thank the stars." Sadra throws her arms around me and squeezes so hard my ribs creak under the strain.

I hug her back, resting my forehead against her shoulder. "I missed you."

"I missed you, too." She leans back, regarding me seriously. "I'm sorry I barked at you that night. I was just so angry. If you died—"

"But I'm not going to," I say as firmly as I can. "I'm going to be a good girl and do whatever Bard says. Where is he? Did he find the Apostate?"

Sadra and Luca exchange a glance.

"What?" I ask, looking from one to the other.

Luca rises and begins to pace. "Bard did find the Apostate. But there's been a change of plans."

"Why?" Dread creeps, cold and sickly, into my belly. "What's happened?"

Sadra looks down, her face puckered. "I'm so sorry Sasha. It's all my fault. I was the one who sent Ari—I mean, the princess. After you left the City, Mother Wenla assigned me to the palace to keep an eye on the investigation into Orean's treason. The House knew about us—at least, about the Apostate. I still don't know how. I sent the princess, but she was meant to *warn* you. And I warned her, I told her not to involve the House! I thought I could trust her. I thought she trusted *me.*"

Sadra breaks off, tears streaming down her face, and I wonder if it's only guilt that bites her so keenly. She cries as if she herself has been betrayed as well. After a brief, uncomfortable pause, Luca picks up the story.

"You're in the palace," Luca says. "It took us nearly three weeks to talk my brother into giving me the writ to extract you from the House. My sister was in a rage, insisting that you would bring down the kingdom and that only the House of Light and Shadow could stop you. I told Costi everything, and Mother Wenla and Porr—the Apostate—confirmed it all. But it was Bard who changed his mind in the end." Luca gives a crooked smile. "We all know how persuasive he can be, don't we? I don't know what he showed Costi, but it worked."

Hope surges in my chest. "So the king believes us? That's good news—isn't it?"

"He believes that the House has overstepped," Luca says. "And he's agreed to an investigation. Porr and the Lord Premier have been going at it for a week now, each one presenting his side of the story. You'll be called on to give your testimony at a hearing before the whole Council as soon as you're well enough."

I gape at him. "What 'side' is there for the House to present? If the king knows the truth, how can they possibly defend what they've done?"

"I can't say for sure," he says. "Costi has kept the meetings private, for the most part. But I can only assume they're arguing that your body is their property. That you're not an individual but a manufactured product, as they've maintained all along."

"That's what Cimari told me." My gut twists at the memory. "She said I'm not real. That I'm an echo."

"She's wrong." Luca returns to my side and squeezes my hand. "Or she's lying. Either way, it's not true."

"As if Cimari is in any position to judge," Sadra adds with a watery snort, and wipes her eyes. "She's barely half a person herself. If you cracked open her heart, you'd find nothing but a pile of ash."

"We know what you are," Luca says. "And we'll prove it to everyone."

"How?" I ask. "How do you prove something like that? How do you even define what is a person and what isn't?"

"The presence of a soul, I suppose," Sadra says. "And *that*, I think we can prove."

"How?" I ask again.

Sadra pokes me in the side and gives me a small smile. "Isn't it obvious? You dance."

en Avant

"Miss, it's time."

A little man with a sour, pinched mouth and a weak chin marches into the room with an air of harried self-importance. Two guards follow and stand on either side of the door, stoic and unblinking. The little man—the steward, perhaps—beckons to me impatiently.

"It's time," he says again. "The Council awaits."

I rise slowly to my feet and smooth the rich, soft fabric of my dancer's costume, which was brought to me this morning. There was no explanation, but I knew what it meant. Only one occasion could warrant my best clothes, flowing trousers bound tight below the knee and a soft, wide-sleeved shirt tied off with a sash, all in tawny gold and cream. Luca had given them to me months ago, shortly after I was Marked at the Temple. I'm sure it wasn't easy convincing the guards to give them to me now, and the gesture gives me the courage I need to step out of the door.

No one has been allowed past the guards outside my door except for a Healer whose name no one bothered to tell me. As neither Luca nor Sadra would abandon me willingly, I can only assume that they're being kept from me. But for what reason, I can't imagine.

Now, it seems, I'm about to find out.

I follow the steward through the twisting corridors of the palace and wince at a fresh, sharp stab of loneliness. I can hardly remember the last time I went anywhere without Kirit padding silently beside me. I hope he'll be there at the trial with Luca. If the Council favors the House, I want to be able to say goodbye.

I begin to shake. I don't even know if Luca will be there. But he has to be—they can't possibly make me do this on my own, can they? For one thing, this is bigger than just me. We're going after the House's whole enterprise—as the complainants, Bard, Mother Wenla, and the Apostate will have to be present at the very least. Unless each witness will be speaking to the Council separately?

Bozhe, I want this over with.

Finally, we stop. The older guard raps twice on an almost shabby looking door and waits. When it opens he walks through, bows, and stands aside. The younger guard behind me gives me a gentle nudge and motions for me to enter.

My muscles tense, and for a moment I seriously consider making a run for it. But then a soft yap grabs my attention and a smile of relief blossoms on my face. Kirit. He *is* here—and wherever he is, Luca can't be far away.

I step through the door to see Luca stationed at the king's shoulder. His face is cool and serious—a soldier's face. But as I straighten up from my bow to the king, I catch the tiniest flicker of a wink. Warmth floods my belly, loosening the knots in my lower back. I take a deep breath and look around.

Atop the dais, the king sits in a sturdy, comfortable looking chair decorated with only a hint of inlaid carving. Arismendi sits beside him, her face white and troubled. On his other side—I suck in a sharp breath, then release it slowly. I should have known. Of course Ismeni would be here. Not only is she the king's lover, she's also a central figure in the trial. But the shock of seeing my former mistress twists the muscles around my spine and through my shoulders so abruptly it's nearly a spasm.

Another breath.

Council members spread to the left and right, curving around in a wide arc. Another arc of chairs is arranged opposite the king and Council members. The people in these chairs sit with their backs facing me, but I recognize Sadra's dark curls and Mother Wenla's shock of white hair immediately. Even Bard's grizzled head and stiff shoulders spark instant recognition. The burly, shaggy figure beside them must be the Apostate. To their right, Cimari sits scowling beside her husband, the House Premier.

"Come forward, child," the king says, his voice stern but not unkind.

I obey, passing between the chairs to stand in front of King Miocostin. For a moment, I'm caught by the familiarity of his features. His resemblance to Luca is uncanny. But he has none of Luca's humor or warmth, only deep, hard lines around his eyes and mouth. His gaze is distant, calculating...and deeply unhappy.

"Some weeks ago, my brother brought me the most astounding tale," he begins. "He tells me that we have been deceived, that the House of Light and Shadow has conspired to exploit and enslave sentient beings. He tells me that you are one such being."

At his expectant pause, I nod and whisper, "Yes, my lord. I mean, my king."

"My sister tells me differently," the king continues. "She insists that you are a deadly threat—though she unfortunately seems unable to provide any greater detail. The House of Light and Shadow tells me differently still. The esteemed Premier believes you to be a harmless oddity, yourself. But he warns me that what you represent could topple the very kingdom. We are met here today to determine the truth of this matter and decide what to do about it."

The silence stretches until he asks, "So, young one...what do *you* tell me?"

I open my mouth to reply, but the Premier cuts me off.

"My king, I must protest," he says. "Of course the creature will parrot the lies it was fed by the Temple of Graces, which has long sought to undermine my House's work."

"I granted your request that this girl be kept sequestered from her fellows," the king says sternly, and I'm relieved to hear the slightest stress on the word *girl*. "I am confident she has not been coached in any way. We *will* hear her." To me, he says, "Go on, child."

I open and close my mouth several times, but nothing comes out. A rushing sound fills my ears as I try to collect my thoughts.

"I'm sorry," I finally say. "I just—I don't know where to begin."

"Tell us your name and how you came to be here," a kindly looking old man suggests.

He leans forward in his seat, which is only two or three away from the king's. His tone is gentle. So are his eyes. I swallow. Hopefully the man is as kind as he looks, and hopefully his proximity to the king is a measure of his influence.

"My—my name is Sasha Nikolayeva," I begin hesitantly. "I was born in another country—another world. I began to see things while I slept…and then, sometimes, when I woke. I saw myself here, in Kingsgarden. I was kept in a cage. I was starved, beaten, branded, and then sold to the lady Ismeni. She kept me as a servant…and as a pet. She called me Cygnet. I can't say for certain how long I spent in her service before I was awakened."

"Awakened," the kindly man says, leaning forward. "How do you mean?"

"I had forgotten who I was," I explain. "I had forgotten a lot of things. I couldn't speak. I had trouble understanding and thinking. Sometimes I didn't think at all. I was…gone. Absent from my own body. Forgive me, it's—difficult to describe.

"After a time, though, I remembered how to dance, and the more

I did it, the more I came back to myself. Then Sadra found me and started teaching me your language. She—well, she bullied me into waking up in the end. I spoke my name, and...and I was myself again.

"She told me about the casting, the shadow, that had stifled my mind and kept me silent. She called it the Pall. She said it was siphoning off my energy and turning it into Light for other people to use. She told me it was the House of Light and Shadow that had done this to me, and that with the Temple's help I could have the Pall removed. I could be free."

I fall silent, and a tide of murmurs and whispering rises among the Council members. The king waves them down and leans back, regarding me thoughtfully.

"Certainly you are not the empty shell we have always believed thralls to be. You speak with an accent, yes, but you speak—something we have long thought beyond the ability of a thrall." The king raises his eyebrows at the Premier. "How do you explain this? Do you deny that Sasha is—or was—a thrall?"

"No, my king," the Premier says, rising to his feet. "A thrall is not a hollow vessel, as many believe—"

"As you have led us to believe," the king corrects in a hard voice. "And neither are they prey to spiritwalkers, as you have stated explicitly—and untruthfully. But go on."

"As I say, they are not—completely—empty," the Premier continues, apparently unruffled. "But neither can they be considered complete, sentient individuals. In short, they are not people."

"How so?"

The Premier folds his hands over his substantial belly and speaks in a smooth, instructive tone, as if delivering a lecture to a group of students.

"There lies in the northern forests a certain singularity. A catalyst, of sorts. Early members of the Temple of Graces—" and here he bows to Mother Wenla "—discovered the singularity some four hundred years ago. They studied it for many years and found that this catalyst attracts various…essences, shall we say, and concentrates them until those essences coalesce to form a body. A living, breathing body, yes, but not a *person*. What lives inside the body is—if anything—merely an echo, an imprint of a mind long dead."

"And how did these investigators come to such a conclusion?" one of the Councilors asks skeptically.

"Every attempt was made to communicate with the creatures," the Premier says. "Each attempt, however, was met with incomprehensible babble at best or violence at worst. The creatures proved incapable of—or even interested in—caring for themselves, and so we did it for them. We cared for them and studied them…and, yes, we made use of them. We found a way to harness their energies—through the Pall, as the creature says. Light was born, and with it the first Lightcrafters of the House of Light and Shadow, who helped the first king of the Garden build the very kingdom you rule today."

The kindly man frowns and clears his throat. "The King's Chalice—"

"Is a tale for children," the Premier says dismissively. "Or at best a highly sanitized edition of the Garden's history. The first king conquered the outlying cities with armies strengthened by Lightcrafters and their workings."

Ignoring the king's narrowed eyes, the Premier continues, "By itself, the singularity is not particularly prolific, producing perhaps two or three thralls per year. House mages developed methods to amplify and concentrate the singularity's effects so that more thralls could be cultivated among the roots of the trees."

"And will you tell them what these methods are?" the Apostate asks, his voice deceptively mild. "Will you tell them how you water your foul garden with the blood of innocents?"

There's a beat of shocked silence, then the room fills with the buzz of whispers and muttered conversations. Luca doesn't speak or even move from his position at the king's shoulder, but his eyes find mine. I cling to the momentary flash of comfort and sit straighter in my chair. Sadra smiles and gives my shoulder an approving pat.

"Order, please," the king says, giving the Apostate a hard look. "You will have your turn to speak. Until then, I must ask you to remain silent." To the Premier, he says, "But do elaborate, if you please."

"Life must be fed with life," the Premier says softly. "This truth is undisputed. We grow our wheat and barley in soil comprised of the once living flesh of other plants and animals and then harvest the living plants to make our bread and ale. We raise livestock and hunt beasts of the forest and field that we might eat. What we of the House do is no different.

"I can attempt to explain the exact mechanics of our processes, but I think it is not necessary. Do not let the words of a malcontent and oathbreaker sway you, my lords. What we produce is livestock, nothing more, to be used as we see fit. That which proves unsuitable to serve as a thrall is used in other ways. We are not wasteful."

"What my former colleague means," the Apostate cuts in, "is that thralls fall into a fairly narrow range of age and physical ability. Those who are too young, too old, too weak, or too unlikely to sell are slaughtered wholesale, their blood and bone harvested for amulets and other workings."

"You have seen this?" the king demands.

"I have, my king." Bard stands and bows. "I have seen children as young as three years old bled like pigs—but more slowly."

"Like pigs," the Premier repeats quickly. "My point exactly. Do you object also to the meat we serve at our tables? Do you contend that the ox should be relieved of the plow? Thralls are no different from any other beast raised for food or labor. They are property—*our* property."

Alternating waves of fire and ice flood my stomach. White lights dance in the corners of my eyes. How can any person spew such filth and mean it? How can anyone hear and not recognize the disgusting absurdity of it? But they can—too many of them can. Half the Councilors look properly horrified, but the other half is nodding, like the Premier's explanation makes perfect sense.

"That's not true." My voice is even, but my body shakes. "I am not a piece of meat. I'm a girl, just like her." I point at Arismendi, whose face has gone pale and hard as marble. "I have—I had—a family. The House of Light and Shadow stole me from them. They pulled me into this world against my will and turned me into a *thing* to be used by whoever had the coin to pay."

King Miocostin turns to a small, mousy woman with graying hair and sharp blue eyes. I hadn't noticed her before, lurking as she was behind the king's chair.

"My lady," he says. "What is your word? Who speaks the truth?"

"I am called a Truthseer, my king, but in reality, I see deceit," the woman says. "All I can say is that neither of them lies. But believing a thing doesn't make it true."

The king sighs. "Then we must proceed and do our best to uncover the truth for ourselves."

"My king," the Premier says. "Might I question the thrall?"

"You may," the king replies shortly.

The Premier turns to me, cool and composed as ever. "You say you lived in another world. Was your life good? Pleasant?"

The question throws me off guard. "I—no. I mean, it was, until…all this."

"The visions, you mean. Tell us more about that, if you please," the Premier says.

"I…I couldn't sleep," I say uncertainly. "Because of the dreams. I couldn't eat. I started forgetting things, and hearing and seeing things that weren't there. I started having…I don't know the word in your language. Fits, maybe."

"In other words, you fell ill," the Premier prompts. "Severely ill, would you say?"

Reluctantly, I nod.

"And at what point did you fully…ah, cross over?" he asks.

"When Sadra—"

"You misunderstand me," the Premier interrupts. "I meant, what was your condition at the time of your transition into this world?"

I hesitate, not sure what he's driving at, but answer as honestly as I can. "I thought I was going to die."

"So, to summarize—and do correct me if I'm wrong—you became deathly ill and then found yourself in Kingsgarden. You remember nothing else—for instance, recovering from your illness," the Premier says. "Is that so?"

"Yes," I whisper.

The Premier asks, very gently, "And isn't it possible that you did, in fact, die? That you are not that girl but an imprint, as I have said?"

"No," I say automatically. "No, it's not—"

"She lies," the Truthseer says promptly.

I take a breath. "I—yes, I suppose it is possible. But I don't think that's what happened."

The king glances at the Truthseer, who nods.

"My king—" The Apostate moves as if to rise but remains in his seat at the king's glare.

"Hold your tongue. I will not tell you again," the king says coldly. "As the accused, the House Premier has the right to present his case first."

"Thank you, my king," the Premier says with a bow. "I would like to question the lady Ismeni next, if you please."

The king nods his assent and gestures for me to sit. I collapse, trembling, into the empty chair beside Sadra. Immediately, her hand finds mine.

On the dais, the king lifts Ismeni's hand to his lips. "Answer honestly and without fear, my love."

Ismeni nods, tight-lipped, and faces the Premier. "What questions do you have for me, my lord?"

"This is the thrall you called Cygnet?" the Premier asks.

Ismeni looks at me—really *looks* at me—for the first time that I can remember. "I…I think so. She looks different. Her hair, her clothes, her manner. And—something else. But yes, I believe it is Cygnet."

"And when the thrall was in your care, did you mistreat it?"

Ismeni shakes her head vehemently. "Never. I was very fond of her."

"She was not starved or otherwise abused, as has been suggested?"

"I—" Ismeni pauses, her gaze flickering toward the Truthseer. "Not by me."

The Truthseer nods. I grind my teeth. Surely everyone can see the giant, gaping hole in her answer. Won't someone speak up? Anger simmers under my skin, echoed by the tightening of Sadra's already bone-crushing grip on my hand. Then, in the moment the Premier draws breath for his next question, a low, clear voice rings out:

"Not by you, my lady?" Arismendi asks. "But by another, perhaps?"

Ismeni winces but doesn't try to avoid the question. "Yes, Princess. Cygnet was once whipped on the lady Cimari's orders."

And nearly raped by her brother. But, as Ismeni herself never knew of my disastrous escape attempt, the omission isn't detected by the Truthseer.

With effort, I swallow a protest. The king is already frustrated by our multiple interruptions, and I don't want to antagonize him further. All I can do is grind my teeth as the Premier moves on with his questioning.

"Over the course of the thrall's service in your household, did you ever witness anything to suggest that it possessed fully human capabilities?"

Ismeni frowns. "I'm not sure I understand you, my lord. Cygnet was clever, certainly—"

"I speak of the hallmarks of humanity, my lady. For instance, compassion or understanding. Something beyond mere intelligence, which all animals possess to some degree."

Again Ismeni hesitates, and this time her eyes come to rest not on the Truthseer but on me. "I don't know."

I nearly choke in my effort to remain silent. How can she not know? She heard Dove speak in her last moments before death. She covered for me then. Why won't she acknowledge it now?

"Answer me this, then," the Premier says calmly enough, though by his narrowed eyes I'm sure he expected a straight *no*. "Based on your extensive experience with this thrall, do you believe that it is the equal of a human being born and bred in Kingsgarden, to be accorded the same rights and consideration due to all citizens of this realm?" He pauses. "In short, do you believe it is a real person?"

Ismeni closes her eyes for several long moments. My heart leaps into my throat with a rush of wild, unexpected longing. Regardless of her answer's impact on the outcome of the hearing, I want her to say yes. I want—I've always wanted—her to acknowledge that I was more than a pet. I want to know that her apparent affection for me was something deeper, something real.

Ismeni opens her eyes and says, "No."

The tiniest of gasps escapes my lips, belying the pain that slams into me like a physical blow. Sadra lets go of my hand and slips her arm around my shoulder, squeezing tightly. I brace myself with my hands on my knees, my head bowed. My insides seem to be crumbling, dry and gritty as desert sand.

"Thank you, my lady," the Premier says, oblivious to my struggle. "And now, my lords, may I present my wife, the lady Cimari, who also possesses first-hand knowledge of the thrall's behavior."

I close my eyes so I don't have to see Cimari's face. But I can't block out her voice, full of self-important complacency.

"The lady Ismeni has indicated that you had this thrall whipped," the Premier says. "Tell us why."

"It was in need of discipline," Cimari says easily. "My good sister was quite lax with all the creatures under her care. What's more, I suspected something was amiss with the thrall. The whipping was in response to unprovoked aggression."

At that, I jerk my head up and stare at her. Aggression? I wrack my brain, trying to remember something, anything, that could have been construed as aggression. What is she talking about?

"Could you be more specific?"

Cimari nods. "It charged me and knocked a piece of food out of my hand."

My mouth drops open. I did not *charge* her. I ran into her, yes, but it was an accident! Rather, I didn't mean to do it—it was no accident. *Unprovoked…* yes, it certainly was that. I grind my teeth.

The Truthseer makes a small noise, drawing an inquiring look from the King.

"Does she lie?" the king asks.

The Truthseer hesitates. "No, but…No, my lord."

The king nods. "Then proceed."

"And when the thrall was punished, did it exhibit any sign of remorse?" the Premier asks.

"None," Cimari says. "What's more, it appeared to feel very little pain, if any. It is my belief that thralls are wholly insensate, closer to beasts than they are to you and me."

My eyes fly to Luca, whose jaw clenches in anger. Even the king frowns in contempt. Hope stirs in my chest. As close as he is to Luca, he has to have spent more than enough time around Kirit to know that the little fox is anything but unfeeling or unintelligent. But the king says nothing, allowing the Premier to continue with his questions.

"Insensate," the Premier, repeats, raising his voice over my garbled cry of protest. "Do you mean they are impervious only to physical pain?"

"No, my lord. I have observed this thrall on many occasions and made particular note of its behavior," Cimari says, her face perfectly bland and innocent. "Behavior which can only be described as utterly impassive, regardless of any stimulus, positive or negative. It appears not to distinguish between kindness and cruelty. For instance, upon witnessing the death of a puppy—a puppy which had been its close companion for many weeks—the thrall showed no sign of distress or, as my husband has said, understanding."

At this, my self-control snaps and I leap to my feet.

"How dare you," I snarl. "How dare you speak of Pretty Girl as if you didn't kill her with your own hands, you filthy, evil—"

"Silence," the king barks. "My lady, has a lie been spoken?"

The Truthseer stares hard at Cimari with a deep frown, dislike and suspicion written in every line of her face.

"No, my king," she says through gritted teeth.

"Very well, then," the king says.

Fury pulses in my veins. I open my mouth to argue, regardless of the consequences, but Sadra yanks me back into my seat.

"You're not helping," she hisses. "Shut up!"

"But she—"

"She's nothing," Sadra growls. "A bloodsucking flea on the back of a rabid dog, nothing more."

The king looks at me with a sort of guarded sympathy in his eyes. "I must say, the descriptions presented seem at odds with what we can see for ourselves. How do you explain this?"

"The thrall is a mimic, my king," the Premier says. "Nothing more. A skilled mimic, I grant you, but then, we know from the lady Ismeni's testimony that the creature is clever enough for its kind. Thralls can be trained, as everyone knows. My…ah, colleagues at the Temple of Graces have had several months in which to produce something that might pass as human to undiscerning or unsuspecting eyes. Such misinformation, if allowed to take root, could seriously undermine the foundation of our House and, by extension, the kingdom itself.

"Make no mistake, my lords: This is a *thrall* we're discussing, not a young woman, not the equal of your wives and daughters. It is a semi-functioning brain inside a body that was not born but *created*. Furthermore, it is a valuable commodity which has been stolen and subverted from its intended purpose. It—"

"That is enough." The king silences the Premier with only a slight gesture. "Have you any witnesses who can confirm that any such training has taken place?"

"No, my king. However—"

"Then I think it's time we heard from the Temple Mother and her witnesses," the king says firmly. "Please be seated, Lord Premier."

The Premier bows his head and takes his place beside Cimari. Despite a wash of relief, I note uneasily that he doesn't seem nearly as discouraged as he should be after what anyone with a scrap of logic could recognize as a flawed defense. But what am I supposed to say to all that? Where do I even begin? And *how?*

My hands and face feel clammy and feverish, and I can't stop shaking. I don't think I can stand, much less defend myself with any degree of coherency. I cast a desperate look at Mother Wenla.

"My king," Mother Wenla says, rising gracefully to her feet. "I fear that my young friend is overwrought by these misrepresentations and half-truths. Might Sasha retire for a short time and begin once she has had a chance to compose herself?"

"Of course." The king nods and sighs. "We could all do with a bit of a break and some refreshment, I think. Go, then. We will reconvene when we are recovered."

Relevé

"Are you alright?" Peering at me worriedly, Sadra pulls me into a small room adjoining the audience chamber. "I'm sorry—of course you aren't. It's just sickening, what they did in there."

"But they didn't lie," I say dazedly, shaking my head. "They never lied. They really do believe that I'm not a person."

"It doesn't matter," Sadra says. "They're ignorant and complacent and what they believe matters not one whit."

But it does. My mind and body are in revolt, churning with helpless, disbelieving rage and despair. Throughout my time with Ismeni, I comforted myself with the knowledge that she simply didn't know. My mask was too good, I told myself. If only I could allow her to see *me* rather than a thrall, she would see the truth. Or so I thought. It never occurred to me that seeing might not be the same as believing.

I sink onto a long couch and sit for several minutes with my head in my hands and Sadra rubbing my back. I lean into her with my eyes closed and for a moment seriously consider running away. With Sadra's skills, we might even make it out of the palace. But my half-formed fantasy is interrupted by the soft click of the door. My head jerks up. A bubble of hope rises—maybe it's Luca—then flickers and pops in surprise. It's not Luca or even Bard or Mother Wenla.

It's the princess Arismendi.

Sadra stiffens beside me. She stares at the princess, her face twisted with something like hate—or maybe only hurt. When she speaks, her voice is harsh.

"You shouldn't be here. You're on the trial council."

"I know." Arismendi's green eyes flick to me, then back to Sadra. "I've come to fetch you both. But first—can we talk?"

Sadra rises and turns to fuss with the hem of my billowing trousers. "This isn't the time or place."

"Sadra, please, let me explain—"

"How could you possibly?" A tear lands on my wrist as Sadra whirls back around to face the princess. "I loved you. I pledged myself to you. I would have broken my vows for you. I betrayed my cause in trusting you, and you betrayed *me*. Sasha might die today because—because—I don't even know. If you want to talk, tell me that—tell me why."

Arismendi, who has grown steadily redder in the face through Sadra's tirade, lets out a puff of scornful laughter. "*You* dare to speak to me of trust? You've been lying to me since the moment we met!"

I reach for Sadra's hand. So it wasn't a man who held her heart after all. I shift in my chair. "Um, maybe I should go…somewhere."

"Yes." Arismendi takes a deep breath and schools her features with visible effort. "They're waiting for you in the council chamber. But first—I'm sorry, Sasha. My Gift is unpredictable, and it took me by surprise. When I saw you, I was terrified. I forgot everything Sadra told me, everything I promised. I knew—I *knew*—that the world was going to end because of you. Now I understand that the world as I knew it *must* end, because I didn't know it at all. And now that I do…it will end. Of course it will."

She frowns, a worried line forming between her brows. "I can tell you that my brother isn't very impressed with the Premier's arguments, and neither were the other council members. But you must be wary. I don't think convincing them is the Premier's primary aim. He relies more on spectacle than logic, and I think he's hoping to make a spectacle of you."

I nod and squeeze Sadra's hand. "Well, I'll give him one. I'm ready."

* * *

Arismendi motions for Sadra and me to enter ahead of her and closes the door softly behind us. The king and Council members look up at our approach, but the Apostate and the Premier are still arguing.

"You are a disgrace to the House and a criminal to boot," the Premier sneers. "Most importantly, however, your theories are completely unsubstantiated."

"No more so than your own theories," the Apostate shoots back. "What real evidence is there to suggest that thralls are only echoes? All you have is supposition, prejudice, and sheer pigheaded refusal to consider anything that threatens your position."

"Be *quiet*," the king snaps, for what must surely be the fifth or sixth time by now. "Sit down, both of you." He glances at me. "Welcome once again, Sasha. I trust you are recovered?"

"I am." I move to stand before him and raise my chin. "I lived for months fearing for my life. I hid the only way I could—with a mask. For months, I was afraid to be seen. But I'm not afraid anymore. I don't need my thrall's mask, and I won't ever wear it again. I'd like to show you something, please."

"And what will you show us?" the king asks.

"The Temple of Graces teaches that the soul withers without knowledge of the beauty in oneself and in the world," I say. "I want to show you that my soul is present, complete, and entirely my own."

The king nods, looking tired. Even so, he gives me a slight smile. "So may it be, child. Show us."

At Mother Wenla's direction, chairs are cleared from the center of the room. Cimari and the Premier stand against the far wall, scowling and muttering to each other, while Mother Wenla settles herself nearby with her harp upon her knee. Bard stands beside her, his eyes fixed on me with an expression I can't begin to read.

Mother Wenla begins to play, rippling scales and arpeggios dancing around a melody that tugs at my memory. It's not until Bard begins to sing that I recognize the tune as one of the many songs of Russia that my grandmother used to play on her ancient record player.

One or two Council members look up in surprise as the foreign words leave Bard's mouth, but the rest keep their eyes on me. I feel the weight of their combined gaze as if it were a physical force. It doesn't bother me. I defied physical forces for most of my life, every time I rose *en pointe*.

I begin to move, swept along and buoyed by Bard's song. It was a smart move on his part: Though comforting and familiar to me, to the natives of Kingsgarden the Russian tongue must sound exotic, almost unearthly, underscoring our claim that we come from another world entirely.

> *"Oh, it's not evening, it's not evening*
> *I was sleeping so small a time,*
> *I was sleeping so small a time,*
> *Oh, and I saw in my dreams..."*

The hair rises on the back of my neck, but I don't falter. I continue to turn and wheel and dip, my movements infused with a kind of smooth inevitability that I've never quite managed to master before now. Though unplanned, each step is executed without hesitation, as if there's only one possible path for me to take.

> *"Oh, evil winds flew,*
> *Yes, from the eastern side,*
> *And snatched the black cap*

From my troubled head."

As the music swells, so does my dance, the gestures and phrases becoming broader and stronger. I catch a glimpse of Ismeni's jaw hanging wide open as I spin in place with the toes of my left foot pointing straight at the ceiling. Another time, I would have laughed to see such an inelegant expression on her face, but I don't have time for her right now. I pour everything I have and everything I am into this, the most important dance of my life.

> *"Oh, it's not evening, it's not evening*
> *I was sleeping so small a time,*
> *I was sleeping so small a time,*
> *Oh, and I saw in my dreams..."*

At the climax of the song, something seems to break free inside me and burst out into the room. At first, no one notices. But then, under Bard's song, a ripple of something strange passes through me. Memories that don't belong to me bubble just under the surface of my own consciousness.

As I dance, I catch glimpses of fire and blood and hear the sizzle of newly branded flesh. I feel the lash of the whip and the impotent, voiceless rage of a newly awakened thrall, the terror of knowing I'm trapped in a world that shouldn't exist.

Slowly, I come to rest and stand with my head bowed, letting the foreign sensations wash over me. Though I've felt it all myself, these memories aren't my own: They're Bard's. I don't know how he's projecting them—I thought his Gift required physical contact—but somehow, it's happening. The memories are nowhere near as vivid as the ones Bard shared directly with me, but even so, the king and Council members shift and shiver in their seats. Whatever they're seeing is evidently clear enough to make an impression.

I lift my head.

"I am myself," I say, speaking not to the king but to Ismeni. "I am my own person. You don't have the right to decide for me what I am."

"I think we are all satisfied on that point," the king says.

"However," the Premier cuts in, "the point is moot."

"Moot?" the kindly man says incredulously. "The girl's status as—well, as a girl—is what we are here to decide, is it not?"

"With respect, my lord, it is not," the Premier says with a bow. "We are here to decide if the House of Light and Shadow has the right to continue making use of thralls. And I say we do, regardless of what sort of mind lives inside the body. While it is admittedly a bit, ah, *uncomfortable* to consider, the fact of the matter is that the body in question was not born but created *by us* and as such belongs to us to do with as we please.

"What's more, the body in question cannot survive without the Pall. It owes its very life to us, which I say gives us the right to decide how to use it. And do not forget, my lords, that most thralls lead pampered, protected lives, knowing nothing of the struggles ordinary citizens face. Does it not seem a fair trade?"

Bard is goggling at the Premier and at the Truthseer, who hasn't said a word.

"No one can be that ignorant unless it's on purpose," he says disbelievingly.

"You have something to add?" the king asks, his eyes flashing.

"We do," the Apostate says, his hand on Bard's shoulder. "The Premier has heard me state clearly and truthfully that Bard was a thrall and that I lifted the Pall from him, and yet he can state with perfect honesty his belief that thralls cannot survive on their own. Such blatant disregard for facts in one's conception of the truth shows a dangerous trend in the House's practices and philosophy which will at some point prove disastrous to your reign and to the kingdom's well-being, regardless of what happens here today."

"He is a fluke," the Premier snaps, finally stung. "My king, I urge you to consider the greater good. The Light provided by thralls supports the infrastructure of the entire kingdom—*everything*, from the economy to the sewer systems. Without Light, your cities would collapse. Your armies would be crippled. Millions would lose their livelihoods. The kingdom would fall into poverty and ruin—and for what?

"For the sake of a few who, for the small price of lending us the necessary energy to continue as we have, lead largely comfortable lives. Perhaps a few could survive without the Pall, but the vast majority could not. What would be gained by killing them and at the same time destroying the realm you are sworn to protect?"

All is silent. The councilors' eyes turn to me. Some are hostile, some troubled, some sympathetic…but I know every one of them is weighing my freedom against their own comfort.

"As distasteful as I find the idea," the king says at last, "it is a valid objection. Porr, what have you to say to that?"

"As to how Kingsgarden will cope with the loss of Light, none of us can say," the Apostate says, shaking his head. "What I can tell you is this: In the world from which our thralls are reaped, there is no Light, and in some ways that world is far more advanced. I say also that the Premier's claim that the majority of thralls would die is incorrect. Approximately three out of every five thralls survive the Pall's removal."

"Little more than half," the Premier points out. "My king, you most graciously allowed this—girl—a demonstration. I beg leave to present my own."

"Granted," the king replies.

Though the king's voice betrays no hint of emotion, the lines around his eyes and mouth seem suddenly deeper. I catch Luca's eyes, and my stomach sinks as I find confirmation there—this isn't going well.

"My dear, if you would," the Premier says to Cimari, who nods and disappears through the door to the corridor.

After a moment, she returns accompanied by two House acolytes and a pale, vacant-eyed thrall. Though clean and clad in a plain but serviceable gown, she bears the undeniable marks of prolonged imprisonment and starvation: white, waxy skin; watery eyes squinting at the light; deep shadows under her eyes…and, of course, the hopeless, mindless indifference of a thrall.

The girl stares straight ahead. A lock of golden hair falls over her face, but she makes no move to push it away. That hair…I look closer, examining what I can see of the girl's face. No, it can't be…but it is! It's Pouter, my nemesis from the Cage. Nausea fills my belly. No matter how irritating I found her then, I don't want her to die now—and I'm sure that's what they've brought her here to do.

"Wait." My voice emerges in a thin, strangled whisper. "No, stop—"

But it's too late. With an exaggerated ripping motion, the Premier tears a strip of—something—out of Pouter. It looks like a shimmer, or a ripple. Something half-seen and half-felt, with undefined edges. I have no more than a millisecond to register it before a raw, agonized shriek erupts from Pouter's mouth.

The king leaps to his feet, shouting, but the Premier continues, tearing the Pall away from Pouter's mind and body. It's over in seconds. Pouter's lifeless body lies crumpled on the ground, her face still twisted in pain and fear. Sweat pours down my body as I fight the urge to vomit. No one should have to die like that. No one.

"That was ill done," the king says, lowering himself back into his seat. Once there, he grips the arms of his chair with white-knuckled fingers. "I gave you leave for a demonstration, not an execution."

"With respect, my king, I felt it necessary to illustrate what it means to remove the Pall," the Premier says. "I see that you are shocked, and for that I beg your forgiveness. But surely it is better that you know what it is these people are proposing?"

"Of course the girl died," the Apostate says, his face flushed with anger. "So would a patient under the care of a violent and incompetent Healer. What's more, you can see for yourselves she was already near death. Look at her! She was skin and bones. She should have been returned to full physical health before any attempt was made to remove the Pall, and it must be done in stages, ideally over the course of several days."

"And yet, even with every proper procedure and precaution, the success rate is anything but overwhelming," the king observes. He spreads his hands. "What am I to do with this?"

"The risk is too great," the Premier says, an expression of sorrowful regret spreading over his face. "Is it not better to live, even in thralldom? I remind you again, thralls live comfortable lives that many of our poorest citizens would envy."

"It isn't better." Every eye in the room turns to me. "It is worth the risk."

A spark of anticipation enters the Premier's gaze. "And you would be willing to take this risk yourself, would you?"

"I would," I say without hesitation. "I am."

He turns to the king. "If I might make a suggestion, my king?"

"You may," the king says shortly.

"The girl presumes to speak for thralls all over the kingdom," the Premier says, though I've presumed no such thing. "Let her demonstrate her sincerity. Let her undergo the removal here and now. Porr contends that the subject must be returned to good health, and so she has been. Porr can even perform the procedure himself if he believes my own skills are not up to the task. Though I think we cannot confine the Council to this chamber for the several days he claims are necessary. Let it be done now, in your presence."

"Ridiculous," the Apostate snaps. "It takes *time*—"

"Furthermore," the Premier goes on, raising his voice. "If she proves unwilling to accept the risk, consider, my lords, that perhaps the possibility of death is indeed enough to justify our continued...custodianship."

"My king—"

Miocostin holds up a hand, silencing the Apostate. He remains silent for several long moments, his gaze distant. But he must be aware of the muttering and shifting of his Councilors. They don't want to think about this. They're only even half-willing to listen now because I'm standing right in front of them. If we release the Councilors for the days it will take to remove the Pall safely, they'll likely go home to their *comfortable* and *pampered* thralls and convince themselves that nothing needs to change, that it's all for the best. My bones turn to jelly as I realize that I am well and truly caught. I can't refuse, and I can't wait.

Finally, the king lifts his head.

"Let it be done now—if Sasha chooses." He meets my eyes steadily, his face betraying no hint of emotion. "You are, as you said, your own person. The decision must be yours."

I don't look at Luca or Sadra. I can't. My own fear is hard enough to bear. I swallow and nod once, my heart pounding

"May I have a moment to speak with the—with Porr?"

"Of course."

The Apostate and Bard are at my side even as the words leave the king's mouth.

"Is it possible?" I ask softly, looking up at this stranger who now holds my life in his hands.

"Yes," the Apostate replies. "But it will be dangerous...and very painful."

"It was already dangerous," I say, more to myself than to him. "And I've been in pain before. I'm not afraid of it."

"Sasha, you don't have to do this," Bard says, clasping my hand in both of his. "It is the king's decision, not the Council's. We can—"

"No." I lay my other hand over his. "Bard—Aleksandr—your daughter's name was Lara. When she was twenty-three years old, an injury ended her career. She went mad. She died—in that world." My throat closes, and for a moment I can't speak. Finally, I whisper, "If anything happens to me…find her, if you can. If she's here."

Bard closes his eyes. "I will, Sasha. Never fear."

He reaches into his pocket and pulls out my moonstone. His fingers shake as he fastens it around my neck.

"We are with you, whatever you choose," he whispers.

I swallow convulsively and nod, unable to speak.

Seeing my difficulty, the Apostate announces for me, "She accepts."

The king shakes his head. "Let there be no confusion. I must hear it from the lady herself."

"I'll do it." My voice is ragged. I step forward and try again. "I'll do it."

"No!" Luca steps forward, ignoring his brother's restraining hand on his arm. "Sasha, don't—"

"The choice is hers, brother." King Miocostin stands and grips Luca's shoulder. To me, he says, "You are certain you wish to proceed?"

"I am." Though my hands shake, my voice holds steady. I look over at Bard's stricken face. In Russian, I tell him, "Thank you…*Dedushka*. I'm sorry."

"Are you ready?" the king asks, still holding Luca by the shoulders.

At my nod, the Apostate steps forward. I turn my head and lock eyes with the Premier. The conviction I see there is chilling. Somehow, despite all he's seen and all he's heard, he believes he is in the right…and that I will die. But it doesn't matter. I will survive, and I will show him that he is wrong.

"Begin," the king says.

The Apostate's hand moves toward me as if pushing through

concrete. Enveloped in an eerie silence, I have time to see and study every detail, right down to his dirty, mangled nail beds and the wiry hairs sprouting from his wrists. And then, in a burst of noise and pain, time speeds up and then simply disappears.

I am nowhere.

I'm gone.

Reverence

I drift through darkness without wondering where I am. It seems completely natural to be without sight. I wonder if I have a body; I touch my hands together. It seems like I do, but how can I really be sure?

The dark is restful and calm. I feel relief, but I don't know what I've been relieved of. Whatever it was, it must have been exhausting. I must have come from somewhere else. I don't think I want to go back.

I don't realize I've been without sound until a faint but familiar melody fills the heavy silence surrounding me. I turn my head, trying to locate its source. It seems to come from everywhere—or nowhere.

> *"I will tell you fairy tales*
> *and sing you little songs*
> *but now you must slumber,*
> *with your little eyes closed*
> *bayushki bayu."*

I know the words. I know the voice. And once I know that, I know myself again.

"Babulya!" I yell. "Baba Nadia, where are you?"

I cast around in the dark until I smack my head on something hard. Reeling backward, I trip over something else. My hand smacks against the wall, and suddenly light flares overhead, blinding me all over again.

Somewhere above me, the song continues.

> *"There will be a time,*
> *after you will learn about life,*
> *When with courage you will*
> *place your foot into the stirrup."*

I look around with watering eyes and gasp. I'm in my own kitchen, and the hard thing that attacked me was an open cabinet. I run for the stairs, calling hysterically for my grandmother.

> *"I will fear for your troubles*
> *far away in a foreign land*
> *Sleep now, as long as you*
> *don't know sorrows,*
> *bayushki bayu."*

I burst into my bedroom, tripping over my own feet in my hurry, and fall onto the old rug where I used to play with my toys. My grandmother sits in a shabby armchair next to my bed, gazing tenderly at something in the bed as she sings. I look closer and realize that the thing in the bed…is me. A younger me, maybe ten.

"Baba Nadia?" I hover in the doorway, torn between hope and disbelief.

"Sasha," she says, turning to me with a radiant smile. "Oh, Sashka, *kotik*, I've been waiting for you."

"But…" I put a hand out to touch her knee. "Baba Nadia, am I dead?"

"No, kitten," she says. "*I'm* dead."

"But you're here," I say. "You're right here with me."

"So I am," she says, a smile creasing her face. "You have to choose."

I back away, shaking my head. I'm not ready.

"Come here," she says, beckoning me with a gnarled, spotty hand.

I move closer, taking her hand and pressing it against my lips. She turns my head so that I'm looking down at my own sleeping face. I touch her—my—cheek and everything around me falls away like a crumbling sandcastle. My mind splinters, trying to take in two—no, three—realities:

Dark lashes flutter against my younger self's milky skin; Luca strains against his brother and two of his guards while I lie writhing on the floor, my whole world alight with pain; Emily calls frantically for a nurse, pointing at my suddenly convulsing body. She holds me by the shoulders, tears falling out of her eyes and into mine as I struggle beneath her.

"Please," she cries, *"Oh God, please…"*

I snatch my hand away and look at my grandmother, aghast. She says nothing. She opens a drawer in the desk beside her and pulls out a rosewood box. My breath hitches as I recognize the deep, rich hue, and I quail at the thought of what's inside.

When Baba Nadia lifts the lid, I twitch in surprise. There's my crown of swans, as I expected, but beside it lies a silver cup. A chalice.

"You have to choose," she says gently.

I close my eyes. I thought I had made my decision. But now, having seen Emily again and felt her tears on my own face…

"What if I can't choose?" I whisper. "What if I stay here with you?"

Baba Nadia shakes her head sadly. "Don't say that, Sashka. Don't even think it. It broke my heart to leave you—would you break it again?"

"Then I should go back," I say. "I promised Emily—"

"Emily returned your promise to you," Baba Nadia says. "You must make the choice for yourself and no one else."

"But I don't know what to do," I whisper, my voice catching on a sob.

For the first time since Baba Nadia died, the long months of accumulated tears escape and cascade down my cheeks in a torrent of grief. Overcome, I hide my face in her lap and weep with the helpless abandon of the very young and the utterly desolate.

Baba Nadia croons meaningless nonsense under her breath and strokes my hair until the fit passes, then wipes my face with an embroidered handkerchief. I press her cool, dry hand against my cheek, screwing up my face against a fresh wave of tears.

"Don't," she chides. "There is no shame in honest grief, nor weakness in tears. You've denied yourself that comfort for too long, *kotik*. It's time to let go."

I shake my head, hard. "I don't want to leave you."

"You will stay with me, *kotik*," she whispers. "Wherever you go."

With a last, brisk pat on my cheek, she tugs the covers up to my younger self's chin and then leans back in her chair, resuming her lullaby. I stare at the little girl in the bed, envying her blissful ignorance. She doesn't know how decent people can be led to do and believe indecent things. She doesn't know the agony of having to choose which loved ones to hurt. She doesn't know loss or grief or doubt.

But she also doesn't know love, not really. What she knows is a child's love. She doesn't—can't—appreciate the true beauty of the thing, having never been without it. She appreciates love no more than she appreciates the air in her lungs or the food in her belly, for she has never drowned and never starved.

She doesn't know strength, despite the long hours of exertion some might consider inappropriate, even dangerous, for a child her age. She has a kind of greedy tenacity, a single-minded drive to obtain what she most desires—but she has never been forced into anything against her will. She has never been pushed, kicking and screaming, to the very edge of humanity. She's never slipped over that edge and then clawed her way back with broken, bleeding fingernails. She doesn't know the core of iron in her bones and in her heart.

But I know these things, and I have broken my chains at last.

I touch the sleeping Sasha's cheek. This time, I don't resist the flood but let it wash over me. I let it drown me.

It's about freedom, not love.

What good is one without the other? My grandmother's hand finds mine, and I squeeze it with all my strength, heedless of the fragile bones. I thought I would never love anyone as much as I love her. But I know, with every fiber of my being, that I love Luca—and Sadra, Kirit, Bard, and countless thralls I've never even met. Thousands of men, women, and children whose chance for their own freedom hangs on my choice: Old promises or new hope? Duty or freedom—to love, to live, to give of myself without reserve? There's a life, a purpose, waiting for me if only I have the courage to take it.

Keeping hold of Baba Nadia, I reach out with my other hand, my fingers hovering over the chalice and crown. I scan the planes of Baba Nadia's face, trying to memorize the soft folds in her cheeks, the curve of her smile. Finally, I look into her eyes.

"I love you," I tell her. "Forever."

I reach for the Chalice...and drink deep.

* * *

"Sasha!" Someone is shouting and shaking me by the shoulders. *"Sasha!"*

I roll over and push myself onto my hands and knees. There's a bitter, coppery taste in my mouth that makes me gag. I spit and then jerk, startled by the sudden splash of red that appears below me. Blood, I realize dimly. I'm bleeding. I swipe a hand over my face and look at the resulting mess. There's quite a lot of it—the blood. Slowly, I let out a long breath and let my head hang for a moment, doing my best to ignore the quick *drip-drip-drip* of blood falling onto the pristine white marble.

"Sasha?" A different voice now, lighter and sharper. "Curse it, Sasha, say something!"

With effort, I lift my head and squint at the faces before me. It takes several moments for the fuzzy, disjointed images to form a picture. Relief flows through me in a cool flood as I recognize Luca and Sadra. I reach out to touch one face, then the other, leaving bloody smudges on each cheek.

"I'm alright," I whisper hoarsely. "I'm—"

"Alive," Luca breathes, and presses his forehead against mine.

He and Sadra help me to my feet and stand by my side, Sadra's arm around my waist and Luca's around my shoulders. The silence of the audience hall is broken only by my own wet snuffling as I attempt to stem my nosebleed. I catch sight of the Premier's face, transfixed with shock and fury, and laugh. Triumph rises in my chest like a balloon, expanding until it fills my whole body.

I'm free. Finally, truly, *free*.

"I am alive," I say, my voice still ragged. "Miocostin. Your brother says you're a good man, and I believe him. So hear me: The mages of the House of Light and Shadow stole me from my home and enslaved me. They believe that they are justified in this. They will continue to lie and cheat and hurt in order to protect their interests, and that makes them a danger to everyone in your care."

The king nods gravely. "The Council will convene—"

He's interrupted by a strange whir and *thunk*. He breaks off, frowning down at the knife protruding from his chest. Luca is already moving, pushing me down to the floor and diving toward his brother through the sudden mess of screaming, flailing bodies. But he isn't fast enough. Another knife appears, this time in the King's throat. He collapses in Luca's arms, blood flowing over his lips and neck.

Something hard barrels into me, knocking me sideways. The floor, suddenly slippery with blood, fouls my recovery and I fall, barely catching myself on my hands and knees. Above me, Bard wrestles with a masked swordsman wearing plain, nondescript clothing. Not a guard, then. Who are these people? What is going on?

I watch, transfixed with horror, as Bard tears the sword away from my attacker and plunges it into the man's stomach. He turns to me, reaches out his hand—and then drops it, a long blade blossoming out of his stomach like a grotesque flower. Another masked man jerks his sword out of Bard's body and takes a step toward me, only to stumble backward again as Sadra loops a small, flexible wire around his neck and pulls viciously.

"Sa…Sasha."

Heedless of the danger surrounding me, I crawl to Bard's side and take his bloody hand in my own. Images and sensations flood my mind, and through it all is weaved a name, repeated over and over again through countless years of longing and loss. *Nadia.* Her face flashes before my eyes in a hundred different permutations: laughing, crying, scolding, radiant with joy and incandescent with rage and defiance, tender and fierce, on and on until finally, a new face emerges.

I see my own eyes and nose and mouth, so similar to Nadia's though twisted with bitterness, and I feel his pain and his guilt. I see myself thrashing and screaming as the Premier rips the Pall away from me, and I feel his fear. I hear myself call him Grandfather, and I feel his joy. I see the blood and tears on my face as I stare down at him in this very moment, and I feel his peace.

"Farewell, *kotik*," Bard sighs, and slips beyond my reach forever.

"No," I choke. "*No.* Come back. *Dedushka—*"

"Sasha, move!"

I scramble backward, out of Sadra's way. She moves faster than thought, feinting and slashing as she tries to get under the swordsman's guard. I look around wildly, trying to find someplace to go. Luca and his soldiers form a half circle around the king—or maybe just the king's body. Arismendi and Ismeni have dragged him against the wall and now bend over him, desperately trying to stanch his wounds. Mother Wenla holds the king's hands in her own and stares deeply into his eyes.

"Sasha!" Luca calls frantically. "Get—"

I push myself to my feet, intending to make for the safety of Luca's circle of swords. But before I can move, I find myself jerked backward by my hair. My back hits the ground hard, knocking the wind out of me.

Cimari smirks down at me, clutching a sword in both hands. Her face is flushed with eagerness and excitement. Her hands shake slightly, more with emotion than strain.

"You should have died," she says, and raises the sword.

I move instinctively, driven in equal parts by long-suppressed rage and fresh, wild grief. My hand shoots out and closes on her ankle. With a snarl, I pull it out from under her and she falls, the sword clattering to the ground beside her. I'm on her in a flash, my fingers tight on her throat. She bucks and writhes beneath me, but I hold her down with strength born of a deep, primal desire to dominate and destroy my enemy.

I squeeze, noting with detached interest the way her eyes bulge and pop. Her lips move, but soundlessly—not a trickle of air slips past my grip. I look more closely at the shapes formed by her mouth, studying them intently until a word emerges.

Mercy.

In another time, another life, I would have granted her request. But I'm not the girl I was. That girl is dead. Just like Dove and Pretty Girl...and Bard.

This monster has beaten me to within an inch of my life not once, but twice, and both times I took it in silence. She killed Pretty Girl without a moment's thought and without even a semblance of regret…and I let her do it.

I watched. I did nothing. But no more. I promised myself that if she ever laid a hand on me again, I would kill her.

And I always keep my promises.

"Let go." Sadra tugs on my wrist, her nails biting into the skin. "Sasha, *let go.* We have to move."

Sadra's voice is distant and muffled. I shake my head, half in denial and half in an attempt to clear it of the cottony feeling between my ears.

With a grunt of effort, Sadra pulls me off Cimari's corpse and drags me free of the melee. Tiny bursts of light flare in my vision, and my breath sounds unnaturally loud in my ears.

"I'm going to be sick," I choke.

"No, you're not," Sadra says. "We don't have time."

She deals me a brisk and businesslike slap across the face, startling me out of my nausea.

"Thanks," I gasp, and we scurry along the wall.

"Stop this."

I freeze, and so does everyone else. Arismendi stalks into the middle of the room, seemingly without care for the swords and knives drawn all around her. She glares around at the few masked fighters still standing. A blood-soaked soldier shoves the Premier forward to sprawl at Arismendi's feet.

"You are defeated," she says coldly. "Lay down your weapons and you will be granted the mercy of a painless death. Resist and I will order my men to take you alive, that you may be publicly flayed before you die."

She pulls the cowering Truthseer to her feet.

"Who is responsible for this attack?" she asks.

"I don't know," the Truthseer wails. "I told you—"

"Try," Arismendi insists. "I believe you may surprise yourself."

The Truthseer, shaking, closes her eyes. A moment later, they fly open again and she points straight at the Premier.

"He is responsible," she says, her voice firm now. "He ordered the attack."

"I thought so." Arismendi's fists clench as she looks down on the Premier. "The trial was a sham. You only needed time and a distraction to move your thugs into place."

The Premier raises his hands. "Princess—"

"Queen." Luca moves to stand beside his sister, his hand steady on his sword. "You are addressing your queen."

My eyes widen and fly to where Ismeni sits with Miocostin's head in her lap. Tears stream down her face. The king is dead.

"My queen," the Premier says, his tongue flicking out like a lizard's. "I know nothing of these men. I—"

"He lies!" the Truthseer shrieks. "He *lies!*"

"This man is guilty of treason and regicide," Arismendi says, her eyes glittering. "Kill him."

But Luca's sword is already in motion. The Premier's head strikes the floor in the same instant Arismendi gives her order.

"It's over." Arismendi takes a shuddering breath, her face pale. "Soldiers, put down your arms."

They obey her at once, loyal and rebel alike laying aside their weapons. All but Luca. He kneels and offers Arismendi his sword, laid flat across his palms.

"Hail the queen," he says softly, and his words are echoed by all who are able to speak the words.

"Rise, Captain."

Arismendi pulls him to his feet and into an embrace. The gesture appears calm, regal. But I see her face crumple as she leans into his shoulder. She steps away after only a moment, her shoulders squared and her chin lifted.

"Come," she says. "There is work to be done."

The cleanup is surprisingly orderly and efficient. Mother Wenla oversees the removal of the injured to the healing wing, and Luca's guards haul the masked men away. The Apostate stands at Arismendi's side, occasionally murmuring responses to her questions. But his eyes frequently find me where Sadra and I sit, tucked away in a corner.

"Shouldn't you go with Mother Wenla?" Luca asks anxiously at one point, hovering over us. "She could give you one of her boosts, at least."

"I don't need them anymore," I remind him. "I'm free. My strength is mine to keep, now."

"And to share," Arismendi remarks. "You're the Chalice, Sasha."

"The Chalice..." I shake my head, dazed.

"It was never a cup," Arismendi says. "The Chalice was a person—a person like you, with your Gift. You make the Gifts of others stronger."

I blink and stare at her stupidly as she continues, "I have seen...so many things. I was right, you know. You will tear down the kingdom."

"I'm sorry," I whisper.

"So am I," she says, a tear sliding down her cheek. "Costi would have done it, you know. He would have put a stop to all of the House's atrocities. He was a good king, a good man. And he died for it."

"And you?" I ask. "What will you do?"

"What will *we* do," she corrects me. "I'm going to rebuild my kingdom...with a Chalice at my side."

Coda

Rebuilding a kingdom, as it turns out, is a hell of a lot of work. I like to think that I would have made the same choice if I had realized what I was in for, but I'm glad I didn't know. Arismendi, in her queenly wisdom, has appointed me the face of her campaign for reform. As a result, I am constantly on display. I now wear a different sort of mask, but a familiar one: a performer's professional, gracious smile.

I'm not bothered by the weight of a thousand pairs of eyes on me, but I could certainly stand to live without the angry, defensive skepticism I encounter from those whose wealth and status are bolstered by Lightcrafting…and even from those who simply don't want to believe they were wrong, that their world isn't what they thought it was.

Every conversation is a sparring match of pointed questions, sneering observations, and outright attacks. They watch my every move, waiting for something, anything that could constitute a hole in my story or in the logic of my very existence. It's exhausting.

Sadra has been a great help, of course, and I have found an unexpected ally in Ismeni. While she hasn't offered anything approaching an apology, she has sought me out on occasion to ask me questions about the Pall and my life under its influence…and about Cimari. She actually listens to my answers, which, as Sadra has pointed out, is more important than getting an apology, especially since Ismeni is also willing to share my information with an army of fashionable young ladies throughout the Terrace and the City.

Right now, though, I am alone and free to set down my burdens for a time. Or mostly alone. Luca watches me from the doorway of the courtyard, but his presence is no more burdensome than that of my shadow. He's a part of me.

"Bayu, bayushki, bayu..."

I sing softly to myself as I raise my arm over my head in a graceful curve, aware that Luca's eyes follow my every move. Though my freedom no longer depends on my barre exercises, I go through the same routine every evening, dancing in the small courtyard that has become my sanctuary, a tiny Eden cooled by the misty breath of the waterfall and covered in moss and vines and beautiful mosaics.

I take my time, enjoying the feel of Luca's admiring gaze as I complete my exercise. Between lessons and meetings and representatives flooding in from all over the kingdom, I've had barely any time alone with him in the two months since Miocostin's death.

But right now there is nothing to be done that can't wait until tomorrow, and I'm looking forward to showing Luca just how much I've missed him. I cross the courtyard and slide into his arms, tilting my head back for a kiss.

"Wait," he says, unwinding my arms from around his neck.

Surprised, I pull away and look at him with a question in my eyes.

"Porr wants to see you," Luca tells me. "He says it's urgent."

My stomach lurches. I can think of only one thing that Porr would consider urgent, inundated as he is with thralls clamoring to be freed from the Pall.

My mother.

The decision to look for her was born first of obligation, buffeted as I was by guilt and the scorching wind of Bard's funeral pyre. I had wasted so much time being angry and defensive and afraid. I had been selfish, unwilling to share myself or my memories of Baba Nadia with my own grandfather, her husband. I had denied a sad, lonely old man any acknowledgment of our shared blood until it was too late. The shame of it may ease in time, but the knowledge will stay with me forever—as it should.

If atonement for cowardice is possible, it can only start with facing my fears. So I spoke to Porr, and, as soon as the dust cleared from the Premier's failed coup, he sent word of my mother to Bird's Path sparrows and fledglings all over Kingsgarden. And now, it seems his efforts may have paid off.

"Do you want me to go with you?" Luca asks. "Or would you rather be alone?"

"No." I hold tight to his hand. "No, I don't want to be alone. Come with me, please."

He gives my hand a squeeze and tucks it through his arm as he leads me from our chambers. I raise a hand to my hair, belatedly wondering if I should have bathed and changed. Too late now, I suppose. My mother, if she's really here, will have to take me as I am.

Porr meets us at the door of his workroom, an eager smile creasing his craggy face. My heart begins to pound, and I can't tell if it's from fear or anticipation.

"It's true, then," I breathe. "You found her."

Porr's smile flickers. "No. But there's someone here you should meet."

He ushers me inside and bows to a dark-haired woman, who sits with her hands clasped before her.

"I present to you Lady Myna," Porr says. "A Bird's Path owl."

"Like Bard," I murmur.

Porr nods and squeezes my shoulder, motioning for me to sit in one of the chairs opposite Lady Myna. I obey, and Luca follows suit.

"Yes," Porr says. "Very much like Bard, though she operated in the auction houses rather than the caravans."

"That's where I met your mother," Myna tells me, her voice surprisingly low and husky. "She was my first nestling."

"Were you…were you friends?" I ask hesitantly. "Did you know her well?"

"I'm sorry," Myna says. "I never spoke to her, not really. I didn't even know her name until I heard you were looking for her. But…she made an impression. I never saw a thrall so determined to survive, before or since."

I nod, my throat tight, and reach again for Luca's hand. "But she's not here, is she?"

Myna and Porr share a brief, inscrutable look. Then Porr motions for us all to sit.

"Just tell me," I say, my fingers stiff and cold in Luca's. "Is she dead?"

"Yes." Myna's eyelids flicker, then her gaze steadies. "She was placed in the plains surrounding the City of Sage. She and her husband raised horses until raiders burned the place to the ground two years ago."

"She had a husband?" I look down at my fingers intertwined with Luca's. "A family? She—was she happy, do you think?"

"I think so," Myna says evenly.

Myna stands. Luca and I rise as well, thinking the interview is over, but Porr holds up his hand for us to remain. He follows Myna to the door and bows to her as she leaves.

"Wait," he instructs us.

Luca and I share a confused glance and sit down again.

We wait in silence, my foot tapping and twitching nervously against Luca's. When I can't stand it any longer, I open my mouth to demand an explanation. But then Porr opens the door and all my questions fly right out of me on the wind of my next breath.

For a moment, I could swear my heart literally skips a beat—or two, or a hundred. Luca stiffens beside me, his fingers suddenly crushingly tight on my own.

"The sun shines on you, my lady, my lord."

A slight, dark-haired girl peeps shyly up at us, Kirit cradled in her arms. Her eyes widen as they meet mine, wonder and confusion mingling together in the cloudy blue. Kirit slips from her arms and she steps forward, every inch of her slender body trembling like a leaf. My fingers slide through Luca's as I move toward her, drawn as if by a magnet.

Slowly, I sink to my knees.

"Who are you?" she whispers, reaching out to touch my face.

I can't speak. I can only stare at her, taking in every tiny, miraculous detail. Her forehead furrows, and a little line appears between her brows, one just like mine.

"Why have they left us?"

I look around and realize that we are indeed alone. Luca, Porr, and even Kirit are nowhere to be seen. I turn back to the girl and try to smile.

"So that we can talk, I think. Is that alright?"

"Yes." She brings her other hand to my face, cupping my cheeks in her palms. "My mother is dead. But you look like her."

A small huff of laughter eases the tightness in my throat. "So do you."

"Lady Myna told me I was coming to meet my family," the girl says. "She said you're going to take care of me now."

"Lady Myna was right," I say. "What was your mother's name?"

"Lara," she says, her lips twisting in a flash of grief.

"Can I tell you something?" I whisper. "Something strange, and wondrous—will you believe me?"

Her eyes widen, and she turns her head so I can whisper in her ear, "My mother's name was Lara, too." Tentatively, I take her small, delicate hands in mine and kiss them. "I'm Sasha. I'm your sister."

"My sister." She says it slowly, as if tasting each syllable. Then she smiles, her face suddenly alight with joy.

My lips tremble as I smile back at her. "And does my little sister have a name?"

"Yes." She giggles and pulls her hands out of mine so that she can hold the end of my braid. She brushes it against her cheek, lightly, and then looks at me with my grandmother's eyes—my eyes.

"My name is Nadia."

About the Author

Kassandra Flamouri made her storytelling debut at age three with "Squirm the Worm," which was warmly received by an audience of assorted beetles. After many years spent exploring a variety of interests, she went on to study music composition at the Sunderman Conservatory of Gettysburg College. She currently resides in Pennsylvania, moonlighting as a folk musician while juggling writing and teaching. Kassandra shares her heart and home with a very sweet and loving man, a very sweet but excitable cattle dog, and an only intermittently sweet, very old black cat.

You can connect with me on:
- https://www.flamourifiction.com
- https://twitter.com/flamourific